Ebb and Flow

Also published by Poolbeg

As Easy As That

Parting Company

Ebb and Flow

Mary
O'Sullivan

POOLBEG

This novel is entirely a work of fiction. The names, characters and incidents portrayed in it are the work of the author's imagination. Any resemblance to actual persons, living or dead, events or localities is entirely coincidental.

Published 2007
by Poolbeg Press Ltd
123 Grange Hill, Baldoyle
Dublin 13, Ireland
E-mail: poolbeg@poolbeg.com
www.poolbeg.com

1 3 5 7 9 10 8 6 4 2

A catalogue record for this book is available from the British Library.

ISBN 978-1-84223 -308-5

Typeset by Type Design in 10.75/14

Printed by
Litographia Roses, Spain

Note on the author

Mary O'Sullivan lives in Carrigaline, County Cork, with her husband Seán. Her novels *Parting Company* and *As Easy As That* were also published by Poolbeg.

Acknowledgements

My life's ambition has been to be a published author. For giving me that opportunity I would like to sincerely thank Poolbeg Press. To Paula, Niamh, David and all the crew, a big thank you.

It has yet again been my privilege to have my work edited by the very talented author, playwright and editor extraordinaire, Gaye Shortland. Thank you, Gaye.

To Karen Kinsella, Mary Lynsky and Mary Malone, I give a big thank you for reading raw first drafts without complaint and for your enthusiasm and encouragement. I have been very heartened by the support I have received since venturing into the world of novel writing. Each and every good wish is deeply appreciated.

To my family: Seán, Owen and Vera in Carrigaline, Paul in New Zealand, Annie and Emmett in Bonn, sisters-in-law Eileen, Rose, Anne and Geraldine in Cork. My grateful thanks and love always.

For Paul and Owen

With warm memories of the children you were and respect for the men you have become.

Chapter 1

Ella knew what he was going to say long before he voiced the words. The whole scene had an inevitability, as if it had been waiting for this moment in the silences and unspoken tensions of their relationship.

He was holding his head, pacing the room, struggling for control. She sat still, wedged into her chair between cushions of guilt and hopelessness. She would have reached out to him, would have put her arms around him and held him close to her, laughed in the way she used to do, made him smile, kissed away his anger. She would have. But she could not.

"You're making no effort, Ella," he said. "There's nothing really wrong with you. Haven't you been listening to your doctor? Have you been listening to anyone else at all? Would you just snap out of it, for Christ's sake!"

Walking over to where she was sitting he stooped down and took her hands in his, the gentleness of his touch a contrast to the anger of his words. She looked into the familiar blue eyes, noticed the dark stubble on his chin, the stray threads of white in his thick, black hair. She examined his features and waited for some stirring of emotion, some vestige of feeling for this man who was pleading with her to respond. He was good-looking in a sophisticated way. A generic handsomeness, born of good breeding and careful grooming. She felt nothing but regret and pity.

"I'm sorry, Andrew," she whispered.

Dropping her hands, he straightened up. He walked to the door and then turned back to face her.

"I give up," he said. "Bury yourself here if that's what you want. But you can stop using your accident as an excuse. That was almost a year ago and you're fully recovered now. You're just being selfish."

He slammed the door shut.

Ella closed her eyes and listened to the sounds of her husband getting ready for the party she was refusing to attend. She shivered at the thought of the noisy, meaningless jumble of prescribed chitchat which passed for party conversation. The type of social occasion she used to love. Maybe she should go. Everyone would compliment her on how well she was looking, acknowledging the level of social acceptability Ella and Andrew Ford had attained, how successful their business had become. Nobody would mention the accident. That would be impolite. A party pooper.

Ella heard the rattle of car keys as Andrew picked them up from the hall table. He banged the front door on his way out. She relaxed and sank further into the blackness, into the only place where her mind would allow her to go.

* * *

Andrew mingled. He was good at that. The noise and vibrancy of the party was such a welcome relief from the silent blackness of Ella that he launched himself into the spirit of it with gusto. 'Resting. Just a little tired,' was his stock reply to the questions on Ella's whereabouts. There were fewer people asking now. An unaccompanied Andrew Ford on the social circuit was getting to be the norm.

He grabbed a drink from a passing waiter. The Cox brothers were not sparing anything in celebrating the completion of their latest apartment block. The wine and champagne were flowing. And so well they might. Andrew had handled the sale of the old brewery to the Coxes. They had bought the derelict building for a song and had converted it into an apartment block. It was all sold now, from the bijou one-bedroom flats to the penthouse suite. At exorbitant prices. This party was in effect an advertising campaign for their next project. Another old building at a knockdown price was due to get the Cox treatment. This time Andrew had found them a disused warehouse and the Coxes would soon transform the grotty building into *the* place to live, *the* address to have. Andrew raised his glass in a silent toast to the enterprising brothers. Being the estate agents for them meant that every time the Coxes made money, so did Andrew and Ella Ford.

"That's a very smug smile, Andrew."

Maxine Doran was standing in front of him, smiling. She looked stunning, her golden skin testament to the fact that she was just back from holiday in some exotic location. Or more likely a shoot. She was one of the more sought-after models.

"Just enjoying my champagne, Maxine. You look wonderful. Is the tan from holiday or work?"

"A bit of both actually. I was in The Seychelles. Where's Ella?"

"She's resting. She still gets very tired."

Maxine nodded in sympathy. "It will take her a long time to get over that awful accident. She was so lucky to survive. I believe she's back at work?"

Andrew nodded. That was one of the most puzzling aspects of Ella's painfully slow recovery. She had been back in the office even before getting medical clearance. And she seemed to have lost none of her business acumen. She had been, and still was, one of the most astute business people Andrew had ever worked with.

"So what do you think about this new warehouse development?" Maxine asked. "Would you advise someone to invest? In, say, a two-bed apartment with maybe a roof garden?"

"Are you interested? I've a copy of the plans in the office. If you call in, I can show them to you. You would want to move quickly though. Interest is brisk already."

Maxine laughed. "Ever the estate agent, aren't you? I'll call to your office if you promise to have a drink with me afterwards."

Andrew held out his hand to her. "Deal. Just ring to let me know and we'll take it from there."

Maxine took his hand, leaned towards him and kissed him on the cheek. Her softness, her perfume, the gentle touch of her lips, all reminded Andrew how much he missed intimacy with Ellen. How much he missed the warmth and sharing they used to have. He pushed the thought out of his mind and smiled at the beautiful woman in front of him.

"Where are you living now?" he asked. "You have a downtown apartment, don't you?"

Maxine signalled to a passing waiter and took another glass of champagne from the tray. Raising her glass, she took a sip and then slowly licked her lips. Andrew stared at the tip of her pink tongue. He felt his breath quicken.

"Why not come to see my apartment now, Andrew? Carry out a valuation. You're at the cutting edge of all this property business. You could let me know where I stand. Financially, that is."

Andrew's blood began to course through his veins. He was not naïve. He knew that Maxine Doran's invitation had nothing to do with valuing her property. He was flattered. And surprised. He and Ella knew the model socially. They usually ended up on the same invitation lists. Of course, he had always admired Maxine but she had never before shown any interest in him. She was usually on the arm of some powerbroker. Even though Ford Auctioneers was growing, it was not yet in the Maxine Doran super-league. He thought again of his wife, of Ella. Poor, sad, depressed Ella. Cold, unresponsive Ella. He took

Maxine's champagne glass and placed it on a table.

"Let's say our goodbyes. I'll meet you in the car park in ten minutes. You can lead the way."

She lowered her eyelids and looked up at him through her long, curling lashes.

"I hope you like where I'm going to lead you, Andrew."

Game on. Andrew knew he was going to be very good at playing follow the leader.

* * *

Ella was still sitting in the same position as she had been when Andrew left for the Cox brothers party. She was held there by the weight of her tiredness, by the heavy pall of guilt, by the replaying over and over in her mind of those few horrific seconds of slaughter and destruction. The accident. Post Traumatic Stress Disorder was the latest official title given to her despair. Selfishness, Andrew called it. They were all wrong. This depression was far deeper and more disabling than reaction or introspection. It was starting again now, the whole scene playing over in her head. She could not outrun, outwit or obliterate the images. Ella closed her eyes and frame by frame, relived the accident.

* * *

It had been raining all that evening. She never liked showing prospective clients around a property on a gloomy grey day. Bad weather always had a negative effect on moods and perceptions. She was sure as she led the way around the five-bedroom house that her clients felt as cold and miserable as she did. She stood on the landing and looked out into the garden. It seemed desolate and bare. Ella frowned. The garden should be one of the best features of this property, the focal point of the beautiful bay windows. Anyway, her instinct told her that these particular clients were not serious buyers. She waited for them as they poked and prodded at everything, leaving no corner unexplored and no door unopened. Glancing at her watch she noticed that it was almost six o'clock. She would have to call back to the office before going home. Getting ready for the dinner party would be a rush. Damn! Time to bring this pointless inspection to an end. She excused herself, allowing the couple time to formulate a polite refusal and giving her a chance to ring Andrew.

"Hi, Andy. Just reminding you that we have dinner with the Mahers tonight."

"Shit! I completely forgot."

Ella laughed. "How did I know you'd say that? I must be psychic!"

"I don't know what I'd do without you. Will you be back soon or will I head home and meet you there?"

"I'm out at The Orchards. I'll see you at home as soon as possible."

"Any good?" he asked.

"WOTS," Ella said, using their code for waste-of-time clients.

"See you soon then. Take care. The traffic will be heavy in this rain."

She had switched off her phone and gone to find her clients who were now opening each and every kitchen press. They all went through the motions of pretending that this was a serious viewing of the property. When they parted company at the front door they knew they would not be meeting again.

It was raining so heavily by now that Ella got drenched when she left the car to lock the gates behind her. The clock on the dash told her it was already twenty minutes past six. Blast! It was all right out here but she knew traffic would be chaotic nearer the city. Maybe she could skip the office and go straight home. But she was waiting on a close-of-deal call and had forgotten to give the prospective buyer her mobile number. If she rang him now, she would seem over-anxious and pushy. It was potentially a huge opportunity. An American with a tenuous Irish ancestry and a fortune in dot.com money to invest in Irish property. It was one call she could not afford to miss. Nothing for it but to wait in the office. Anyway, there was a seven o'clock deadline on the call and these Americans were usually as punctual as they were wealthy.

Ella was seeing the road ahead through wavering rivulets of rain. The windscreen wipers were walloping over and back but were fighting a losing battle with the torrents of water. The channels at the side of the narrow road were beginning to overflow. The sooner she got off the miserable soon-to-be-flooded little strip of tarmac the better. She pressed her foot on the accelerator. The car aquaplaned. One second she was driving forward and the next she was being borne helplessly towards the ditch on the opposite side of the road. Her hands were glued rigidly to the steering wheel, her breath stuck somewhere between lungs and mouth. Then she felt the tyres grip. She turned the steering wheel and the car responded. Control returned as quickly as it had been lost. Her breath gushed out and the blood she had not realised had left her face rushed back.

"Fuck!" she said softly, the profanity a mixture of relief and fear.

Back on her own side of the road, she slowed down to a crawling pace. There was a hairpin bend ahead and besides she was shaking with fright. That had been so close. Too close. This was her last coherent thought. The four-wheel drive lunged at her from around the bend, looming huge and menacing and already out of control. Ella knew then that the skid had only given her a scare, a forerunner of the terror which gripped her now. It filled her with the knowledge that she might never see Andrew again, never hear him laugh, never see another sunrise or feel the wind on her face.

The woman at the wheel of the Land Cruiser was screaming, her mouth open wide, her eyes staring. She had one hand reaching behind her towards the back seat and Ella realised there must be a child or children there. Real time stopped. Sound and vision were swept into a maelstrom of intense, slow-moving emotion. Fear was the overriding feeling but it was tempered with fascination. Minute details burned onto Ella's brain, as if her senses were grabbing at the last smells, sights and sounds they would ever perceive. She smelt the scent of her perfume mixed with perspiration and knew it was the smell of fear, heard the thunderous crunch of metal on metal as the two vehicles crashed, saw an intricate spider-web pattern creep across the windscreen of the 4x4 as the woman's blonde head hit it with force. Ella struggled for breath as her airbag pushed her back and the impetus of the motor pushed her forward. Her car began to spin out of control. The Land Cruiser was heading for the opposite ditch. When the 4x4 mounted the stone wall, Ella was turned in that direction. A child's face was glued to the back window. A beautiful child. A little boy, blonde-haired like his mother. He was crying, calling out for help. Ella's car spun again and this time it landed in the deep roadside channel. It had overturned. The rest of Ella's nightmare was viewed from this upside-down perspective, until finally, mercifully, when the hell became too much, she lost consciousness.

* * *

Ella shook her head now and stood up. Why was this happening? Why did she have to relive this nightmare over and over? It had not been her fault. The inquest had said so. Andrew had said so. The man who was the husband of the woman and father of the little boy had said so. Why couldn't she forgive herself? And why was she sitting here, full of self-pity, when she should be at the Cox brothers party? By her husband's side. She looked at her watch. It was twelve fifteen. Where had the night gone? She must have slept without realising it. Too late to go out now. "Too late," Ella muttered out loud as she thought of the person she had been before that horrible day. Sometimes she imagined that the bright, ambitious, fun-loving Ella had died in the crash and was replaced by this manic-depressive zombie who was also named Ella. Maybe she was just plain exhausted. Sleep was now just a series of hellish re-enactments of the accident.

She went to the medicine cabinet and took out two of the sleeping tablets the doctor had prescribed for her. Two little nuggets of oblivion. She swallowed them with a glass of water and then went to bed. She fell into a drug-induced, gloriously dreamless sleep.

★ ★ ★

Maxine's apartment was just what Andrew would have expected her to have. It was chic, spacious and tasteful. He examined the artwork on the walls with interest.

"You have quite an eye for up-and-coming talent, haven't you?" he remarked.

"My talent lies in knowing the right people. It pays to know who to talk to."

Andrew looked sharply at her, surprised and a bit disappointed at the crass comment. She laughed at him. "C'mon, Andrew! Don't be a hypocrite. You haven't built up your business without kissing some bottoms. You might like to call it networking but it's the same thing. How many of your clients, the big ones, the money-spinners, do you actually like?"

Taking the drink she offered him, Andrew sat down on the cream leather sofa. She was right. He had to deal on a daily basis with gobshites but he smiled at them and agreed with their points of view and went to their parties. With few exceptions he had learned that the bigger the account, the more obnoxious the account-holder. He shrugged.

"You're spot on, Max. If kissing arse pays, why not do it? Let's drink to that!"

They touched glasses and then she sat down at the opposite end of the couch. Kicking off her shoes, she settled cushions behind her back and gracefully put her long legs up onto the soft leather. Andrew held tightly onto his glass. His fingers needed something solid to hold, something to distract them from following in the direction his mind was already travelling. He imagined how soft her skin would feel. Smooth and cool. She was unpinning her hair now, shaking her head as the blonde shining tresses came loose and tumbled around her face and shoulders.

"Comfortable?" she asked, stretching out one leg towards him and touching the side of his thigh with her perfectly shaped, tanned foot.

He gripped his glass even tighter. He was hypnotised by the slow movements of the model's red-varnished toenails as her foot stroked his thigh. Blood-red varnish. Blood. Like he had seen pour from Ella's head. He shivered, remembering his wife after the accident, her waxen face, her bruised and swollen eyes, remembering how he had prayed for her survival, bargained with any god who might listen.

"It must be a year now since Ella's accident," said Maxine, almost as if she knew what he was thinking.

Andrew nodded. It would be exactly a year next week. Twelve months of absorbing the horror of the crash, the deaths of the young mother and her child, the seemingly endless wait for Ella to come out of her coma, the joy when she opened her eyes. Then the inquests, the therapy and the pain of realising that the Ella he had known and loved was gone forever.

"Do you think Ella has changed? Events like that can alter people's personalities."

"I don't want to talk about my wife," Andrew said abruptly.

Maxine swung her legs down from the couch and, smiling, took his hand. "Of course you don't. You want to value my apartment. Come with me and I'll show you around. There are only two bedrooms but the master bedroom is big and has a Jacuzzi. Maybe you'd like to see it?"

Andrew put his glass down and cleared his mind of all Ella thoughts. He was not really being unfaithful to her. Twelve months of celibacy was all he could take. He needed sex and obviously his wife did not. He needed this beautiful woman who was leading him by the hand into her bedroom. It was just a fuck.

"I may need to try the bed too," he said to Maxine.

"Of course," she smiled. "Nothing quite like hands-on experience, is there?"

Her smile and her words freed Andrew. He took Maxine with all the hunger and passion of a man deprived of sex for a year. Then he took her again with the tenderness of a man making love to a beautiful woman.

* * *

As Andrew dressed, Maxine noticed in the dim light that she had left a scratch on his back. She felt sated, totally satisfied, as she had never been before. This had not been part of the plan. She had meant to be the one in control. And she had been for a while. The man had been desperate for her. For any woman. It seemed like stuck-up Ella Ford was holding out on her husband. Not surprising maybe after the trauma of that fatal accident. Silly bitch. She could have found rehabilitation in her husband's arms. Maxine stretched and put her hands behind her head, knowing that she was showing off her breasts to their best advantage. She smiled at Andrew.

"Funny, isn't it, that we have known each other socially for so long and yet we never got together before now?"

"I'm married," he answered sharply.

And guilty, Maxine thought. Better let him work that one out for himself. She was not worried. Andrew Ford would be back. Of that she was sure.

Chapter 2

Ella swam through thick layers of exhaustion. She lay still and concentrated. Satisfied that she had not dreamt or had nightmares last night, she sat up and threw back the duvet. Her legs felt heavy. She hated the side effects of those sleeping pills but loved the safe, dreamless void they created. She looked at her watch. It was seven fifteen. She could hear the shower running. Andrew was already up. He must have slipped away early from the Coxes' party last night.

Breakfast always consisted of coffee and toast. Ella put on the kettle, popped some bread in the toaster and opened the patio door. It was a foggy morning. Stepping onto the patio, she breathed in the moist air. It floated, cold and damp, into her lungs. She pulled her dressing-gown more closely about her and went down the steps into the garden. Autumn berries were just a memory now. Shrubs and trees were bare but had a stark beauty in the diffused light. She touched her finger to a branch and watched as a droplet of water swelled and wavered and finally plopped onto the grass. The greyness of the scene resonated with her mood. She closed her eyes and tried to visualise the summer garden. Roses, lupins, sunflowers, begonias, trailing clematis and geranium. The blooms sat, overblown and grey, in her mind. Even her memory was stripped of life and colour. Except red. Blood red.

She opened her eyes and started to make her way back to the kitchen. As she turned, her attention was caught by a spider's web. It was delicately balanced between twigs, intricate and beautifully crafted. Tiny specks of moisture beaded each fine strand, leading the eye towards the closely woven centre. And there, enmeshed in the web, was the face of the blonde woman. Karen Trevor. The woman was terrified, her eyes huge and her mouth wide open. Blood was trickling from the wound in her forehead and seeping into the strands of the web. Just as it had on the evening of the crash. Ella's face mirrored the terror, her eyes dilated and her mouth wide open in a silent scream. Her mind filled with fear and left her body standing, icy cold and mindless, in the winter garden. She became Karen Trevor, hurtling towards death, out of control and terrified.

"Ella! Ella! What in the hell are you doing standing out in the wet garden? You'll catch your death of cold."

Andrew's voice reached through the capsule of fear surrounding Ella. Karen Trevor's face faded. Bleeding and terrified, the image shrank. There was nothing left now but a misted spider web. And despair. Slowly, Ella made her way back to the kitchen.

* * *

Traffic was heavy. It was backed up for six kilometres into the city. Andrew switched off the engine. Normally, he would be verging on road rage but he was glad of the chance to get his head together this morning. His mind was racing in all directions, his body still tingling from last night. Maxine Doran. Beautiful, sexy Max.

His excitement was tempered by guilt. Being unfaithful to Ella did not sit easy with his conscience, even though he had reasoned that the dour, depressed woman who hung over his life like a dark shadow was not his Ella. Her depression was getting worse. He made up his mind. Today he would contact her doctor. Before she arrived into the office. He shivered as he remembered her this morning, standing in the wet garden, absolutely terrified by a spider's web. She had not told him that of course. Ella did not confide in him any more. But the fear had been obvious in her staring eyes and ashen face.

He allowed himself think of Maxine again. A smile crossed his face. He had never before experienced the intensity he had felt when he made love to her. Her body was lithe, smooth, warm. More than that, there had been a chemistry between them. An instinctive knowing of each other's bodies and needs. Except that he had a scratch on his back to prove it, he would imagine their coupling had been nothing more than an erotic dream.

The beeping of car horns behind him brought him back to reality. He had not noticed traffic ahead beginning to move on. He waved his hand in apology and started his car. He would have to wait until later to figure out why Maxine Doran had targeted him, wooed him, and slept with him. Or maybe that was something he would never know.

* * *

The office was busy. It was always busy. Ford Auctioneers had gone into business at the right time. He and Ella had opened their doors just as the property boom had begun its meteoric rise. Luckily for them, the demand for property, especially in the urban areas, was rising almost as fast as the property prices. Long may it continue, thought Andrew, as he looked at his staff busily taking calls and dealing with customers. A chorus of respectful "Morning, Andrew" greeted him as he made his way into his office.

Logging onto the computer he looked up his address book and found the number for Ella's specialist. He should just about get the call in before Ella reached the office. The doctor's secretary put him on hold. He drummed his fingers impatiently on his desk as he listened to an endless stream of tinny holding music. By the time Dr Edmund Quill finally came on the line, Andrew was in no mood for pussyfooting around.

"Good morning, Dr Quill. Andrew Ford here. I'd like to talk to you about my wife."

"What's the problem, Mr Ford? Has something happened?"

"Nothing has happened. That's the problem. My wife's

condition has not changed. If anything she's worse. Shouldn't this depression, or whatever it is, be lifting by now?"

"I did advise that you would have to be patient. She suffered a very severe trauma. You have to understand that full recovery will take time."

Edmund Quill's patronising tone was the final straw for Andrew. The previous twelve months of worry, fear and frustration poured out in a torrent of angry words.

"I can't accept your wait-and-see attitude any more. What are you doing for her? Sweet damn all! A few counselling sessions and a handful of sleeping pills and anti-depressants. Her treatment is not effective. Why aren't you listening?"

"Ella is my patient, Mr Ford. I'm not willing to discuss her condition with you. Certainly not over the phone. Accompany your wife on her next appointment. If she agrees, I will talk to you both then. Civilly. Good morning."

Andrew slammed down the receiver in disgust. The prick had cut him off. It was so easy for the doctor to advise patience. He was not the one who had to live under this perpetual cloud. Edmund Quill was supposed to be the best. He certainly charged the most. But somehow, some way, Andrew was going to have to persuade Ella to see another doctor. Before it was too late to save her sanity. And their marriage. Getting out the phone book, he began trawling through the medical directory in the belief that in amongst the small print was a person who could bring the real Ella Ford back to life.

* * *

Maxine was tempted to skip the gym today. She stood in front of the mirror and examined her body. It was honed to perfection and today it had a special glow. Andrew Ford had been stupendous. He had teased a response from her that she had never experienced before. Even her eyes seemed brighter and her hair shinier. Maybe if she continued burning off calories in bed with Andrew she would never have to walk sweaty miles on the treadmill again. He was funny too and kind. And married. Besides, she had only slept with him because Jason told her to.

Her afterglow faded as she thought of Jason Laide, entrepreneur and shagger of young girls. Custodian of a video of a very young Maxine, nude and willing to perform anything, anything at all for his camera. She turned her back to the mirror, unable to meet the shame in her own eyes. Despite her effort to blank the memories, her mind travelled back.

Maxine Doran had been born with the knowledge that she would have to, just must, rise above her background. She hated it with a vengeance. Hated the mean streets and pokey little house, the continuous striving to make ends meet, the drunkenness of her father and coarseness of her mother, the lack of ambition of her siblings.

"That one is a throwback to her great-grandmother," her father would always say as he watched his youngest daughter isolate herself from the rough and tumble of the family way of life.

Her paternal great-grandmother had hailed from a high-class family. She had been disinherited when she eloped with a stable lad. Maxine often thought about her. How had the lady survived in the tiny, terraced red-bricked house her stable boy called home? The very house in which Maxine herself had been reared. Had she felt sick with disgust when she had to use the backyard toilet, when she had to cook and clean, when she had to dine at the scrubbed timber table and eat off thick pottery plates? Or had her love for Maxine's great-grandfather, stable boy Thomas, been so great that it overcame all cultural differences?

Maxine walked over to her dressing table and unlocked the top drawer. Carefully she removed the tattered photo album. The red velvet cover was faded and bare in patches. She held it up and sniffed the musty aroma. It fell open at the page she always went to. The portrait of her great-grandmother Harriet. The corners were curled on the sepia photograph but the dignity and pride of the sitter shone through. Her great-grandmother had been beautiful then, tall and slim, her blond hair swept up underneath her hat with the ostrich plumes, her hands clasped genteelly together on the folds of her silk skirts. But it was the eyes that attracted most. They still shone, hypnotic and lustrous, through the browny-yellow tincture of time and wear.

Maxine snapped the album shut and, putting it back into the drawer, locked it safely away. This always happened. Every time she looked at Harriet's photograph she began thinking like a member of the gentry. And if there was one thing Maxine Doran knew herself not to be, it was a lady. She washed and dressed quickly and then went for a four-mile jog. By the time she reached her apartment again, she was too exhausted to worry about her background or her confusing feelings for Andrew Ford.

* * *

Ella stood in front of her office building and took a deep breath. She felt the strength flow into her, felt all the foggy greyness lift as she focused her mind on work. The door slid open and her business smile slipped into place. For an instant she wondered yet again how she could achieve this state of near normality for work but yet her personal life was controlled by what she had come to call her demons. Shrugging off the thought, she walked through the public area, saluting staff and customers, and went into the private office she and Andrew shared. He was on the phone. He waved to her and continued on with his call.

While Ella was logging onto her computer and checking her appointments for the day, she was half listening to Andrew's side of the of the phone conversation. When she heard him mention Ballyhaven, she stopped what she was doing and gave the phone call her full attention.

"Of course, I would have to discuss it with my wife,"

Andrew was saying. "It's in joint ownership."

She indicated to him to put the call on speaker but he signalled to her that it was almost at an end.

"We'll certainly have a think about it," he said. "Give me a week or so and then I'll get back to you." He laughed at something the caller said before putting down the phone and turning to Ella. "Well, well! You'll never guess who that was."

"Probably not," she agreed. "You'd better tell me."

His smile faded as the dullness of her tone washed over him, dragging his mood down to the murky depths of her self-pitying sadness. He shrugged. "It was Garry Cox."

"And? Why were you talking about Ballyhaven? Was it about our site?"

Andrew frowned. More to the point, why was Garry Cox talking about Ballyhaven? Of what interest could it be to the Cox brothers? Maybe it was time to look again at Ford's fifty acres in the country.

"I think there must be some rezoning in the air," he said slowly, more thinking out loud than answering his wife. "Ballyhaven is forty kilometres outside the city but at the rate the suburbs are expanding that's no distance. Isn't that why we bought it in the first place?"

"We bought it because we had money to invest," said Ella flatly.

"Yes. And because fifty acres of scrubland in the middle of nowhere was all we could afford six years ago. Jesus, Ella, what has happened to you? Has your memory been wiped clean of all good things? Can't you remember the day we went to view the fields? How excited we were, how we felt we had finally made it? Does your life start and end now with the accident?"

Ella stood and picked up her bag. She walked over to Andrew's desk and, staring solemnly at him, spoke in a near-whisper. "You weren't there. You don't know what it was like. What it's still like."

"Tell me, for fuck's sake! How can I know when you won't even talk to me?"

"I'm going to see a client now. I expect, when I come back, that you will have got control of your temper."

She turned and walked out of the office, leaving her husband no right of reply, no chance to tell her that he had made an appointment for her with a new doctor, or that Garry Cox was interested in buying their fifty acres of agricultural land in Ballyhaven. To hell with her, Andrew thought, as he began to sort paperwork.

* * *

Maxine was annoyed with herself. She should have taken this whole week off. The Seychelles job had paid exceptionally well but she was exhausted. Her problem was that she could never turn down an assignment. She was twenty-four now. Soon she would be past her sell-by date in modelling terms. This thought always drove her on. Her retirement scheme was not yet fully funded.

Reluctantly, she packed her make-up and hairpieces and prepared for her appointment in the studio. This job would not pay much money but the prestige and publicity involved in a feature in *Looking Glass* magazine more than made up for the lack of bucks. It would be the usual. "How do you stay in shape? What advice would you give young girls starting out on a modelling career?" Run-of-the-mill trivia. Then it would be on to the photo-shoot. That is where Maxine knew she would shine. No matter how tired or down she felt, the camera lens revived her. They had a mutual love affair, she and the camera. A safe, noncommittal relationship.

As she was about to input the code on her alarm, her phone rang. Very few people had her landline number. It could only be one of a handful of people, any of whom would expect her to answer. She dropped her bag by the door and went back to pick up the phone.

"How are you, Max? Enjoy the party last night?"

It was Jason Laide. She had suspected it might be.

"You know I did, Jason. You were there."

"I'm talking about the real party. The one you had with Andrew Ford."

"Yes. Everything went fine. We got on well."

"And did you get the information for me?"

"Of course not. I could hardly come straight out and ask him, could I? He'll have to trust me first."

"Losing your touch, Max? There was a time you could screw the information out of anybody, man or woman, in ten minutes."

Maxine felt her skin go hot and then icy cold. Jason, in a way that only he could, was referring to the girl-on-girl video he had of her. He knew she had never had sex with a woman. Not off camera anyway. Bastard!

"You don't want him to be suspicious, do you?" she

asked as casually as she could manage. "He's an intelligent man. He needs careful handling."

"You're the girl to give him that. Don't take too long about it. I want to know as quickly as possible. I'm not the only one after the information."

"Okay. I'll contact you soon."

She put down the phone before he could deliver any more veiled threats. And then she smiled. At least there was an upside to this. She could contact Andrew Ford again with a clear conscience. She had not been given an option.

* * *

The day passed quickly and relatively demon-free for Ella. It was so much easier to escape her nightmares when she was working. The challenge involved in her job seemed to draw her mind away from the things which haunted her. Away from Karen Trevor.

She was standing now in front of a long bay window, gently stroking the rich fabric of the curtains. It was Indian silk, cool and delicate. The maroon background was embroidered with an intricate design in gold thread. Hand-embroidered. Countless hours of ceaseless and most likely underpaid labour. The hands which had created this beautiful pattern were probably cracked and sore. Lifting the cloth to her face she rubbed its coolness against her cheek. She felt the raised pattern of the tiny, painstaking gold stitches.

"Are you alright, Ella? Do you need a drink of water

or something?"

Ella dropped the cloth, aware that she had lost concentration. Not good. Not while working. She forced the smile back onto her face and turned towards her client.

"Just admiring your drapes, Sharon. They lend the room an air of formality but yet the colour is warm and inviting. Perfect with the Indian teak dining suite. Do you intend selling this house furnished or unfurnished?"

"The whole idea in selling is to have a change. I don't want to bother with any of this stuff. You'll sell it either way. You and Andrew are the best at this property game."

Ella smiled and it was a genuine smile this time. Her first of the day, maybe of the month. She still had pride in her work and appreciated the compliment. She knew she could get a good price on this property. It was a spectacularly large house and the interior design was state of the art. And then there would be the replacement property. The budget available seemed to be unlimited. Just a matter of finding the right place. Jason Laide had deep pockets.

"Where exactly would you and Jason like to move to? Does your husband have any preferences?"

"Blondes and redheads," Sharon laughed.

Ella had of course, like everyone in their circle, heard of the Laides' open marriage yet she was surprised at Sharon's casual reference to her husband's affairs. But then, according to rumour, Sharon had her own share of extra-marital relationships, many of them with men almost young enough to be her sons.

Ella stood and shook the other woman's hand.

"That's it for now so. I'll work up the ads and run them by you before we commit."

"I'm sure it will be fine. Besides, I'll be away for a while. A ski trip actually. But don't worry about access. Jason will be here. You come and go as you please. I'll be looking forward to seeing the 'Sold' sign when I get back."

Ella relaxed a little. Sharon Laide would not be a difficult client to satisfy. Change was all she needed. Ella left with a sneaking admiration for Sharon Laide's attitude to life. Maybe a little change was all anyone needed.

Chapter 3

It had been the usual unhurried, silent Sunday morning they had both come to dread. That was until Andrew mentioned he had made an appointment for Ella to see another doctor. Ella had been hurt at first. Then anger and outrage at her husband's arrogance took hold.

"You had no right," she had shouted at him but when she calmed down she realised that Andrew would not have done something like this unless he was feeling desperate. In a moment of understanding, she tried to imagine what it must be like for him. She knew she had become silent and morose. What other way could she be with a head full of death and destruction?

"He can't be up to much, can he?" she asked. "What specialist would take an appointment over the phone without a referral and without actually speaking to the patient? Not very professional. Or is it that you spun him a good story?"

Andrew took a deep breath and she could see him

struggle for calm and almost succeed. Almost. She knew him too well. His anger and resentment still shone through his blasé words when he spoke.

"It's entirely up to you, Ella. Your choice. Stay the way you are or try to move on."

The words were so subdued, so falsely neutral, that Ella realised this new doctor had coached Andrew in what to say. Appropriate language to coax the reluctant patient. An incompetent, incapable patient. Fuck! He must be a psychiatrist!

"Have you made an appointment with a psychiatrist for me? You think I'm mad, is that it? How dare you! How could you?"

"How could I not? I can't cope with your black moods. I can't cope with the hours of silence, with seeing you getting more and more withdrawn. You've cut me out of your world, Ella. I don't know what's going on with you. Edmund Quill is certainly not helping. What else could I do?"

Ella put her head in her hands and closed her eyes. What could anyone do? Maybe she *was* mad. How sane was it to be seeing a dead woman's face day in, day out? Awake and asleep, Karen Trevor relived the horrific moments of the accident over and over again in Ella Ford's head. That was not sane, not normal. Karen was refusing to die and refusing to allow Ella live. Why? Why? Why?

"He's not a psychiatrist. He's a psychologist."

Ella lifted her head and looked at Andrew. "And that makes a difference?"

"Well, yes. I'm not saying you're mentally ill. Just that

you need help getting over the accident. You've made it very clear that you don't want to communicate with me. Maybe you would find it easier to talk to a professional."

Ella thought about it. Maybe she could explain to someone who was used to dealing with every demented aspect of the human mind. Fuck! How had she come to this? An instant of slaughter and a lifetime of nightmares.

She bowed her head into her hands again and squeezed her forehead as tightly as she could. Still her thoughts kept swirling around that wet road and the out-of-control Land Cruiser. Andrew touched her shoulder. She felt her body instantly stiffen. He dropped his hand angrily and walked away from her. She tried to feel sorry but there was no pity for the living in her psyche. She was too obsessed with the dead. Or more correctly, she thought, with those who were supposed to be dead. A tear, hot and salty, tracked down her cheek. She felt the heat and wetness of it and none of the relief the shedding should have brought. Out of the corner of her eye she noticed that Andrew was standing at the door, his knuckles white on the hand grasping the door handle.

"Your appointment with Dr Peter Sheehan is for tomorrow afternoon. I'm leaving the details on the hall table. Please let his office know what you decide."

Ella listened to him speak in cold, clipped tones. She did not care. He did not touch that place inside of her which felt the pain.

It was some time before she noticed that Andrew had left the house.

* * *

Andrew tried to convince himself that he was not following a plan, that phoning Maxine Doran was only a whim. He just happened to have her number in his phone. He was in need of a little normal company, someone soft and feminine and sane. The excuses built as he listened to her phone ring out. It had been a long shot anyway. She could be in another country, away on one of her glamorous assignments. Or more likely out to lunch with a moneyed boyfriend.

He pulled onto the hard shoulder of the road. Where to now? It was early Sunday afternoon and here he was sitting in his car not knowing how to spend the rest of the day. He could go into the office. He could go to the park and feed the blasted ducks. He could go anywhere except home. Or at least the place he used to regard as home before Ella had her accident. Guilt began to nag at him. Maybe he should go back to her, try to get through her layers of hostility. He shivered at the thought. Ella protected her suffering as if her life depended on it. The suffering was her life. Outside of work, she did not allow anyone or anything else to share in her martyrdom. He could not go back to her for more rejection, more pained looks, more silence. It was a beautiful day, unseasonably warm and bright. He would not allow his wife to rob him of the sunshine. "Fuck her," he muttered as he turned the key in the ignition.

Just as he had the car in gear, his phone rang. He

glanced at it, deciding not to answer if it was Ella. It was Maxine. The ring tones seemed to shiver with her perfume, her warmth, the sheer animal sexuality she exuded. Andrew grabbed his phone.

"Hi, Maxine. How are you?"

"Sorry I missed your call. I was in the shower."

He took a deep breath, closed his eyes and allowed himself a moment to enjoy the image of Maxine Doran, wet and naked, emerging from her shower.

"Are you still there, Andrew?"

He opened his eyes and shook his head to clear it. He was behaving like an adolescent.

"Just wondering if you're busy," he said, forcing himself to sound casual. "I'm going for lunch now. Would you like to join me?"

"It'd be great to get away from the city for a while. How about we find a nice quiet country pub?"

"Sounds perfect. I'll pick you up in fifteen minutes. Okay?"

"See you soon," she said and to Andrew's ears her words were full of the promise of glamour, excitement and glorious sex.

* * *

"Well done. I shouldn't have doubted your powers of persuasion."

Maxine looked at Jason Laide and felt her stomach churn. He was sprawled on her bed, beads of sweat trickling from his ginger-haired chest onto the white mound of his belly. Bastard, she thought as she smiled at him.

"I told you I'd get your information. Haven't I always done what you wanted?"

"Am I to assume then that this prissy little Sunday lunch is going to be somewhere near Ballyhaven?"

Maxine nodded. She had not thought of that but it seemed like a good idea now. A natural way to bring up the topic she needed to discuss with Andrew. She walked over to the bed and sat on the edge, far enough away so that Jason could not touch her.

"I want our agreement in writing, Jason. We are quits after this job. I want the video back."

He rolled over onto his side and his eyes narrowed as he stared at her from underneath his ginger brows.

"I call the shots. You're free if and when I say so. You owe me big-time. You'll never be able to pay me back, you little trollop! You're nothing more than a high-priced whore."

Maxine stood up quickly and began to dress. Name-calling was usually Jason's prelude to sex, anger his aphrodisiac. She slipped quickly into a top and jeans and grabbed her jacket.

"I'll ring you later," she called back over her shoulder as she left her apartment to wait for Andrew in the lobby.

★ ★ ★

Ella dragged the ironing board from the utility room into the lounge. She had a mountain of ironing to do.

When everything was organised, she switched on the television and began to press and fold, press and fold, finding peace in the repetitive actions. She occasionally glanced at the home makeover programme on the television, amused at the frantic activities of the crew.

She had got halfway through her pile of ironing when the doorbell rang. Iron in hand, she froze. Who in the hell could that be? Nobody, but nobody, called to see Ella Ford any more. Small blame to them. She had made it very clear that she was no longer interested in their chatter and did not need their pity. The doorbell sounded again. She could not ignore it because whoever was there would have heard the television and seen her car on the driveway. It rang again. It was obvious they were not going to go away either.

After unplugging the iron, she began to make her way slowly to the hall. The bell rang for the fourth time just as she raised her hand to open the front door. Annoyed, she pulled the door open quickly and then just stood there staring at the man on the doorstep. A wave of icy cold washed over her and she held onto the doorjamb for support.

"Mrs Ford! Ella! Are you all right? I'm sorry. I've startled you. I should have phoned first."

Ella's eyes were riveted to a point just left of his head. A shadow wavered there, shimmering and swirling. She knew, with every fibre of her being, that Karen Trevor was bleeding and screaming and dying inside that shadow. She would see it all again, the terror, the pain, if she could not find the strength to look away. Ella dug deep.

"Come in, Mr Trevor."

"Call me Rob, please," he said as Ella led the way to the kitchen.

"Tea or coffee?" she asked, her hands shaking as she filled the kettle.

"Coffee would be fine."

They were silent as Ella busied herself with mugs, sugar and milk.

"It's been a long year, hasn't it?" he said when she'd handed him his coffee and sat opposite him.

Ella looked at the man sitting at her kitchen table and was not sure how to answer him. It would be a year tomorrow. Three hundred and sixty-five days since the accident. Yet Ella was not altogether aware of the passing of time. It seemed to her that she was still stuck back in that day, on that flooded little road, locked into the horror of the crash.

"Yes," she agreed. "In some ways it has."

"I know what you mean. Sometimes I feel it was only yesterday that my wife and son were with me, laughing and full of hopes and dreams. Other times, it seems like they never existed at all. That Karen and Ian are only a figment of my imagination."

Ella gripped her coffee mug tightly and thought about that. Suppose it had all been imagination. Suppose Karen Trevor had never existed. Had never given birth to the blonde-haired little boy named Ian. Then Karen could never have crashed her Land Cruiser, never have lost her own life and destroyed Ella's. She looked closely at Rob Trevor and saw in the dark circles under his eyes and the deep wrinkles on his face that he was suffering too.

"It must be very lonely for you now," she said and then remembered how annoyed she got when people tried to second-guess her feelings. She expected an angry reply, a curt response to her insensitive remark. She had not expected the tears that welled up in his eyes.

"You know Manor House. It's historic and beautiful. But I'm afraid it has lost all its beauty for me. Every room, every painting, the gardens, the stables, all remind me of Karen and Ian. I will never come to terms with what has happened as long as I am living there."

"Are you thinking of selling?"

"That's why I've come to see you today. I believe you're back at work these past six months. Will you handle the sale for me?"

Ella's first reaction was an instinctive no. It was hell enough living with the memory of the accident and Karen's continuous presence in her life without involving herself further with the Trevor family. But then some half-remembered piece of psychobabble made her realise that maybe that was exactly what she needed. Face her fear. That was it. How could she be afraid of Karen Trevor if she was handling the sale of her home, getting rid of her earthly ties, finally burying her? Admitting to herself that her line of thinking was illogical, if not insane, Ella stood up from the table to get the coffee pot.

"More coffee?" she asked.

Rob nodded, never taking his eyes off her face as she poured.

"I'm sorry," he said. "I think I've upset you. I just felt

that Karen would want you to be the person to do this."

"I didn't know her. I never met her."

"You were the last person to see her alive."

The words hung in the air between them. Was he blaming her for surviving when his wife and son had died? He had not been like this when he'd come to visit her in the hospital. Understanding and sympathy and complete exoneration of any blame had been his message to her then. Maybe they had both changed in the intervening time. She noticed suddenly that his hair had got greyer, his body thinner. What a fucking mess!

"All right," she agreed. "I'll value the property for you, explain our terms and outline your options. Then you can decide if you wish to go ahead with the sale."

"I must. I have no choice."

The despair in his voice struck a chord in Ella's mind which reverberated long after Rob Trevor had left to return to Manor House.

* * *

It would have been nice to go to a crowded place. A place where he could show off the beautiful woman by his side, where he could revel in the envy of every man who laid eyes on Maxine Doran. Even though she was dressed casually – jeans, a wispy top and a faux-fur jacket and high-heeled boots – she still exuded glamour and that indefinable factor which set beautiful women apart from the merely attractive. Andrew realised as he drove further from the city that he was far enough away from his home ground not to be recognised but that Maxine would probably be known wherever she went. It would have to be a very quiet pub for lunch.

He began to feel nervous, gauche, in the company of this much-travelled, sophisticated, successful woman. Glancing across at her he noticed that she seemed relaxed, her long legs stretched out, casually admiring the scenery whizzing past.

"Anywhere in particular you'd like to go?" he asked.

"I see a signpost for Ballyhaven ahead. Why not go in that direction? It's a very nice area."

Andrew indicated to turn off the motorway. This was perfect. He would not have to lie now. Not really. He could tell Ella he came here to look over their site. If she asked, which she probably would not.

"Do you know Ballyhaven well?"

Maxine smiled. "What's to know? A few shops, a church, a pub and endless acres of farmland."

"I own fifty acres there."

"Really? I couldn't picture you in Wellington boots and a peaked cap. Wait a second though . . ."

She closed her eyes and threw her head back against the headrest, smiling as she described her image of Andrew going to feed the pigs wearing *only* green wellies and a tweed cap.

"I hope it's a warm day in your imagination or else I'll get pneumonia!"

"It's gloriously hot," she said, opening her eyes and laughing now, enjoying her little game. "But there's danger. You're being chased by a dairymaid named

Maxine. She's wearing pink wellies and a white frilly bonnet. She's running very fast. Oh, no! You've slipped and fallen. She's just about to . . ."

Andrew brought the car to a stop outside Ballyhaven's only pub just as Maxine's fantasy was about to get very interesting.

"We'll never know now what the dairymaid would have done," she said softly, putting on a very pretty pretend-pout.

"How about we go to my site after lunch? Maybe you'll remember what happened next."

They were laughing as they walked arm in arm into the Ballyhaven Inn.

* * *

Lunch had been a stodgy affair. The mounds of mashed potato and thick slices of roast beef sat heavily in their stomachs.

"Let's walk your fifty acres," Maxine suggested. "Burn off those calories."

It had been a very long time since Andrew had visited his site. He had forgotten how beautiful and tranquil the setting was. Or maybe viewing it with Maxine made him see it in a different light. They had laughed and even giggled over lunch. He felt happy for the first time in a whole year. He imagined himself young, free and totally enthralled with the woman by his side. That was the magic of Maxine.

The fields were wild and overgrown, the ditches in bad

repair. He had toyed for a while with the idea of letting the fifty acres out in conacre but had never got around to following up on the plan. He parked beside a rusty gate where they would have easy access to the fields. He was surprised to see Maxine take off her high-heeled boots and put on a pair of walking shoes.

"I wondered what you had in that big bag," he remarked. "What else do you have in there? A frilly white bonnet?"

Zipping up her bag, Maxine put it back into the car with her jacket, turned her back on Andrew and headed for the gate. She scaled the rusty bars and began to run.

"Come on, lazy boots! Let's see how fit you are!"

Andrew trotted after her, soon realising exactly how unfit he was. He was puffing before they reached the second field and he was suffering badly by the time Maxine stopped in the shade of the woods which sprawled across the bottom of the site.

"You're in good shape," he gasped as he reached her.

"It's my job."

He looked sharply at her. Had there been a note of bitterness in her voice?

"Don't you enjoy modelling?"

"I enjoy the success. The money. What else is there?"

"Job satisfaction?"

"You mean like you get from selling a property? Tell me, Andrew, would you feel the same satisfaction if you sold at no profit, or even a loss?"

He shook his head and took her point. It was all about making money. She was stooping down now and feeling the thick carpet of pine needles with her hand.

"It's dry," she said. "Why don't we sit down and take a rest? We can put our backs to this big tree trunk."

They sat in silence until Andrew's breathing became regular again. The pine needles were soft underneath them and the rays of sun slanting through the branches bathed them in a golden pine-scented light. They held hands and breathed in the sylvan peace.

"So what are you going to do later on? I mean when you're tired of modelling?"

"You mean when I'm too old and fat and wrinkled to get any more work."

Andrew lifted his hand and stroked her shining hair, murmuring that she would always be beautiful.

"And practical," she answered. "I want to open a restaurant. A high-class restaurant, a place where everybody who is anybody will want to be seen. I want to provide an elegant dining experience, with international cuisine in beautiful surroundings. I want to –"

She stopped suddenly, aware that she had already said too much. This was her secret, her plan. She had never meant to share it. Remembering why she was here, she turned to Andrew.

"And what about you? Are you going to retire from Ford Auctioneers, a grey-haired, crabby old man, or are you going to sell these fifty acres and live on the profits?"

Andrew frowned. This was a coincidence. The second time in the past few days he had been asked about his plans for these fields.

"Depends," he answered. "If these fifty acres were

rezoned as residential, I might consider selling. And since Garry Cox is interested, there is some move afoot. I must give my contacts in Planning a call."

Maxine smiled. Jason Laide would be furious that the Cox brothers were sniffing around the Ballyhaven site. She would love telling him he had strong competition. Then her smile faded. This was not good news for her. The quicker Jason got his hands on the land, the quicker she would be rid of him. For good. She put her head on Andrew's shoulder.

"Let me know what you decide. I might be interested in buying. Build my restaurant in this glade here. What do you think?"

Andrew raised an eyebrow. Was she fantasising again or did she really earn the kind of money that would allow her build her dream?

Whatever the answer to that, he was sitting here, now, alone in the woods with the most beautiful woman he had ever known. He laid her on the pine needles and, skin caressed by cool breeze and warm sunshine, Andrew and Maxine made love.

Chapter 4

Ella welcomed the sound of her Monday morning alarm call. She took her time getting ready, breathing deeply, putting on her favourite shoes, forcing herself to concentrate on the day's work ahead. Andrew would already be behind his desk, phoning, faxing, emailing, doing all the things that made him such a successful auctioneer. Finished with her make-up, she examined herself in the full-length mirror. She saw a well-groomed, attractive, dark-haired woman, wearing very nice shoes. There was no trace of torment in the reflection, no despair in the hazel eyes, no sign flashing to say that today was the first anniversary of the accident.

Satisfied that she had turned off everything in the kitchen, she checked the rest of the house and was surprised to find her ironing still in the lounge since yesterday. She had a vague memory of abandoning it when Rob Trevor had called but she could remember little now of the rest of the evening after he had left.

Maybe she had slept.

Annoyed with herself, she tidied up the mess in the lounge and rechecked the kitchen appliances. It was as she was picking her car keys off the hall table that she saw Andrew's note about the new doctor. She took the piece of paper and put it into her bag. She would ring Dr Peter Sheehan as soon as she got into the office and let him know just what she thought of his collusion with her husband. The anger she felt against the two men was the spur she needed to kick-start her day.

* * *

Andrew was puzzled when he put the phone down. He had just had a baffling conversation with his contact in the Department of Planning. Oliver Griffin was far more than just a business contact. They had gone to school together, played on the same teams, chased the same girls, attended the same college. Oliver was holding out on him now. He had been evasive when Andrew had mentioned Ballyhaven. There were some ideas being thrown around, he had said, nothing concrete that he knew of. Bullshit! As if anything could happen in that Planning Office without Oliver Griffin's say-so. He was Chief Planner. The uncomfortable silences and forced bonhomie of the conversation after Ballyhaven had been mentioned was baffling.

Andrew picked up a biro and began to scribble. He always thought more clearly with a pen and piece of paper. He wrote Ballyhaven and underneath it Oliver Griffin. Then he wrote down the name Garry Cox and put a circle around it. Next he penned Maxine Doran in big bold letters. Could there be a link between all of them and the fifty acres of scrubland in Ballyhaven? Where did Maxine Doran fit into the picture? She mixed with the high and mighty and the Cox brothers were quickly climbing to the top of the entrepreneurial heap. Was she working for them, deliberately getting close to Andrew, trying to screw the fifty acres out of him? But what would be the point in that? Garry Cox had asked Andrew directly about the Ballyhaven site. Why should he need Maxine as a go-between? She must be working on someone else's behalf. Unless of course, she was telling the truth and her concern with Ballyhaven was purely personal.

Trying to forget her smooth skin and her firm breasts, Andrew thought about the little he knew of Maxine Doran and her very recent, very intense, interest in him. In fact, he wondered if anybody knew anything about her. All the information in the public domain was what Maxine or her agent chose to publicise. Her career and her love life were well documented. But who was she really? She must certainly be a wealthy woman by now. But would she be able to raise the kind of capital needed to build a high-class restaurant? In any case, she was lying when she said she would consider building it in Ballyhaven. Even if the area was going to be developed – *if* – it would not be the place to build a gourmet restaurant. So why the charade?

Without realising what he was doing, Andrew found that he had sketched a reasonably good likeness of

Maxine. If he had not been so obsessed with financial security, maybe he could have made it as an artist. Just as he was shading in the area where her waist narrowed in, he heard the door open. With a deftness and speed spurred by guilt, he had the scribble page in the shredder across the room before Ella had reached her desk.

"I'm going to ring Dr Peter Sheehan now," she announced.

"Good."

Andrew tried hard to remember Peter Sheehan's advice. Play along with her, let her make her own decisions, or at least let her believe that she was making them for herself. Stupid advice really. Ella did just as she pleased anyway.

"I'm going to complain about him to the Medical Board for discussing my health issues with someone else without my permission. I'm not even his patient."

He felt his calm fade away as his anger rose. "The 'someone else' is your husband. Or at least, the man who is trying to be a husband to you. I need you to get better, not just for your sake but for mine too."

"And going behind my back, treating me as if I was incapable of handling my own –"

She stopped mid-sentence and, taking off her jacket, sat down at her desk. She logged onto her computer as calmly as if she had not just been shouting.

Andrew shrugged. He could not fathom her moods.

"Rob Trevor wants to put Manor House on the market," she said.

"How do you know? Who's handling the sale?"

"We are. He called round yesterday. Asked me to organise it for him. Pity you weren't there."

"I went to Ballyhaven to look over our site," Andrew said much too quickly.

Ella gave him one of her cold stares and he was not sure whether she was telling him that she suspected he was with another woman or if she was not even seeing him at all. The probability was that she did not care either way.

"Why do you think the Coxes are interested?" she asked. "Why don't you ring that slimy friend of yours in the Planning Office? He should be able to tell you."

"I did and Oliver was very evasive. And he's not slimy by the way."

She wondered how Andrew would feel if he knew that his great school friend had tried every trick in the book to get her into bed with him. He was a scumbag but an influential one. She flashed one of her business smiles at her husband.

"Ballyhaven is your baby anyway. I'm working on the sale of the Laides' property. Let me know if you come across something huge and expensive that might suit them as a replacement."

Now there, Andrew thought, was a genuinely slimy character. Jason Laide was all gold chains and shiny suits and pots of money from some mysterious source. His haulage business seemed to have become an overnight success. From one truck to international haulier in the blink of an eye. He now had enough wealth to be able to buy his way into the best society in town. One of those people you could not afford to ignore. Ella seemed to be getting on with them all right.

"What's she really like? Sharon Laide, I mean."

Ella put down the sheet she had been reading and looked at Andrew with a puzzled expression. "The answer to that question is that I don't know. One minute she's the soul of charm and elegance, just as she seems on social occasions, and the next she's crass and . . . a bit dangerous maybe. Reckless."

"Well, she *is* married to Jason Laide. Laid more women than Casanova as he likes to say."

"What do we care once we get our commission for selling his house?"

Andrew nodded. At least this was one thing on which they could agree. "What about Manor House? Do you think the Laides would go for it? They might like the image."

Ella shivered. She had to face that demon today. She had promised Rob. More importantly, she had promised herself. Standing, she picked up her bag.

"Actually, I'm going out to Manor House now. I'm assuming we can market it at around the six million mark but I want to check the condition of the buildings."

By the time she had reached the door of the office, Andrew had already returned his attention to valuation documents. Ella stared at the bowed head for a moment before she spoke.

"I've decided to see Dr Sheehan after all. I want to tell him face to face exactly what I think of him."

Andrew just nodded and kept on with his work. He sighed in relief when he heard the door closing.

* * *

Maxine smiled as she examined herself in the mirror. Just as well that it was a winter collection she was modelling for the charity show tonight. She had a big red mark on her bottom where a pine needle had pierced her skin. It would not have looked very attractive in a bikini. She laughed out loud now as she remembered the passion, the exquisite pleasure, of yesterday afternoon. It was as if Andrew Ford's body had been designed specifically to match hers. Even as she remembered her overwhelming physical reaction to Andrew's lovemaking, Maxine admitted to herself it was more than that. It was the safety and security she felt when his arms were around her. For the first time in her life, she felt protected. She closed her eyes now and imagined that Andrew was standing beside her, stroking her hair, looking into her eyes, smiling . . . Her eyes flew open as she heard a key being fitted into her door-lock. Fuck! She grabbed her dressing-gown and tied the belt tightly around her waist.

"Not dressed yet, Maxine? Lazy cow! Or were you waiting for me to help you put on your little bits and pieces? You know I prefer taking them off."

Maxine glared at Jason Laide and her stomach heaved. How had she ever got involved with this piece of shit? Bile rose in her throat as a treacherous voice in her head told her that there had been a time when she would have done anything for Jason. A time when she had done every perverted thing he asked of her.

"I have a friend, a very important friend, coming to visit," he said. "I need you to keep him sweet. You know what I mean."

Maxine knew only too well what he meant. She might be a supermodel on the world stage but when the cameras stopped running she was still Jason Laide's property. That meant she was also available to his friends and those thugs he liked to call his business colleagues. She looked at him and for one hate-filled moment imagined how good it would feel to strangle the life out of the bastard. She somehow managed to smile.

"Who is this person and why is he so important?" she asked.

"All you need to know is that you must make sure he enjoys his visit. Show him the sights. And anything else he may care to see. That shouldn't be too difficult for you. You've had plenty of practise."

"Why don't you show him around yourself?"

"I will. But I won't fuck him. That's your job."

Jason narrowed his eyes and glared at the beautiful woman standing in front of him. She tightened her dressing-gown around herself and stared back. Huge deep-blue eyes met narrowed ice-blue slits.

"You're beginning to believe your own publicity," he said softly and the gentle tone carried more threat than a shout. "You need reminding just who you are. I could very quickly land you back in the gutter where you belong. Don't ever forget that."

"No, Jason. I won't ever, ever forget."

Jason smiled in satisfaction, enjoying the feeling of

being in control. Happy that Maxine was now as respectful towards him as he deserved, he told her about his friend, Dirk Van Aken, and the entertainment he expected her to provide.

When he left, Maxine picked up a Belleek vase and smashed it onto the tiled floor of the kitchen. She felt less angry but much sadder as she swept up the shards of the once beautiful piece of porcelain.

* * *

Ella drove slowly and carefully, all the time prepared to be bombarded by overwhelming emotions. Metre by metre, she got closer to the crash site. The scene of the accident, the place where Karen Trevor had died and Ella Ford had stopped living. This was not her first time driving here since that day. She had passed by many times and on each occasion she had felt exactly as she did now. Nothing. It was just a sharp bend on a narrow road leading to some of the most valuable real estate in the western suburbs. Nettles and grass clogged the drains which had been flooded with water a year ago today. Brambles, bare and woody, clawed the stones of the boundary ditches. There was no blood, no twisted metal, no broken and dying bodies. After rounding the bend, she put her foot on the accelerator and drove the five kilometres to Manor House at a more normal speed.

Rob Trevor was waiting for her at the entrance gate.

"Thank you for coming, Ella. I thought you might like to park here and we could walk around the grounds and outbuildings first."

She got her clipboard and camera and followed him as he led the way through the shrubbery, the rose garden, the orchard and then onto the well-kept lawns. Even at this time of year, there was scent and colour in the gardens.

"It's beautifully kept," Ella remarked.

"We have a good gardener."

Of course. That's how these people lived, wasn't it? They enjoyed the spoils of someone else's labour. The gardener, the cook, the nanny. The estate agent. Ella looked at the man walking beside her and flinched when she saw the pain in his eyes.

"You're sure you want to sell, Rob? Maybe you should wait a little while before making up your mind. It's a very big decision. Maybe now is not the right time to make it."

"I must. I have no choice."

They walked in silence towards the stables. Ella's heels clicked on the cobbles as they crossed the courtyard. Taking out her camera she began to shoot the stables from different angles. They were perfect for conversion to apartments. With proper planning it would be possible to fit eight, maybe ten, good-sized apartments around the central cobbled yard. A definite bonus selling point.

"I gave the horses away," Rob said quietly. "Karen was a great horsewoman. Talented. Ian was beginning to show some promise as well."

He stopped abruptly and stood staring at the stable with the red half-door. Ella assumed that must have been where Karen had kept her horse. She walked towards it and peered into the gloom. It was large inside, much larger than most inner-city apartments. The roof and walls seemed in perfect condition. Even though the stable was cleared out, the warm, musty aroma of straw still lingered. What a privileged lifestyle Karen Trevor had lived. Why couldn't she have been more careful? How arrogant had it been to speed along that little road in the lashing rain? But she would have been an arrogant woman, wouldn't she? Stables and rose gardens were the stuff of arrogance.

When Ella turned, Rob had gone. She shivered. The courtyard seemed threatening now, the click of her heels eerie as they echoed around the quadrangle formed by the stables. It was a relief to get back onto the driveway and see Rob waiting for her at the front door.

"Shall we see the reception rooms first?" he asked.

Ella just nodded, awed into silence by the splendour of Manor House. She was used to seeing luxury, multi-million euro homes full of designer chic. This was different. The good taste here was not bought and paid for. It had evolved over centuries and was passed from generation to generation in the upper-class bloodline. The hall was vast, with a magnificent staircase sweeping upwards from the black-and-white tiled floor. Portraits lined the walls. Ella's eyes were drawn to the largest portrait at the bottom of the stairs. As she walked towards it, it began to happen again. She felt the coldness, the fear, the horror. Karen's face peered at her from the painting, the eyes wide and staring, the mouth open in a silent scream. Ella wanted to close her eyes, to shut out the vision, to stop the nightmare, but she could not move. She stood paralysed with fear, as blood trickled from Karen

Trevor's smashed forehead.

"That's Karen's great-aunt."

Rob's voice brought Ella back to reality. She turned and looked at him, wondering if he had noticed that she was behaving oddly. Insanely.

"She was very beautiful," Ella replied as she now examined the portrait as the artist had depicted it. The sitter was young, maybe sixteen or seventeen, her blonde hair swept up underneath a hat with a large plume, her hands resting on the silk folds of her dress. There was something about the way the girl held herself, the proud tilt of the chin that reminded Ella of someone she knew. Not Karen, even though there was an obvious family resemblance.

"What was her name?"

Rob laughed and Ella looked at him in surprise. She had expected reverence where ancestors were concerned. Of course, these were Karen's family. This was Karen's house. At least it had been before she went and crashed her four-wheel drive on a flooded little by-road.

"She was a feisty lady. Karen never liked talking much about her. The black sheep of the family. She eloped with one of the stable lads. That is Harriet. Lady Harriet Wellsley."

Ella examined the portrait again and this time she saw beyond the fine silks and plumes. There was a fierce pride and determination in the lift of the chin but it was in the eyes that the real character of Harriet Wellsley shone through. Even on canvas they shone with passion. This was a woman capable of either great love or great hate.

"And what happened? Did she stay with her stable lad or did she come back into the fold?"

Rob shuffled his feet and seemed a little uncomfortable. "I don't know what happened. I told you the Wellsleys didn't like talking about her. She never came back into the family anyway. At least, not that I know of."

"But yet they kept her portrait hanging in the hall."

"Probably because it's worth a lot of money. It may be a Collier portrait."

Ella glanced quickly at him, surprised at the sharp tone. She had vaguely heard of John Collier, society portrait painter of the late nineteenth and early twentieth century. If Rob said this might be a Collier, he was probably right. Rob was a well-established art dealer and Karen, an only child, had inherited all the old Wellsley money. Had money been an issue between himself and Karen? They must have had a very comfortable lifestyle. Except, of course, that the upkeep of this house would cost a fortune. Maybe the vulgarity of money had spoiled the elegance of Karen's inheritance.

She followed on as he led her into the splendid drawing room, still wondering about his offhand comment.

It took them almost an hour to examine all the rooms from the ground floor to the top floor where the household staff used to sleep in their cramped quarters after a hard day slaving for the Wellsleys' comfort. The house was in excellent condition.

"It's been very well maintained," Ella remarked. "We should have very little trouble finding a buyer. Do you mind if I take a few photos now? Get some ideas for a brochure. I assume title deeds are in order?"

"Yes. Ready to go as soon as you find a new owner."

She spent another half an hour taking shots of the grandeur of the interior. When she had finished, she found herself drawn back again to the portrait of Harriet Wellsley. Standing in front of it, she tried to remember just who the lady resembled. She had definitely seen that face before, seen those lustrous eyes.

"She fascinated Karen too."

Ella jumped when Rob spoke. She had not realised he was standing beside her.

"She is, or was, very beautiful," she said. "A timeless type of beauty. Do you mind if I photograph her. Just for myself?"

When Rob nodded his agreement, Ella began to click. Zooming in on the face, she was even more fascinated by the lustrous eyes, more certain that she knew somebody who looked just like Lady Harriet Wellsley.

As she drove out through the pillared gates, Ella felt satisfied. She had faced one demon by going into Karen Trevor's home. She had stood in the dead woman's kitchen, incongruously modern in the old house. She had seen the bed where Rob and Karen had created the little boy who was destined to die in the wrecked four-wheel drive. She had poked and pried in Karen's life. And she had survived. Maybe she could yet learn to live with Karen's death. Glancing at her watch she realised it was almost time for her doctor's appointment. Getting into her car, she smiled. She was ready now to tackle Dr Peter Sheehan.

Chapter 5

The blues and greens of the waiting room annoyed Ella intensely. The colour scheme was obviously designed to pacify, to lull neurotic patients into a false sense of calmness. Peter Sheehan must be the sort of doctor who thought he could cure his patients by controlling their moods, their thoughts. A manipulative, controlling man. By the time his secretary led her into the holy of holies, into the divine presence, Ella had built up a huge resentment against Peter Sheehan.

He was standing behind his desk. Tall and broad-shouldered, dark hair short and neat, skin tanned, he exuded an aura of confidence which irked Ella even more. His choice of clothes was the final straw. He was wearing a fine wool sweater and jeans. Dressing down so that he could fool his insane patients into a false sense of camaraderie. What a prick!

"Mrs Ford. How nice to meet you. Sit down please."

Ignoring the chair he had indicated, Ella walked

towards him and stood directly in front of him. Up close, he was handsome. His green eyes, clear and very alert, were carefully watching her. She stared back at him, noticing the dark thick lashes and the crinkles at the corners of his eyes. He had probably got them from laughing at his idiotic patients. Fuck him!

"I won't sit, thank you. I won't be staying long. I just came here to tell you that I think you're a disgrace to the medical profession. How dare you collude with my husband behind my back? I did not make an appointment to see you and I most certainly do not want to be treated by you. You have behaved unprofessionally and I intend taking this matter further. I'm going to make a complaint to the Medical Board."

He sat. Like a huge, green-eyed cat, he lounged on his chair and regarded her with interest. No anger, no shock. Just curiosity.

"I see," he said quietly.

His voice had shades of the calming blues and greens too. It was deep and still. Ella knew he had sat so that she would not feel intimidated by having him tower over her. She sat now so that she could look him in the eye, not allowing him to take the initiative.

"Do you usually handle cases without proper referral? Is a phone call from a family member enough for you?"

He smiled and the flash of white teeth was so startling in his tanned face that Ella almost responded by smiling herself.

"Yes. I've been known to oblige people by cutting through the red tape. Especially friends."

"Well, I'm not your friend."

"But Andrew is."

"What do you mean? Do you know my husband?"

"Andrew and I are from the same neighbourhood. We were practically inseparable for twelve years. Terrible twins. Then my family emigrated to Canada. We stayed in touch for a long time but you know how easy it is to get too involved in your own life. We lost touch at the college stage. I'm surprised he hasn't told you."

Embarrassed, Ella conjured up her business smile. How had Andrew allowed her to make such a fool of herself? Damn! He could have warned her. He should have warned her. Then she shrugged. Her attack on Peter Sheehan was as big a slur on Andrew as it was on her. She could almost read the doctor's mind now, noting the lack of communication between husband and wife, wondering why Andrew Ford had married such a hysterical shrew. To hell with both of them. She stood.

"Since you and Andrew are practically related then, would it not be inappropriate for you to treat me? It was interesting meeting you. Goodbye."

She held out her hand to him but he ignored it.

"I believe you were involved in a very serious car accident, Mrs Ford. Do you want to talk about it?"

Something about the green eyes, the calm voice, made Ella stop and think. Maybe she should challenge him to take her on, to give her back a normal life, a peaceful night's sleep. See how he would cope with her recurrent vision of a dying woman.

"Do you have expertise in the area of Post Traumatic

Stress Disorder?" she asked.

He sat up straight then and his casual wait-and-see attitude fell away from him.

"Yes, I do. I've worked for six years in a military hospital in the States. As you probably know PTSD is very prevalent in war veterans. Vietnam, Afghanistan, Iraq. No end of wars and war victims."

"I'm not a victim."

"From where I'm sitting, you're a victim of your own unwillingness to face your problem. Why don't you stop being angry and just sit and talk?"

"So! You're a Reality Therapist too. Not going to take any excuses for my behaviour?"

He smiled at her again and suddenly Ella realised that she was behaving like a petulant child. Determined to prove that she could be mature, she sat and began to speak.

"I'm stuck in a time warp. What happened exactly one year ago today is happening over and over again. I can't sleep, I can't eat. I can't live like this. Can you help me?"

"I will help you to help yourself," Peter Sheehan said with such conviction that Ella dared to believe him.

* * *

Every time Andrew reached for the phone he had to stop himself dialling Maxine Doran's number. He had been like this all day. He knew all the reasons he should not. She was far too sophisticated and ambitious to have any interest in a moderately successful estate agent. She was yachts and ski slopes and Caribbean islands. She was fantasy. And he was married. Sighing, Andrew dialled Gary Cox's mobile number.

"Ah! Andrew. You've made a decision on Ballyhaven?"

"No. Not quite. I wanted to ask you a question. Why are you interested in it? It's agricultural land. As far as I can find out, there are no plans to rezone the area. So why do the Cox brothers want to buy fifty acres of waste land?"

"Why did you and Ella buy it?"

"Because we hoped at some stage it would become residential and we would make a killing."

"Well, there you go. We're thinking along the same lines. We're offering you a good price."

Andrew grunted a noncommittal reply. It would be a very good price for the fifty acres as they stood now. He could not shake the idea that everybody knew of plans afoot for Ballyhaven. Everybody except Andrew Ford.

"I'll think about it, Gary. I'll get back to you."

"Don't take too long. We won't leave this offer on the table forever. There are other investments we're looking into as well."

Andrew quelled his instinct to tell Cox to shove his deal. He had not offered the site for sale. But he owed the Cox brothers, Gary and Noel. Besides he was in no mood for making business decisions. Unable to put the image of Maxine Doran out of his mind, he finally rang her house phone. Getting no answer, he rang her mobile. He left a bumbling hesitant voicemail on her message minder. Then he rang again and again, just to hear her voice on the answering machine. It took fifteen minutes for him to admit to himself just how adolescent his behaviour was.

And to add guilt to shame, he had forgotten to ring Peter Sheehan to warn him of Ella's attitude. A glance at the clock told him he was now too late.

* * *

Dirk Van Aken looked like a blonde version of Jason Laide. As the two men sat side by side in the restaurant after lunch, Maxine thought they could be twins. Both wearing silk suits and expensive open-necked shirts, both with gold chains around their necks, both sleazy. Jason glanced at his watch and winked at Maxine.

"My wife is off on another of her ski trips. I must see her before she leaves."

He turned towards Dirk and smiled. "I hope you don't mind. I'll leave you with Maxine. She'll show you around."

Dirk flashed back an identical smile. A sneer, full of the promise of debauchery and barely contained violence. Jason stood up and then strutted out of the restaurant, leaving Maxine to do the job expected of her. She turned to Dirk.

"A walk around the city? Wine bar? What would you like to do?"

"I would like to see your city now," he answered glancing at his watch. "I need to walk. Get a little exercise. But later, a club. A little party for you and me maybe?"

Maxine answered him with a smile and hoped that he read as much threat in her smile as she did in his. She could not tell this piece of shit exactly what she thought of him. Jason had said he was important. But she could think what she liked and all her thoughts now were murderous ones.

"How long have you known Jason?" she asked.

"We have been acquainted for some time. We have mutual friends but we are not long in business together. Well, serious business anyway."

"Really?" Maxine asked, hoping her curiosity was not too apparent. Jason Laide must have done his training in the KGB. He was so secretive about his business affairs that Maxine had no idea, even after all the years, exactly how he made his money. Of course there was his haulage business. Laide Transport was the biggest national haulier and had a good share of international business too. The public face of Jason Laide. A money-spinner. But the overheads must be huge. Insurance, maintenance, wages, tax. The profit margins could not be high enough to support the Laides' lifestyle.

Maxine had lost track of how many foreign properties the Laides owned. She was probably not even aware of all of them. Sharon Laide seemed to spend most of her time visiting one or other of the properties abroad. Probably the only way she could manage to stay married to Jason. Maxine had also heard rumours of an art collection.

She turned now to the sleazebag beside her, wondering if he too had been warned by Jason to keep his mouth shut. She smiled at him.

"So Jason's thinking of doing business in Holland?"

"He already is," he answered quickly. Then the ice-cold eyes narrowed. "I don't want to talk about business. I want to talk about you. It's not every day I get to share some time with a supermodel. Is Jason a good friend of yours?"

"I've known him forever," Maxine replied and she was not being smart. It felt like forever since Jason had spotted her in her school uniform and had offered to get her a starring role in a film. Stupid, stupid child!

"Shall we go then? It's a nice day. I'd like a walk."

Maxine had to drag her attention back to Dirk. She stood and led the way out onto the street. Several people glanced at her and some just stared. She could almost hear them telling their exciting story later: 'Guess who I saw? Maxine Doran. The supermodel. Strolling around with a tough-looking guy.' They would probably think he was her minder. Jason knew she would attract attention. He must not care about exposing Dirk to speculation. One thing was sure, nobody would believe that the aloof Maxine Doran, supermodel, was escorting this Dutchman around because if she did not Jason Laide would distribute a pornographic video of her. She shivered. Thinking she was cold, Dirk put his arm around her. She raised her chin, squared her shoulders and stilled the scream in her head. Then she led Dirk Van Aken on a walking tour around her city. As requested.

* * *

Just as Ella thought she could not absorb any more information, Peter Sheehan stopped talking and smiled at her. More of a grin, full of fun and mischief.

"Bet you're wondering if I'm ever going to stop

lecturing and start treating? But it's important that you understand Post Traumatic Stress Disorder. It's a multi-faceted disorder. We will have to treat it on all fronts."

Ella nodded her agreement. Since Peter Sheehan had explained all the biological changes associated with PTSD in addition to the psychological problems, she felt less helpless, less of a hostage to her damaged memory function, her out-of-control emotions. Couching her nightmares in scientific and medical terms somehow empowered her again.

"If you are agreeable, Mrs Ford, I would like you to go to the blood clinic in the hospital where I work and have some tests done. Hormone levels, thyroid function and a few more. I'll write a letter for you."

He was assuming that she was going to become his patient. She had come here to tell him how unprofessional she considered him and now . . . now what? She had told him all about her visions of Karen Trevor, about the screaming terrified face she saw over and over in spider webs and teacups and traffic lights. She had confessed it all. Everything she had been ashamed to tell Dr Quill. Or even Andrew. The dreams, the sense of isolation, the feeling that the Ella she knew was still in a coma and that Karen Trevor had taken her place. The guilt. The crushing guilt of the survivor. The horrific loss of control. She looked across at him and saw sympathy in his eyes. Not pity. Not condemnation. Not irritation at her weakness and lack of character. Not a hint of 'pull yourself together' or 'here, take this pill and shut up'.

She smiled at him. "Yes, Dr Sheehan. I'll go for the

blood tests. What then?"

"I'd like to see you again. Talk more. Also I would like you to keep a log of episodes. We'll talk through them next appointment and we will decide together how best to deal with your situation."

"Therapy? Medication?"

"Probably a combination," he said. "Too soon to give you a definitive answer."

Ella stood and shook his hand. "Sorry about the less than polite way I introduced myself. I'll make an appointment with your secretary on the way out."

He stood then and walked her to the door. When she went out onto the street later, her step was a little lighter, her shoulder muscles less tense, the cold space around her heart slightly warmer than it had been before she had met Peter Sheehan.

★ ★ ★

Andrew felt restless. He had plenty of work to do but nothing so urgent that it required his immediate attention. Walking over to the window of his office he looked at the traffic on the street outside. It was building nicely towards the bumper-to-bumper chaos of the evening rush hour. The walls of the office seemed to shrink and close in about him. He had not heard from Ella. He regretted his call to Peter Sheehan now. Suppose Ella had carried out her threat and had angrily confronted Peter? What would the perfect Mr Sheehan think of Andrew Ford's wife then? What would he think of

Andrew Ford? Opening his door, he walked through the main office, stopping to tell the receptionist that he would be gone for a little while.

Out on the street, he looked in both directions. He could turn left and go to the newsagent's for an evening paper or turn right and go for a walk in the park. The thought of trees, gravelled paths and the duck pond won out. Turning right he headed for the park. Everyone seemed to be leaving as he entered. The path was packed with buggies, children on bikes or rollerblades and toddlers pursued by harassed mothers. Andrew made his way towards the pond, remembering the seating there. Maybe sitting watching the ducks paddle and waddle would calm the restlessness inside him.

He found a vacant seat. The traffic was just a distant buzz and he could hear the rustle of wind in the trees, the gentle lap of the water against the edge of the pond, the quacks of ducks, the squeals of excited children and the barely controlled hysteria in their mothers' shouts. Maxine Doran seemed to have peeled away his protective skin. His feelings, his senses, his perceptions, were all sharper now. It was as if Maxine had reached inside him and turned him inside out, leaving the most vulnerable, sensitive part of Andrew Ford to absorb the sights and sounds, the pain and joy of living.

Annoyed at his fanciful turn of mind and at allowing Maxine into his conscious thoughts again, he stooped, picked up a pebble and threw it into the pond. It landed in the water with a splashy sound. Little waves billowed out from the point of impact. He watched as the circles grew wider and wider, hypnotised by the gentle, unstoppable motion.

He continued staring until a tinkling sound, a familiar laugh, caught his attention. It was unmistakable. Sweet and pure and, for him, heart-stopping. His head snapped up and he saw Maxine, laughing up at the man by her side. They were walking towards the pond. Andrew swallowed to rid himself of the sharp knot of jealousy that stuck in his throat. The man was blonde, stocky, wearing an opened-necked shirt and a silk suit. Gold chains around his neck glinted in the feeble evening light.

Andrew stood as they approached.

Maxine's laugh faded as she saw him. "Andrew! What a surprise! I didn't think you were a feeding-ducks type!"

"I'm not," he replied sulkily. "And ditto."

"I'm just showing Dirk around," she explained. "Dirk Van Aken from Holland. Dirk, meet Andrew Ford. One of our leading estate agents here."

Andrew shook the Dutchman's hand. What in the fuck was Maxine doing with a hoodlum like this?

"Your city is very beautiful," Dirk said, "and so full of energy. It really is at the cutting edge of progress, isn't it?"

"Are you just visiting?" Andrew asked curtly.

"I'm carrying out a feasibility study. I may invest here. If the conditions are right."

"What line of business are you in?" Andrew asked and was not surprised when Dirk answered, "Entertainment". It figured that this scummy-looking person would be involved in lap-dancing and maybe strip clubs or something even sleazier. What was his connection with

Maxine? Why was this beautiful, successful woman spending time with a man who was obviously a pimp?

"I enjoyed our trip to the countryside," she said, smiling at Andrew.

Andrew was taken aback. It was careless of Maxine to mention that they had shared time together. But then this Dirk person did not know and most probably did not care that Andrew was married.

"I own a few acres of land out there," Andrew explained. "Max and I just went to look over the site."

"I see," Dirk muttered.

His stare sent a shiver down Andrew's spine. He took a step back from the man with the gold chains, furious with himself for making an explanation to this piece of gilded shit. Glancing at his watch he saw that it was almost closing time in Ford Auctioneers.

"I've got to get back to the office," he said. "Enjoy your stay, Dirk."

Turning to Maxine, he wanted to warn her, to tell her be careful of the Dutchman. Instead he just said a quick goodbye.

"I'm off to Paris tomorrow for a couple of days," she said. "A catwalk job. I'll call you when I get back."

Maxine looked so beautiful, so delicate and frail in the evening light that Andrew wanted to take her in his arms and then punch the Dutch gangster. No. He would flatten Dirk first and then take Maxine . . .

Realising that he was making a spectacle of himself staring at Maxine, Andrew nodded curtly and strode off in the direction of his office. By the time he reached the street again he had admitted to himself that Maxine Doran was probably well capable of taking care of herself. She had not needed Andrew Ford to get her to where she was and she certainly did not need him to keep her there.

Maxine had watched Andrew go, then turned to the man by her side and began to walk at a pace that had him gasping for breath. She walked and walked from monument to monument until both she and Dirk Van Aken were completely exhausted. Especially Dirk Van Aken.

* * *

Ella arrived back at the office at exactly the same time as Andrew. Unless Andrew was mistaken there was a new energy about her, a slightly less dark shadow around her. She threw a package on her desk and took off her coat.

"I collected the photos of Manor House. Would you look through them with me? I'll have to pick out a few for the website and the brochure."

Andrew walked over to her desk and sat opposite her. Up close his earlier impression was confirmed. Her eyes were definitely brighter, her shoulders more relaxed.

"Did you go to see Peter Sheehan?"

She glared at him. "Why didn't you tell me you knew him? I was embarrassed when he told me."

"You didn't give me a chance. Anyway, how did you get on with him?"

Ella stopped opening the package on the desk and frowned. How had she got on with Dr Peter Sheehan?

When she was in his office, under his green-eyed gaze, she had felt his compassion and understanding. She had been confident that he would solve all her problems. She had imagined herself to be safe and even sane. Now she was not so sure. Vulnerability gnawed at her insides again.

"I made another appointment with him."

There was no need to say more. Andrew nodded in satisfaction. He did not like Peter Sheehan. He never had, despite the fact that they had been inseparable. Peter had always been a Goody Two Shoes. But he had an international reputation for working with PTSD patients. He would have.

Ella had the package opened now and photos were strewn around the desk top. One by one they examined the pictures. The gardens, the stables, the façade of Manor House, the interior. They sorted through the photos, putting some aside as possible brochure pictures, discarding others, working in harmony until there was just one picture left.

They both stared in shocked silence at the portrait of Lady Harriet Wellsley.

Andrew saw Maxine Doran staring back at him. He saw Maxine's lustrous eyes, luxuriant blonde hair, delicate nose and high cheekbones. The resemblance was uncanny. It was as if Maxine had put on a plumed hat and a satin gown and sat for an artist.

"Who is she?" he asked in a whisper.

Ella did not answer. When Andrew looked at her she was staring wide-eyed at the photograph.

Ella was seeing Karen Trevor. She reached out to touch

the picture where Karen Trevor's endless dying played on relentlessly. The contact with the smooth, cold paper stilled the image and Lady Harriet Wellsley came back into focus. Ella sat back in her chair, at once exhausted but relieved. The dying image had been shorter, less intense this time. Maybe Peter Sheehan would live up to his promise to return her to normality. She turned to Andrew.

"That's a portrait of Karen's great-aunt. Lady Harriet Wellsley. A feisty woman by all accounts. She reminds me of someone but I can't put a name on her. Can you?"

"No," Andrew muttered but when Ella's attention was elsewhere he slipped the photograph of Lady Harriet Wellsley into his inside pocket.

Chapter 6

Jason Laide woke the following morning with an unfamiliar feeling of loneliness. He looked across the wide expanse of his seven-foot bed at the space left vacant by his wife. Sharon was gone again. Another young man. Another Adonis to entertain her for a little while. She would be back. She always was. Sated and amused, she would return to briefly fulfil her role as Mrs Jason Laide.

Her next spell at home would have to be longer. She had decided to move house again. Jason tried to remember how many times they had moved in the five years they were married, their homes getting progressively more ostentatious. At least this time he could benefit from whatever deal they made. He had been very satisfied to hear that Ford Auctioneers were to handle the sale of this property and the purchase of the new one. Trust Sharon to do the right thing! He now had a very good reason to deal directly with the Fords himself. And he might need to. It was very bad news that the Coxes were sniffing around the Ballyhaven site too. How in the fuck did they find out about it and how many more vultures would be trying to grab it? He was disappointed that Maxine Doran did not seem to be making good progress with Andrew Ford. The fifty acres in Ballyhaven were still in Ford's name. Maxine was not trying hard enough or else she was losing her touch. Her success was going to her head. She was becoming more and more difficult to handle.

Jason reddened with anger as he thought of the way Maxine looked down her nose at him, her distaste undisguised. There were times when he wished he had left the little slut where he had found her. In her crummy back street. But that would not have been her life-path in any case. Maxine, with her extraordinary beauty and overriding ambition, was never going to be left to smoulder in the mean streets. Not for her the job on the factory line, the drunken husband, the drudgery of childbearing and rearing. The life style her sisters had chosen. Yet she was beginning to outlive her usefulness to Jason Laide. Getting to be more trouble than she was worth.

Throwing the duvet back he got out of bed. His toes curled into the thick pile of the carpet. He stood for an instant, enjoying the warmth and softness, remembering the cold linoleum and chilblains of his childhood, the black moulds and stains of dampness that traced patterns of neglect on the walls and ceilings, the buckets and basins strategically placed to catch leaks. The incessant blood-chilling, mind-numbing drip-drip of poverty. He shivered. He had worked hard, done things he would rather not remember, in order to leave that childhood behind. He had one more goal. One more achievement to make before he could finally bury the poverty of his past. Neither the snotty Fords nor Maxine Doran were going to get in his way.

He dressed carefully, putting on even more bling than usual. It was vital that Dirk Van Aken and everybody else realised just how successful a man Jason Laide had become. Then he drove down town, fifteen minutes early for his appointment with the Dutchman. They had some very important business to do, a very important person to meet.

* * *

Ella went to her bag for a tissue and saw the letter Dr Peter Sheehan had written for the blood-testing clinic. She took it out and held it in her hand, trying to decide what to do. It was sealed. Of course she could open it. It was, after all, about her. But how would that help? Probably just a page covered in illegible doctor's squiggle. No. What she must decide now was what to do about it. Go to the clinic, have the tests and continue on with Peter Sheehan? See where the treatment took her, see if he could deliver peace of mind. Or she might go back to her previous doctor, Edmund Quill. And nightmares. Not an option.

She looked across the office at Andrew. He was gazing out the window, a frown creasing his forehead. For a moment Ella felt guilty. Her sickness, phobia or disorder, whichever terminology applied, had robbed Andrew of his smile. That crashing, death-filled instant which had taken Karen Trevor's life and that of her child, had forever changed the Andrew and Ella that used to be.

On impulse, Ella stood and walked across the office to her husband. Reaching out her hand she touched his cheek, remembering how she used to love the prickly feel of his strong stubble. He turned his gaze on her and she saw all the trauma of the past year reflected there. For the first time since the accident she really saw him, her husband, the man who used to be the centre of her life. Tears filled her eyes.

"I'm so sorry, Andrew," she whispered. "This has been terrible for you. I've been selfish. Focused on my own problems. Not thinking of you at all."

Andrew caught the hand touching his cheek and gently kissed it. The fingers stiffened, the hand withdrew.

"I'm getting help," Ella said, with an edge of panic in her voice. "Peter Sheehan is going to devise a recovery programme for me. And medication too. We'll be alright, Andy. Won't we?"

Andrew looked at the semi-hysterical woman standing in front of him, totally traumatised because he had kissed her hand. He wondered if any doctor, even the renowned Peter Sheehan, could ever fix her damaged mind. If they would ever be together again as man and wife.

He smiled at her. "Yes, Ella. We'll be fine. It will just take time."

Ella knew then that she would go to the blood-testing clinic that afternoon. She must.

* * *

Jason led the way into the cottage. It had the cold feel of an unoccupied dwelling. He flicked on the heating and brought Dirk Van Aken and Oliver Griffin into the kitchen-cum-dining room. It was sparsely furnished. Just the bare essentials. Cooker, fridge, microwave, kettle and in the dining area a huge table and six chairs. Jason indicated to the two men to sit at what he thought of as the conference table. Buying this cottage in a quiet suburban area of town had been one of his better ideas. It was the sort of area where people came and went and nobody asked questions. There were no concerned neighbours or nosey do-gooders. All his sensitive meetings were conducted here, safe from prying eyes. None more so, in his view, than the one they were about to begin now.

Sitting at the head of the table he looked at both men. Dirk Van Aken he recognised as his own double. His doppelgänger. Same backgrounds, same ambitions, same taste in clothes and women. Just born in different countries.

The Chief Planner was a different story. Oliver Griffin had come from the right side of town. Best schools, best opportunities, best reputation. A snob. The type of person Sharon could relate to with ease. Same background, same unshakable self-esteem. Fuck him, Jason thought as he watched Oliver glance disparagingly around the cottage. The shit never turned up his nose at his money. The man's class was only as deep as his designer labels.

Jason cleared his throat. "Let's get on with it. We all know why we're here. I'd like to hear from you first, Oliver. You can talk openly in front of Dirk. He knows everything about the proposed plan. In fact, he's part of it."

Oliver sniffed and straightened his immaculate cuffs. Jason felt his anger rise and had to make an effort to appear calm as the Chief Planning Officer spoke down to them.

"I'm not sure what you want me to say, Jason," Oliver said. "I've already told you that my contact in the Dáil has assured me about the Bill."

"Can you trust him?" Jason asked.

Annoyed at the implication that anyone would try to fool him, Oliver snapped a reply.

"He's a friend of mine. I went to college with him. Of course I can trust him. Besides, the agreement has already been made. My friend's party will vote with the Government on the controversial new Gambling Bill. It will be pushed through quickly with all the amendments necessary to enact it."

"Wait . . . wait!" There was a tinkle of metal as Dirk put up his hand and his bracelets slid down his wrist. "The Dáil, I believe, is your Irish Parliament. Yes? I understood that the politician in your pocket was a member of the party in power. Someone with clout. Are you now telling me that our plan hinges on a mere member of the opposition?"

Oliver's stomach did a flip. Who was this Van Aken guy? He seemed to be the most lethal of creatures: a gangster with brains. Jason Laide didn't appear to know the difference between a member of the government party and a member of opposition. That suited Oliver well. The last thing he needed now was a smart-ass thug informing Jason Laide.

"Pascal McEvoy is a very influential man!" Oliver snapped. "Whatever he says carries weight. And he's not 'in my pocket' as you put it. He's a friend. Can you understand that?"

Jason watched as little beads of sweat appeared on Dirk's forehead. He had always known Oliver Griffin was an idiot. The last person they needed to alienate was Dirk Van Aken. Dirk was getting perilously close to losing his monumental temper now. Time for some oil on troubled waters.

"Let's all show each other a little respect," Jason said, looking directly at Oliver. "The thing we really need to know is what's happening with the Gambling Bill now. Did your contact give you any idea?"

"Don't worry. It'll shortly, maybe in a month or two, be before the house. They'll vote for the changes. The bill will pass. There will be a super-casino licence up for grabs."

"But how many licences will they sanction and what will the terms of granting be?" Dirk asked.

Oliver turned and glared at the Dutchman. "I'm not clairvoyant. I can only tell you what's happening now. The proposal recommended by the advisory committee is for the granting of one licence in a designated area. All sides seem to be in agreement with that. You should be happy that things are looking so positive. What's your interest in it anyway?"

"Dirk owns the biggest gaming-machine company in Europe – he'll be supplying equipment for the casino," Jason answered quickly. "But actually that's none of your business. We just need you to use your political contact and to ensure our casino plans are accepted when they reach your office. How can we be sure that they'll all agree to Ballyhaven as the designated site? What does this politician guy want? What makes him tick? Money? Entertainment?"

Oliver looked at the two glitzy gangsters sitting in front of him and his stomach heaved. How had he come to this point in his life? The answer of course was gambling. The unstoppable urge to make a bet, to wager money he had not got, to gamble everything on a horse, a dog, a match, a white Christmas, roulette, black jack. It was excitement. Fulfilment. It was debt and cover-up. It was doing Jason Laide's bidding. Or appearing to. It was ensuring that this sleazy syndicate got a licence to turn Ballyhaven into the Vegas of Ireland. Or else . . . He smiled at the two men.

"No need for any sweetener. My contact, as I told you, is in favour of this Bill. Everything is going according to plan. Just have patience and it will all work out. In the meantime though, I would advise you, Jason, to buy that little pub in Ballyhaven. It would look better on paper if you already had an interest in the leisure business."

And that, thought Jason, was confirmation of the fact that Oliver Griffin was not as smart as he liked to think.

All that education was wasted on him. He should have worked out by now that Jason did indeed have a big stake in the leisure business. Jason Laide was the owner of the Eureka Club in town. The place where Oliver had gambled and lost and then gambled some more. Jason smiled. He was pleased for two reasons. One, obviously his own involvement in Eureka was well disguised, and two, Oliver had just made a bloody good suggestion. He would make the Ballyhaven pub owner an offer he could not refuse. He would also go to see Andrew Ford. Those fifty acres the Fords were sitting on in Ballyhaven were essential to the plan.

He would also have to turn his attention to Oliver Griffin's political friend, Pascal McEvoy. The passing of the Gambling Bill was too important to leave to chance. It was time to discover the politician's dirty little secrets. Jason never doubted for a moment that he would find one. Just in case. He always did.

* * *

Sitting at her desk Ella rolled up her sleeve and gently prodded the plaster on the inside of her elbow. The blood tests had not been nearly as traumatic as she had anticipated. The no-nonsense nurse taking the test had jabbed the needle in, filled a few vials, withdrawn the needle and slapped a pad of cotton wool on the puncture site before Ella even had time to consider fainting, screaming or otherwise making a complete spectacle of herself.

She patted the plaster thoughtfully now. For the first

time since the accident she felt a modicum of control. She believed she had taken a step towards recovery, found a path through the maze of nightmares and delusion. Soon, very soon, she would be able to part company with Karen Trevor. But would Karen let go? Would Karen find her own path? Realising that she was speculating on the future behaviour of a woman who had died over a year ago, Ella frowned. She may have taken the first step towards recovery but Peter Sheehan had a lot of work to do before Ella Ford was normal again. Work was the answer. Time-consuming, mind-absorbing work.

Logging on to her computer she began to examine her two new projects: the Laide property and Manor House. Both brochures were coming together nicely. Using a split screen she compared the properties side by side. As she was editing them, the door opened and Andrew came in. Ella noticed that he looked pale. A bit tired, a bit down.

"Busy?" she asked.

"Yeah. I've been to the old brewery site with the Coxes. They're really going to push the boat out on this one. We're talking roof gardens, basement gym and swimming pool here. With matching price-tags."

"Will they sell?"

Andrew went to his desk, picked up a thick folder and waved it in her direction. "Enquiries. Interested buyers. Not a sod turned yet and this is a list of potential clients who don't need to ask the price. Long live prosperity!"

"Amen," Ella said and turned her attention back to her computer screen.

Her breath froze in her lungs, her eyes widened in

horror. Karen Trevor stared back at her from the screen. Karen was standing on the front lawn of Manor House, her head broken and bleeding, her mouth open in a scream of terror, her arms outstretched. Ella tried to move, to tear her gaze away from the haunting image but Karen's bloody eyes held her in frozen horror. Somewhere, a tiny space at the back of Ella's head, told her this was illusion, hallucination, her malfunctioning flight or fight reaction, her altered brain function, her unbalanced hormones. All those things that Peter Sheehan had talked about. But nothing explained the horror in the dead woman's staring eyes, the persistent plea for help, the reaching out to Ella. What in the fuck did Karen Trevor want? Why could she not just die, bury her restless spirit with her decaying body?

"You can't use that picture," Andrew said. "Look, there's a flaw. A dark shadow on the lawn."

Ella had not noticed him cross the office to stand behind her. He was pointing now, leaning over her shoulder to place his finger on the section of screen where she was staring. His finger touched the spot where Karen Trevor stood. The image of Karen disappeared and Ella's breath exhaled in a rush.

Interpreting this as an impatient sigh, Andrew said, "A nuisance, I know, but you took plenty of shots, didn't you?"

Ella nodded, glad that Andrew was not aware that she'd had another of her delusional episodes. Her hands were shaking as she opened a drawer to get out the photographs she had taken of Manor House. She flicked through them and soon found another suitable shot to scan. Just as she was tidying them back into the holder, she noticed there was a photo missing.

"Remember the portrait in Manor House? The photo I took? Lady Harriet Wellsley. Did you see it? It's not here."

Andrew shrugged his shoulders. "You don't need it anyway, do you?"

Ella shook her head. She did not need that photo but the familiarity of the face in the portrait still niggled at her. She must remember who it reminded her of. She must remember that Karen Trevor was dead. She must forget the accident. She took a deep breath.

"I'm wondering if the Laides would be interested in Manor House. It seems a logical progression for them. Do you think I should suggest it to them?"

"Definitely. And by coincidence Jason Laide rang today while you were out. He seems anxious to close a deal on their new home as soon as possible. He's calling in here tomorrow."

Ella was about to mention that Sharon was away on a ski trip but then remembered that Mrs Laide had not seemed to be particularly worried about where their new home would be. As long as it was luxurious. Manor House would certainly fit that bill. And it was apparent that money for upkeep would not be a problem for the Laides. Yes, she would strongly suggest to Jason Laide that he view Manor House.

"Have you heard any rumours about Ballyhaven?" Andrew asked.

"No. Should I have? What kind of rumours?"

"I don't know. It's just that the Coxes seem very anxious to get hold of our fifty acres there. They upped their offer again today. There must be a reason other than long-term investment. Yet Oliver Griffin said there were no plans for the area."

"Slimeball," Ella muttered underneath her breath at the mention of Oliver Griffin.

She turned her attention back to her work. The presentation for Jason Laide tomorrow must be good. What a relief it would be to sell Manor House, to be rid of it and all its trappings of grief and tragedy. Another step on the twisty road to recovery.

Sitting at his desk, Andrew surreptitiously patted his inside pocket to make sure the photograph of Lady Harriet Wellsley was safely there. It was. Maxine Doran had flown out to Paris on an assignment this morning but she would be back tomorrow. There must be, there had to be, a connection between the Victorian lady in the portrait and Maxine. He intended to ask her when they met again. If they met again.

* * *

Jason felt pretty satisfied as he drove back from Ballyhaven. Glancing at his watch, he saw that the timing was perfect. He turned to his passenger.

"We'll just swing by your hotel, Dirk, to collect your luggage, then we'll have a drink at the airport when you've checked in."

"Suits me," Dirk answered. "We'll raise a glass to a good day."

It had been. The owner of Ballyhaven's grotty little pub had only hesitated for a moment before accepting Jason's generous offer for his rundown premises. Their respective lawyers would start drawing up relevant papers tomorrow. More importantly, Dirk had seemed impressed by the general area. "A good location for the development," he had announced.

"What about this planning officer guy?" Dirk asked now. "Is Oliver Griffin kosher? He seemed a bit of a bullshitter to me."

Jason laughed. "He *is* a bullshitter. But no worries about him. He depends on me to keep the bailiffs from his door. He has to deliver and he's got the contacts."

Dirk was quiet then, his eyelids drooping as they drove along. Jason guessed that he would not be sleeping though. The Dutchman never let go of control long enough to really sleep. His mind always ticked over, always aware of threats, always planning and scheming. The power he wielded and his mega-wealth were testament to his shrewdness. That was why Jason was surprised that Dirk had not mentioned the problem of the fifty acres. The heartland of the new development. The area where the casino itself would be located. The hub of the custom-built Casino Village. Maybe he thought Andrew and Ella Ford could be bought off as easily as the pub owner and Oliver Griffin.

Jason frowned. The only card he had up his sleeve now was Andrew's few shags with Maxine Doran. He would use it if he had to but it might not be worth much. It was possible that the snotty Ella Ford was glad to have her husband satisfy his needs elsewhere. People said she had become a bit peculiar since the car accident she had over a year ago. He put the problem to the back of his mind now. He would sort it when he met the Fords in their office tomorrow. Everybody had a price. Besides, he still had some very serious, and very secret, arrangements to make with Dirk Van Aken. Jason Laide had moved on from comfortable wealth to join the ranks of the powerfully rich.

Chapter 7

Ella was surprised. Jason Laide was smooth. His appearance and the few brief meetings she'd had with him on social occasions had led her to believe otherwise. She had assumed him to be rough, uncouth, as loud and vulgar as the gold chains around his neck. The quietly spoken man sitting in the office this morning was the antithesis of her preconceived idea.

She smiled at him. "Your wife didn't give me any specific idea about the type of property you're looking for, Mr Laide. Do you have any preferences?"

He laughed. "I would like to buy a property so big and grand that Sharon would never want to move again. I've lost track. As soon as a property is decorated, she wants to move on."

"I think we could help you there," Andrew said. "Ella is handling the sale of Manor House. Big enough? Grand enough?"

"Manor House? On the west side of the city, huge

grounds and stables? Wasn't the owner of that house involved in an accident? A car accident?"

As soon as the words were out of Jason's mouth, he realised that he had made a blunder. Ella Ford's face had gone white and her husband looked as if he was ready to leap up.

"I'm very sorry," Jason muttered, silently cursing his own stupidity. "I've just remembered that you were involved in that tragic accident, Mrs Ford. I should not have mentioned it."

Ella sensed his upset. This had been no trick to upset her, no deliberate barb. Jason Laide had made a genuine mistake.

"Yes, it was tragic," she agreed. "A little boy lost his life too. Rob Trevor, the owner, wants to move on. Too many memories in Manor House for him. Would you like to see the brochure?"

Jason nodded, glad that his faux pas seemed to have passed off without causing serious damage. The last thing he needed to do was upset the Fords. Bringing up the question of their fifty acres in Ballyhaven was not proving as easy as he thought it would be. They were reserved, both of them. Very polite but cold. Snobby. Hypocrites like all their sort. Andrew Ford was not the class act he pretended to be. Nobody could bed Maxine Doran and call himself a gentleman. The temptation to wipe the superior look off Andrew's face was overwhelming. There would be a right time but not now.

He held his hand out to Ella and took the brochure. "I'll read this and have a chat with Sharon. Then maybe I could make an appointment to view Manor House?"

"Certainly. Just let me know. And I'm glad to tell you that we already have a lot of interest in the property you're selling. Two very definite potential clients. Possibly more."

"That's what I like to hear. A bit of competition."

Jason stood then, still wondering if he should mention Ballyhaven. This pair were making him feel inadequate. Insecure. Fuck them! They were no better than him. Charging inflated prices for properties, driving the housing market mad just to line their own pockets.

"I'm looking out for a few investment properties too," he mumbled. "Long-term investment. Maybe in an area not yet developed. A terrace of houses, a few acres. That kind of thing. Something I could let sit there until progress caught up with it."

Andrew looked at him and frowned. It was almost as if this mobster was trying to get rid of money. But then, Jason Laide was too successful and too astute to invest funny money at home, wasn't he? He appeared to have oceans of liquid assets, however he came by them. Maybe it would be worth testing the waters.

"Actually, we do have something you might be interested in," he said. "An old factory twenty-five miles east of town. Forty acres of arable land with it. The area is nowhere now but if you're interested in the long term . . ."

Too quickly Jason shook his head. "That's not really what I was thinking of. More a neat plot of land. Near a village maybe."

"I see," Andrew nodded. "I'll keep an eye out for you now that I know what you want."

As soon as Jason had left, Andrew began to pace the office.

Ella glanced at him. "You're like a cat on hot bricks. What's the matter?"

"I don't trust him."

"We don't have to trust him. Just sell his house, buy him another one and collect the commission."

Andrew laughed out loud. That sounded like the Ella of old, the Ella he had not heard from for a long time. He was smiling as he sat at his desk again. His suspicion that Jason Laide was trying to buy the fifty acres in Ballyhaven was ridiculous. So ridiculous that he banished the thought from his mind and got on with his day's work.

* * *

Ella already had three customers interested in Sharon and Jason Laide's home. She was standing in their house now, waiting as the third set of viewers looked around. They were making some very promising remarks. Ella had only to sit back and let the clients outbid each other.

She glanced at her watch as she waved the people off. Just enough time to get to Peter Sheehan's office without rushing too much. By now, he should have the results of her blood tests and a programme organised for her recovery. He should have. He must.

She had to wait ten minutes in reception before Dr Peter Sheehan finally came to the door of his office and called her in.

Today he was wearing a beige sweater and snug jeans.

He seated her in front of his desk and then went to sit behind it himself.

"How have you been since I saw you last, Mrs Ford?"

"You tell me. What did my blood tests show?"

"They don't tell me how you feel. Only you can do that."

Words like hopeful and hopeless, confident and despairing, tumbled around Ella's head. Opposites. Feelings pulling and dragging in all directions. From the terror of Karen Trevor's perpetual dying to the desperate need to regain control of her mind, of her life.

"I thought I was finding a way back," she said. "I felt strong after talking to you. Confident. But then . . ."

To her shame, Ella felt tears behind her eyelids. Hot and salty, they welled and spilled over onto her cheeks. She dashed them impatiently away with her hand and took a deep breath. Peter Sheehan was regarding her impassively with his clear green eyes. Not commenting, not helping. Just sitting there like a judgemental green-eyed statue, mentally noting every tear, every quivering breath. God damn him!

"It's still happening. All the time. Everywhere. Anywhere. It happens."

"What happens?"

"Don't play the psychiatrist game with me! You know. I told you. I see Karen Trevor. Injured and bleeding. Dying."

"Karen Trevor, who died in your accident."

"Did she? She figures a lot in my life for a dead woman."

Ella heard the hysteria and anger in her own voice.

Suddenly she felt mortified. Andrew would be embarrassed if he knew she was shouting at his old school friend. Fuck Andrew too! Why wasn't he here with her? Where was the support from her husband, the understanding? True, she had told him very little about her . . . visions but he had not tried very hard to reach her, had he?

"Andrew probably thinks I'm mad," she blurted out.

"Probably?"

"Well, we never actually discuss his opinion of my mental state."

Realising how very bitter and petulant she sounded, Ella dropped her head, shielding her face from Peter Sheehan's perceptive gaze. He asked her for the log of events he had advised her to keep. She had to admit then that she had forgotten, maybe deliberately, to commit any of her mental torture to paper. That would have given the visions of Karen Trevor an authenticity she was not prepared to handle. She heard him get up from his desk and walk to the other side of the room.

"Come and sit here, Ella. Do you mind if I call you Ella? Make yourself comfortable." He indicated an armchair.

When she was settled, he seated himself in the upholstered chair opposite. "Now," he said, "you are going to tell me everything you remember about the accident. Every little detail of that day. Everything you felt. Are you ready?"

Ella was ready. Without difficulty she recounted all the events of that day from the torrential rain to her last memory of Karen Trevor's wrecked 4x4.

"You've been back to the accident site?" he asked when Ella had finished.

"Many times," she replied. "That road leads to some very exclusive properties. We've been involved in selling two of them during the past year. I don't have a problem with the actual site of the accident. And you can also record, Dr Sheehan, that I don't have a problem driving or with work."

"I see. And do please call me Peter."

"No, Peter, you don't see. Nobody does. It's . . ."

He put up his hand to stop her and then stood and walked to his desk. Picking up a page, he handed it to her.

"This prescription should help you sleep. That's all for today. I'll see you next week."

Ella felt as if he had slapped her across the face. She had confided in him, trusted him and cried in front of him. He had even told her call him Peter. And now he was dismissing her. Pig! She stood up abruptly and took the prescription from him.

"Time up. Get out. Is that it?"

"For today," he smiled, unruffled by her obvious anger. His eyes crinkled at the corners and the lovely white teeth flashed.

If Ella had not been so angry with Peter Sheehan she would have thought him a very attractive man. Just as well she was furious.

* * *

Jason would have said he felt vulnerable if he had recognised that quality in himself. Instead, he thought himself to be at a loose end, to be somehow unnecessary.

He had spent the morning wandering from one of his enterprises to the other. Everything was rolling along nicely. He did not need to involve himself with the day-today running any more. Just the more sensitive projects. The haulage business was being run very efficiently by the expensive team of managers he employed. He recruited them for their education, their nice accents, their image. The respectable face of Laide Haulage International. Even though he paid their wages, or their remuneration as they preferred to call it, their respect for him was only skin-deep. He knew it. Mr Laide to his face and, behind his back, 'that lout from the wrong side of the city".

It was the same story in his chain of dry cleaners, the printing business, his fleet of taxis, his portfolio of apartments all over the city. His club. The Eureka Club. That thickly carpeted, plushly decorated, private members club where the cream of society went to secretly indulge their need to have a gamble. Poker schools, roulette tables, blackjack. It was all there in Eureka. Van Aken supplying equipment, a management team running the place and Jason, out of sight, taking the profits. Very few people knew of his association with these businesses. He had front men in place. Apparently respectable, socially acceptable people who had all exposed some weakness which Jason had been able to exploit to his benefit. They might think he was a piece of shit but they could never, ever, allow that thought to escape.

Restless, he drove towards home. A nice long bath and a few drinks might cheer him up. As he turned the key in his front door, he admitted to himself that all the alcohol or bath oil in the world could not ease the ache in his belly. Throwing his keys on the hall table, he went upstairs and straight to the bedroom. The door was opened back. He hated open doors. Hated letting his privacy out or other people into his private space. He remembered that Ella Ford would probably have been showing clients around today. Nosey fuckers, poking and prying into his home. Into his bedroom for Christ's sake! Peering at the four-poster where he and Sharon slept, where they made love.

Tossing his jacket on the bed, he walked into the ensuite bathroom and turned on the taps in the sunken bath. He searched the cabinet until he found the blue bottle of bath oil which Sharon used. When he tipped some into the water the scent of Sharon instantly filled the room. He closed his eyes and inhaled deeply, longing for the sight and touch of the only woman he had ever loved. His lady. His wife.

Stretched out in the fragrant, warm water, he fell asleep.

Jason woke with a start and almost slipped under. The water was cool now. Shivering, he got out of the bath and dried himself off vigorously, getting angrier with each rub of the towel. What in the fuck was he doing here on his own while his wife was off enjoying herself on the ski slopes of Austria? Screwing someone else! Opening those smooth, long legs to some gigolo! Going into the dressing room, he grabbed clothes and threw them on, put on his shoes, combed his hair and then stood there. Lost. Lonely. Longing for Sharon.

Remembering the brochure on Manor House, he went out to the car to get it. He brought it into the study. He liked to sit here in the room that Sharon had decorated especially for him. The walls were oak-panelled and the shelves were lined with leather-bound books he had never read. And never would. Turning on the green desk lamp, he spread the brochure out and examined it. From the rose gardens to the stables to the magnificently spacious rooms, this house was Sharonesque. Class. Style. He flipped over the page and gasped. It should be bloody class. It should be fucking Buckingham Palace for the price! He quickly worked out the Fords' commission and decided they would definitely owe him a few favours if the sale went through.

Picking up the phone, Jason dialled the international code for Austria and then tapped in the local area code for Salzburg.

As it rang he pictured the three-storey building on Junkergasse, Sharon sitting by the huge open fireplace in the lounge, glowing after a day on the ski slopes. It had been the place where he and Sharon had spent most time together in the early days. Not too much time. Not even then, when she could not seem to get enough of him. Then too, everything had been on her terms. Dispensing just enough sharing to keep him happy, enough sex to keep him interested. He had always felt uncomfortable in the Junkergasse house. Not in control. It was her property, bought by her with money she had inherited from her father. Her house, her rules.

The ring went on and on, persistent and unanswered. Just like the question Jason tried to silence in his head. Persistent and unanswered. Why in the fuck had Sharon married him in the first place and why did he allow her to continue to use him? Humiliate him?

He slammed the phone down. Maybe she was not in Salzburg at all. Or maybe she had been lying naked on the thick rug in front of the log fire in Junkergasse, a muscular young man lying beside her, both laughing as they listened to the phone ringing.

"Ignore that, it's just my husband," she would say in that smoky voice which sent shivers down his spine.

He could ring her mobile but did not want to know it if she was with one of her lovers.

He stormed out of the house and jumped into his car. He drove quickly. He knew exactly where he could go to regain his feeling of control. He knew exactly the woman to restore his masculine pride. To make him proud of himself again.

* * *

Deep in the cellar which ran underneath the entire length of the house on Junkergasse, Sharon had been aware that the phone upstairs was ringing. She had ignored it.

Nearby the gas boiler hissed as it pumped heat throughout the three-storey building, the freezer hummed, stacks of unused furniture and discarded bric-a-brac surrounded her, racks of wine bottles glinted in the light from the bare bulbs which hung low from the ceiling. She had come down here on a sorting mission. What to put in storage and what to discard. Seasons of melting snows had seeped through the foundations of the house and a fine mould now laced the lower walls. The cellar would have to be cleared by next week, when work was due to begin on dry-lining the leaky old cavern.

Sharon shivered. This was the only area of the house where she felt uncomfortable. More than that. Terrified. Every time she came down the steep stone steps into the dark space, she relived her nightmare. Her eyes were drawn now to the furthest corner where hampers of old linen were piled high. That was where she had hidden from Jason on that awful night five years ago. That was where Jason had found her, curled up and shaking. He had beaten her almost senseless. She walked slowly towards the corner now, one roll of green stickers and one roll of red in her hand. A guide for the workers. Green to keep and put in storage. Red to discard. Dump. Destroy.

Her fingers shook as she peeled off a red sticker and stuck it onto the bottom hamper. Some very fine linens were stored in there but nothing was so fine that it could obliterate the memory of that night. Working faster now, she put a red sticker on each hamper. Her legs began to shake too, just as they had on that night as she had run down the cellar steps and hidden here. A refuge from Jason's rage. She had felt so safe in Junkergasse up until then. Had thought herself clever and resourceful. And she had been. She had managed to buy this house, book her flight, wind up all her affairs in Ireland and come here without Jason ever suspecting that his wife, his new bride, was about to leave him. She had not reckoned on the depth of Jason's anger or the far reach of his influence. He had tracked her down and beaten her up. He had kicked and punched while she had pleaded for mercy.

She slid down the length of the wicker chests now and dropped onto the floor as she had then. She heard their voices again, hers whimpering and weak, his piercing and trembling with rage.

"Bitch!" he had roared as he grabbed her throat. "Nobody runs out on Jason Laide! You're my wife. You'll always be my wife. You'll never, ever, escape from me. You're mine."

"I'm leaving you, Jason," she gasped. "This marriage was a mistake. For both of us."

He had put his hands around her throat then and squeezed. As consciousness faded she saw his eyes water with tears of rage. When she had woken, those same teary eyes were staring at her. Jason Laide was crying, swearing eternal love, vowing that he had never meant to hurt her.

"Don't ever run away from me again, Shar! We're meant to be together."

Weak, terrified, in pain and fear for her life, Sharon had then made the second biggest mistake of her life after marrying Jason. She had agreed to stay with him. Sorry now that he had hurt her, afraid that his reputation as a macho man would suffer if she left him, he had agreed to her terms and she to his. And so the farce of Laides' open marriage had been born. Separate lives in different countries but yet spending enough time together to appear to be a couple. Enough to fool onlookers but not enough to fool themselves. Not Sharon anyway.

She levered herself up from the floor now. It was time to take control. This mockery of a marriage would have to end. Coming down here to the cellar had made her face her fears. He could, and would, kill her and worse still, those she loved most, if he knew the truth about her life in Salzburg. His arrogance had protected her up until now. He believed she was too terrorised to do anything he would not approve of. He was right. She *was* terrified. But there were stronger emotions than fear.

He was talking now about buying a bigger house in Ireland, getting more insistent about her spending time there, hitting her harder when she would not agree quickly enough.

She hesitated before opening the safe. Her life, her freedom depended on her instinct being right. Jason's papers were in there. The taped and sealed envelopes he always asked her to bring back with her when she was returning from Ireland. And always with the warning that he would break her neck if she ever opened them. She prayed, her lips moving silently, as she picked up the first envelope and tore open the tape that secured it. If she was right, if these envelopes contained evidence of illegal deals, tax evasion and undeclared income, then she would have something with which to bargain, something to barter for her freedom. To outwit him.

Ten minutes later, ripped envelopes, torn bindings and papers lay as she had dropped them. All covered in Jason's handwriting. She had found what she was looking for. The records of offshore accounts and shell companies were here. So too was page after page of extortion, bribery and blackmail. There were photographs and videos too, all neatly labelled. And now she knew why he would resort to any measures to protect this hoard of filth. This evil on which his empire was built.

A noise sounded. A whispery creak. It was the gentle groan of ageing timbers but it made Sharon jump. Her shocked senses snapped back and she heard herself sob. Jesus! How could she have been so cowardly? Why had she allowed him to bully her into being his courier for all this filth? Stupid, stupid woman! To think that she had married this creature! An apt partner for a man idiotic enough to detail his every crime in his own handwriting and then to store the evidence.

Sharon closed her eyes. She had tried to be so clever. To take control. A double life? No problem! And she'd thought it had worked. Jason had indulged what he believed to be her penchant for foreign property and young lovers. Because, in his way, he loved her. She was probably the only person in the whole world for whom Jason Laide felt genuine emotion. She had only ever intended her ploy as a temporary solution anyway. A stopgap until . . . until what?

Everything was changed now. No more waiting for the

right moment to rid herself of Jason Laide. No more running back to Salzburg and pretending for a few glorious months that he did not exist. Her repulsion now outweighed her fear. It was time to do what she should have done a long time ago. It was time to divorce Jason.

A video in the pile caught her eye. She picked it up. It was labelled in Jason's childish handwriting: *Marie Murphy aka Maxine Doran.* Then she climbed back upstairs and put it in the video machine. She switched it off after a few minutes and brought it back to the cellar. There was no need to see any more. She knew now why Maxine Doran always seemed to be at Jason's beck and call. She did not have the stomach to check the other videos or photos. They would all be the same. Just different victims.

Slowly, carefully, Sharon put all Jason's papers, videos and photographs together in a neat pile and carried them up to her bedroom. She locked them into a drawer and poured herself a very stiff brandy. Then sitting on the side of her bed, she cried for the girl she had been and for the woman she had become.

* * *

Maxine hated night flights. Or more accurately, she hated night landings. After dark, all airports had a sameness. The lit-up runway and city lights beneath her now could equally be Beirut or Cairo, Dublin or Delhi. She could have waited until morning. Maybe she should have. When she'd left Paris, the rest of the fashion crew were preparing to go clubbing, living it up in the city where style and glamour were ingrained in the very fabric of the infrastructure, in the air the elegant Parisians breathed.

The touchdown was bumpy and they seemed to taxi very quickly along the runway. Maxine closed her eyes and waited for the plane to come to a halt. Home was all she could think of now. A hot bath and bed. Sleep. Tomorrow she would try to sort out all the confusing thoughts in her head.

She began to nod off to sleep in the back of the taxi on the way to her apartment. When she got out, the cold, damp air woke her up again. She paid the driver and took the lift to the first floor. She had the door unlocked before she realised that there was someone in her flat.

Jason was sprawled on her couch, his feet up on the coffee table.

"Welcome back, Maxine. I was hoping you'd decide to come home tonight."

Maxine dropped her cases on the floor and slowly closed the door behind her. She glared at the man draped over her couch and for a very intense second she hated Jason Laide enough to murder him. Hated herself for being in this position.

He read her thoughts, like he always did. He grinned.

"C'mon, Max! Smile. It's not every girl gets a welcome home like this."

"True," Maxine agreed and went to the kitchen to put on the kettle. "Coffee?" she called out.

"Fuck off with your coffee!" Jason answered.

She heard a glass tinkling and liquid splashing as he

poured himself a drink. It would be whiskey. Neat. He would drink half the bottle and then want to have sex. He would not be able. As usual. His dick was as limp as his brain. Then he would try to blame her, to force her into the most demeaning acts in order to revive his flagging libido. He would threaten. Blackmail. "The video, Maxine. What would the Press think of your performance? What would your glamorous friends think? How many modelling assignments do you think you'd get after they see it?"

Maxine's hand shook as she spooned instant coffee into her mug. She could hear him filling his glass again. The first drink had disappeared down his slimy throat even more quickly than usual. She poured hot water into her mug and brought it into the lounge. Jason already looked drunk. Little beads of sweat stood out at his hairline and his nose had a purplish tinge. Her stomach churned and she knew that she could not, would not, do whatever he wanted tonight. The sight of his flabby white body with the network of purple veins and fuzz of ginger hair was more than she could endure. Fifteen years old she had been when first she had seen Jason Laide in his hideous nakedness. Nine years of fear and revulsion crowded in on top of her. What could be worse than this? What could be worse than touching that greasy flesh, than kissing this sweating heap of ugliness, then exposing herself to the particular brand of cruelty that Jason Laide considered to be masculinity?

"Sit!" he ordered, nodding to the empty space on the couch beside him.

Maxine cradled her mug of coffee in both hands as if she could draw strength from it. She remained standing. Jason sat up straight, the animal in him alert to danger, the bully in him aware of a threat to his power.

"I'm tired, Jason. I've just come back from a gruelling day's work. I want to sleep."

"And so you can. When I say so."

"I want to sleep now!" Maxine said and the fingers curled around her warm drink shook with a mixture of fear, despair and anger.

Jason took in a sharp breath. His nostrils and his lips whitened as his veneer of civilisation slipped. He became an animal in silk shirt and gold chains, a sadistic primate. Maxine wanted to throw the hot coffee at him, to see it dribble down his evil face, to hurt him. She held tightly onto her drink. He would enjoy that, see it as foreplay, the only type he could respond to.

Walking over to an armchair she sat down opposite him, far enough away not to hear his snorting breath. She put her mug on the table beside her, out of harm's way.

"I'm tired, Jason. Tired of working and tired of your games. It's time we had a talk. Reached an agreement."

He burst out laughing. The sound echoed around the apartment, bouncing off walls and wooden floors. She waited for the mocking sound to stop and for the anger to start. She did not have long to wait.

"You piece of filth! You slut!" he shouted at her. "Do you think just because you drape yourself in designer gowns that you are less a whore? I know what you are, Max. Don't ever forget that. And I can tell the whole world if I want to. I can show the whole world!"

All the thoughts which had been swirling around her head in Paris, all the confusion and despair, seemed to find focus now. Maxine could no longer stay under the control of Jason Laide. If exposing herself as a child porn actress was the price of her sanity, she had at last reached a stage in her life when she was willing to pay that price. She smiled at him, hiding her fear, not giving him the thrill of control.

"Do whatever you must, Jason. I don't owe you anything any more. I've done your bidding for long enough. I've paid you back. Now get out of my apartment!"

His mouth hung open and his icy blue eyes glittered. A string of saliva seeped unnoticed from his lips. He became a solid mass of seething hatred.

Maxine could no longer hide her fear. She lifted up her chin and tried to outstare him, to defy him. He was gone beyond manipulation. She had never seen him so vicious. He lunged across the room at her and before she could protect herself, had his hands around her throat.

"I could ruin you, bitch!" he hissed into her face, spraying her with flecks of spittle. "You're my discovery. My property. Mine to use as I see fit. Slut!"

His hands were tightening, his thick fingers spanning the entire circumference of her slim neck. Maxine's eyes filled with tears.

Then as suddenly as he had pounced, Jason let go. He walked back to the whiskey bottle and poured another glassful. He drained the glass in one gulp and came back to stand in front of her. Her hands went instinctively to her throat again.

His voice was gentle when he spoke. Wheedling. "I'm willing to forget about this, Max, on condition that you get the Fords' fifty acres in Ballyhaven for me. Deal?"

Terrified, cowed, fearing for her life, convinced now of this man's mental instability as well as of his innate evil, Maxine nodded agreement. Jason pushed her roughly ahead of him into the bedroom.

Chapter 8

When Ella woke next morning, she felt energy flood through her. She stretched, enjoying the novel sensation of rested and revived muscles. There had been no nightmares last night. Maybe that was due to the new sleeping pills Peter Sheehan had prescribed or maybe Karen Trevor had got tired of her hauntings. Perhaps she had at last decided to float off to wherever it was that restless souls found peace.

Ella sang as she showered. Her singing had not improved since last she had sung. Over a year ago. She was still tone deaf but the joy in the inharmonious sound lifted her spirits. Andrew's too.

"Did I hear you singing?" he asked when she came into the kitchen.

She nodded and smiled, glad to share this little sign of hope with him. "I slept well. I feel much stronger today. Happier than I have for a long time. Happier than I have been since . . ."

"Since the accident?"

Ella nodded.

They stood looking uncertainly at one another, he wondering if he should embrace her, she wondering if she wanted him to. Neither moved.

Ella's feeling of wellbeing began to dissipate in the bewilderment and confusion of Andrew's stare. What did he expect from her? Instant recovery from her near-death experience? Smiles and laughs and mind-blowing sex under the shadow of Karen Trevor's persistent presence? How was it that she knew this man's favourite colour, the food, music and reading he liked, his history, his hopes and yet she felt she did not know him at all? She read the same questions about her in his troubled eyes and knew that he was no nearer an answer.

The toaster popped and they both went towards it. They laughed awkwardly, each realising that they were married to a stranger, that the path back to their easy relationship of a year ago was twisted and fraught with obstacles. The only common ground they shared was work. Safe, solid ground. He stepped on it now.

"What will I say to the Coxes about Ballyhaven? Should we let it go or hold out for another few years?"

Relieved that emotional issues were firmly back in their hiding place, Ella got her toast and began to butter it. The Cox brothers' interest in the fifty acres in Ballyhaven was puzzling.

"You're sure Oliver Griffin told you the truth?" she asked. "Did you go to the Planning Office yourself?"

Ella knew by the swift strokes Andrew was using to

plaster butter onto his toast that her question had annoyed him. It had to be asked though. There was something peculiar about the Coxes' interest in a green site so far out of town. And with no hint, apparently, of any development or rezoning in the area. Besides, she never had, and never would, trust Oliver Griffin.

"Yes," Andrew replied curtly. "I went there myself and looked at the projections. No mention at all of Ballyhaven in the five-year plan."

Ella poured her coffee and brought it to the breakfast counter, but it grew cold as the germ of an idea took hold in her head.

"I miss the sea," she said.

Andrew smiled. That statement used to mean only one thing. "Are you telling me it's holiday time again?"

Ella shook her head. "No. I don't mean the blue, tepid waters of some Mediterranean resort. I mean the powerful, grey, rolling Atlantic. I mean seaweed and rocks and pools and towering cliffs. I mean salty spray on my lips and cold, clean, ozone-laden air in my lungs."

"You mean home."

Ella nodded. Home. Cuanowen. That little coastal village on the western seaboard. The place she had grown up in and left behind so many years ago.

"Why don't we sell the fifty acres? Even with planning, we could not hope to get much more than the Coxes are offering now. Then we could buy a cottage in Cuanowen. Right on the beach. No mortgage. We could look on it as a retreat and an investment at the same time."

Andrew drained his coffee and put his mug into the

dishwasher. So much for his half-formed hope that Ella was about to regain her sanity. She was just looking for a new place to hide, a new escape from reality.

"You've never gone back to Cuanowen since your parents died five years ago. How come you miss it now?"

Ella shrugged. She didn't know. But she certainly had a strong urge, a longing, to be there this minute, to feel the wind in her face and the gritty sand beneath her feet. To be back in a time and place where there was no Karen Trevor. No accident. No disapproving, disappointed Andrew.

Shocked into action by her train of thought, Ella stood and began to pack her handbag for the day ahead.

"Think about it," she said.

Andrew nodded and gave a little wave as he went out the door. He forgot the conversation very quickly. He had a lot more than a seaside cottage to think about.

★ ★ ★

Maxine tore the sheets from her bed and threw them into the washing machine. They stank of Jason Laide. Turning the programme to hot wash, she added some disinfectant with the detergent. She was probably ruining the delicate silk but she did not care. Thankfully Jason had been gone when she woke. It was just the evil whiff that lingered. And the disgust.

She made her coffee black and strong and brought it over to the table. Then she sat and sipped and tried to hold back the tears. Neither crying nor self-pity was going to help. She had got herself into this situation and now she would just have to get herself out of it. She had nobody to turn to. Ironically, that is the way she had planned her life.

Looking around her now, Maxine saw the trappings of success. Expensive décor in her expensive apartment. Designer clothes in her wardrobe. Money in her deposit account. Even more money in her savings account. With the art on the walls and in the bank vault and the apartment itself included, Maxine Doran was worth a lot in monetary terms. Her life, on the other hand, was worth nothing. It was Jason Laide's to play with as the mood took him. Enough!

Maxine went to her computer and logged onto her online bank. Satisfied, she logged off again. The bottom lines on her accounts could represent freedom. She could sell up. Emigrate. Change her name again. Change her appearance. Disappear. Run. Hide. But she knew there was no hiding from Jason Laide. No place safe from him. He had contacts everywhere. Maybe she should just do what she had said last night. Stand her ground. Let him do his worst. Let him send his vile video to the press, to her agent, to all the people who knew her as the cool, sophisticated supermodel who only fucked someone worth more than a million in assets. Her modelling career was nearing its time limit anyway. She had no intention of hanging around until she was reduced to modelling thermal underwear. She could open her restaurant. Follow her dream. But how could a disgraced supermodel whose name had been dragged through the tabloids hope to have any respect, any credibility as businesswoman and entrepreneur?

As always in times of crisis, Maxine went to her dressing table and unlocked the top drawer. Carefully she removed the tattered photo album with the red velvet cover. It fell open at the portrait of Great-grandmother Harriet. Maxine sat still, looking into her great-grandmother's eyes, seeing the dignity and pride there, the confidence of a beautiful and privileged woman. Had Harriet ever felt as desperate as her great-granddaughter did now? Had she plotted and planned to escape the poverty and vulgarity into which her impetuosity had led her?

When her text alert sounded, Maxine jumped with fright. She carefully closed her album and put it back in the drawer before reading the message.

It was from Andrew. Andrew Ford. *'Hope you enjoyed Paris. Would like to see you when you have a chance. Have something interesting to show you.'* Maxine smiled. Something interesting? Everything about Andrew was interesting from his dark blue eyes to his laugh full of warmth. Andrew was so very strong, so vibrant that he made her feel alive, in touch with her own feelings as no other man had ever done. And Maxine realised, as she sat there, phone in hand, that Andrew Ford would be horrified if he knew the real Maxine Doran. The girl that Jason Laide had found and exploited. The Maxine in the video. The Maxine who must remain secret.

She texted Andrew back. *'Tonight?'* Then she sat and waited for his reply.

* * *

Ella had a headache. She rubbed her temples but still the band of pain encircled her head. It was a pressure headache. Too many thoughts vying for attention at the same time, jostling each other inside her skull. Annoyed, she dropped the papers on which she was working onto her desk and went to get a drink of water. Her phone rang just as she reached the water dispenser. Cursing under her breath, she went back to pick it up.

It was Jason Laide, wanting to view Manor House. Today. Now! Ella patiently explained that she would contact Rob Trevor and try to arrange a viewing as soon as possible but that today might not be convenient.

"Does he want to sell it or not?" Jason snapped.

Ella felt like snapping back at him but had to remind herself how big the commission on the sale would be. "I'll contact you as soon as I can arrange a viewing, Mr Laide."

She rang Rob Trevor but there was no reply. She left a message. Maybe he was at some art exhibition, or perhaps he was out somewhere on the vast grounds of Manor House. Jason Laide would just have to wait.

Ella got a glass of water and took some paracetamol. Closing her eyes, she sat back in her chair, waiting for the pain to lift. It didn't. A new worry began to nag. Could this headache be a side effect from the sleeping pills Peter Sheehan had prescribed? He had not mentioned that this might happen. He should have. Anger replaced the nagging worry. Peter Sheehan was so cavalier! Ending her session yesterday just when she needed to talk more and then giving her pills that were putting her through agony. The headache grew in proportion to her resentment.

When Andrew came into the office he looked at his wife with concern. He should have known that the fleeting good humour of this morning would not last. She seemed distraught now, distracted and angry.

"Something wrong?" he asked.

"Just a headache," she replied dismissively and Andrew knew she had retreated back into her own world of suffering and silence and that he was not welcome there. Jesus! How much more of this depressive behaviour could he be expected to tolerate? Was there no light at the end of this dark and lifeless tunnel?

"Jason Laide has been on the phone, demanding to view Manor House."

Andrew whistled. "He's keen! When are you showing him around?"

"As soon as I can contact Rob Trevor. You should really be there too."

"Fine, as long as it's not this evening. I'm meeting the Coxes. A discussion about marketing their new development."

Ella looked sharply at him. "I thought that was all finalised."

Andrew looked away from her, unable to meet her eyes. He mumbled something about organising a property exhibition. He was glad when her phone rang. He did not like lying to her.

She finished her call and sat back in her chair.

"Pity about your meeting tonight. That was Rob Trevor. I'm going to let Jason Laide know now that he can view Manor House this evening. Just like he demanded. This deal could be closed very quickly."

It was a pity. Andrew should be there really. Jason Laide would expect the full treatment. Flattery and bowing and scraping to his spending power.

Ella would have to do that on her own. Andrew had already replied to Maxine's text. There was not a sale big enough to make him cancel that arrangement.

* * *

Jason met Ella at the imposing gates of Manor House. They drove in convoy up the tree-lined avenue and parked on the gravelled circle in front of the house. When he got out, Ella could see that Jason was awestruck. He bent his head back and looked up towards the turreted roof. She walked over to him and shook his hand.

"Pity it's dusk now, Mr Laide. You're not really going to see the gardens at their best. I can assure you, though, they're spectacular. Would you like to view the outside buildings first? The storerooms and stables?"

Jason nodded and followed where Ella led. The courtyard formed by the stables was eerie in the dusk. Their footsteps echoed loudly in the enclosed space. Jason poked around, opening stable doors and peering in.

"If you were interested in development, these stables would easily convert to some very classy apartments," Ella said.

He just grunted a reply and she knew then she had said the wrong thing. Jason Laide was obviously vetting Manor House as his future home, not an investment and had been insulted that Ella should think otherwise. He was standing inside the stable with the red door now, his jewellery glinting, his ginger hair glowing in the semi-darkness.

"My wife is a good horsewoman," he said defensively. "You know Sharon. Gymkhanas and all that kind of thing."

Ella just nodded. She should have remembered that Sharon Laide stabled horses in the county and that she rode out at times. When she was home. Ella should also have remembered to bring the torch she always kept in the boot of the car with her. In semi-darkness, Jason was pacing the area of the red-doored stable. Ella watched on as he trod the length and breadth of the very stable where Karen Trevor had kept her horse. This man could afford to buy the whole estate and more but yet he could not trust anyone's measurements except his own. If he really was going to pace the entire property, then it could be a very long time before a decision was made.

"I think maybe we should go back to the house, Mr Laide. It's getting too dark to view the gardens."

"When I'm ready."

Ella shrugged and leaned against the stable door as Jason Laide continued to pace around the big, dark, empty space, just to make a point. He obviously was laying down some markers. He was the one with the money and she should show him deference. And Ella would do that. The commission from this sale added to the revenue from the sale of the site in Ballyhaven would mean that they could buy a cottage in Cuanowen. If Andrew agreed.

The longing for Cuanowen which had struck her this morning had increased throughout the day. Through her headache, which had by now abated, and a million annoying little jobs. She closed her eyes and pictured the shoreline, scattered with driftwood, flecked with foam, dotted with the jagged rocks that stubbed your toe unless you were careful.

She had just begun to mentally scan the horizon when a shout brought her back to reality. Her eyes flew open and she focused on the dim reflection of Jason Laide's gold chains and iridescent hair at a much lower level than she had last seen them. Ella had to smother a laugh. The stupid man had fallen on his backside in the middle of the stable. He was clambering up as she walked towards him, brushing himself off.

"Are you alright, Mr Laide?"

"Yes! Yes," he said impatiently. "I want to get out of here. Show me the house."

Just the words Ella had been hoping for. She didn't feel too comfortable out here alone with Jason Laide anyway. Yesterday she had been surprised and even impressed by his gentleness, despite his awesome appearance. This evening she sensed a barely repressed violence in his impatient manner. How had Sharon Laide, a cultured woman for all her bohemian lifestyle, ever got involved with this Neanderthal? They walked in silence to the double front doors of Manor House. Ella rang and waited for Rob to answer. He had obviously noticed their arrival because he opened the door instantly.

"Good evening. Come in, please."

Ella motioned for Jason to precede her into the vastness of the black and white tiled hall.

"Thank you for seeing us at such short notice, Rob. I'd like you to meet Mr Laide. Jason Laide."

Rob offered his hand but Jason was standing still, his mouth hanging open, staring at the portrait at the bottom of the sweeping staircase.

"Mr Laide?" Ella prompted, embarrassed now by her client's rudeness.

Jason brushed past her and walked over to stand in front of the portrait.

"Who's that?" he demanded.

"Lady Harriet Wellsley," Rob said, going to stand beside Jason. "My late wife's great-aunt."

Ella tried not to follow on, tried to stay away from the portrait but she found herself drawn towards it.

"She was a very beautiful woman, wasn't she?" she said softly.

Neither Jason nor Rob replied. As they stood in silence, in front of Lady Harriet's portrait, Ella was powerless to prevent the image changing, powerless to look away as the features wavered and changed into the death mask of Karen Trevor. Karen bled and cried and reached out to Ella from the portrait of her great-aunt.

"Fucking creepy!" Jason said.

Jason's words brought Ella back to reality. She blinked and Karen disappeared.

"What do you mean?" she asked Jason.

"Just what I said. That Lady Harriet whoever is a double for someone I know. You must know her too. Everyone does."

Ella nodded her head. She remembered her nagging feeling that she had seen Lady Harriet's face before, seen those near-perfect features and those bluest of blue eyes. "Yes, I believe I have seen that face before. Who is it, Mr Laide?"

"The likeness is fucking creepy."

Ella cringed. Jason was doing a good job in convincing Rob Trevor not to sell Manor House to him. At any price. Unless of course Rob so desperately wanted to be out of here that he did not care who took it off his hands.

Jason interrupted her thoughts. He had said a name: Maxine Doran. Of course! She knew she had seen that face before.

"The supermodel?" Rob asked

"The very one," Jason answered. "Who would have thought that she had any decent blood in her veins?"

"She may well have," Rob said quickly, "but it's not Wellsley blood. Maxine Doran has no connection to this family. None at all."

Ella was not so sure about Rob's quick denial. The grace, the dignity with which Maxine Doran carried herself was natural, not acquired. Something innate. Something inherited? Why could Maxine Doran not be one of the Wellsley clan? Looking at Rob's closed features now she saw that he was not willing to discuss this any more.

"I'll leave you both to look around the house," he said. "Feel free to wander. I'll be in the library if you want to ask me anything."

He turned and walked quickly towards a carved and panelled door on the right-hand side of the hall. The door closed with a heavy thud.

"Fucking creepy," Jason said again as he and Ella began their tour of Manor House.

Chapter 9

Before Maxine had even said good evening she bundled Andrew into her lounge and began to lock and bolt her door and put a safety chain across it. He watched in puzzlement as she turned her apartment into Fort Knox.

"Nervous about intruders, are you?" he asked. "You seem to have invested in a lot of security since I was here last."

She turned around and stood facing him with her back against the fortified door.

"We don't want to be disturbed, do we?"

He let his eyes wander over this beautiful woman from her shining blonde hair to her toes with the red-varnished nails and he agreed. He did not want anybody to spoil their precious time together. Maxine looked extraordinarily beautiful tonight. Her black dress fitted like a second skin and a single diamond on a gold chain glittered tantalisingly in the cleft between her breasts.

She walked slowly towards him, swaying her hips in

that elegant way which had made her so famous. In her four-inch high heels, she was almost as tall as Andrew. She put her arms around his neck and brought her body close to his. Andrew gasped as her softness settled against him.

"This is our space, our time," she whispered.

Andrew closed his eyes and kissed her. He wanted to talk to her about her trip to Paris, about the amazing photograph in his pocket, about their relationship and where it was going but first he had to follow the dictates of his body, his soul. He had to make love to the beautiful woman in his arms. He picked her up, carried her into the bedroom and gently removed her shoes, her dress, her silky underwear. Then he paid homage to the most perfect body he had ever seen. Inch by inch, he venerated the perfection of Maxine Doran and claimed her as his own. The gentleness gave way to a desperate want and they became the sum of their need, crying out as that need was fulfilled. Exhausted, replete, stunned by the intensity of their union, they lay back on the silken sheets and held each other closely. They drifted off to sleep.

When Andrew woke, he reached out to an empty space beside him. He sat up and listened to the sounds of ware tinkling in the kitchen. Getting up, he was about to reach for his clothes when he noticed a dressing-gown draped across the bottom of the bed. Navy terry towelling. A man's robe. A sudden bolt of anger shot though his post-coital calm. Who else had worn this dressing-gown? Was Maxine so expert in entertaining men that she had all the little details down to a fine art? Had the Dutchman who was with her in the park, the Van

Aken person, worn this robe? He remembered whispers. Rumours. Maxine and one business magnate and another. How many had there been? Had she cried out in ecstasy with all of them? Kissed them and held them with the intensity she had just bestowed on him?

Naked, he sat on the side of the bed and tried to reason himself out of his fit of petty jealousy. He had no right. He was the one who was married, the one who had lied to his wife this evening. Maxine had every right to sleep with whoever she pleased. Whenever. He did not.

The door opened and Maxine stood there in a white towelling robe, the light from the corridor behind her turning her blonde hair into a halo.

"Get up, sleepy head! Dinner's ready. Try on the robe I bought you. I wasn't sure about the size but I think it'll be okay."

Guiltily, Andrew put on the robe which fitted perfectly. She had bought it specially for him. He smiled at her.

Together they went to the kitchen, served up the delicious lasagne and salad Maxine had prepared and brought the dishes to the dining room. Glass and silverware glistened in the flickering candlelight and Andrew thought he had never seen Maxine look more beautiful. Her hair was loose and tumbling around her shoulders and she looked innocent and vulnerable wrapped in her towelling robe. In this dim light she bore an even stronger resemblance to the lady in the Manor House portrait. He would show it to her when they had finished eating.

After chocolate mousse dessert, they brought their

coffees into the lounge. Maxine lit the soft lamps and put on a CD of Nat King Cole. Andrew was surprised at her choice.

"I thought you would be much too young to appreciate this type of music."

Maxine turned towards him and there were shadows in her magnificent blue eyes. "I was young a long, long, time ago. I had to grow up quickly, Andrew."

Andrew raised his hand and touched her hair, her soft cheek. "I want to know about you, Max. Not just your media hype. I want to know the real Maxine."

She laughed and the sound had an edge of sharpness. "Believe me, Andrew, you don't. What we should really be talking about is 'the something interesting' you said you must show me. Have I already seen it or is there more?"

Andrew frowned. She was telling him not to ask any questions. Telling him not to try to get close to her. Maybe she was right. But her warning was too late for him. He already felt closer to Maxine in the short time they had been together than he ever had to his wife. Or to any other human being. He stood up.

"The 'interesting something' is in my coat pocket. I'll get it. Bet you'll be surprised."

When Andrew came back into the lounge, he flicked on the overhead light so that Maxine could see the photograph of Lady Harriet Wellsley's portrait clearly. The irony of the situation was not lost on him. Here he was, presenting a woman who could now be considered his mistress, with a photograph taken by his wife. Tragic, sad Ella.

Handing the photo to Maxine, he waited for her squeal of delight, her laughter. He was not prepared for the shock on her face, for the tears that welled in her eyes.

"Where did you get this?" she whispered.

Andrew put out his hand to touch her, to try to comfort her but she shrivelled back into her robe, a hunted, terrified expression replacing the earlier shock.

"Where did you find it?" she shouted. "Tell me! Have you been poking and prying into my private life? What do you want, Andrew Ford?"

Andrew stood up and walked to one of the armchairs. Obviously Maxine was terrified of him now. Maybe he could make more sense of this if she calmed down a little. If he put space between them, showed her he was no threat. He had, after all, over a year's experience in dealing with emotional trauma. And here it was again in the last place he had expected to find it. Ella, yes. She had good reason to be 'upset', as he liked to term her impossible moods. But Maxine? What in the fuck was wrong with her?

"Calm down, Max, please. I would never do anything to upset you. I thought you'd have known that. This is a photo of a portrait hanging in a property we are selling."

"What property? Where?"

"Manor House in the western suburbs. Do you know it?"

"I know where it is. The owner and her son were killed in a . . ."

Maxine stopped talking and Andrew knew that she was putting the pieces together.

"Yes," he said. "Karen Trevor of Manor House and her son died in the road accident in which my wife almost lost her life too. Now, a year later, Rob Trevor, Karen's husband and father of the little boy, is selling up. He no longer wants to live in that big old house alone. Can't blame him really."

Maxine continued to stare at the photograph in her hand. Andrew knew his first instinct had been right. There must be a connection between the woman in the portrait and the beautiful woman sitting across from him in a state of agitation. She looked up at last and asked the question he'd thought she should have asked long ago. Would have asked had she not already known the answer.

"The lady in the portrait. What's her name?"

"Lady Harriet Wellsley."

Maxine whispered the name and allowed the sound of it to sink into her mind. Lady Harriet Wellsley. Great-gran Harriet Murphy? The legend of the Murphy family. The woman who was only whispered about, her existence only hinted at. Surely, looking at the portrait in Manor House, great-gran Harriet and Lady Harriet had been one and the same person. Had she left her stable boy, gone back to Manor House? No, she had not. Maxine remembered some drunken mumblings of her father about his snotty bitch of a grandmother. How cold and "highfalutin" she had been. Could she have been around the mean streets of Maxine's childhood long enough to make an impression on her grandson? Maxine's father. All stable lad and no Manor House. Harriet's airs and graces had skipped two generations.

"Is she related to you, Maxine, or is the resemblance only coincidence?"

Maxine looked across at Andrew, at the concern on his handsome face. How had she doubted him and what must he think of her now? That she was neurotic, unbalanced? Maybe she was. Great-gran Harriet was her most prized secret. Her comfort. Her security blanket. It had been a shock to discover that somebody might have been invading her secret territory. Also a shock to discover the name of Harriet's family. Wellsley. The name suited the lady in the plumed hat. It had dignity and poise. It fitted. But what about Andrew? How much should she tell him? How much could he bear to hear? She gave a long look into his dark blue eyes and then went to the top drawer of her desk.

Taking out the red album, she opened it at Great-gran Harriet's photo and handed it to him.

"Here. Tell me what you think. Is Lady Harriet Wellsley the same woman that I know as Great-gran Harriet?"

Andrew looked from the photo Ella had taken in Manor House to the sepia picture with the curled edges in Maxine's album. The pictures could be of the same woman. It was hard to be certain when one was in colour and the other just muted shades of browns and tans. He held them side by side and scrutinised them. Maxine was standing over him. Hovering, anxiously awaiting his verdict. He looked up from his examination of the pictures.

"I'm almost sure," he said. "The eyes, the nose, the

mouth. Your eyes, nose and mouth, Maxine. Your face. I'd bet it's your great-grandmother in Ella's photo. Even the plumes are the same. In fact, the more I look the more certain I become. That's definitely the same lady in both pictures. Why were you so shocked when I showed you my photo? Is your connection to the Wellsleys a secret?"

"I knew nothing about it, Andrew. I just knew her name was Harriet and that I am supposed to resemble her. In personality as well as appearance. I never knew her family name."

"So the Dorans kept Lady Harriet a secret?"

"My name is not Doran. It's not Maxine either."

Andrew waited for her to go on. Silently she took her photo album back from him and locked it into her desk. As the key turned he knew Maxine, or whoever she was, was not going to talk any more tonight. She came to him and put her head on his chest. He held her for a long time as she cried. He rubbed her back, her hair, stroked her face, did every soothing thing he could think of, but Maxine cried until, at last, she fell asleep in his arms.

* * *

Ella had been glad this evening that Jason Laide had driven himself out to Manor House. The thought of travelling back to the city with him sitting in the passenger seat made her shiver. Yet she could not afford to turn her nose up at him, despite his crudeness and the aura of suppressed violence that clung to him. He could be one of the best clients they had ever had.

On impulse Ella called to Ford Auctioneers on the way home. She always liked the quiet of the deserted office at night. It was relaxing with no phones ringing and no clients looking for attention. Sitting back into her chair, she swivelled it gently, enjoying the soothing motion. Maybe she should come to live here. At work. Where Karen Trevor rarely bothered her. Here she was Ella. Not quite the Ella she had been. Not the person who had greeted each new day with a smile, the person who had resented sleep as an intrusion on the life she could not wait to live. The person who had been whole and complete. In love with her husband.

Ella got up and walked over to Andrew's chair and sat in it. If only she could slip into his mind as easily. She used to always know what he was thinking. They would say things simultaneously, finish sentences for each other. A unit. Andrew and Ella as fellow students, as boyfriend-girlfriend, as husband-wife. Andrew and Ella as lovers, as business partners. And now? Karen Trevor had split them in two, sent Ella spinning into a world of darkness and despair and left Andrew resentful, to live his life alone.

Karen's pleading and silent screaming had been more strident this evening. As Ella had stood in front of Harriet Wellsley's portrait with Rob and Jason Laide, she had believed for an instant that Karen's hands would reach out and touch her. So much for Peter Sheehan's therapy. He had mentioned "Survivor's Guilt", suggesting that maybe Ella felt guilty because she'd survived the accident and Karen and the child had died. Bullshit! Karen had caused the tragedy. She had been driving too fast. There was nothing Ella could have done to save her. Karen Trevor had taken Ella's life too. She had taken the fun and the joy and the love. But she had not left guilt in its place. No. Smart-ass Peter Sheehan, with his white smile and green eyes, was wrong. Whatever it was that was haunting Ella and making her existence hell, it was not survivor's guilt. Besides, the sleeping pills he had prescribed had given her a headache today, hadn't they? Maybe his great reputation was not well deserved.

The more she thought about Peter Sheehan, the angrier she became. She had a good mind to ring him now, to let him know that his treatment was ineffective. She was still getting flashbacks, still tense and nervous, still depressed. And he had not bothered to tell her the results of her blood tests. She had the phone in her hand before she realised his office would be closed by now.

As she was about to replace the receiver, she noticed a message flashing. This was Andrew's line but it would be a business call anyway. Ella tapped in the number for the message minder and Noel Cox's voice echoed around the empty office.

"Hi, Andrew. Just letting you know that Gary and I will be out of the country for the next few days. We'll touch base when we get back. You might have a decision on the Ballyhaven site for me by then."

Ella checked the time the message had been sent and played it again. Just to be sure. She switched it off and sat staring into space. She recalled, word for word, what Andrew had said to her this evening. He was going to meet the Coxes tonight to finalise plans for marketing their new development. He had lied. Why? Why?

When the answer came to her, Ella was still spinning in the world of despair and darkness into which Karen Trevor had catapulted her but she knew now, with a cruel knowing, that even though Andrew was still resentful, he was no longer alone.

* * *

Jason flicked on every light switch as he went through his house. He still felt a bit less in control than he should be. Going into the lounge, he went over to the custom-built bar and poured himself a large whiskey. The liquid seared his throat and dribbled hotly into his gut but the creepy feeling still lingered. He must be losing his fucking marbles! But yet he could not forget the feeling in the stable that someone, or something, had pushed him in the back. And then there was that portrait of the lady. The Maxine Doran look-alike. It was as if Maxine had dressed up in a big frock and feathery hat and had her picture painted but this lady person had died years and years ago. Yet she could not be really dead because Maxine was walking around with the lady's perfect face.

Jason banged his glass impatiently on the bar top. He was definitely cracking up. Anyone would think he had tried some of Dirk Van Aken's merchandise. Jason straightened his shoulders back proudly. Whatever else he had been guilty of in his lifetime, and that covered nearly everything, he had never, ever, taken drugs. Lately he had started to buy them from Van Aken, ship them, deal them.

Yes. But ingest them? Never! They were just a means of funding his future plans. And how! The profits were mindboggling.

Manor House was all that Sharon could want. Everything she deserved. At least that is what Jason thought from what he had seen tonight. The gardens, stables, the huge reception rooms, even servants' quarters. Maybe it would be the place where Sharon would finally settle. Maybe she would turn Manor House into a home. And stop her fucking travelling.

Jason filled his glass again. He would have to ring Sharon now. Tell her that he had gone to see the place where he thought they should live. If she was not on the other end of the line tonight he would be very, very angry. Over and over again he had told himself that he would not take her coldness, her indifference, her lack of respect any more. And over and over he crawled to her, topped up her bank account, paid her credit-card bills, waited for her to come home. Stuck to their deal. He would like to travel with her. Sometimes anyway, if he wasn't too busy. But Sharon didn't want him. Her travel time was her time and hers alone. Except of course for the young men who shared it with her.

Jason had worked himself into a rage by now. He dialled Sharon's number in Junkergasse. She answered immediately and the sound of her velvety voice poured instant balm over his anger.

"How is the skiing going, Shar?"

"I haven't done any yet. I've just been around Salzburg for the past few days. A bit of shopping. A few concerts."

"All that classical stuff?" Jason asked, remembering Sharon's attempts many years ago to whet his interest in the scraping and screeching she called music.

"This *is* the birthplace of Mozart, Jason."

The impatience in her tone told Jason that his ignorance had annoyed her. Yet again. Yes, he knew Salzburg was the birthplace of that Mozart guy. How could he not when the whole city was a monument to its most famous son? They even stamped his face on their chocolate. But he just had no interest in the long-dead old fucker. The here and now was what counted.

"I went to view a property this evening, Sharon. I think you'll love it but I want to make sure before going any further. Manor House is the name of the place."

"Where the Trevors live?"

"Yeah. Do you know it?"

"I was there once as a child. A birthday party for Karen Trevor. Karen Wellsley as she was then. Poor Karen. So Rob is selling out?"

"Yeah. And as it happens Ford Auctioneers are handling that sale too. Ella Ford showed me around the place this evening. I think it is you, Shar. Stables and all."

"Can you afford Manor House?"

Jason was taken aback by her question. Since when had Sharon cared about their financial situation? She just took and never asked where it came from or how much was left.

"Just you leave the money side of things to me. I only need to know if you're interested in Manor House or not."

"Who wouldn't be?" Sharon asked and her question

brought a smile to Jason's face. He might yet impress Sharon enough to gain her respect. Then he remembered something else that would probably interest her.

"There are a lot of paintings, family portraits, that kind of thing in the house. But the oddest thing, there's a huge portrait of Lady something Wellsley and you would honestly believe that Maxine Doran had dressed up and sat for the artist. The likeness is creepy."

"That would be Lady Harriet," Sharon said. "She was a renowned for her beauty but there's some story about her. She disgraced herself somehow or other. Interesting character. And now that you mention it, she was reputed to have the same type of blonde-haired, blue-eyed beauty as Maxine Doran has. So you'll be making a bid on Manor House?"

Jason thought for a moment. He had a lot of irons in the fire at present. The Ballyhaven project, when it kicked in, would soak up the money. And of course he had just bought a pub there. Setting that up would cost too. But he would never have a better opportunity to impress Sharon, to tie her down here for a while. Sure, he could afford it. He could afford anything since he'd made the deal with Van Aken. A couple of consignments of Dirk's merchandise, channelled safely through Laide Transport, would soon sort out any shortfall.

"Yeah. Since you like the idea. I'll get an engineer to look over it for me. One of ours. He'll bring the price down. When are you going skiing?"

"We leave for Lech tomorrow. The snow is good."

"Enjoy. Take care, Sharon."

"Will do. See you soon."

Jason held the phone in his hand long after Sharon had cut the connection. "We," she had said. "We leave for Lech tomorrow." She didn't even try to hide it any more. Why should she? They had long ago decided on this openness shit. This living of separate lives. It was the price he had to pay to hold on to her. It was a price that Jason, up to now, had been more than willing to pay.

Sharon had done her part. She had opened doors for him that otherwise would have been slammed in his face, she had helped him make significant contacts, introduced him into her social circle, made him respectable. But she had not given him a family. An heir. Nor had she ever, in all their years together, given him her respect.

He banged the phone down and made up his mind. Manor House would be his last concession. Sharon would have to settle down, make a home for him, have his child before it was too late. She was thirty-four now. No longer the young thing he had fallen in love with. Nor was he any longer the street hustler she had fallen for. He was a powerful businessman in his own right. Fuck Sharon and her bloody Mozart and her boyfriends! She was taking him for granted. Nobody did that to Jason Laide and got away with it.

Chapter 10

Ella had taken her sleeping pills last night, just as she had all over the weekend. Possible headache was a far superior option to certain heartache. She did not want to know what time Andrew came home, what lies he would tell. Nor did she want to smell the lingering traces of another woman on his skin or see the satisfied afterglow of sex in his eyes. Peter Sheehan's pills had dropped her into a dreamless sleep.

She opened her eyes this Monday morning to a room flooded with clear light. It was late. Lying still she sensed the empty space beside her. Had Andrew already gone to work or had he not come home at all last night? Afraid of the answer, Ella lay on her back, her eyes focused on the ceiling light. It had a cream shade, circular, heavy, diffusing warm tones when the bulb was lit. Very gradually, blink by blink, Ella edged her gaze away from the ceiling and towards Andrew's side of the bed. There was a dent in his pillow. An imprint of where his head had rested. The duvet was tossed back. Slowly, Ella leaned over and sniffed the space where Andrew had lain. She smelt nothing except the odour of her husband. His aftershave, his deodorant, him. Essence of Andrew.

She showered and dressed in a cocoon of drug-induced drowsiness. Coffee would dispel the remaining traces of sleep. Coffee would allow the day, the truth, the questions to begin. She was halfway down the stairs when Andrew came into the hall, briefcase in hand. He looked calm, responsible. A busy man on his way to work. Not a trace of lies or deceit on his open face, in his dark blue eyes.

He smiled at Ella. "You looked so peaceful this morning, I decided to let you sleep on. Did you have a good rest?"

"Yes, thank you."

She stopped then, mouth shut, staring at her husband, not knowing what to say next. Should she tell him? Should she let him know she had discovered his deceit? Ask him why he had lied? Who he had been with?

"Are you all right, Ella?"

She nodded. Of course she was all right! Why wouldn't she be? She had Post Traumatic Stress Disorder, survivor's guilt and cuckolded wife's dementia but what the hell! Fuck you, Andrew Ford! She smiled down at him from her perch on the stairs, from her lonely place halfway up and halfway down, half-awake, half-asleep. Half alive.

"I'll see you in the office," she said.

"Yeah. See you later," Andrew answered airily. "There are some things we must talk over."

Then he turned on his heel and walked out the front door.

Ella began her slow descent of the stairs, her slow entry into a day she would rather not face.

⋆ ⋆ ⋆

Andrew was getting ready to leave the office just as Ella arrived in.

"Glad you're here," he said. "I've had Jason Laide on the phone. He's getting an engineer to vet Manor House for him."

"Good," Ella answered, dropping her bag on her desk, holding back the words she really wanted to say.

"Maybe," he agreed. "But I've just had a call from another client who wants to view the house. It's not a done deal for Jason Laide yet."

This was good news. Ella got the distinct impression that Jason Laide was totally overawed by Manor House, that he believed he could buy into its history and its inherent dignity by buying the property. He would outbid any other potential customer in order to stake his claim on respectability. The bigger the selling price, the bigger the commission.

"Well, who is it?" she asked, wondering if it was somebody who could challenge Jason Laide's resources.

"Nobody you know. It was just an inquiry anyway. We'll wait and see."

He had gone out the door before Ella could pin down her uneasy feelings. Just as the door shut, she realised

Andrew was lying to her again. About a potential client for Manor House?

A tight band of tension clamped around her head. The same as yesterday. And the day before. In another few minutes the pain would start.

Angry, she picked up the phone and dialled Peter Sheehan's number.

His secretary was apologetic. "He's at the hospital this morning, Mrs Ford. If it's urgent, I could fit you in for an appointment this afternoon."

Ella made the arrangements. It *was* urgent. She urgently needed to tell Peter Sheehan that the sleeping tablets he had prescribed were giving her a headache, that his treatment, or what he termed as treatment, was not working. That she was sadder. Madder.

The bureaucracy of buying and selling property generated mounds of paperwork. Ella could not concentrate on it. She pushed it aside and logged onto the web. Trawling around, she found the website of an auctioneer in Cuanowen. That was easy. There was only one, Cuanowen Properties Ltd. Cuanowen. Home. Or at least it had once been home for the young Ella.

Several properties were shown for sale in the area but only one appealed to her. More than appealed. It was a new build bungalow right on the coastline. How had they got planning permission? Enlarging the picture, she examined the details. Four-bed, all ensuite, glass-fronted, overlooking the sea, wooden floors, under-floor heating. Fully furnished. Price on application. As Ella well knew, that meant a very high price tag, one that could kill all enquiries if it was published. Nevertheless she took down the contact phone number and logged off. She looked at her paperwork again but all she could think of was the way Andrew had slid out the door, disappearing before she could ask him any more questions. As if he had been trying to hide something else from her. Something about Manor House. That should be easy enough to check. All she had to do was cross the office and go to Andrew's desk.

When Ella checked the calls-received list on Andrew's phone she recognised Jason Laide's number instantly. Their accountant had called too. Just the two calls directly to Andrew's line this morning. Could the accountant be the person interested in Manor House? Maybe Andrew didn't want to say it until he had something definite. Only one way to find out.

"Good morning, Gerard," she said brightly to the Ford Auctioneers accountant when she had been put through to him. "I was just wondering if you have all the documents you need for our annual accounts."

"Yes, Ella, thank you. As I told Andrew this morning it will be another week before your tax returns are sorted out. I'll let you know as soon as they are ready." If he was puzzled, he kept it out of his voice.

"Fine, Gerard. Anything else you'd like to know? Any more information. On sales, projections, anything?"

Ella could almost hear the "she's barmy after the accident" thought forming in his head. She could sense everything except an interest in Manor House. She finished the call with as much speed and dignity as possible. The inquiry about Manor House must have come to Andrew through the front office. Knowing that her behaviour had a manic edge to it, Ella dashed out to reception and asked for a list of all calls that morning. Clutching the page, she dashed back into her office and pored over it. Caller, time, enquiry and follow-up were all logged on the page. Not one call referred to Manor House. If Andrew had got a call about Manor House, he had taken it on his mobile, which meant it was from a personal friend. Or else he was just lying. For what possible reason? To pretend he was showing someone around the property when he was elsewhere, just as he had done with the Cox brothers meeting?

Ella dropped her head onto her hands. The headache was pounding now. What in the fuck was she supposed to do? Should she confront Andrew with what she knew, accuse him, question him? She had a right. But he would probably lie again. Deny. Should she demean herself by searching through his pockets, his clothes, for telltale signs, for clues that he was seeing, holding, laughing with, loving someone else? Wave evidence in his face? A ticket stub, a hotel receipt, an item of silky underwear. Every letter that Ella had ever surreptitiously read in the agony columns of magazines came into her mind now. She had never bothered reading the answers, preferring to think these problems were all fictitious and that anyway they had no relevance to her life.

Grabbing her bag, Ella walked out of the office. She held her head high as she passed through reception, wondering how many of the staff knew that Andrew was playing around behind her back. Had he asked them to cover for him?

When she reached the street, she noticed it was a nice day. The sunlight made her feel very exposed. She felt a need for clouds and darkness, for shelter. For a hiding place. Humiliating tears welled in her eyes as she realised that she had no safe place. There was no shelter for Ella Ford, no refuge from all the chaos in her head. Then she remembered Ballyhaven. The fifty acres that had meant so much to herself and Andrew when first they had bought it. It was a place of shadows and secret nooks. She rang reception to say she would not be back until later in the afternoon. Then she went to the car park, got in her car and drove to Ballyhaven.

* * *

Maxine dressed even more carefully than usual this morning. When she examined herself in the full-length mirror she was satisfied that she had achieved the effect she wanted. On the outside anyway. She was dressed in John Rocha, all clean and subtle lines. Making a statement. This woman is beautiful, slim and clever. Well bred and successful.

Leaning closer to the mirror she looked past her black suit with the straight skirt and fitted jacket, into the face reflected in the unforgiving light. Minute lines were beginning to appear around her mouth. So tiny that only she could see them. As yet. The effort of trapping words inside, of holding her thoughts hostage for years on end was beginning to show on her face. There were no lines around her eyes. She had never laughed enough to create them.

Turning sideways, she examined her figure. Still perfect. Unusual that she should feel a degree of satisfaction with any part of her physique. As she examined herself now, for a moment she was able to look through Andrew's eyes. She saw her figure, honed to perfection, her legs, appearing even longer in her high heels. Her stock in trade, the tools of her craft. What made Andrew Ford different to any other man she had ever met was that he saw beyond her physical appearance, beyond the barriers she had built. He spoke to her, listened to her. Shit, she had shown him her precious picture of great-gran Harriet!

As Maxine stared at her reflection she saw the dark shutters fall over her eyes, the minute lines tighten imperceptibly around her mouth. Andrew could never know the real Maxine. He was enthralled by the image, out of love for the time being with his neurotic wife. If he knew the truth . . .

The intercom sounded. Maxine did not bother answering it. She just picked up her bag and went down to the lobby to meet Andrew. His admiring glance told her he liked her businesswoman image.

"Great that you were able to arrange a viewing so quickly," she said.

"Your wish is my command," he laughed as he ushered her to his car.

The nearer they got to Manor House, the more

nervous Maxine felt. Suppose when she saw the portrait in reality, it did not resemble great-gran Harriet at all? Would she still think her plan was a good one then, would she still be interested in buying Manor House?

"Will Rob Trevor be there?"

Andrew shook his head. "He's away in London for a few days. He left early this morning. Some art exhibition or auction. Something arty anyway. But I cleared the viewing with him before he left."

Maxine relaxed a little. She would feel more comfortable seeing the house with just Andrew. Apart from the whole idea of opening a restaurant there, she needed to find out if Manor House was indeed part of Maxine Doran's past. Part of her heritage.

* * *

Ella had tried everything to open the rusty old gate leading into the Ballyhaven fields. It looked as if a good kick could knock it to the ground, but it would not budge for her. Glancing along the length of the narrow country road to make sure she was alone, she began to climb the corroded bars. There was a precarious moment as she straddled the top of the gate, her leather-soled high heels slipping on the bars, her skirt riding up her legs. Thankfully she dropped, feet first, onto the ground on the field side. She should have gone home for walking shoes before coming here. In fact, she should not be here at all. Traipsing through her past in unsuitable footwear.

Keeping her eyes focused on the stand of trees in the

distance, she began her uncomfortable totter through grass and rutted earth. She tripped several times but kept forging ahead. A thistle snagged her tights, a nettle stung. She kept going. When she reached the shade of the trees, she stood and breathed in the mustiness. Then she walked without hesitation towards the glade. The place where she and Andrew had celebrated their purchase of these fifty acres and their love for each other. She sat with her back against the big tree and remembered.

It had been summertime six years ago. They had just completed the sale of a block of flats. They had disposable income. For the first time ever. And they had bought these fifty acres from a farmer who was about to retire. They had plans. Maybe they would develop this site in years to come. Maybe they would build a huge house here and fill it with children. Some time in the future. Then they had sealed the bargain by making love. Under the branches of this big old tree, bathed by dappled sunlight. Ella had cried out. And so had Andrew. They had pledged eternal love and both of them had meant it at the time.

That moment, that sun-drenched, triumphant moment had been the highest point of their relationship. Their love had teetered on that brink for a while before sliding gradually downwards and then staying totally behind in the aftermath of the accident. Or had it been fading, losing its depth in the shallowness of day-to-day life long before Karen Trevor had crashed into their lives?

Angrily, Ella picked up a twig and snapped it in pieces. The signs had been there. They had gradually begun to speak more of work and had stopped talking about children. It was as if Andrew and Ella had ceased to be a couple and had become a corporation. Their relationship was one long business meeting, with a few shags thrown in for the sake of correctness. Affection had succumbed to acquisition.

Ella cried out, just as she had six years ago in this very spot. But the cry was one of anguish now. She remembered things she had not allowed herself to know at the time. Little things, like forgotten birthdays, like not sharing laughter any more, like not holding hands. It had all disappeared and neither of them had missed it or mourned its passing. The horrible truth, highlighted by the flood of memories, was that the eight-year marriage of Ella and Andrew Ford was dead. As dead as Karen Trevor and her beautiful little boy.

Ella was suddenly filled with new understanding of why she obsessed about Karen, about the accident. By focusing on that, she could blot out other traumas. She had known before the crash that she and Andrew were in trouble and had not wanted to face it. She did not want to face it now either but she could no longer deny the truth of it. Nor would she.

Reaching into her bag, she got a tissue and make-up and tried to repair the damage to her tear-stained face. She did not succeed very well. Her eyes were still puffy and full of pain. The deceit was what really hurt. So Andrew had fallen out of love with her. They had been very young when they met. Freshmen in college. Perhaps they had just grown in different directions. But having an affair? Lying to her? To hell with him!

Tucking her bag under her arm, she began her trek back across the fields. It was easier now. Anger gave her impetus.

She attacked the climb over the gate, throwing her leg over the top with abandon. She was sitting there, her skirt right up to her panty line, when a car came speeding along the road. Jason Laide tooted the horn and jammed on the brakes. Furious, Ella tried to pull down her skirt and at the same time dismount the gate with dignity. She failed on both counts, landing awkwardly on the road and managing to twist her ankle in the process. Jason jumped out of his car and ran to her side.

"Are you all right, Mrs Ford? I'm sorry if I startled you."

Ella took the hand he offered and stood up straight with as much pride as she could muster. She had to bite back her angry retort. He was, after all, a very important client.

"I'm fine, thank you. What are you doing out here, Mr Laide?" she asked.

"Actually I've bought the little pub in Ballyhaven village. Do you know it?"

Ella nodded. It was a dingy little bar, not much changed since it had first been opened in the 1950's. God! Was Jason Laide intent on buying up the whole country?

"Would you like to come there now? Let me buy you a drink, a bowl of soup, something to apologise for scaring you?"

Ella wondered if he noticed that she had been crying. Of course he had. Maybe he was just displaying that gentle streak she had seen in him the first time they met. She smiled at him and tried not to let the pain of her ankle show.

"I've an appointment this afternoon but a quick bowl of soup sounds good. I'll meet you in the pub."

"Can you drive with that ankle? Would you prefer to come with me?"

"I'll be fine Jason, thanks. It's my left ankle and anyway my car's automatic."

Jason smiled at her as she got into her car. He almost rubbed his hands together in glee. Well! Feck Maxine Doran! He might not need her after all. Not for the site in Ballyhaven anyway. It seemed like Mrs Ford was vulnerable at the moment. Getting her to agree to the sale of the fifty acres should be a piece of cake.

Chapter 11

Andrew thought that Maxine looked like a child playing pretend grown-up in her mother's clothes. It wasn't that the clothes were too big for her. They fitted perfectly. The child was in the wonder in her eyes, in the awestruck expression on her face as she strolled around the gardens of Manor House.

"It's so beautiful, Andrew," she whispered and he could have sworn that her voice belonged to an excited seven-year-old exclaiming over a new toy. He just smiled and followed on as she glided elegantly over the pathways and walks of the intricately laid-out gardens.

"There must be a gazebo," she said as she headed almost instinctively towards the Manor House summerhouse. Going in she stood in the middle of the octagonal, open-sided building with the tiled roof, gazing around her as if she could not believe her eyes. "I knew it would be just like this. I can almost see Victorian ladies sitting on that timber bench in their beautiful clothes, gossiping, all speaking such proper English, their hair piled up in complicated styles. And they probably had some secret meetings here too. Trysts. Affairs."

Andrew stood with his shoulder leaning against one of the uprights, smiling at Maxine as she let her imagination run riot. She seemed to glow in the dimmed light of the summerhouse, her blonde hair taking on a golden hue.

"What about the house itself, Max? Are you ready to see it?"

She came to stand beside him and her expression immediately became more guarded.

"Yes. I'm ready."

The housekeeper answered their ring on the double front door. A flash of recognition lit her eyes when she saw Maxine but the older woman remained tactfully silent as she led them into the hall.

"Mr Trevor said you were to have access to any part of the house, Mr Ford. If there's anything you need, please tell me. I'll be in the kitchen."

Then with another surreptitious glance at Maxine, she drifted off down the hallway. Maxine stood on the elaborately designed black-and-white tiled floor and looked upwards at the magnificent chandelier, at the cornicing on the ceilings, at the sweep of the wide stairs. Her eyes were drawn to the portraits that lined the staircase. One forbidding portrait after another glared down at her. Men in wigs and some in military uniform, women seated on little stools with lapdogs resting in the folds of their dresses. Dark-haired, solemn women, with rouged cheeks and tight rosebud mouths.

"Where is she? Lady Harriet?" she whispered to Andrew.

Andrew walked over to the bottom of the stairs. He was positive, he knew, the photo Ella had taken of Lady Harriet Wellsley's portrait had placed it just here. At the bottom of the stairs. In the place where now hung a gilt-framed painting of a very ferocious-looking man in a powdered wig and ridiculous pantaloons. Standing on the first step of the stairs, he closely examined the embossed wine wallpaper. The gilt frame was bordered all around by an inch of richly coloured paper. Paper that until very recently had not been exposed to light. Obviously because it had been covered by a larger frame. The frame that had held the portrait of Lady Harriet Wellsley.

"She's gone," he answered Maxine. "She's been removed. I wonder why?"

"Are you sure? Maybe she's somewhere else in the house."

"We'll see."

They walked slowly from room to room, from the luxury of the vast reception rooms, to the elegance of the dining room, to the solemnity of the library and then up the staircase to the sleeping area. Maxine twirled around on parquet floors and Persian rugs, reverently touched Royal Doulton and Belleek, peered into cabinets at Minton and Spode ware, ran her fingers over mahogany furniture gleaming with the patina of age, lay under the canopy of the huge four-poster bed in the master suite. She revelled in the dignity of the old house, in the solidity and permanence of it, in the space and elegance. Then they climbed the crooked little stairs that led to the servants' quarters. These rooms were abandoned now, packed with boxes, trunks and discarded pieces of furniture, dusty, musty and draped with cobwebs.

"I would open these rooms up again," Maxine said. "Knock a few walls, bring the plumbing up here. There must be another stairs leading to the turrets. In fact this whole floor could be the most luxurious part of the house. The tower suite. For hire to princes, footballers and rock stars."

Andrew laughed at her enthusiasm as he led the way back down to the kitchen. The housekeeper was standing just inside the door, as if she had been waiting for them.

"You can tell Mr Trevor I will be in contact with him," Andrew said. "By the way, the portrait of Lady Harriet Wellsley – do you know if it has been moved recently?"

The housekeeper looked at Andrew as if deciding whether she should trust him or not. Obviously remembering Rob Trevor's instruction to help in any way possible, she answered reluctantly.

"Mr Trevor took it to London with him."

"Oh! I see."

Andrew thanked her and followed as she led the way back to the front door. But he did not see at all. Why had Rob Trevor removed Lady Harriet's portrait? Had he really taken it to London with him? Maybe he was just having it valued. But then that was his profession. He knew the monetary value without hauling it to London. The housekeeper stood at the door and waved them off.

When they were halfway down the drive Maxine told

Andrew to stop.

"I can't leave yet," she said. "I must have another walk in the gardens."

They strolled back to the summerhouse and sat side by side on the bench. Andrew drew in a breath to say something but Maxine gently put her fingers to his lips.

"Just listen."

He did but he heard nothing. A slight rustling of leaves maybe, a bird singing. Silence.

"Peace," Maxine said. Her eyes were shining and her lips were curved in a smile. How could a woman who knew the excitement of the catwalk, of fame and success, of New York and Paris and Rome, be ecstatic in the stillness of an old garden?

"You like Manor House? I hope you're not too disappointed about Lady Harriet's portrait?"

"I love Manor House. I love everything about it. The gardens, the rooms, the furniture. Even the servants' quarters. I'm disappointed not to have seen the portrait of course."

They were quiet again and this time the bird too respected the profound silence. Maxine seemed content to sit there but Andrew was feeling the nearness of her. He needed to, he must, touch her, kiss her. He bent towards her but she leaned away from him.

"I must think, Andrew. I don't think very well when you are so close to me."

Hurt, Andrew stood, but she caught his hand and pulled him down beside her.

"Remember I told you about my ambition? To open a restaurant?"

"A lovely dream, Max, but Manor House is big money. I mean serious investment."

"Are you saying that I couldn't afford it? How do you know?"

Her chin had lifted and her perfectly groomed eyebrows were raised, waiting for an explanation. He knew he had hurt her feelings, insulted her, but a dose of realism was called for.

"Max, Manor House is one thing but it stands on thirty acres of prime land in one of the most expensive suburbs of the city. The grounds are worth way more than the house. Mega money."

"What are you trying to tell me? That it can only be bought by a company, a corporation? A filthy-rich film star?"

Andrew laughed. "Actually, we have somebody who is very interested but he could hardly be called a film star. He appears to be filthy-rich though."

"Who is it?"

"You know I can't say. I wouldn't tell anybody you were looking at it either."

"The housekeeper will. She recognised me."

True. It was obvious that the woman had recognised Maxine but Andrew believed she would not say anything. Discretion was written in every pleat of her navy skirt and every neat grey hair on her head. He caught Maxine's hand.

"I know how important this restaurant idea is to you but Manor House would be a bit ambitious. Why don't we search for a smaller premises, something nearer town?"

Angrily, she snatched her hand away. "Don't patronise me. I'm meeting my accountant tomorrow. I've made some very careful investments over the years. You must remember, I've been working since I was sixteen. I've been clever with my money. But there's more than that, Andrew. You know it. Manor House feels right for me."

Andrew nodded his head in agreement. There was a completeness about Maxine and Manor House, a feeling of something that was meant to be.

"Are you going to tell me who you are?" he asked.

Maxine stood, walked to the opening of the summerhouse and stared at the turreted roof of Manor House. Then she turned to Andrew and smiled.

"I am Maxine Doran. Supermodel."

She began to walk back towards the car, her head held high and proud. Andrew watched as her hips swayed, her hair shone in the sunlight, her long legs strode gracefully forward. She had an innate grace and dignity which had not been acquired on the catwalk. She was Maxine Doran now but who, Andrew wondered, had she been before the world came to know her as one of the most successful models ever?

★ ★ ★

The soup was thick and rich. Vegetable, served with chunks of brown soda bread. Ella forgot the nagging pain in her ankle as she tucked in. She had not realised she was hungry until she started eating.

Jason Laide smiled at her as she finished off the last of

her soup. "More? Maybe some roast beef? Coffee?"

Jason clicked his fingers and the owner, soon to be the ex-owner, came running to serve them. Ella asked for coffee. She felt surprisingly relaxed in this tatty little pub. With this tatty little man. Guilty at this thought, she tried to think of something nice to say.

"This pub is a lot more comfortable inside than you would think from passing. It's cosy."

"I have plans for it," Jason said. "The paperwork will be sorted soon. Then I'm going to apply for planning. I'll build a proper dining area, a games room, a beer garden. Give it the treatment."

Ella frowned. Far be it from her to tell Jason Laide his business but investing in a public house out here in Ballyhaven did not seem to make much sense. Where was the population to support the expanded pub? Where was the passing trade? And what made him think he could put gaming machines in here? Surely he must know that was against the law. Yet he was obviously an extremely wealthy man. He would not make an ill-informed decision.

"So, you think Ballyhaven has a future, Jason?"

He nodded. "It might have. I'm willing to speculate that it will. I can afford to."

That seemed to be very true. Apart from his transport business which practically had a monopoly, the solid gold chain draped around his thick neck must be worth a ransom.

"If you come across any more property for sale here, let me know," he said.

Ella picked up her spoon and began to stir her coffee.

She stirred and stirred as an idea began to form in her head. She should talk to Andrew first of course. He might have made some promises to the Coxes, said something to them she should know about. He had done something else she should know about, hadn't he? Fuck him. She stopped stirring and looked at Jason.

"Would you be interested in a green site? Agricultural land, no planning as yet but you said you're willing to speculate."

"In Ballyhaven?"

"From where you saw me almost topple off the gate right down to the wooded area. Fifty acres of agricultural land."

Jason appeared to hesitate and for a moment Ella regretted her impulsive offer. She had not thought it through. An offer to this man could be difficult to withdraw. She began to feel hot, her ankle suddenly more painful. He seemed to come to a decision.

"Right. I might be interested," he said. "Could you maybe show me around? Walk the site with me?"

"Yes, I could."

"Who owns it?"

"My husband and I own it. And yes, I'll make arrangements to show you around."

"Why not now?"

Ella looked at her watch. It was almost time for her appointment with Peter Sheehan. She could cancel that. No. She needed to see him, to tell him exactly what she thought of him. She needed to finish with him. Closure. Anyway her ankle was too uncomfortable for traipsing around fields.

"I'm sorry, Jason. I've got to go now but why don't you ring the office and make an appointment for when it suits you? And thanks for lunch."

Jason smiled at her as she arose and Ella saw again the kindness, the charm of the man. She understood a little better now what Sharon Laide had seen in him. He wasn't all vulgarity and meanness. Not really. She said goodbye and walked to the door. Then, remembering, she turned back.

"There's something you should know, Jason. Andrew and I already have an offer on our site."

Jason shrugged. "I'll better it. And I'll pay you cash."

Ella knew he would. A hint of Jason Laide's ruthlessness had just peeped through his veneer of charm. Ella shivered and pulled her jacket more closely around her as she hobbled to her car.

* * *

By the time Ella had found a parking space and made her way to Peter Sheehan's office, she was already late for her appointment. A flushed face and untidy hair now added an extra dimension to her puffy eyes and mucky shoes. She limped into his office, an apology for her lateness on her lips.

"Whatever have you done to yourself?" Peter greeted her before she could say a word. Ignoring the question she hobbled towards a chair, gratefully sticking her swollen ankle and muddy shoes out of sight under the desk.

Peter got up from his seat and came to stand beside her. She was surprised to see the way he was dressed today. A dark navy suit, blue shirt and tie. Very professional. Very handsome.

"Did you have an accident?" he asked.

"I'm prone to accidents."

"Your ankle. What happened to it?"

"I fell off a gate."

"Really?"

Returning to his place on the opposite side of the desk, he sat back and calmly regarded her. His green eyes did a radar sweep over her dishevelled appearance and flushed face. Ella could see him formulating theories about her condition, diagnosing phobias, manias, deciding on treatments, crisis interventions. What did he know about her? Prat!

"I just came here to let you know that I'm discontinuing treatment with you."

"I see."

"Of course you don't see! You didn't when I last spoke to you and you don't now. I don't need your help. I can sort my own problem."

"What problem would that be?"

"Karen Trevor of course and why I keep seeing her! How could you possibly help me when you haven't even been listening to what I've been saying?"

"I've been listening to what you haven't been saying. That's where the answer to your problems lies."

Smart-ass! Ella fumed with anger and her ankle throbbed with pain. She glared at Peter Sheehan and tried desperately to think of some way to ruffle his calm.

"The sleeping pills you prescribed are giving me a headache and as well as that you never bothered to give me the results of my blood tests. That's not satisfactory."

Putting his elbows on the desk he leaned towards her. Ella could smell his aftershave. She looked away from his clear green gaze. It was too penetrating.

"Your headache could not be from the pills and your blood tests were perfectly normal."

"So now you know. And no doubt I don't have Post Traumatic Stress Disorder either."

"I didn't say that."

Ella closed her eyes for a moment and took a deep breath. She made a conscious effort to control her anger, to stem the flood of bitter words which threatened to overflow. It was Andrew she was angry at. Andrew was the one who had hurt her. There would be no point in behaving like a shrew towards Peter Sheehan. In fact, there would be no point in behaving that way in any case. She stood, carefully balancing her weight on her uninjured foot.

"I won't be seeing you any more, Dr Sheehan. Thank you for your time."

She offered him her hand across the desk and, standing, he took it. His skin was warm, his fingers strong and for a microsecond Ella wondered if she was doing the right thing. He smiled at her.

"Your choice, Mrs Ford. Ella. But remember you're welcome to call me any time, even if it's just for a talk. I could recommend some good marriage guidance counsellors to you if that would be of any help."

Ella stared, open-mouthed, at him. "What do you mean?"

"I thought you said you had identified your problem?"

A blush of embarrassment began to creep up along Ella's neck. She flopped back onto her chair. Fuck! Did everyone in the whole world know that Andrew was screwing someone else, that their marriage was a farce? Her words tumbled out now, trying to explain herself. Trying to maintain some self-respect.

"I've just figured that I could not move forward from the accident because I was trying to prevent myself from looking back to what was going on before it. So my subconscious got stuck on that moment when Karen Trevor died. That was my excuse. Am I right? Does she pop up every time I don't want to confront the real issues?"

Peter nodded slowly. "A bit simplistic but accurate. The question now is what do we do about it?"

Ella stood again and this time she went to the door. "Not we. This is an issue I must resolve myself. Goodbye, Dr Sheehan."

By the time Ella reached her car again, her ankle was throbbing. She thought about going to the hospital, to the Accident and Emergency. Maybe she had broken a bone. Then she decided, broken bone or not, she could not face a hospital. Not now. She would drive home and put her foot up. Put a bag of frozen peas on it.

In fact, the thought struck her that maybe she should freeze everything. Her life, her marriage. Put everything on hold until she was ready to deal with it. But wasn't that her problem? That's exactly what she had been doing. Putting her life on hold. No more. Andrew's days of conducting an affair behind his almost catatonic wife's back were over. Ella's days of being the catatonic wife were over. The time to finally bury Karen Trevor had arrived.

Ella eventually fell asleep on the couch with the bag of frozen peas on her ankle. Andrew woke her when he came in, fussing over her. She ignored him and he soon went away and left her in peace.

More than could be said for Karen Trevor. Karen did not seem to know that her time in Ella Ford's head was up. She haunted Ella's dreams that night with the same intensity, the same goriness and desperate pleading as she had done ever since the day she and her son had died in the mangled four-wheel drive.

Chapter 12

It was a mild morning but before Maxine left the taxi she tugged her hat low on her forehead and pulled up the collar of her coat. As she paid the fare she carefully examined the driver for any signs of recognition. There were none. He obviously did not know her. Or else, more likely, he did not care who his fare was as long as he was paid.

"Will you collect me here again in an hour's time, please?"

He nodded and drove off, leaving her standing in the surroundings which had once been so familiar to her. The place she used to call home. Looking around she noticed that the buildings had changed. A shopping centre, its windows barred and shuttered, now sprawled along the area where the tower block flats used to be.

She began to walk, heading back towards the older streets, to where the artisan cottages huddled together under the chimneystacks of the old steel foundry. The streets got narrower and the graffiti more explicit. She kept her head bowed but then everybody around here walked with bowed head. To meet someone's eyes was to issue a challenge.

Three pairs of legs, moving towards her in unison, came into her line of vision. As they neared, Maxine clutched her bag more tightly under her arm, afraid to look up. Maybe it was just a group of innocent kids, on their way to play basketball. Nearer now, she saw that they were all wearing pants with the legs so long that they trailed over the heels of their shoes, fraying from the constant friction with tarmac. The group stayed in line on the pavement. They were not going to give way. Maxine veered to her right and walked on the road. One of them jeered. Another whistled. Maxine walked quicker and did not slow down until she came to the narrow turnoff which led to the inappropriately named Mountain View Terrace. The only mountains visible from this row of red-bricked dwellings were made of concrete.

She stood for a whole minute outside the door of number six before finally raising her hand and knocking. The bang echoed hollowly around the square formed by the cottages. A curtain twitched on a window a few doors down and Maxine wondered if the Dunphys still lived there. She burrowed her face further into her collar and turned her back on the house of twitching curtains in case Assumpta was the person doing the peeping. Assumpta had always been number-one gossip in this area, assiduously gathering and spreading information. If anyone were to recognise the tall woman knocking on the door of number six it would be Assumpta Dunphy. But then, not even Assumpta would link the skinny, shorthaired child Maxine had been to the tall elegant woman she had become. If Assumpta thought about it at all, it would be to tut and maybe gloat at the rumour that the skinny child from number six had come to a bad end on the streets of London.

Maxine knocked again, more loudly this time. Assumpta Dunphy opened up her window.

"You'll have to keep knocking. Paddy is probably still in bed."

Maxine heard a shuffling inside the door. Someone muttered, mumbled and then fumbled with the latch. The door opened a slit. Paddy Murphy peered through the narrow opening. When he saw who was standing there, his sleepy eyes opened wide.

"It *is* you, isn't it?" he asked. "What're you doing here?"

Maxine grabbed the door, opened it wider and slipped inside. The smell of stale cigarettes and alcohol assailed her as she stood in the tiny hallway. Paddy, drool sliding from his open mouth, was staring wide-eyed.

"Get dressed. I want to talk to you," she said, trying not to look at the wasted figure of her father. When last she had seen him he had been taller, stronger. Eight years younger. She pushed past him now into the kitchen. It was a mess. Discarded take-away cartons, empty bottles and overflowing ashtrays littered every available surface and the sink was piled with ware.

"Did you come here just to look down your nose at

me again?"

Maxine turned around and regarded her father. The stubble on his chin was white and the head that used to have a magnificent shock of auburn hair was sparsely strewn with lank strands. Stains dotted the dressing-gown draped over his stooped shoulders.

"Of course not," she said with as much conviction as she could muster. "I just came here to ask you a few questions. What's wrong with you? You don't look well."

"What in the fuck do you care? You turned your back on your family a long time ago. Not good enough for you. We were never good enough for you, were we? Not your mother, your sisters and certainly not me. Too muck-common for Marie Murphy and her notions, weren't we?"

Marie! Marie Murphy. The name fell over Maxine like a thick fog, smothering her, blanking out her years of pride and achievement, her success, her money. Marie Murphy, the skinny, lanky child with a driving ambition to escape from the meanness and vulgarity, the crudity of Mountain View Terrace. The little tramp who sold her soul for freedom from poverty. Maxine's legs began to shake. She flopped down on the chair nearest to her, not noticing that it was piled with newspapers.

"You broke your mother's heart!" Paddy accused. "What kind of a daughter wouldn't send her mother a birthday card? Wouldn't even come to see her when she was dying?"

"I did. I saw her in the hospice," Maxine whispered.

Paddy was quiet for a moment, absorbing this bit of

information. "You snuck in when we weren't there, is that it? Hung around waiting for your common family to go away? You're a disgrace to the Murphy name! Why weren't you at her funeral?"

"I was in America when she died. Working."

"Bullshit! You should have come home. If you had any streak of decency in you, that's what you would have done."

Tears began to well in Maxine's eyes as her father's words trawled up memories of that lonely, guilty time. The model agency had sent her away on assignment just before the burial. They had probably been afraid she would go to the funeral which was sure to have been drink-sodden. The agency had invested a lot of time, PR expertise and money obliterating her Mountain View Terrace background, creating a mysterious, barely hinted at, sheltered childhood lived somewhere on the north side of the city. A background to match her transformed appearance until even she did not recognise herself any more. They had turned the skinny child into a beautiful woman, the poverty-stricken girl into wealthy socialite. It had been easy for Maxine to go along with their scheme. It was what she wanted too.

Maxine had tried to mourn her mother, tried to feel sadness at her passing. Instead all she had felt was pity for the suffering that cancer had inflicted on the woman and a huge regret that they never had, nor could they ever have had, a mother-daughter relationship. Any relationship.

"Good job Jason Laide looked after us. Lucky for you

too. He persuaded your sisters not to go to the papers and tell them what a bitch you are. He still keeps them in line. Not that they'd betray you anyway. They're real Murphys. Loyal to the death, even though you don't deserve it."

Maxine clamped her lips tightly shut. She could have told her father that she had paid for her sisters' silence. Was still paying for it. That the pension he thought Jason Laide was so generously providing for him came out of her pocket, that it cost her more every time one of her sisters decided they must go to the papers. She had furnished their houses, paid for their holidays and was obviously providing plenty of drinking money for her father. She owed them nothing. And they believed they owed it all to Jason Laide.

"I can't work for Jason any more," her father said. "I've arthritis. But he still looks after me. He has more loyalty to this family than you have."

Loyalty! Jason! Jason the carer. The protector. Could her father really be that naïve, that stupid? He had worked for the scumbag long enough, loading and unloading his lorries, driving his forklifts, sweeping his floors. Didn't he know what a complete shit Jason Laide was, what an uncaring, cruel user he could be? The man standing over her in the filthy dressing-gown was no longer her father. He had sunk even lower than the loud, aggressive, hard-drinking man he had been in her childhood. The cunning in his rheumy eyes was an animal cunning. It was all about where the next drink was coming from. Maxine knew then that the silence money she was paying via Jason Laide was killing her father.

"Get dressed, Dad," she said quietly. "I'll make some breakfast. We'll talk then."

Sensing that his daughter was not going to take no for an answer, Paddy shuffled off to dress. Maxine rang the taxi company and cancelled the return car she had ordered. It would take a lot longer than an hour to clean up here. She started by dumping the take-away cartons and empty bottles and washing the ware. Then she boiled kettles of water and added a generous dash of washing-up liquid, the only detergent she could find in the chaos, and scrubbed until she considered it safe to have a cup of tea in the small but now clean kitchen.

Finding a loaf of relatively fresh bread, she popped some in the toaster and put on two eggs to boil. When her father came to the door of the kitchen he looked around in surprise.

"It's like as if your mother was back again," he said.

He sat at the table and waited for Maxine to serve him. Just like her mother used to do. Even though Eileen Murphy had been ten years younger than her husband she had always looked as old as him. Having four daughters one after the other, Maxine being the youngest of them, had taken a toll on her. And looking after Paddy and matching him drink for drink had done nothing to improve her health.

As Maxine made tea for her father now she noticed that he seemed even thinner in his clothes and his skin had an unhealthy yellow pallor. She put the mug of tea and the boiled eggs and toast on the table in front of him and sat across from him.

"Have you been to see a doctor, Dad? Are you on treatment for your arthritis?"

The sly, cunning look came back into his eyes. He picked up his mug of tea and Maxine noticed how much his hand was shaking.

"They know sweet fuck all. They let your mother die."

"She had cancer. They did what they could. Stop lying about arthritis and get some help with your drink problem."

The knuckles whitened on the hand holding the mug, his nostrils flared, his eyes blazed. Maxine saw a flash of the angry, violent man who had terrified her when she was a child.

"How dare you! You think you can swan back here after all these years and then start insulting your father! Just because you get paid for showing off those stupid clothes doesn't make you any better than the rest of us. You're still one of the Murphys from Mountain View Terrace, no matter how you try to deny it."

"I don't deny it. I don't have to. How could anyone associate Maxine Doran with a place like this?"

"We're decent people, not like those shites you mix with now. Your crowd are the type who smile at you one minute and then stab you in the back the next. You're young now, successful. Wait until you're old, fat, sick. How many of them will be there for you then?"

"What are you trying to say? That you'll be there for me if I need you? That you were ever there when I needed you?"

Insulting the quality of his parenting was a step too far

for Paddy Murphy. He banged his mug down. Some tea slopped over on the newly cleaned table and formed a little pool that dribbled over the edge onto his clothes. He was too angry to notice.

"I worked my fucking fingers to the bone for you and your sisters!" he shouted. "Ye were always the best-dressed children in the terrace. Who do you think put food on the table for you, put shoes on your feet? You're an ungrateful little bitch. Your mother and myself did without to give to you! Your sisters and myself have kept our mouths shut about you for years and this is the thanks we get!"

Maxine got up and found a cloth to mop up the spillage. When she came back, her father was topping his egg, tucking into his breakfast. He had always been the same. Roar, shout, bully and then behave as if nothing had happened. Maxine sat opposite him and tried to see the tired, sick old man he had become. There was still too much of the rough bully left for her to ignore.

"You never listened to me," she said. "Neither you nor my mother."

"You always talked bullshit. From your first words. You were different to the rest of us. A throwback to your great-grandmother. A snotty cow, like her."

Maxine's breath caught in her throat. This was it. This is what she had come here for. She would have to be careful now. Not make him angry any more. Calm him down. Besides, she had to admit that Paddy was sincere. By his standards, he had been a very good father. He had provided food and clothes and a roof over their heads. The essence of a happy childhood. Anything more would have been beyond his ken.

She wanted to reach across to him now and touch his shaking, veined hands. Her fingers remained curled around the mop-up cloth, refusing to move. The gulf between them was too wide, spanned too many hurts and rejections, for a mere touching of flesh to bridge. She looked away as a little river of egg yolk dribbled out of his mouth and onto his chin. Focusing her eyes on the cloth in her hand she spoke quietly to him.

"You've always said that I was like great-gran Harriet. I want to know about her, Dad. Who was she, where did she come from, what kind of a life did she live before she came to Mountain View Terrace?"

Maxine sensed that her father was sitting up straighter, that he had tapped into an area of awareness in his alcohol-dazed brain. He took in a deep, rattling breath.

"What do you want to know about that old bag for? I can't tell you much anyway. I never knew her."

"What was her name?"

"Harriet of course. Harriet Murphy. Married to Thomas Murphy, your great-grandfather."

"No, before that, who was she? What was her maiden name?"

Maxine looked up and saw the cunning look come to the fore on her father's egg-stained face. He seemed to be calculating how much the information he had was worth to his wealthy daughter. Or maybe he had none but would make something up. Paddy Murphy had been a good liar. Probably still was. She picked up her bag from the chair where it rested and took out the photograph of Lady

Harriet Wellsley's portrait that Andrew had given to her.

"Is this great-gran Harriet Murphy?" she asked, pushing the photo across the table to her father.

Paddy picked it up and made an issue of peering at it and holding it close to his rheumy eyes. "Where did you get this?"

Maxine paused before answering. Should she tell him or wait to see if he knew anything of his grandmother's background? Play him at his own game.

"I saw it in an art gallery," she lied.

He was still staring at the photo. "There was a photograph of her. An old tattered, browny one. Your great-grandfather, Thomas, kept it in his pocket until the day he died."

"I know. I have that photo."

Paddy ignored her as he examined the picture in his hand. "Yes, this is her. See the head in the air? The way she looks down her nose? Just like you do. That's why I always said you were so like her. She thought she had married beneath her and she let everyone know, including my henpecked grandfather. Thomas was a decent man. Gifted at handling horses. Not so good at handling women though. He should have taken a whip to the old biddy."

Maxine cringed.

He put the photo down and peered at his daughter.

"Why have you really come back here, poking into the past? Are you trying to find royal connections or something? Pretend that you are one of her crowd?"

"Who were 'her crowd'? What was her family name?"

"How the fuck should I know? Nobody ever said.

Some kind of aristocracy I think. She had disappeared well before I was born. My grandfather never talked much about her. Not to me anyway. All I know is that her son, my father, married in 1925 and she wasn't here then. My father often spoke of her though. He said she was a tyrant, a stuck-up cow."

"She disappeared? What do you mean?"

"I mean she just wasn't here any more. My father said one day her place at the table was empty and nobody said why. Those were the days when children spoke only when they were spoken to. Even though he was nearly twenty by then he couldn't ask or he would have got a clip on the ear. Proper order too. Not like now –"

"Did she die?

Paddy just shook his head and, suddenly losing interest, dropped the photo onto the table.

"Angela has four children now," he announced.

Maxine just nodded. She had no interest in the size of her sister's brood. It was obvious to her that her father knew very little about his grandmother. Communication had never been the forte of the Murphy clan and as far as Harriet was concerned they seemed to want to forget her. Except of course the recollection that she was snooty. Just like her great-granddaughter. Just like Maxine.

"Remember that old biscuit tin Mam had with all the old papers in it? The one with the garden scene on the lid? Is that still here?"

Paddy shook his head. "Naw! I threw that out after your mother died. She was a fright for hoarding." Then he narrowed his eyes and peered at Maxine. "Oh, I see! You're looking for certificates. You think you'll find out who Harriet was if you see her marriage certificate to Thomas Murphy. What's your game, Marie? Are you trying to get an inheritance or something?"

Maxine did not bother answering him. She wasn't sure of the answer anyway. She got out her phone and ordered a taxi, cleared off the table, gave her father a fistful of cash and then for the second time in her life turned her back on Mountain View Terrace.

Chapter 13

Jason smiled as he put down the phone. What a way to start the day! He had just had a very satisfying conversation with Dirk Van Aken. It was nice doing business with Dirk. This was only the third shipment he had handled for the Dutchman but when he saw the incredible profits he regretted not being involved a long time ago. Jason was a wealthy man now. No denying that. But he had worked his butt off, slaving and scheming, building up his portfolio of blackmail and threats in order to get ahead. He could have been mega-rich a long time ago if he had met Van Aken sooner.

He and Dirk had evolved their own shorthand for their phone conversations. Just in case some nosey fucker was listening in, prying into places where they had no right. In the course of their seemingly innocuous conversation, they had arranged that Dirk send gaming machines to Jason. For the Eureka Club. An innocent exchange. Money for machines. Jason grinned as he thought of the deal he had struck. In Holland, the gaming machines were packed with some high-grade cocaine and heroin before crating. Dirk only supplied the best. The crates were then loaded on a Laide Transport container and would duly arrive at the main Laide depot in Ireland for unloading, then the goods filtered to buyers through the distribution network Jason had set up. The operation worked like a dream. This little shipment would pay for the pub in Ballyhaven and also, hopefully, the Fords' fifty-acre site there. That should free up a lot of resources for the purchase of Manor House and the inevitable alterations Sharon would want to do. A few more shipments would help set up the Casino.

Jason reached into his jacket now and took out his notebook from the inside pocket. Carefully, in his childish hand, he wrote the details into his little leather-bound book. It wasn't that he particularly distrusted Van Aken. It was just that he didn't trust anybody. Just as well to have all the agreement down in black and white. As soon as this notebook was full he would transfer it to the Salzburg safe. Sharon had her uses.

Apart from wheeling and dealing, nothing excited Jason Laide as much as controlling a woman. He had the best of both worlds now. Maxine Doran had proved yet again that she was not strong enough to stand up to him, and Ella Ford, the hard-nosed businesswoman, had shown him a vulnerable side. That was a double-edged sword though.

It was obvious that Mrs Andrew Ford had been crying yesterday. Walking the fields, falling off rusty gates and crying. Jesus! Maybe the rumours that she was completely off the wall since her car accident were true. But it was much more likely that she had somehow found out that her husband was playing away from home. Did she know that Maxine Doran was the slapper in question? And there was the downside. If she did know, then Jason no longer had as strong a hold over Andrew Ford.

Jason shrugged. What the hell! It would be a lot more entertaining to screw the fifty-acre Ballyhaven site out of Ella Ford. She was a very attractive woman in a dark-haired, well-groomed, cultured sort of a way. A little like Sharon.

The happy, in-charge mood dwindled as he thought of his wife. The multi-million-euro home he was buying for her deserved some appreciation, a modicum of gratitude and respect. Sharon didn't seem to care. Of course she was interested in owning Manor House. As she had said "Who wouldn't be?". But the fact was, she had made no effort to come home. She was still skiing in Salzburg or one of those unpronounceable resorts. Flying down the slopes with a young man in her wake, laughing with him, making love to him on a rug in front of the blazing log fire. Doing all the things she never did with her husband. Bitch!

For the first time since they had met and married, Jason resented Sharon and regretted the compromises he had made to stay married to her. He didn't need her any more. Not for his business anyway. He had bought his own way into respectability now. A few more shipments from Van Aken and he could buy the fucking country, let alone the respect of the gobshites who ran it. His fingers drummed impatiently on the desk as he considered what he would say to her. Get your ass back here or else stay with your gigolo? How would she react to that? Probably just with a shrug of her shoulders.

It was a complication that Sharon was the keeper of the documents, photos and videos which had been the foundation of his empire. His precious blackmail stash. His insurance against ever seeing a poor day again. She had them all locked away in the safe of the Junkergasse house in Salzburg. The one in the creepy basement with all the old furniture and wine bottles. They had never discussed the stash but Jason was sure that she would not have gone through it. He was sure for two reasons. One, she would be terrified to disobey his strict orders never to poke into his private business – she knew what she had coming if she broke that rule. The other reason had to do with the thing Jason most admired in his wife. Her breeding. In her book prying into someone else's business would be rude... Even your husband's. She had obviously chosen to keep her eyes closed and her hand out. Or had she? She was a very clever woman.

Jason's fingers stilled. His breath stopped. His heart skipped a beat as he at long last began to suspect Sharon of having a plan. A very clever plan. Why the fuck had he never seen it before? How had he been so idiotically stupid? It was not in his nature to trust, yet he had given her all the information, all the evidence, all the ammunition to destroy him. She was custodian of everything from Maxine Doran's porn video right up to

Oliver Griffin's IOUs. She could, if she wanted to, go to the police, show them a list of his offshore account numbers, his shell companies, his money-laundering system. His blackmail cache of dirty little secrets. Fuck! How had Jason Laide, the tough guy who had dragged himself up by the bootstraps, so stupidly put himself in such a vulnerable position?

Jason stood and began to pace as he admitted the answer to himself. He could pretend it was sex. And it had been in the beginning. Sex with Sharon was different to sex with anyone else. It was wild and abandoned. Satisfying. But that had been just the bait, the lure that had reeled him in. The truth was he had been equally as enthralled by her beautiful pronunciation, her social grace, her manners and culture, as by her dark-eyed beauty. He had wooed and pursued her until she had agreed to marry him and he had never asked himself why a socialite like her would marry a working-class upstart like him. Nor had he ever really asked himself why he had so desperately needed her to become his wife. She had opened doors for him, yes. Given him a veneer of respectability, introduced him into the circle of powerbrokers that ran the country. But the truth, the fact that he had hidden so carefully from himself, was that he loved Sharon. Soppy, sentimental, mind-bending, gut-wrenching love.

Jason stopped pacing and stood stock-still. He began to feel angry. This was a weakness in the strong character he had perceived himself to be. He knew himself to be. No more! He'd show Sharon who was boss in their relationship. Striding over to the phone, he quickly dialled the number in Salzburg. It rang out. He dialled Sharon's mobile. It was switched off, out of range, silent.

Needing to do something to alleviate his anger, he pulled off his wedding ring and threw it as hard as he could across the room. It skittered along the floor and rolled to a stop underneath a chair. He looked at it, glinting dully from its hiding place. Jason decided at that moment that he was never going to put it back on his finger.

If Sharon would not talk to him on the phone, he would go to see her. As soon as he had a few things straightened out here, he would go to Salzburg. Sharon would discover what a dangerous game she was playing. A game that she would never win.

⋆ ⋆ ⋆

Andrew was thinking about Maxine as he went into his office. He was a bit worried about her fixation on Manor House. He had understood yesterday that she had just wanted to see the portrait of Lady Harriet Wellsley in situ. He had had no idea that she was so carried away with the idea of actually buying the property and developing a restaurant there. There had been no dissuading her. She even had an appointment set up with her accountants for this afternoon. Maybe they could talk sense into her. On the other hand, maybe she really had the funds and he was the one who needed the talking to.

He put his briefcase on the desk and tried to put Maxine out of his mind. Not an easy thing to do. She seemed to have infiltrated every fibre of his being. Closing his eyes, he allowed himself to indulge for a few seconds in thoughts of her. Then he sat at his desk and got out his 'to do' list. It was busy, busy, busy. Some major decisions to be made. The Coxes would be back soon. They would be wanting an answer on the Ballyhaven site. There were a number of clients to be seen about the new Cox apartments. The units were selling off plan as quickly as if they were going at a bargain price instead of the exorbitant money they were costing. Then there was the deal to close on Sharon Laide's house. That had gone for way over the guide price too. Ella should be handling that. She had dealt with the buyers.

Andrew sighed in frustration as he thought about his wife. When he had gone home last evening, she had been lying on the couch, a bag of frozen vegetables on her foot. She said she had tripped over a section of broken pavement and twisted her ankle. She had seemed flushed, agitated and even a bit shifty. She had refused his offer to bring her to the hospital for an x-ray. In fact she had refused his every offer of help. In the end, he had given in and left her in peace. She had slept on the couch last night and was still asleep as he was leaving this morning. Maybe he should ring Peter Sheehan, see what his opinion of her condition was. He might later on.

Just as Andrew was about to contact the first person on his client list his phone rang. He recognised Jason Laide's rough voice instantly.

"It's your wife I wanted to talk to," he said rudely.

"I'm afraid she's not here at the moment, Mr Laide,"

Andrew said, gritting his teeth and hoping that he sounded cooler than he felt. He had an instinctive dislike of this vulgar man despite his buying power.

"When will be she back?"

"I'm not sure. She had a slight accident. Tripped over a broken pavement actually. Hurt her ankle."

"Really? Tripped, did she? On a pavement?"

Andrew heard the mockery in Jason's voice and he was furious. It was obvious that Jason was implying Ella had been drunk. If the sale of Laide's present home and the potential sale of Manor House were not so profitable, he would tell this barely disguised thug where to go. Pragmatism won. Andrew found his polite business tone again.

"May I be of any assistance, Mr Laide?"

"Just tell her my engineer's report on Manor House will be back tomorrow. I'll make my final decision then. And do tell her to watch where she's walking."

Without waiting for any reply, Jason cut the connection. Just as well Ella was dealing with him. Andrew would probably end up throttling him with his gold chain.

Shrugging off his annoyance, Andrew rang Oliver Griffin again, much to Oliver's irritation.

"I told you, Fordie. There are no plans for Ballyhaven. Not that I know of anyway. I believe you even checked the five-year plan yourself. What's your problem? Don't you trust me?"

Andrew furiously backpedalled, assuring Oliver that he trusted him implicitly. He could not afford to alienate his friend in the Planning Office. Yet when he put down the phone, he was no nearer a decision about the fifty acres. Whether Oliver Griffin knew it or not, there was definitely something in the air for Ballyhaven. The Coxes would not be interested otherwise. The question was, should he and Ella sell now or wait and see what was going to happen there?

He must talk to Ella again. See if she still had her mind set on selling the site in order to buy a seaside cottage in Cuanowen. A little bolthole for her. An escape route. Maybe that was the right idea after all. They both needed an escape from the marriage which was daily becoming colder, more hostile. Or was he just thinking this way because it was what he wanted? Weren't there more urgent priorities now than an escape route for either of them? Questions, questions, but how was he to get the answers? Ella just shut down, allowed a pall of blankness to drop over her every time he tried to discuss their relationship.

Angrily Andrew kicked his desk. He felt better. Before he got back to work he vowed that they could not carry on any longer the way they were. Ella and Andrew Ford had to make a decision about their future. And they would. When the time was right.

* * *

Ella was very pleased. Her ankle seemed to have healed itself overnight. It was still slightly tender but the swelling had gone down. There would not have to be any embarrassing visit to the Accident and Emergency Department. As she put on her make-up, she wondered why she had lied to Andrew. She had never done that before. But then he had never lied to her before either. They were both bringing their relationship to a new low. Besides, such lying was risky. One chance remark from Jason Laide could reveal how she had really hurt her ankle.

She would have to talk to Jason today about Ballyhaven. She was determined now to sell their site. The more she thought about Cuanowen, the more she wanted to be there. If only she could be on Cuanowen beach this minute, walking along the shoreline, the thunder of waves in her ears, the wind whipping her hair, blowing all her problems out to sea. If only. And why not? Jason Laide would top any offer the Coxes made. It was just a matter of convincing Andrew.

Because she was late going into work, traffic was light. She paused as usual on the steps of Ford Auctioneers and focused her mind on work. Fleeting images of Karen Trevor flittered past and faded. Smile in place, she walked through the front office, saluting, acknowledging greetings.

She allowed her smile to slip when she opened the door to the office she and Andrew shared. Her husband was sitting at his desk, absorbed in paperwork and on her desk was the largest bouquet of flowers she had ever seen. It was a riot of colour and texture, artfully arranged and presented. She looked at Andrew's bowed head and felt like throwing the flowers at him. How crass! A sop to his conscience. Screw someone else and ease the guilt by buying flowers for your wife.

Andrew did not look up from his work as she picked up the bouquet and read the card. *'Sorry to hear you tripped on pavement. Hope your ankle gets better soon. Regards. Jason Laide.'*

A lucky escape. He could just as easily have said *'Hope you got over that fall from the gate . . .'* Ella dropped the card back into the arrangement. How did Jason know about her cover story anyway? She could not help but smile. He had an unexpected sense of humour. But the carefully worded card held a warning too. Jason was not a man to underestimate.

"Were you talking to Jason Laide?" she asked Andrew.

He glared at her. Ella felt a very unworthy sense of satisfaction. He must have read the card. He was furious. Jealous. Great!

"Yes, I was. And so were you judging by the size of that bouquet. Just how personal is the service you're offering him?"

"I'm giving him the time and attention due to a good client. So should you. I hope you were polite to him."

"I tried to be. It's not easy. He says his engineer's report on Manor House will be back tomorrow. He'll decide then whether he's going ahead with the purchase."

"Did you tell him we're hoping to close the sale on his old house today?"

"No."

Andrew's sullen answer told Ella that the conversation with Jason must have been tense. She would have to ring him herself, thank him for the flowers, smooth things over. Pave the way for the sale of the Ballyhaven site. Unless . . .

"Andrew. The site in Ballyhaven. Have you made any commitment to the Coxes?"

"No. They're away now anyway. Why?"

Ella was tempted to tell him she knew they were away. But that would mean admitting that she had heard Noel Cox's message to Andrew. That she had pried. That she knew he had lied to her.

"Because Jason Laide is interested in buying the fifty acres too."

"Jesus! What *is* going on there? I was onto Oliver Griffin again and he swore blind there were no plans for the area. So why the sudden interest from Cox and Laide?"

"Jason has bought the pub in the village too. You know, that grotty little place with the huge unkempt garden at the back. He has plans to expand it. He said he was going to make a beer garden and put in gaming machines there."

"Gaming machines? Didn't I read something about new legislation coming in about gaming and betting? More relaxed laws?"

Ella shrugged. Since the accident her interest in current affairs had not gone beyond the affair she now suspected her husband of having.

Andrew sat back in his chair and tried to figure out the mystery. Either Oliver Griffin was lying or it was a huge coincidence that two separate groups of very astute business people had suddenly decided Ballyhaven had a future in which it was worth investing.

"We could play them off against each other. Push up the price. What do you think?"

"I don't agree," Ella said shaking her head. "Jason Laide is too valuable a client to play games with."

"That's a stupid point of view! The Coxes have been the backbone of our business. If either of them should have a preference, it would have to be Noel and Gary."

"Jason said he would top any offer they made."

"What? Have you discussed it with him without even consulting me? Since when do we work independently of each other?"

How about since you started lying to me, pretending to have a business meeting with people who were not even in the country? It was what she wanted to say but something told her this was not the right time to let Andrew know what she knew. He could too easily talk his way out of it.

"It just came up in conversation with him," she said as calmly as possible. "So have you given any thought to the idea of buying a holiday home in Cuanowen?"

"I have and I think it would be a nice escape hatch but I don't see that it would be a good use of money at the moment. If we sold Ballyhaven – *if* – we could open another branch of Ford Auctioneers. I'd like to open up in the next county. People are beginning to move out there. Now is the time to set up –"

Andrew suddenly stopped talking. What was he thinking of, suggesting he and Ella open another branch of the business they ran together? Less than half an hour ago he was wondering if their marriage could survive.

Ella didn't seem too impressed by his idea either. "But we work too hard as it is. In fact we do nothing but work. What quality of life would we have if we added a far-flung office to the one we already run?"

They were both silent as they thought of the dismal quality of their lives at the moment. Each of them clung to their own dreams of escape. Andrew to his growing fascination with Maxine and Ella to her belief that a home by the sea, a safe, clean, Karen Trevor-free environment, was what she needed to begin to live again. To regain her sanity.

Ella picked up a printout and walked over to Andrew's desk. She handed it to him.

"This bungalow is for sale on the shoreline in Cuanowen. I want to sell our site and buy it."

Andrew glanced at the page with little interest. "You just want to run away. To hide. You're not thinking this through."

Ella smiled at him as she picked up her bouquet of flowers to put them in water. "I'm sick of thinking things through, Andrew. I want this bungalow. You think about it and let me know your decision."

Then she walked out of the office, the flowers in her arm, leaving her husband wondering just how much more of his wife's erratic behaviour he could tolerate.

Chapter 14

The taxi dropped Maxine in the city centre. When she got out she stood for a moment, breathing in traffic fumes, listening to the engine sounds and footfalls of the busy main thoroughfare. People rushed past, each intent on their own mission, each focused on their own particular goal. Maxine took a moment to hide in the anonymity of city life. To feel safe.

Glancing at her watch she realised she would be late for her appointment with her accountants if she didn't hurry. She took off her hat and shook out her hair. As it tumbled around her shoulders she got the slight aroma of cigarette smoke and mustiness. The stench of Mountain View Terrace. The lingering scent of poverty.

Charles Rea was waiting for her, her files on the desk in front of him, a welcoming smile on his broad face. He was the founder of Rea & Co Accountants and dealt personally with only his most prestigious clients. Maxine flashed a smile of satisfaction back at him. It had taken her a long time and a lot of hard work to earn this type of attention in Rea & Co.

She began her rehearsed speech, outlining her plan. Charle's face got more incredulous with each passing minute. By the time she finished, he looked stunned.

"Why ever would you want to go down this road, Maxine? You risk losing everything you have accumulated."

"But I could also multiply everything tenfold. Manor House is a big investment, yes. But it's a good one."

"It's too risky. You'd be using all your resources to buy the property. Manor House is old. What kind of condition is it in? I assume you couldn't open it up as a restaurant without conversions and repairs. You would have to employ staff, spend money on advertising. You would be looking at big borrowings. And it takes time to build up a clientele in the restaurant business. You have no track record in catering. Have you thought this through at all?"

Maxine stared at him, knowing that despite her careful management of her earnings, Charles Rea still thought of her as a dumb blonde. She had been the one who had invested in biotechnology company shares when other people did not even know they existed, the one who had bought artwork from little known artists and had watched her investments appreciate as the artists became household names. She had an instinct for making money but yet this blob in the suit in front of her did not respect or appreciate that. Besides, buying Manor House was far deeper than just an instinct. It was a need. It was her fate. Karma.

"I don't think you can have been listening to me, Charles. The sale of Manor House includes thirty acres of prime real estate. I intend applying for planning permission and then selling the land off in parcels. Have you any idea how much money I could make on that alone?"

"Have *you* any idea how long that process would take? What are you going to do for income in the meantime? If you intend keeping on your modelling career, how are you going to get the restaurant up and running? If you retire from modelling, where will the money to service overheads come from? This is not a good plan, Maxine. I must advise you against it."

"You advised me not to buy Plantok Biotechnology shares. Remember? Two years before they discovered the cure for Alzheimer's Disease."

Charles shifted his broad butt uncomfortably on his throne-like seat. He had the grace to blush a little. "Well, yes," he admitted begrudgingly, "you do have a good nose for a successful investment. And before you mention it, I admit your art buying is inspired. You have a very valuable collection now. But nevertheless, buying Manor House and going into a business you know nothing about would be risking everything you have worked for. Unless you share the risk. Form a partnership with another investor."

"I work alone, Charles. No partners. I need to know from you how best to manage the resources I have in order to buy Manor House. So . . .?"

Charles nodded slowly, his jowls wobbling as his head bobbed. His scowl was soon replaced by a well-practised neutral expression. "As long as you note my words of caution, Maxine. I don't want you coming back to me in a year's time asking me why I didn't stop you in this foolishness."

Maxine smiled at him. "Don't worry, Charles. I take full responsibility. Now would you please get down to work?"

It was an hour before Maxine left the offices of Rea & Co. By then she knew that it would be possible, if very risky, for her to put in a bid on Manor House. She also knew it would be impossible for her not to.

* * *

When Jason reached his cottage in the quiet suburbs, Oliver Griffin's car was already parked outside. Oliver got out of his car and they walked to the door together. As soon as the front door had closed behind them, Jason turned the full force of his fiery stare on Oliver.

"What in the fuck is wrong? Why do you need to see me so urgently?"

"It's Andrew Ford," Oliver said, nervously turning his car keys in his hand.

"What about him?" Jason demanded.

"He's prying. Asking a lot of questions about Ballyhaven. I can't keep putting him off much longer."

Jason stormed into the kitchen, filled the kettle and plugged it in. Oliver followed meekly, standing, not sure what to do next.

"Sit down for fuck's sake," Jason said impatiently. "Tell

me what's going on."

As Jason made tea, Oliver told him of Andrew's inquiries about Ballyhaven.

"He even came to the office and looked up the five-year plan."

"Of course he did. He's an estate agent. He needs to know what the plans are. They all do it. In fact anyone is entitled to look at those plans. For Christ's sake! Is that what you called me here for?"

Oliver picked up his keys and began to twist them nervously in his fingers again. Suspicious, Jason sat down at the table opposite him and stared as Oliver began to stutter and stumble over his words.

"Well, there's something else. Umm … you won't like this. Our man, our politician, Pascal McEvoy, says the Gambling Bill is going before the House next month."

"So? Isn't that good?"

"Yes. But I'm afraid there's a lot of opposition building up. It's not going to be as easy to get through as he thought."

Jason began to spoon sugar into his tea as if he had not heard. Oliver cringed. He knew this man's quiet anger was more cruel and vicious than his exploding temper. He waited while Jason stirred and then drank a big mouthful.

"I can destroy you. And that poxy politician too," Jason said softly.

Oliver bowed his head. There was no denying the truth of that. There was no denying either that Jason Laide was not the only power working behind the scenes of this Gambling Bill. There should have been months, even years of bumbling debate, argument and counter argument, select committees, house committees, pressure groups, interest groups, mothers of seven, Opus Dei, white papers, green papers. Instead, after decades of archaic gambling and lottery laws, amended to allow the National Lottery take place, this new Bill full of sweeping changes was being rushed through. Of course gambling in general, particularly online betting, was generating increasing amounts of revenue, but the super casino proposed would be in a different league. Mega investment, mega profits.

"What do you know about the Cox brothers?" Jason asked. "The building contractors and developers?"

Oliver looked at him in surprise. What was there to know about the Coxes except that they had turned their once-small building business into a multi-million-euro goldmine through astute investment? And also that they were nice people, Noel and Gary, not like the piece of shit Laide.

"I met them several times on planning issues. They're working on a warehouse development at the moment. Why?"

"Because a source tells me the Coxes have put in a bid on the Ballyhaven site too. They're trying to pressure Andrew Ford into selling to them." Jason frowned as he thought of his source. All the five foot nine of smouldering sexuality that was Maxine Doran. She was too slow on this job. Ballyhaven should belong to Jason Laide by now.

"Do you think they know it's the designated area for a super casino?" Oliver asked and immediately regretted his question.

Jason's glare was full of scorn. "You moron! Of course they know. Why else would they want to buy land in the arse-end of the county? What else would make them want to move out of the city? Besides, it was always obvious that little clause couldn't be kept secret for long."

"Well, I'm surprised the exact location has leaked out so quickly. It was decided less than two weeks ago. Only a handful of people know."

"We know, don't we? Have you any brain in your head? This super-casino licence is a licence to print money. Whoever gets it will have it all. Profits, status, prestige, power. People would sell their souls to get their hands on it. You can't believe we are the only ones who realise that. Shit, man, I should have let the loan sharks wipe you out a long time ago."

Oliver could feel a net closing in around him. The time was fast approaching when Laide would realise that Oliver had no influence over Pascal McEvoy and that Pascal McEvoy had very little influence over the passage of the Gambling Bill. It had seemed so simple in the beginning. The fact that Jason Laide was ignorant and ill-informed had made it easier. All Oliver had to do was promise that Pascal McEvoy would support the new Gambling Bill when it came through. Easy. There had been no undue pressure involved. Pascal was a forward-thinking politician. He supported the Bill. He truly believed that a Vegas-style gambling village would attract tourists to Ireland and boost revenue. Pascal felt comfortable discussing the progress of the Bill with Oliver. They were old friends. They could trust each other.

Since Ballyhaven had been chosen as the designated site, Oliver as the Chief Planning Officer for the area had a professional interest too. Besides, Pascal was his friend. A classmate. One of the gang which included Andrew Ford.

Now Jason's demands were growing with each step forward the Bill took. Oliver's fabrications had grown in tandem with the increased demands. When the politicians decided on one super casino licence, one designated area, Jason demanded that his name should be the only one given serious consideration. And out of fear, greed, cowardice and desperation, Oliver had guaranteed Jason that Pascal McEvoy would support his application.

To date, given Jason's unreasonable demands, everything had gone surprisingly well. Oliver had managed somehow to wheedle information from Pascal without arousing his suspicion and to pass on enough to Jason Laide to keep his vicious temper at bay. But Oliver had not reckoned on someone else playing the same game. If his own neck had not been on the line he would have felt some satisfaction.

"Listen, dickhead," Jason said. "Gary Cox is married to an American. It didn't take much effort to find out that her old man runs a casino in Vegas. Cox does business with Andrew Ford. Even you should be able to put those pieces together."

Oliver nodded and held his hands tightly together under the table. He had to. The urge to punch the leering thug across from him was overwhelming.

"So what do you want me to do now, Jason?"

"Find out who the Coxes' political contact is. It must

be someone with clout or else they wouldn't know about Ballyhaven."

Oliver nodded agreement, relieved that was all he was being asked to do. The relief was shortlived.

"There's something else," Jason said. "Tell Pascal McEvoy I was asking for him."

Oliver tried to appear calm. Inside he was shaking with fear. He knew Laide well enough to read the threat in that seemingly innocent remark. Jason was implying that he would soon approach Pascal directly. Oliver's stomach churned at the thought of Pascal McEvoy, or any of his friends, ever knowing that Jason Laide was an acquaintance of his. Ever knowing that Oliver Griffin was a hopeless gambling addict in the grip of a piece of scum. Ever knowing that he had abused his lifelong friendship with Pascal.

Oliver was once the most likely to succeed. Now he was the one with three separate lives: professional, domestic and underworld. All of his lives were nightmarish. Out of his control. Slowly but surely beginning to tangle together. And there was nothing Oliver could do to stop it.

* * *

Ella walked to the door of Ford Auctioneers with her satisfied clients, wishing them well in the house on which they had just put a deposit. Jason and Sharon Laide's house. The legalities would take a while longer but to all intents and purposes the house was sold. For a very good price and quickly too. Paving Jason's way to an equally quick purchase of Manor House and maybe the Ballyhaven site. Definitely the Ballyhaven site also if Ella had anything to do with it.

This led Ella to thinking of Cuanowen again. When she got back into the office, she took the printout of the seaside bungalow from Andrew's desk where he had left it. The views were spectacular. This photo had been taken on a blue-skied sunny day of course. Ella smiled. She would have done the same. Dark clouds and stormy seas were not the stuff of advertising.

On impulse she picked up her phone and rang the auctioneer in Cuanowen. By the time the conversation was finished Ella had arranged with the secretary to view the bungalow on the coming Saturday. She smiled with satisfaction as she entered the date in her diary. Andrew could come along if he wanted. If he didn't want to he could stay at home sulking or doing whatever it was that occupied his time these days. Or, more likely, whoever.

She looked around her office, for once feeling bored and not interested in her work. Her eyes fell on the bouquet of flowers from Jason Laide. That was something she must do. She must thank Jason for the kind gesture and let him know she did not give a fiddler's damn that he knew she was lying about how she injured her ankle. Unlike her husband, she had nothing to hide. She drowned the little voice in her head which reasonably suggested that Andrew might not have anything to hide either. Maybe, like her, he had lied just for the sake of it. Like hell!

Looking up Jason's file, she found his mobile number and dialled.

He answered immediately with a curt "Yes?".

Knowing from his tone that she had chosen a bad time to ring, Ella spoke as politely as possible.

"Ella Ford here, Jason. I just wanted to thank you for the beautiful bouquet. It was very kind of you."

"Ah! Ella. You're welcome. Those pavements are a disgrace, aren't they? There should be something done about them. How's your ankle?"

"Much better, thank you. I may not sue the corporation after all," Ella laughed and was surprised to hear an answering laugh, full of genuine good humour, from Jason.

"I'm just winding up a meeting here but since you're recovered from your unfortunate accident, how about showing me around that site we were talking about yesterday? Would that be possible?"

Ella looked around her at the stack of paperwork and the four walls closing in around her. The decision was easy.

"Fine, Jason. How about I meet you in Ballyhaven in, say, two hours' time? Give me a chance to go home and get walking shoes in case there are any more cracked pavements."

"I'll meet you by the gate then in two hours. Thanks, Ella."

He had put the phone down before Ella had a chance to say goodbye or before she could remember when she had given Jason Laide permission to call her Ella. He probably had assumed it after she had begun to call him

Jason. Cosy. A little too cosy, Ella thought as she drove home to get her walking shoes.

* * *

Andrew was about to ring Ella to inquire if she wanted to join him for a late lunch when he remembered her defensive attitude, her depression, her plethora of bloody problems. Having just come from a meeting with a newspaper which was going to run a feature on Ford Auctioneers he felt all out of patience and charm. A little peaceful time alone was what he needed.

He parked in his usual spot near his office and then walked back the street to his favourite local pub. When he had collected a cold plate from the carvery, he got a pint of beer and made his way to a corner table. The whole pub was gloriously quiet this time of day. His meal eaten, he got out his newspaper and flicked through it. Then he began again, reading more carefully this time.. His attention was caught by an article on page two. It was about the new Gambling Bill which was shortly to come before the Dáil. He remembered Ella saying this morning that Jason Laide had bought the old pub in Ballyhaven and was going to fit it out with gaming machines.

Andrew drained his pint and sat back to read the article. By the time he had finished reading it he was frowning. There was something going on here he should have been aware of. This licence for a super casino seemed to have slipped into the new Gambling Bill without much fanfare. Andrew would have assumed a public outcry against licensing gambling on that scale, rallies and debates against glamorising a pastime which could potentially ruin lives. Maybe everyone was like him. Caught unawares by the speed of this new legislation. Then he shrugged at his niggling thoughts of impropriety. There were too many checks and balances, too many safeguards built into the legislative system for an inadequately debated Bill to be pushed through without transparency. He must have missed all the lead up to this stage. Probably too involved in Ella's accident and recovery. Or what passed for recovery. One thing was sure though, he would have to find out all he could now. If anybody was going to build a custom-made gambling village, as reported in the article, Andrew Ford wanted to be the one to sell the site for the development. It was with that thought Andrew began to put the Ballyhaven site, the casino and Cox Brothers together. Jason Laide fitted somewhere into the picture too.

As soon as Andrew got back into his office, he opened his contact page and found Pascal McEvoy's phone number. It was some time since last they had spoken but that didn't matter. That's how the old boys' network operated.

* * *

Because she had her flat shoes on Ella had been able to enjoy her stroll around the fields. Jason seemed to have been impressed too. He had stopped walking on several occasions and had just stood looking around him, a faraway look in his eyes. It was obvious that he had plans for this site. The little brook at the edge of the glade seemed to have made up his mind.

"Can you imagine if this area was landscaped?" he asked. "Keep some of the old trees, maybe plant some willows by the stream. It would be a beautiful feature."

Ella nodded agreement at first but then began to worry. If Jason was this enthusiastic about building here, did that mean he was no longer interested in Manor House? He had his back to her now, facing towards the setting sun. The sky was infused with shades of orange and yellow light but it was already getting dark in the woods. She felt a little uncomfortable and for the first time questioned the wisdom of being in this isolated area with a man she barely knew. She patted the pocket of her coat, feeling for her mobile phone. She felt its outline just as Jason twirled around to face her.

"That then would be south," he said, pointing over her shoulder. "I like all my buildings to be south-facing. Maximise natural light and heat."

"Of course. But shouldn't we be getting back? It's dangerous walking the fields in the dark."

"Yes," Jason agreed. "We might trip and hurt our ankles."

They were both laughing as they made their way back to their cars. When Jason suggested a drink in the pub he would soon officially own, Ella did not hesitate in agreeing. There were questions she needed to ask Mr Jason Laide.

The three customers in the bar looked as if they were

part of the décor. Shabby, old and dull, they faded into the background and Ella soon forgot they were there as she and Jason chatted about Sharon and Salzburg, about skiing and the type of holidays they liked, about trivial and surprisingly entertaining things. Jason was in his nice mood. A good time to broach the subject of Manor House.

"I believe your engineer's report on Manor House is due tomorrow. You'll be making a decision then, Jason?"

"I've already made my decision. Sharon likes Manor House. She wants it. Subject of course to what the engineer says. You never know with these old buildings. They can look beautiful but still be in terrible condition."

Ella fiddled with a coaster on the table, pushing it around in circles. She must find out what this man's interest in the fifty-acre site was but she knew instinctively, if not from experience, how volatile his moods could be.

"Spit it out," he said.

She smiled at him, glad that he had paved the way. "I'm just wondering what your interest in the fifty-acre site is. If you're going to build there, why would you want Manor House?"

"I intend building there. But not my home."

"I see. But you're becoming pretty involved in Ballyhaven, aren't you? First the pub, now the site. And there are other people showing interest as well."

His eyes narrowed and immediately his face lost its pleasant expression. His mouth tightened a little and a purplish tinge spread up from his neck. Ella had to suppress a shiver. This man was a Jekyll and Hyde.

"I'm sorry if you think I'm prying, Jason. I was just wondering if you had lost interest in Manor House. That's all."

He leaned across the table towards Ella and fixed her with his penetrating icy-blue gaze.

"I know there are others interested in your fifty acres. I want it. As you so rightly guessed, I have plans for it. I'll give you a thousand more per acre than your highest offer, whatever that is. What do you say?"

As he spoke he reached across and caught her hand. Ella stared at the thick fingers with the ginger hairs and square nails as they closed around her pale, slim hand. A thrill of fear, revulsion and excitement ran through her. There was a warning and a promise in the touch. She could imagine those same chunky fingers crawling gently all over her body or strangling the life out of her.

"I'd have to talk to Andrew," she said. "The site is in joint ownership."

"Do you think your husband talks to you about everything? Are you aware of every deal he does, every move he makes? You're an intelligent woman. You must know he has secrets from you. Private things he would prefer you did not know. Do I have to say any more?"

Ella tried to withdraw her hand but the entrapping fingers tightened. She did not want to think about what Jason had just said. She could ask him. Obviously he knew something about Andrew. He probably knew who Andrew was seeing, which tramp he was screwing. Everybody must know. Tears of humiliation began to fill her eyes. Jason let go her hand and gently touched her cheek. His thick fingers were tender as they trailed from her cheekbones to her chin. The tears spilled over and he wiped them away. Ashamed, Ella opened her bag, got out a tissue and blew her nose. How had the dignified and sophisticated Ella Ford come to this? Sitting here crying in front of a barely civilised man. It was Andrew's fault. Fuck him! She put the tissue back in her bag and clicked it shut. Closing her eyes for a second she visualised Cuanowen, the strand, the cliffs, the cleanness and freedom of it. The new build bungalow with the under-floor heating. Andrew owed her. She opened her eyes, forced herself to smile at Jason and offered him her hand.

"Deal," she said. "A grand plus the highest offer we receive per acre."

"On condition that the contract is signed soon. Very soon."

Jason took her hand and then, leaning across the little table, kissed her on the cheek. She smelled his expensive aftershave and felt the sweat on his bristled cheeks. Grabbing her coat, she stood and left the pub as quickly as she possibly could. Too quickly to see Jason nod to the three customers who had witnessed the deal being made.

* * *

Ella drove speedily away from Ballyhaven, anxious to leave the memory of the thick, ginger-haired fingers and the sweaty cheeks behind her. The smell of Jason Laide's aftershave was still in her nostrils as she pulled up at Ford

Auctioneers. The front office was in darkness. Glancing at her watch, she realised it was after closing time. All the staff would be gone home. As she reached the front door she saw that the lights were on in the back of the building. Andrew must be doing some overtime. Probably biding his time until he went to meet his mistress, his bit on the side.

Ella's anger grew as she stormed through the empty reception area. All residual traces of guilt about making the deal with Jason Laide dispersed in the heat of her anger. She looked forward now to seeing Andrew's face when she told him. See how he could explain to his precious Cox brothers that they were pipped at the post where the Ballyhaven site was concerned. She threw the door of the office open. Andrew was sitting at his desk. He looked up, startled, as Ella stood motionless in the doorway, her eyes staring, her mouth hanging open in shock, her face ghastly pale.

Ella could not move. She felt as if her limbs had turned to stone, as if her heart had turned to ice. Karen Trevor was sitting at the desk opposite Andrew, her face turned towards Ella, the blood trickling down her forehead, her mouth open in a scream of terror, her hands reaching out, pleading for help. Karen stood and began to move towards her in slow, determined steps, the hands, the staring eyes getting nearer and nearer. Ella tried to move but her feet were cemented to the ground. She tried to breathe, to call out but her lungs were paralysed. Karen was nearer now and she could feel the deathly cold of her. Somewhere deep inside, she knew that if Karen reached her, if she touched her with her ghostly hands, then she too would be condemned to eternal terror. Forever screaming silently and begging for help. Karen made a sudden move forward. The image began to waver in front of Ella, the room began to darken. She knew she was going to faint but she did not want to fight it. Unable to breathe, unable to move, she welcomed the darkness which engulfed her.

Maxine caught Ella just as she was about to hit the floor. She was too late to prevent her hitting her head against the doorjamb.

"Jesus!" Andrew shouted as he dashed across the office to where his wife had fallen. He cradled her in his arms and examined the cut on her forehead. It was deep and already blood was streaming down her face.

"Call an ambulance," he ordered Maxine.

When she had made the call Maxine came back to the door where Andrew was still holding Ella in his arms.

"I'm very sorry, Andrew," she said. "This is my fault. She must know about us."

Andrew looked up at Maxine. "Of course it's not your fault, Max. Ella has problems since the accident. Who knows what goes on in her mind? There's no way she could know about us. Anyway, you were here on business, weren't you?"

Maxine nodded. True, she had come here to officially express her interest in buying Manor House. To make a bid. But whatever Andrew wanted to believe, Ella must know that they were having an affair. What else could have caused this intense and extreme reaction? Maxine felt a huge wave of sadness engulf her then. The only meaningful relationship she had ever had in her life was nothing more than an affair. How could the feelings she and Andrew shared be described by that one tawdry word with all its implications of furtiveness and sleaze?

Her thoughts were interrupted as Ella stirred in Andrew's arms. Maxine picked up her bag. "I'll ring," she mouthed to Andrew and she left Ford Auctioneers as quickly and quietly as possible.

As she reached the end of the street Maxine heard an ambulance siren in the distance. It would not be long now before Ella Ford would be taken to the hospital. Maxine tried not to feel resentful of the fact that Andrew would be by his wife's side, holding her hand, brushing her hair back from her forehead, being there for her. Loving her. She tried but she did not succeed. She walked to her apartment, ignoring the stares and remarks and whistles. Nothing impinged on her dark mood. By the time she reached her apartment block she had one fact settled in her mind. Andrew Ford was the only man she had ever loved and even though she had been with him for only a short length of time, Maxine Doran knew in her heart that he was the only man she would ever love.

Chapter 15

Ella heard the sounds first. Strange and varied they impinged on her consciousness. She tried to sort through the layers, from the whisper of rubber-soled shoes on tiled floors to the high-pitched beeping she recognised as a monitor. They were familiar background noises to someone who had spent time in hospital. She sniffed and breathed in the mixed smells of disinfectant and mass-catered meals. Her returning memory went into overdrive. The accident! A four-wheel drive enmeshed in a stone wall, a woman bleeding. A child somewhere in the wreckage. Pain, spreading from the top of her head to the tips of her fingers. Burning, stabbing pain, trapped inside her body. The woman in the 4x4, the woman with the smashed head, began to drift towards her, reaching out to her. Ella tried to force her eyes to open, tried to replace the writhing nightmare with the solidity of real images. She heard voices. Someone caught her hand. Someone else said "Sedative". Her muscles relaxed as her system was flooded with chemical tranquillity. Peace drifted into her mind. She slept.

When Ella woke again her room was awash with bright light. Sunlight. She reckoned it must be morning or early afternoon. She tried to sit up but pain shot through her head and she flopped back against her pillow again.

Andrew was suddenly standing over her, his face anxious and pale.

"Ella! How do you feel?"

For a moment she felt happy. Then the questions began to tumble around in her head. Where was she, why was she here, how long had she been in this condition of suspended animation?

"Just rest now," Andrew said. "You fainted in the office last evening and banged your head on the door. You've had stitches in the wound but you'll be fine."

He was lying, hiding something. Now he was pressing the emergency bell.

"Why did you do that?"

"The doctor wanted to see you as soon as you woke."

Immediately the door opened and a man in a white coat walked quickly to her bedside. It was Dr Peter Sheehan.

"What are you doing here? I fired you."

Peter laughed. "That answers one of my questions, Ella. At least you have some re-call. Now tell me, can you remember what happened immediately before you came in here?"

"I fainted in the office and hit my head."

"And before you fainted?"

Ella turned to Andrew and raised an eyebrow. He just stared blankly at her. She shrugged.

"We'll go over the events of yesterday. See if we can jog your memory," Peter suggested.

"Am I in a psychiatric hospital?"

"No. You're in the City General. I'm on call here. Besides, Andrew asked me to monitor your recovery. Is that okay with you?"

As Ella looked into his clear green eyes he flashed his white smile. She figured that if she needed a shrink it might as well be a handsome one. Peter Sheehan certainly fitted that bill.

She smiled at him. "I can always fire you again if I want to. And as for yesterday, I remember closing the deal on Jason Laide's house, then I went to Ballyhaven."

"Why did you go there?" Andrew asked sharply.

"To walk the site with Jason Laide. I agreed to sell it to him."

"You *what*! You had no right!"

Peter turned to Andrew and looked sternly at him. "Andrew, we need calm now, please. Let Ella speak. You can discuss business later."

Andrew nodded agreement and bowed his head but Ella could sense his anger.

"I went to the pub in Ballyhaven with Jason and then drove to the office," she continued. "I saw that the lights were on in the back so I knew Andrew was there."

Andrew looked up and their eyes met. Ella saw guilt and apprehension in her husband's eyes. He seemed to be holding his breath, waiting to find out just how much she remembered. Peter Sheehan was probably aware of it. She looked away from Andrew then, realising that she was adding paranoia to her already impressive list of mental illnesses.

As she turned towards Peter Sheehan, the memory of what had happened in the office came flooding back. Her fingers grabbed a bunch of stiff white hospital sheet and curled around it as she remembered the image of Karen Trevor, walking towards her, getting closer than she ever had before. Almost touching her, almost dragging her into the world which only the living dead inhabited. She remembered the fear, the sensation of icy cold, the darkness engulfing her. The fear and cold gripped her again now and she began to shiver. Peter Sheehan reached down and loosened her fingers from their grip on the sheet. His touch was warm and comforting.

"I think that's enough for now, Ella. You should get some rest. We'll talk more later."

Ella smiled gratefully at him. She felt drained. Sleep was exactly what she needed now.

"You look as if you need sleep too, Andrew," she said. "Go home. I'll see you later."

Andrew kissed her on the cheek and then both men left the room. Ella wriggled around until she found a reasonably comfortable position on the hard mattress. Then she fell into a peaceful sleep.

* * *

Andrew and Peter watched through the glass panes on

the door until they knew Ella had settled into a deep sleep.

"Have you time for a coffee?" Andrew asked.

Peter nodded and led the way to the staff canteen. "A bit quieter here," he said. "Easier to chat."

When they were seated Andrew regretted not going straight home. He felt uncomfortable surrounded by doctors and nurses. Peter was gazing at him with a superior attitude. Not judging. Not condemning. Just knowing, like he had always done. Even in short pants.

"What in the hell is wrong with my wife, Peter? Will she ever recover from her accident?"

Peter lifted his cup and drank some coffee. Careful. Honing and polishing his words before he allowed them the freedom to fly. "She was involved in a pretty major trauma. Recovery takes time. She needs a lot of support and understanding."

"Are you saying I don't give her the support she needs? Jesus! Have you any idea what life has been like for me over the past year? First the accident itself and the tragedy of the loss of life and then not knowing whether Ella was going to live or die. And finally, when she came home, months of living with her zombie-like state..."

Andrew suddenly became aware that his voice had risen, attracting curious stares from the people around them. The thought crossed his mind that he must sound as mad as Ella. He was immediately struck by guilt. How could he think like that about his wife? He bowed his head and tried not to feel Peter Sheehan's analytical gaze.

"Would you like to tell me exactly what happened to

Ella last night?" Peter asked. "It could be helpful in her treatment to have a full account of events."

"I was in the office with a client. Ella came to the door, looked at both of us, went into some kind of shock or trance or something, fainted and banged her head."

"A client?"

Andrew glared back at his one-time best friend. "Yes. A client. Somebody interested in making a significant investment in a property we are selling. At least she was. After all this fuss –"

"She?"

"What are you implying? That Ella witnessed some impropriety? That I'm lying to you about what Ella saw?"

Peter did not answer. Andrew nodded his head slowly. Peter Sheehan knew. He knew that there was another woman in Andrew's life and that Ella had seen that other woman in the office.

"I'm not making any judgements," Peter said. "I just need to know all the facts so that I can help Ella in the best way possible."

"I don't want to hurt Ella. I still love her. At least I love who she was. I don't think I can live with the person she has become since the accident. She's cold. Totally self-absorbed."

"And the client?"

"She's warm. Beautiful. Fun but mysterious too. A fascinating woman. Way out of my league. I haven't known her long but I am savouring every minute of sharing I have with her. She'll soon move on. So do you think Ella knows?"

Peter nodded assent. "She knows subconsciously that there is someone else in your life. She's having difficulty admitting it to herself."

"So what do I do? Stop seeing . . . my friend?"

"That's totally your decision. But as Ella's therapist I think the best way to help her is by being honest with her. Then maybe she can be honest with herself and begin to truly recover."

They were silent then as the buzz of other people's conversation drifted around them. Andrew stood. He was exhausted and stressed. He could no longer tolerate Peter Sheehan's self-righteous attitude or the smell of the hospital. He offered his hand to his one-time friend.

"Thank you for looking after Ella. We'll talk soon."

He turned and walked away before Peter could read the despair in his eyes.

* * *

It seemed to Andrew that he had only just fallen asleep when his alarm rang. He jumped out of bed. Two hours of rest was all he could afford to take. He must get into the office before going back to the hospital. As he showered his head buzzed with all the things he needed urgently to do. The Coxes were back. They would want an answer about the Ballyhaven site. He'd have to put them off until he found out exactly what Ella had said to Jason Laide. And there was yet another problem. Jason Laide's engineer's report on Manor House was due today and his final decision on purchase would be made. But judging from Maxine's conversation last night before Ella's dramatics, it seemed that Maxine too was a serious contender to be the new owner of Manor House. Fucking Jason Laide! He seemed to be popping up everywhere.

When he got into the office Andrew knew from the discreet enquiries and pitying glances of his staff that they had not fully believed the story about Ella tripping and banging her head. They thought that she had had a nervous breakdown. It was written on every concerned face. He was glad to get into his own office and close the door on their sympathy.

His desk was piled with memos. Not for the first time he reminded himself that he and Ella kept too tight a hold on the reins of power. His staff were competent. There was no reason not to delegate more and then things would not be so fraught in emergencies. Like now. Like every second week since the blasted accident. That car crash had been tragic, yes. For Rob Trevor. But even he was moving on with his life now. Only Ella had to continue with the melodrama, reliving those few seconds of slaughter, wallowing in it.

Before Andrew could gather his wits together to start work, there was a knock on the door of his office. Without waiting for an invitation, Jason Laide walked in. He dropped a file on the desk and pulled a chair out for himself.

"My engineer's report on Manor House," he said. "There's a lot of work to be done on that place. It's not in as good condition as you told me."

There was a challenge in the icy blue eyes. Andrew

stared back and felt his instinctive dislike of this man come to the fore. He was too tired, too troubled, to find his neutral business tone.

"I don't remember telling you anything about Manor House, Mr Laide. To the best of my knowledge, you've been dealing with my wife."

"True. Where is Ella? Is she out on some job?"

"Actually, no. My wife tripped and banged her head last night. I'm afraid she's in hospital at the moment."

Andrew caught a flicker of annoyance cross Jason's face. Ella's absence was obviously an inconvenience to him. He must be finding it easy to wind her around his little finger, to bend her to his will.

"I'm sorry to hear that," Jason said. "She's very accident prone, isn't she? Which hospital is she in?"

"She just needs rest at the moment. She'll be fine. Is there anything I could help you with, Mr Laide?"

"Read that report. I'll have to spend at least two hundred thousand rewiring, damp-proofing, insulating and re-roofing Manor House. I'd want that knocked off your asking price."

Andrew picked up the detailed engineer's report and pretended to read it. Words and figures flicked past him in a blur. His main concern at the moment was to stall Jason Laide until he knew exactly what Maxine wanted to do. He looked across at the money-rich, charm-deprived man and tried to smile.

"Leave this with me, Mr Laide. We'll see what we can do."

"Don't take too long. I won't leave my offer on the

table forever. I have a lot of projects in the pot at the moment. I want to get this one wound up."

Andrew nodded, waiting for Jason to mention the other projects or to talk about the Ballyhaven site. Instead, Jason stood and pushed back his chair.

"I'll be going to Salzburg at the weekend to see Sharon. I want to be able to tell her that I have secured Manor House for her. Okay?"

Jason didn't wait for an answer. He just assumed Andrew's assent and went out the door, banging it roughly behind him.

When Jason got as far as the front desk he stopped and smiled at the receptionist.

"Bad luck that Mrs Ford had another accident, isn't it? Where did it happen?"

The girl looked at him with a puzzled frown and then obviously figured that since he had been in the office with Mr Ford it was all right to discuss Ella with him.

"Yes. It's unfortunate. It happened in the office here."

"Lucky she was so near a hospital."

"True. I believe the ambulance arrived in minutes."

Jason winked at the girl and moved on. City General was the only hospital minutes away. He now knew where to find Ella.

* * *

Maxine smiled broadly when she cut the ribbon. The applause rippled around as yet another shopping centre was declared officially open. She could play this part in her sleep by now. The celebrity role. Another deposit in her savings account. A few more minutes of posing for cameras, scissors in hand, a sip of champagne and then she could decently slip away, her obligation fulfilled. Glancing at her watch she knew the taxi she had ordered would soon be here for her. She quickly said her goodbyes and left the group of managers and hangers-on to finish the drinks and hors-d'oeuvres.

When she was seated in the taxi, Maxine got out her phone and dialled Andrew's number.

"How is she?" she asked as soon as he had said hello.

"Sleeping," he said and Maxine could not gauge from his tone whether that was good news or not.

"Is she still in hospital?"

"Yes. I'll be going to see her shortly. Where are you? Could you pop into the office soon?"

"I'll be with you in fifteen minutes," Maxine said and was taken aback at how strongly her heart beat at the thought of seeing Andrew. She was even more surprised when, fifteen minutes later, she sat opposite him and saw how pale his face was and how dark the rings underneath his eyes. She wanted so much to reach out and touch him, to hold him in her arms and soothe away his deep sadness.

"Has she said anything about us?" she asked.

Andrew shook his head. "No. But her psychologist thinks she knows. He didn't ask me directly but he guessed and I didn't deny it. He said she's just not admitting it to herself."

"Well, she saw us, didn't she? She must know."

"She saw us in the office, yes. But she had no reason to

believe you were anything other than a client. I really don't know what goes on in her head any more. I think she probably blanks out when she doesn't want to face reality. Anyway, enough about Ella and her problems. What about the conversation we were having last night before the drama? Are you really serious about buying Manor House?"

Maxine tossed her blonde hair back and lifted her chin. She was annoyed at the implication that she was only playing at investing in Manor House. It was her accountant Charles Rea all over and she had not expected this from Andrew.

"I'll start again and hope that this time you take me seriously. I've seen the property, I have plans for it. I've spoken to my accountant and I can afford it. I want Manor House. Is there any reason why I can't put a bid in for it?"

Andrew flinched. He had made her angry and he never wanted that. But Maxine would have to understand just what a huge undertaking she was considering. And just who she was up against.

"There's already a bid in on the property. Ella was handling it. It's fairly far advanced. The client seems to have huge resources and I think he would not hesitate to outbid any opposition."

"Andrew, you know what Manor House means to me. I'll start off by offering ten thousand more than your present bid. I can up that as necessary. Apart from my business plan for opening a restaurant, there is the coincidence or whatever of the portrait of Harriet Wellsley. Manor House is more than just an investment to me."

Andrew unlocked the top drawer of his desk and took out the copy photograph of Lady Harriet he had made for himself before giving the original to Maxine. He glanced from it to the girl sitting in front of him now and was struck again by the resemblance. More than just a passing resemblance. The only thing distinguishing one from the other was the way they were dressed. And over one hundred years. Extraordinary.

"Have you done any research? Surely you could trace who your great-grandmother was. Family photos, letters, certificates, that kind of thing."

A shiver went down Maxine's spine as she remembered her recent attempt to get the family history from her father. For a second she could sniff the must and poverty of Mountain View Terrace again. She shrugged her shoulders to rid herself of the memory.

"I tried with no result. My family were never ones for preserving their heritage."

"I could help you. We could go to the Registrar's office. Find birth, marriage and death certificates for Lady Harriet. It should be easy enough to trace."

A closed look came over Maxine's face and Andrew knew he had gone a step too far. She did not want him to know who she really was. Or rather where exactly she had come from. The vague 'north side' of the city in her publicity material gave nothing away. And neither did Maxine.

"I intend applying for planning permission and selling off most of the estate," she said, her voice business-like. "I will keep the gardens around the house of course and probably develop the stables as well but I won't need the thirty acres. When I sell them, I will recoup my investment. And more."

Andrew put the photograph back in his top drawer and locked it in. Obviously Maxine wanted to keep this meeting impersonal and her private life very private. Her choice.

"Well then, I think you should know that the other bidder brought his engineer's report on Manor House in here today. I haven't had time to go through it but I understand the house needs extensive renovation. At huge cost. Not that I trust this man much."

"Who is he?"

"You know I can't say. Unprofessional."

Maxine smiled at him and pushed a page across the desk to him. "You don't have to say a word. Be professional."

Andrew wrote the name Jason Laide on the paper and pushed it back across the desk to her just as there was a tap on the door. One of the secretaries came in inquiring about a property which they had recently sold. Andrew went to his filing cabinet to get the appropriate folder. When he turned back, Maxine had gone. Nothing of her left except a lingering trace of her perfume.

Andrew sat at his desk and put his head in his hands. It seemed to be his fate that the women in his life were highly strung to put it mildly and hysterical to put it bluntly.

★ ★ ★

By combing her hair down over her forehead Ella was able to conceal the plaster on her stitches. She had only needed four. With any luck she might not scar and, even if she did, it would be easy to hide. She felt much better since showering. Unable to get dressed because the clothes she had worn last night were bloodstained, she got back into her hospital bed. It was only a matter of waiting now for the discharge paperwork to be completed. Peter Sheehan had already made an appointment for her to visit him in his rooms next week. She was just about to ring Andrew to bring in clean clothes for her to wear going home when Jason Laide arrived in the door of her room. He was grinning. Ella pulled the sheets up around her chin, embarrassed by the hospital gown she was wearing.

"You, Ella, are a disaster area. Are you always falling over?"

She had to laugh. It did seem ridiculous. He walked over to the bed and handed her a gift-wrapped box, then plonked himself on her bedside chair.

"These should help," he said. "You can change them if you want."

Ella took the parcel from him and tore away the wrapping. Inside was a shoebox. When she lifted the lid she saw a pair of flat shoes. They were made from beautiful soft, red leather. She looked at the size. Five. Perfect.

"You can't fall off them, can you?" Jason asked.

"They're lovely, Jason, but I can't accept them."

"Why not?"

What could she say? That they were an inappropriate gift from someone, a man, she barely knew. That they were expensive and she did not want to be under a compliment. That she did not trust him.

"How did you know my size?"

"You look about the same as Sharon. Anyway, how are you? Are you up to talking business?"

Surprisingly, she was. Ella felt energised. Her forehead was a little sore but nothing she couldn't cope with. As for the rest, the nightmares, the visions, the ghostly images, they seemed to be at peace. She had some control back and had promised herself that she would never, ever, lose it again.

"Manor House?" she asked.

"I brought the engineer's report in to your husband earlier. My man says that old house is half falling down. I'll have to spend a fortune on it to fix it up."

Ella knew this was blatantly untrue. She was not an engineer but she was experienced in valuing properties and Manor House was in very good condition for a building of its age. The Trevors had spent a lot of money modernising and maintaining. Jason was obviously trying to lower the price. Exactly what she would have expected him to do.

"I'm sure Andrew will give your report his attention and then talk to you."

"When will you be back at work? I started this deal with you and I'd like you to see it through."

"Andrew and I are a partnership. We work together on things."

"Not on everything."

Not wanting to get into a conversation which was obviously about her marriage, Ella thanked him for the shoes. He dismissed her thanks with a wave of his hand.

"I'm going to Salzburg this weekend to see Sharon. She'll be delighted to know everything is fixed up with Manor House. What about Ballyhaven?"

Ella's head began to throb again as the memory of her promise to Jason returned. Unless her recall was totally screwed up she had agreed to sell the fifty-acre site to him. Without ever talking to Andrew about it. Shit!

"The fifty-acre site. You walked it with me yesterday and then agreed to sell it to me. Remember?"

"No. Actually I don't. The bang on my head must have caused more damage than I realised."

Jason narrowed his eyes and moved close to her. Ella instinctively tried to move away from him but she had nowhere to go. He hissed at her and a fleck of his spittle landed on her cheek.

"Don't even try to do the smart-ass with me, Ella. I have witnesses to the deal you made. The three old men in the pub all saw you shake hands on the deal."

Frightened, Ella picked up the alarm bell and held it in her hand.

Jason sat back. "There's no need for that. I won't hurt you. Not if you keep your word. But nobody reneges on a deal with Jason Laide and gets away with it. Just remember that. You sign the deal and get your husband to do the same and everything will be all right."

Jason stood and walked to the door. He stopped there

and turned towards her.

"I'll be in touch. Take care. No more accidents."

For a long time after he had left, Ella just sat in the bed, the alarm bell in her hand. What had she done? Her logic told her she did not have to keep her verbal agreement to sell the Ballyhaven site to Jason Laide. Besides, legally, it was not hers alone to dispose of. Andrew would have to agree too. But her instinct told her Jason had no respect for the finer points of the law. He wanted that fifty acres and would stop at nothing to get it. The instinctive knowledge that Jason Laide would sink to any depths to get what he wanted kept Ella rigid with fear until Andrew arrived into the hospital to bring her home.

Chapter 16

For the first time in her career, Maxine found it difficult to find her famous smile this morning. It was never genuine anyway but now the seventeen muscles needed to produce a smile were refusing to co-operate. The sultry pout would have to do.

"You might pretend you're enjoying this just a little bit," her male partner whispered.

"Passion!" the photographer shouted. "I want to see passion from you two. This perfume is supposed to get you all horny and ready for action. Throw back your head, Maxine. Show us that lovely neck! Look at Clive as if you want to jump into bed with him."

She did smile then as she felt a shiver of distaste ripple through Clive's perfect body. She always liked working with him. There was no hidden agenda with Clive. He was gay and required nothing more from her than a professional relationship. This was the fourth series of shoots they had done together for this particular perfume.

It was a heavy, cloying scent. The only thing Maxine liked about it was the huge amount of money she got for the promotion.

Making an effort to put everything else out of her head, Maxine tried to concentrate on her work. She thought she was getting there, beginning to find her rapport with the camera, when the photographer called a halt again.

"Maxine, you have dark shadows under your eyes. When did you last sleep? Make-up! Where's the make-up person?"

The studio began to buzz as people ran around, slapping highlighter under Maxine's eyes, retouching her hair, rubbing another coat of oil onto Clive's already slick skin, rushing and racing to avoid the wrath of the temperamental photographer.

Clive leaned towards Maxine. "Something wrong, Max? Are you all right?"

"I'm fine, Clive, thanks. Just a little tired. Let's give this guy what he wants. Get it over with. I need to be out of here."

Maxine made a huge effort to put Jason Laide, Manor House and Andrew Ford out of her mind. She turned her face to the wind machine and let it blow her mane of blonde hair back from her face. She found the zone. The work zone where only she and the camera existed. After another two hours, everyone was satisfied with the morning's work and the shoot was wrapped up.

Looking at her watch Maxine saw that she had an hour to spare before meeting her agent. An hour to relax, maybe do some shopping, a stroll around town, a walk in the park. Something enjoyable, like normal people did. She wanted to ring Andrew, needed to hear his voice. She took out her phone and then put it back in her bag without switching it on. What could she say to him? Sorry I ran away from your office? How could she explain to him that he had given her the worst news possible? That he had destroyed her dream of owning Manor House by letting her know that Jason Laide was the other bidder? That she could never tell him the truth.

Maxine said a quick goodbye to everyone in the studio and went out onto the street. She began to walk towards the city centre with no particular plan in mind. Her pace quickened in an attempt to outrun her thoughts. They were all Jason thoughts – how much she hated him, how much she wanted to destroy him, to make him suffer. Head down, she forged forward, not noticing anyone, almost knocking people down in her rush to nowhere. Suddenly she ran out of steam and stopped on a broad footpath just off the city centre. People walked around her, some staring at the tall, vaguely familiar figure disrupting the flow of pedestrians.

Maxine looked around her and suddenly realised her mad dash had not taken a random path. She was standing in front of the Registrar's Office. The place where Andrew had suggested she go to trace her background. To find the paper trail that could lead to Lady Harriet Wellsley. Or not.

Without waiting to think any more about it, Maxine turned and went into the building. The lobby was big and draughty and busy with people coming and going. *'Registrar of Births, Marriages and Deaths'* she read on a signpost pointing to the first floor. A group of people were waiting for the lift. Maxine took the stairs and then followed more signposts until she came to a large room with little tables and chairs dotted around and staff behind a counter at the head of the room. The people at the tables had big leather-bound books open in front of them, heads bowed, turning page after page. The silence was church-like, disturbed only by intermittent coughs and the low mutter of staff as they dealt with customers.

A queue was snaking its way towards the counter. Maxine joined it. She listened as each person in turn asked for what they needed. Marriages 1949-1954. Deaths 2001. Births 1890-1895. Some were foreign, some Irish. All seemed to know exactly what they were looking for. One by one they each received their big leather-bound volumes of official entries in the Register and found their own table where they could search for the information they had come here to get.

The nearer Maxine got to the counter, the more she began to panic. What did she want? What should she ask for? What year had Lady Harriet been born, where and when had she married? Should she look for Wellsley or Murphy? There was only one person in front of her now. A girl behind the counter waved her forward. Jesus! Just as Maxine reached the counter, her courage failed. Muttering an apology to the girl, she left the queue and headed for the street.

What had possessed her to go in there, totally

unprepared? She would have to think this through, know approximate dates, names and places. Bottom line, all Maxine Doran knew of her background began and finished in Mountain View Terrace.

By the time Maxine reached the footpath outside again, she realised she would be late for her lunch appointment with her agent if she did not hurry. Rushing suited her now. It left her no time to think. When she reached the restaurant, Blanche Foley was already seated at the table, a forbidding frown on her forehead. Maxine sat across from her agent and apologised for her lateness. All Blanche's clients knew that keeping her sweet assured them of work. You upset Blanche at your own risk.

"The shoot ran a little over time," Maxine lied.

"You look tired," Blanche accused.

Maxine smiled at her. "You work me very hard."

"I hope you're not complaining about that? And talking of work, how would you feel about doing a show in Amsterdam? Next week. DiAngeli has suddenly decided to launch his new range there. Don't ask why. You know the man is quite mad. I don't know how he's so successful. Top rates for his show as usual. Are you interested?"

Maxine nodded her head slowly in assent. Yes. She was interested. Very interested. Not in DiAngeli's fashion show, spectacular as that usually was. No, her interest was in the germ of an idea which was taking root in her mind.

Yes. Maxine was really looking forward to her job in Amsterdam.

* * *

Leaning closer to the mirror Ella added a touch of blusher to her make-up. She was quite pleased by the effect. With her fringe brought low on her forehead and her war paint, nobody would ever guess she had been in hospital only yesterday. Clear hazel eyes looked back at her from the mirror. They seemed calm and trouble free. In fact, the brown-haired woman reflected in the mirror wearing cream suit, coffee-coloured cami-top and tan high heels, was a picture of quiet control. Ella did not know her at all. Inside, where the real Ella lived, she was struggling to find a place for her raw emotions from the past few days. Feelings of confusion, hurt, betrayal and fear swirled around inside her head, blurring her thinking. How could she see the way forward when this fog of emotions was shrouding all escape routes?

Realising that staring at herself in the mirror was not going to get her anywhere, Ella picked up her bag and car keys, locked up the house and headed for the office. By the time she got there she had the beginnings of a schedule for the day planned. It all revolved around Jason Laide. And Andrew. She must somehow persuade Andrew to sell the Ballyhaven site to Jason and to close the deal on Manor House. It was the only way they could be rid of the frightening, barely disguised thug.

Her plan began to unravel the minute she opened the office door and saw Noel and Gary Cox sitting across from Andrew. They both looked tanned, relaxed and happy. Andrew's reaction to seeing her was far from welcoming. In fact, he seemed angry.

"What are you doing here, Ella? I've just been telling Noel and Gary about your accident. You should be resting."

"I'm fine, thank you," Ella said, walking over to her desk and sitting down. Turning to the brothers she asked them if they had enjoyed their break.

They both nodded but as usual Gary was the one to do the talking.

"Yeah, we had an interesting, if very short, holiday. As you know my wife is American. We stayed with her family in Vegas. It's a crazy place."

"The gambling capital of the world really, isn't it? What do you say we go there for a holiday, Andrew? It would be fun."

Andrew didn't answer her. He was agitated, shuffling papers around on his desk. Ella realised she should not have mentioned them going on holiday together. It had just been a throwaway remark, an attempt at social chitchat but it had obviously upset him. He must think she was trying to publicly force him into a commitment to their future he did not want to make. Fuck him!

"Anyway, you'll have to excuse me. I have work to do," Ella said as brightly as possible.

"Same here," Andrew said. "You'll have to excuse me, guys. I've an urgent appointment in ten minutes' time. I should be gone by now actually."

The brothers stood up at exactly the same instant as if they were responding to a signal only they heard.

"We'll talk again soon," Gary said looking towards Andrew. "We must have a decision as quickly as possible on the matter we discussed this morning. We can't let it drift on much longer. We're putting a deadline of next week on our offer. Okay?"

Andrew nodded in agreement and stood as the two brothers drifted towards the door.

Ella frowned. The "matter" they had discussed this morning. Did the Coxes not want her to know? Had they forgotten she was an equal partner in this business?

"Hope you're feeling better soon," Gary said to Ella as he passed by her.

She had a gut instinct then that they considered her unfit to handle their business any more. They would, in future, or until she waved a certificate of sanity in their faces, only deal with Andrew on business matters. Ella sat there, barely saying goodbye as the brothers gently closed the door behind them. The implications were huge. If the Coxes considered her unfit, how many other clients would think the same? The one constant in her life was her work. She was bloody good at that. How dare they!

"What did you say to them about my accident?"

"Which accident?" Andrew asked sarcastically and Ella knew that he shared the Cox brothers' low opinion of her competence.

"How could you pass derogatory remarks about me? For God's sake, Andrew! I'm your wife!"

Andrew laughed. A humourless sound. "It's over a year since you've been a wife to me. But this is not the time or place to go into that. What we must do now is try to sort out the Ballyhaven mess."

"I thought you had an urgent appointment?"

"I just wanted to get rid of the Coxes."

Ella raised an eyebrow and stared at her husband. How easily lies seemed to come to him and how smoothly he passed them off as truth. Had he always been a liar? Till death us do part. Had that been a lie too? He left his desk and came to sit across from her.

"Exactly what have you said to Jason Laide about Ballyhaven? Have you committed us in any way?"

Ella shuffled uncomfortably on her seat. Obviously "the matter" discussed this morning with Gary and Noel Cox had been the Ballyhaven site. It appeared that they wanted it as badly as Jason Laide. And Andrew apparently was determined that the Cox brothers should have it. She shivered as she thought about Jason Laide's anger if she reneged on her promise to sell the fifty acres to him.

"I shook hands on the deal. Isn't that commitment enough?"

"Did you sign anything?"

"How could I? You're co-owner. Any agreement would need joint signatures."

Andrew relaxed. He sat back in his chair and smiled at Ella. "That's okay then. I was afraid you had made some promises we couldn't go back on. The Coxes must have that site. We need to keep them on-side."

"Not so quick. I don't agree. We have just sold Jason Laide's house and got a nice commission from it. When Rob Trevor signs the Manor House contract with Jason, we'll have a very good bonus. Enough to buy the bungalow in Cuanowen. He's a good client. I want to keep him."

"For heaven's sake! Where's your common sense? The Coxes are the best clients we have. They have a history with us. And a future if you don't mess it up."

Ella thought again of the Jason's purple infused face leaning over her in the hospital bed. He was not a man to issue idle threats. The promise of violence and evil was plain in the icy blue eyes. He would use anything to get what he wanted.

"Jason came to see me in the hospital yesterday. He said he has witnesses to the deal I made with him. I don't think he's going to take no for an answer. Maybe we won't have a choice."

Andrew thumped the desk in uncharacteristic rage. "Jesus! Ella! You're getting us into a real mess. You've got too familiar altogether with that man. You know nothing about him. Couldn't you have picked somebody decent to befriend?"

"Like you did?"

Andrew opened his mouth as if to speak. The words did not come out. He just sat there, looking sheepish and guilty. He didn't have to say anything. Ella should not have been shocked or hurt. But she was. She pushed the feelings back into the fog of her mind. They could be dealt with later. She managed to smile at her husband.

"As you said this is not the time or the place to discuss personal matters. We'll do that when we are both ready. Now tell me about the engineer's report on Manor House."

"That report is a sham. I'm having it vetted by a man

I can trust. Anyway, it may be quite irrelevant. We have another offer on Manor House."

"Really?"

"You saw the bidder. Here in the office before – before you collapsed. Don't you remember?"

How well Ella remembered. Too well. Karen Trevor walking towards her, reaching out to her, pleading, begging, asking too much of her. Of course her logic told her that Karen could not have been there. She was not altogether mad. But why had she not seen someone else? How could she not have noticed a client in the office?

"Who was it?"

It could have been the way Andrew hesitated before he said the name, or the soft way he spoke the words that sent shivers down Ella's spine. Or maybe it was because of the beautiful portrait in Manor House that Jason Laide said resembled the girl. Whatever the reason, the second she heard him say the words "Maxine Doran" she knew beyond doubt that this was the woman with whom her husband was having an affair.

* * *

Jason was standing outside the door of Maxine's apartment when she got out of the lift. She could see his sweaty, purple-faced anger from twenty feet away.

"Why did you change the fucking locks?" he raged as she approached.

"There have been a lot of break-ins around here," she explained reasonably as she let them both into the apartment.

Jason threw himself onto the couch and ordered a drink. When Maxine brought it to him, he grabbed her wrist and pulled her down beside him. Pushing his face so close to hers that she could feel the heat from his skin, he began to harangue her, spitting the usual obscenities. It soon became clear that the Ford's site in Ballyhaven was the cause of this particular manic bout.

"I don't ask much of you. I let you get on with your life. Just an odd favour every now and then. You owe me, you bitch!"

Maxine smiled at him. She had to. "Yes, Jason. I know. You could destroy me any time you wanted to. I appreciate that. But I've really tried my best with Andrew Ford. I even told him I wanted to buy his site for myself. But you do realise that his wife is joint owner. She would have to agree to sell it too."

"She has agreed, you silly cow! I've made the deal with Ella Ford. She's off her fucking head but I could still make that agreement stick. Have you completely lost your touch? You must be well gone past it, Max. How could you not get Andrew Ford to sell a few fields that he doesn't even want?"

"The trouble is, Jason, as I've already told you, you're not the only person who's interested in that land. Noel and Gary Cox are after it too. There must be oil wells underneath it."

"None of your business. I have to force Andrew Ford's hand now. And quickly. I want evidence. Photos. You know what I mean. Home movie sort of thing. The more explicit and embarrassing the better. At least that's one thing I know you can do."

"But I think Ella already knows Andrew is with somebody else. Maybe she doesn't care."

"Of course she doesn't fucking care! She's too absorbed in her nervous breakdown. Spending her time falling around the place. But he'd care if his business colleagues knew, wouldn't he? There are newspapers that would love to have the pictures. You know the ones. Can you imagine the headlines? Leading Business Man Exposes His Assets?"

Needing breathing space, Maxine got up to put on the kettle. Her mind was in over-drive. What in the hell should she do now? She would not, could not, do this to Andrew. There was only one choice she could make now: never to see him again.

Better to have him believe that Maxine Doran had dumped him rather than have him discover her involvement with Jason Laide and all the murky history that entailed. But then Jason would very gladly destroy both of them if she refused. She would just have to play along with Jason. For now. Hoodwink him.

She jumped when she felt Jason's breath on the back of her neck and realised that he had followed her into the kitchen and was standing behind her. Turning to face him, she fixed a smile on her face.

"Fine, Jason. I'll go along with that idea. See if we can make Andrew Ford sign on the dotted line."

Jason grabbed her roughly around the waist and pulled her close to his body. "You have no choice, slut. The newspapers would also love to see supermodel Maxine as she was in her teens, wouldn't they? I want a set of your new keys. I'll have one of my men come here to set up cameras. I want that site in Ballyhaven at any cost and anyone that tries to stand in my way gets what they deserve. Understand?"

Maxine understood perfectly. It was a fight to the death. Either she destroyed Jason Laide or he destroyed her. To her relief, Jason relaxed his grip on her then.

"I know you're gagging for it, Maxine, but sorry, I'm in a hurry. I'm going to Salzburg tomorrow and I have a lot to do before then."

"Give Sharon my regards. When will she be home?"

"Just as soon as the contract for our new place is fixed up. I'm buying Manor House. Do you know it?"

For an instant Maxine thought of the kitchen knives on the counter behind her. How shiny and sharp the blades were and how easily they would sink into Jason Laide's fat, white flesh. What an abomination! This piece of filth getting his mucky hands on Manor House, sleeping in the canopied bed, walking on the magnificent floors and in the gardens, polluting the peace and dignity of the old building with his vulgarity and cruelty. She took a step away so that the knives were out of her reach.

"You must come to see it, Maxine. There's a portrait of some old biddy hanging in the hall and I swear to Christ she's your double. You wouldn't believe it."

"Really?"

"Anyway, you know Sharon. She'll be throwing plenty of parties there. You'll see the portrait then. That's if you get the business with Andrew Ford fixed up. If you don't, you may not even be around."

With that threat delivered, Jason turned and walked away. Maxine waited until she heard her front door close. Then she went to her diary and found the phone number she needed. This was her last chance, the only one she might ever have to rid herself of Jason Laide. Her fingers shook as she dialled the number.

Chapter 17

Ella liked the city on Friday mornings. It always seemed to buzz with anticipation, an energy and willingness to get on with the day so that the weekend could begin. At least she used to like it when she had weekends to look forward to. That of course had not been the case for the past year when every day had been tinged with the dogged determination of Mondays. To be endured rather than enjoyed.

As she stood this Friday morning outside the main office of the business she and Andrew had built from scratch, she decided that another weekend of playing host to Karen Trevor was more than she could take. Looking around her on the busy street she could see people carrying weekend bags, dressed up in their best, anxious to get duties done and be on their way. Escaping. Living.

At the door she took her usual deep breath, fixed her business smile in place and, shoulders back, walked through reception into the private office she and Andrew shared. He was at his desk, his hair tousled. Not a good sign. He always ran his fingers through his hair when he was frustrated or even angry, leaving it standing up in little tufts.

"Everything all right?" Ella asked as she settled down at her desk.

"Bloody fine. Why wouldn't it be with everyone on my back? I've had another call from Gary Cox. Just a little reminder that he will want an answer on the Ballyhaven site. Jason Laide has been on looking for you too. You've really botched this Ballyhaven thing up."

"I've got a promise from Jason Laide that he'll top any other offer by one thousand euro an acre. That's not what I call botching it up."

"Really? You never told me that."

Ella did not answer him. Instead she logged onto her computer and searched for a hotel near Cuanowen. Finding one within a five-kilometre radius, she put in a request for details and then turned to her husband.

"Remember I told you I've made arrangements to view the bungalow in Cuanowen? I've decided to spend the weekend there. Take a break. Why don't you come too? How about it?"

"Don't be ridiculous! I can't go swanning off with all this hanging over our heads."

"What can you do to change things over these couple of days? Wouldn't it be better to get some fresh air and rest? Then we could see more clearly how to sort things out. We need the time together, Andrew. We have a lot of things to talk about."

His hands went to his hair again and he began to run his fingers through it. As Ella watched him she subconsciously crossed her fingers. If he said yes, then maybe there was some hope for them, for their relationship, for the Ella and Andrew that used to be. If he said no . . .

"I'm sorry, I can't go. I've a very important meeting tomorrow."

"I'm sure you have. What's her name?"

The bitter words had left Ella's mouth before she could stop them. She had not meant to sound so waspish. That was not true. She had. She wanted to hurt him as he was hurting her. But she did not want to appear unreasonable while doing it. She should not give her husband yet another excuse to go off to his floozy. His bit on the side. To Maxine Doran. Bitch!

He crossed the office now and came to stand in front of her desk, his eyes glittering with a rage she had seldom seen before in Andrew Ford.

"What goes on in that twisted mind of yours, Ella? As a matter of fact, I'll be meeting Pascal McEvoy and Oliver Griffin for a drink tomorrow night. I must. I believe they know what's going on with Ballyhaven. They're the people to tell me why the Coxes and Jason Laide are both so determined to buy our site."

"What has Pascal McEvoy got to do with it? He's a politician."

"Exactly. So he can tell me, one old friend to another, if Ballyhaven has anything to do with the new legislation on gambling."

"Gambling? Andrew, what are you talking about?"

He sat on the chair opposite her and she could see worry lines on his face she had not noticed before. With a start she realised that Andrew was beginning to age. As she was too. Their lives were passing by and they weren't even living the time they had. All their youth and energy had gone into Ford Auctioneers. Their hopes, their dreams, maybe even their marriage, had been sacrificed at the altar of commercial success. And on the grave of Karen Trevor.

Andrew put his hands on the desk and leaned towards her. "We've been caught napping, Ella. We missed all the lead up to this new legislation. From what I can gather now, the government are going to issue a licence for a super casino here in Ireland."

"But what has that got to do with us?"

"This casino has to be built somewhere, doesn't it?"

Ella thought for a moment and then nodded slowly. "I follow your line of thinking. You suspect that Ballyhaven as been earmarked as the location for the casino. Am I right?"

"That's what I intend to find out."

At last Ella uncrossed her fingers. She had lost the gamble. Andrew was not going to spend the weekend with her. But she was still determined to go herself. Maybe he was telling the truth about meeting his two old college friends. Or maybe he would spend the time with this person, this other woman. Maxine Doran. The woman who wanted to own Manor House. The beautiful woman who wanted it all. Andrew seemed to be telling the truth now but he had proved himself to be an accomplished liar. She shrugged her shoulders in defeat.

"Suit yourself. I'm going anyway. In fact I think I'll go this evening."

"Fine. Enjoy Cuanowen but do not, under any circumstances, make any more deals without my agreement. See that bungalow, get information on it, but no commitments – okay?"

"And likewise. I have a client for Manor House and the Ballyhaven site. I don't want you making any new agreements without my say so."

When Andrew nodded his head Ella went online to book a single room for herself in the Seaview Hotel near Cuanowen.

* * *

Knowing that he would be pushed for time in the evening, Jason packed for his Salzburg trip before leaving his house. Not a very demanding job. He was going only for a couple of days. Besides, Sharon kept a stock of everything he might need carefully stowed away in Junkergasse. Probably well out of sight of her toy boys. Just for a moment Jason regretted having let her know he was visiting. He had been considering the idea of a surprise visit. But what difference would it make if he caught her with her lover? She would probably introduce them to each other without even a blush. He had even, for one moment, considered hiring a private detective to find out just who she was spending her time with in Salzburg.

Having to explain to someone, even a stranger, that his wife was whoring around the continent was enough to kill that idea. He might think about it again later.

As he zipped up his weekend case, he looked around the house. It already felt as if he was intruding even though the final papers for the sale had yet to be ratified. In fact, he had to admit, he had never felt at home here. Sharon had a talent for creating beautiful spaces but the ability to create a home seemed to have eluded her. For the first time it struck Jason how impersonal the house was. No photographs, no holiday mementos, no sign that a family lived here. A sad reflection of the truth. He and Sharon were not a family. They were a chemical reaction that sizzled and flared and faded with monotonous regularity. Gladly, he turned the key in the door and, throwing his bag into the car, headed into town for the first of his calls.

The staff of Laide Transport deferred to Jason with their usual pseudo-respect when he called in to the main office. As he inspected the current work log they assumed he was checking up on them. Normally he would have been doing just that, making sure the shower of hypocrites were earning their money, but this morning was different. His only interest was in the shipment from Dirk Van Aken. With relief he saw that the container was almost safely here. Very soon it would be landing in Ireland. In fact, he could oversee the unloading of the gaming machines before his flight tonight if everything went according to plan. Calling the deliveries manager, he left instructions that he be contacted as soon as the ferry carrying the container docked.

"I want to know the second she drops anchor. Understood? And I want a lorry on standby. That container has some urgent supplies I need delivered straight to our own yard here before anything else is unloaded."

"Yes, Mr Laide."

"Don't mind your arse-licking. Just make sure you do as I say."

Satisfied that his manager was intimidated enough to do exactly as he was told, Jason left the office and went out into the yard. He stood for a moment, enjoying the sight of the state-of-the-art warehousing complex which surrounded the central open space. A good portion of his profits came from storing the goods his lorries transported until the customer was ready to take delivery. Jason was never in too much of a hurry for people to collect their goods, unless of course it was a consignment from Dirk Van Aken. In that case the quicker the goods were delivered to the end customer, the better.

Warehouse number six was situated at the furthest corner of the yard away from the office. Jason began to walk in that direction, saluting people as he passed, answering the hoots of passing lorry drivers with a wave. When he reached it, he walked through the rows of neatly stacked crates and barrels and headed for the little office at the back.

He knew he would find Gussie inside, sitting as usual on the high stool he preferred, his hooded eyes deceptively sleepy. Nothing passed Gussie by. He noticed things. Little things. Like who might be asking too many questions, who could be trusted with the most important jobs, who should be got rid of without delay. He had spotted Jason's progress across the yard from his vantage point on his high stool.

"She's on time," he said by way of greeting.

Jason nodded. The ferry was indeed on time. He and Gussie understood each other without a need for too many words.

"I'm going to Salzburg this evening. I'm hoping to have distribution under way before I leave."

"No problem," Gussie said. "They've all been contacted."

Jason closed the door to the little office and stood with his back to it. Just a precaution. There was no one near enough to overhear anyway.

"I have one special drop. It's very important. Have you contacted O'Shaughnessy?"

Gussie nodded.

"I want to make sure he delivers to the contact for the Alexander Private Secondary School. You know the one?"

"I do."

"How far would you trust O'Shaughnessy?" Jason asked.

Gussie's hooded eyes narrowed so that they appeared to be closed. The seconds ticked by but Jason knew better than to try and hurry an answer from his right-hand man.

"I'd trust him with my life," Gussie answered at last.

That was good enough for Jason. He walked the few steps it took to cross the little office and stood in front of Gussie.

"I want to make sure that a kid named Hugh McEvoy gets some merchandise. For free if necessary. And I want a record, maybe a photo, of the hand-over. Understood?"

"The politician's son?"

Gussie understood. Young McEvoy was just a kid. But he was already a customer. Small stuff. Like a lot of the rich kids. Playing at being cool. Jason must need some favours from this kid's father.

"I'll have O'Shaughnessy look after it," Gussie said.

Jason breathed a sigh of relief. He would not have trusted anyone else with this job. He smiled at the solemn man sitting on the stool.

"Thanks, Gus. It's very important to my future plans that I have some influence with this kid's father. You have my mobile number. Just text me and say 'the film is in' when the job is done."

Gussie nodded silently again. They shook hands, sealing their deal. They always looked out for each other, Jason and his old friend. Then Jason turned and recrossed the yard. He had lots more to do before he got on the plane for Salzburg.

* * *

Maxine took the business card out of her purse and stared at it, as if by concentrating on the small lettering she could find the answers she needed, written between the lines. It was an innocuous card: *Dirk Van Aken, Manufacturer and Distributor of Gaming and Lottery Equipment*. She would try his mobile number one more time, just as she had been doing since yesterday evening. If there was still no reply, she would ring his business number. The one on the card in her hand.

She was so convinced that the mobile number would ring out again that she was speechless for a moment when Dirk Van Aken's coarse voice answered.

"*Hallo. Wie zit spreken?*" Dirk asked impatiently in Dutch.

Maxine breathed deeply and used her most seductive tone. "Dirk! How nice to hear your voice. This is Maxine Doran. You remember? We met in Ireland."

"Ah! Maxine the model. Yes? Jason's friend."

"That's right. I will be in Amsterdam for a show next week and I was wondering if we could get together for a drink?"

"The DiAngeli show?"

Maxine was surprised that he knew about the show. Maybe that was the power of the Jason Laides and Dirk Van Akens of this world. They made everyone else's business theirs.

"Exactly," Maxine said. "I was hoping we could spend some time together while I was in Amsterdam."

"Sounds good. Why don't you ring me when you're here and I'll return the favour you showed me in your city? But maybe this time we won't walk quite so far."

Maxine was shivering in disgust by the time she put the phone down. Then she straightened up her shoulders and stopped feeling sorry for herself. Dirk Van Aken was her only chance. Her only way forward. She had nothing more to go on other than gut instinct but she knew in her heart that Dirk Van Aken could tell her things that would help even the score with Jason Laide. Maybe even help to destroy him before he destroyed her. Besides, the only favour she had shown him in Ireland was to exhaust him by walking him around for hours on end.

Maxine went for a run then and left her phone behind. She had to. Otherwise she would have rung Andrew Ford. Just to hear his voice. Just to tell him how much she needed him.

* * *

Skittish was the only word Ella could think of to describe the way she felt. She should be sad, squashed underneath the weight of her black cloud of depression. Her husband had, after all, refused to spend the weekend with her and would probably be spending it with his girlfriend instead. Yet her mood was inexplicably light. She smiled at the receptionist as she left the office.

"I'm going to an early lunch," she told the girl. "If anyone is looking for me I'll be back after two."

The girl's surprised expression said it all. She was convinced that the workaholic Ella Ford had finally lost it. Falling, fainting and now early lunches! What next? Ella smiled as she silently answered the unasked question. What next indeed! A weekend of sea air and cool breezes, of peace and harmony and quiet.

The good mood lasted all the way through lunch. Until coffee. That's when Jason Laide suddenly appeared at her table, teeth bared in his growling parody of a smile.

"They told me I'd find you here," he said.

"They shouldn't have," Ella answered. "I'm on my lunch break."

Jason looked at his watch and then back at her. She shrugged, refusing to explain herself to him. He might be a client but he had no right to interfere in her private time.

"Can I do something for you, Jason?" she asked coldly.

"That's a loaded question," he sneered, "but for now closing the sale of Manor House will do. I'm going to Salzburg this evening. I hope I can tell Sharon the deal is done and that she can be mistress of the Manor when she comes home."

"We're looking at your engineer's report. You found quite a few faults with the property, didn't you? I'm surprised that you still want to buy it."

Jason leaned across the table towards her and the ice glittered in his pale blue eyes. Ella realised that she had totally misread the situation. Jason was not here just to give her a gentle reminder. His glare, the hunch of his shoulders, carried a warning that had nothing to do with gentleness. Or even civility.

"Andrew is having your report looked at," she said hurriedly.

"Checked out, you mean."

"Well, yes. Of course. You did make a lot of claims. And we're giving them due consideration. Also, you must remember that there's another client interested in the property."

"Is there? Who?"

"I can't say that. How would you like it if I started telling people your business? What I can tell you is that this is a genuine client who deserves the same level of our professional service as you do."

"Cut the crap, Ella. You're talking to someone who has witnessed your unprofessional falling around the place and having nervous breakdowns or whatever it is you do. And your husband isn't much better. I'm sure he wouldn't like his lifestyle too closely examined. He thinks he has secrets."

"Are you threatening us?"

Jason sat back in his chair but his glare seemed to intensify with the increased distance. "What do you think?"

What Ella thought was that Jason Laide would make sure everyone knew of her frailty and also Andrew's affair if he did not get his own way. In other words, ownership of Manor House and the Ballyhaven site. But it was obvious that even if he did know Maxine Doran was the person Andrew was having the affair with, he did not have any idea that she was the other bidder for Manor House. He would not have been able to keep that little gem of information to himself. If indeed Maxine was still interested in the old house.

"I'll need to speak with Andrew. He's handling the offer for the other client. I'll obviously have to talk to Rob Trevor as well. The ultimate decision will be his."

Jason shook his head. "That prick will do as you advise him. You'd better advise him right, Ella."

Then he stood and swaggered out of the restaurant, his

squat broad figure seeming to clear a path ahead of him. No one stood in his way. No one interfered with his progress. And that, thought Ella, was how Jason Laide lived his life.

* * *

Andrew put the phone down. Maybe Maxine was working, too busy to answer her phone. Maybe she did not want to talk to him. He started guiltily as the office door opened and Ella came in. The animated mood of the morning seemed to have left her. She appeared agitated.

"I thought you were taking a long lunch," he said.

Ella shrugged. "I was but Jason Laide came to see me in the restaurant."

"How did he know you were there?"

"He knows everything about everyone." She sat down opposite him. "I need to talk to you about Manor House. How serious is Maxine Doran's offer? Can she compete with Jason Laide?"

"I don't know," Andrew answered honestly. He didn't, did he? He really knew very little about the woman who was occupying his every waking thought and a lot of his dreams.

"So should we just sell to Jason Laide then? What's the point of delaying if she's not a serious contender? "

"We don't know that either. She's made a mint on advertising contracts. Maybe she has more real money than Laide. Anyway she has made a bid and we must respect her as a potential client."

"He's getting nasty, Andrew. I don't want to antagonise him. He seems to believe he has something on you. He keeps hinting about secrets."

"What could that thug know about me? Don't be ridiculous!"

Ella's answering glare left Andrew feeling defenceless. Did Ella know about Maxine? Did Jason Laide know about Maxine?

"Did you tell him who the other bidder was?" he asked.

"Of course not! I still have some professional ethics left."

Ella stood up abruptly and gathered her coat and bag.

"I'm going," she said coldly. "Ask Maxine for a firm decision on Manor House. Make sure she understands that Jason Laide would be willing to outbid her. He says he has cash in hand for an immediate deposit. Offer her another property instead. I'll see you Sunday night or maybe Monday morning."

Andrew sat still for a long time after his wife had left the office. He could not shake off the feeling that Ella knew Maxine Doran was the woman with whom he was sleeping. It took longer again for him to shake off the feelings of sadness and betrayal his wife left in her wake.

* * *

Traffic heading out of town was heavy. Ella could not concentrate on the road. The thud of the front door of her home closing behind her echoed in her head. A lonely, faraway sound, as if her whole life with Andrew had been thrown into a deep well and was being sucked to the muddy bottom. But there had been joy in the sound too. The light gurgle of a spring rising high up in the mountains. A beginning instead of an ending. She was leaving Andrew behind, to maybe spend the weekend with his mistress, but she had found the strength to pack a bag and leave, if only for a few days. She had taken some control back. She would make a safe space for herself in Cuanowen, one hundred and twenty kilometres to the west of here. A little oasis in time to gather her strength, to find Ella again.

Driving past Manor House had not been a conscious plan. In fact doing so brought her in the wrong direction. Ella was already approaching the driveway before she allowed herself admit where she was headed. It must have been a business decision that led her this way. A need to discuss the sale of the house with Rob Trevor. If he was here. As she rounded the bend on the sweeping driveway, the house came into view and in front of it was Rob's Jaguar.

Ella parked and, getting out of her car, looked around her. The gardens were shrouded in dusk by now, shrubs and bushes dark shadows in the fading light. Craning her neck she scanned upwards past the numerous windows towards the turreted roof. Manor House was a conglomeration of differing architectural styles, added to by many generations of Wellsleys. For a fanciful moment she felt Manor House was looking back at her and that it found her wanting. A breeze rustled through leaves and branches. The gentle sound brought Ella back to the present.

She mounted the steps and rang on the immense double front door. Rob answered almost immediately. Ella's prepared speech faded when she saw him. He looked sick. Pale and drawn.

"Do come in, Ella," he said politely but even his voice seemed weak.

"Are you all right, Rob? You don't look very well."

"I haven't been sleeping properly," he answered abruptly as he led the way through the black and white tiled hallway. When he turned at the kitchen door to say something to Ella she was not behind him. Looking back he saw that she was standing at the foot of the stairs, staring at the bottom portrait.

"Where is Lady Harriet?" she asked as she pointed at the portrait of the male Wellsley ancestor who had taken Lady Harriet's place.

"I brought it to London," Rob answered, standing waiting for Ella to join him near the entrance to the kitchen.

Ella walked slowly towards Rob, trying to analyse her feeling of disappointment. The grand hall did not seem as imposing without the extraordinary portrait of Lady Harriet. London? Surely Rob had not sold it? Lady Harriet was as much part of the fabric of this house as the chandeliers and the turrets. Or was her letdown feeling caused by the fact that she had really come here to confront Karen? A shiver rippled along her spine as she remembered the last time she had stood here gazing at

Lady Harriet's portrait. She remembered how the beautiful features of Harriet had wavered and swirled until Karen had been enclosed in the gilt frame, silently screaming, bleeding, pleading. Dying.

"Something wrong, Ella?"

She started as she realised Rob was looking curiously at her. She smiled at him and nodded. "I'm fine. Just like you. Not sleeping very well."

Rob led the way into the kitchen and held a chair out for her at the huge timber-framed granite-topped table. She was struck by the same thoughts she had the first time she had seen this kitchen. It was incongruously modern in the old house. The solid oak units looked relatively new and the wine tiles and stainless-steel appliances were too up-to-the-minute to be any more than a year old. As if he had read her mind Rob told her that Karen had had this kitchen fitted just weeks before she died.

"She loved the old house," he said, "but she liked convenience and comfort too. She had a talent for renovating without destroying. Tea or coffee?"

"Coffee, please," Ella replied quickly without giving her answer much thought. She was too preoccupied with thinking of Karen, imagining how the dead woman had planned this kitchen, how she must have looked forward to using it. Yet she could not feel Karen's presence here, nor could she get any sense of the woman who haunted her sleep and a lot of her waking hours. This kitchen was Karenless. Rob had his back to her, head bowed, busily pouring water into the percolator.

"What's disturbing your sleep, Rob?"

He stood still. He muttered one word. Ella thought he said his wife's name.

"Karen?" she asked.

He turned around to face Ella and her breath caught in her throat when she saw his white face. Mirrored in his eyes she saw the same confusion and fear she sometimes felt, the same terror.

"I know this sounds heartless, Ella, but I sometimes wish Karen would just go away and leave me in peace. She haunts my sleep."

"You dream a lot about her then?"

"Yes. She always seems upset. Angry. Accusing. Pleading."

That was the Karen who visited Ella's dreams too. And sometimes her waking moments. Her hands shook now as she tried to decide how much she should reveal to Rob Trevor. He was just mentioning bad dreams. What would he think if she told him she did not have to be asleep to be terrorised by his dead wife? Probably the same as any logical person would think. As she herself would have thought a year ago. Nonsense. Hysteria.

Abandoning his coffee-making, Rob came to the table and sat opposite her. He was even paler now, his eyes dark and shadowed.

"I must talk to someone," he said softly. "I think I'm going mad."

Ella smiled at him and reached across to touch his cold hands. "Talk, Rob. I'll understand."

His lips quivered as he attempted to smile. This vulnerability must be torture to a man as self-possessed as

Rob Trevor always appeared to be. Tears glittered in his eyes as the last vestiges of his dignity dissolved. His voice was barely above a whisper when he spoke.

"I'm trusting you not to laugh at me, Ella. I have the instinct that you've been going through some of what I'm suffering. I saw your face the first day you looked at the portrait of Lady Harriet. You had the same expression on your face as Karen used to have when she looked at that portrait. What did you see when you looked at Lady Harriet? What did Karen see? What was it that kept her standing for hours in front of that likeness? Do you know? "

Shock flooded through Ella. Either she and Karen shared the same madness, the same mental disorder or else . . . What if Karen had seen the identical image in Harriet's portrait? What if she had seen herself all broken and bruised and bleeding? Ella dismissed the thought, afraid that she again was beginning to lose her hold on reality. She looked across at Rob and pity overrode all her other emotions. What would she say to this troubled man? What could she say? Which words could possibly capture the fear invoked by writhing images of dead people? Maybe the truth was the only panacea to all the un-dead hurts.

"Your wife has become part of my life too. I never spoke to her when she was alive, never shook her hand but yet she somehow lives on inside my head. Always screaming, always pleading with me. I don't know what she wants. Do you, Rob?"

"I never knew what Karen really wanted when she was here. I certainly don't now."

The vehemence of Rob's statement stunned Ella. She had made an assumption that Karen and Rob had been a very contented couple. Why not? They had wealth and privilege and a beautiful son. But then a lot of people probably made the same assumption about herself and Andrew. She waited now for Rob to go on. She saw his inner struggle reflected on his face. His jaw muscles twitched as if trying to trap thoughts which were fighting to escape.

"Karen changed after she had the baby. She was treated for post-natal depression. But it went on and on. Ian was four at the time of the accident and Karen was still supposedly suffering from the after-effects of giving birth to him."

"Supposedly?"

Rob spread his hands on the table and stared at them as if the answer to the awkward question was written on his well-manicured nails. When he looked up, Ella saw that he had made a decision. A painful one.

"I don't know how much longer we could have gone on. Our situation was almost impossible. Karen was withdrawn. Moody. Uncommunicative. She spent hours standing in front of that goddamn portrait of Lady Harriet. She seemed obsessed by her ancestor yet she would never talk about her. I know there was a scandal. Lady Harriet eloped with one of the stable lads. It was the big shame of the Wellsley family. But I don't know what happened to Harriet after that and I certainly don't know why Karen became obsessed by her."

Ella looked around the kitchen again. It was bright and

warm and welcoming. Not the design you would expect from a woman who was as depressed as Rob seemed to imply. He followed Ella's gaze now around the brightly lit space and nodded in agreement.

"I know what you're thinking. Not the work of a manic-depressive. But she was in good form while this work was being carried out. We had agreed to sell Manor House. To move on. To try to save our marriage. I lied when I said we did the kitchen for comfort and convenience. We renovated to make the place more saleable."

"So Karen was well at the time she had the accident?"

Rob got up from the table and went over to the percolator. He busied himself preparing two mugs of coffee, concentrating on the task in silence. Ella took the time to try to make sense of what he was telling her. Karen had been depressed since the little boy Ian had been born. Yet she was happily planning a new kitchen and a house move just before she died. And now it seemed she did not want to be dead at all. Rob brought a tray to the table and laid out sugar, cream and the two coffees. He settled in his chair again, a determined look on his face.

"The truth is that Karen was totally distraught on the evening she died. After the work on the kitchen was finished we began to plan for the sale of Manor House. That's when she seemed to change her mind, to get even more withdrawn than she had ever been. The nightmares and sleepwalking, which had been intermittent, became nightly affairs. Even Ian was becoming afraid of his mother. She practically wore a patch bare standing on the hall floor in front of Lady Harriet's portrait. She wasn't eating or sleeping much. On the evening she died, I . . . I threatened to leave, and take Ian with me."

Ella heard the guilt and regret in his voice. The pain. It seemed as if Karen had taken matters into her own hands.

"She left, with your son?"

Rob nodded his bowed head. "I should have tried to stop her. I knew she was irrational. Over the edge. Ian was crying. He didn't want to go with her and I did nothing to help him."

"Where was she going?"

"I don't know but I do believe she meant to kill herself. To kill both of them. It was not an accident."

Ella released a long breath she had not realised she had been holding. Maybe it was a sigh of relief. This was total exoneration for her and confirmation of the suspicion she had held but had been reluctant to admit. She examined the sequence of the accident as it rolled past her yet again. The jeep thundering around the corner of the narrow road, Karen's face, opened-mouthed and wide-eyed, her hand reaching back to instinctively protect her child. Squinting her eyes, Ella tried to see if there was any emotion other than fear on Karen's face. Maybe determination or vengeance. The image faded. She turned her attention again to the distraught man sitting across the table from her.

"She was driving very fast, Rob. And conditions were bad."

"She told me she was going to do it. I didn't believe her. I suppose I should have told the police. I would have if they had asked directly. That is why I tried so hard to reassure you as soon as you came out of your coma. I knew it wasn't your fault. Karen was the architect of her own horrible end. And Ian's too."

They were silent as Ella wondered if it had been pride or insurance considerations which made Rob keep the real reason for his wife's car crash to himself. There surely would have been financial implications if her death was officially found to be suicide. Ashamed of this mean thought, she reached across the table and touched Rob's hand.

"I'm sure it was an accident, Rob. The inquest said so. And if it wasn't, the situation was out of your control anyway. You must stop blaming yourself."

"Karen must stop blaming me."

Ella suddenly felt claustrophobic in the large kitchen, as if the walls in the big room had slithered forward to enclose her. She stood and gathered her coat and bag.

"I must go," she said. "I've a long drive ahead. I'm on my way to Cuanowen on the west coast. I just popped in to let you know there are two offers on Manor House."

"I know. Your husband rang me about Maxine Doran's offer."

Ella tried to hide her reaction but knew that Rob had caught the flicker of shock tempered by annoyance which crossed her face. Andrew could have told her he had contacted Rob. Should have. Rob stood and held her coat for her as she put it on. "I'm sorry," he said. "I spent a lot of time talking about myself. You've gone through a lot too. Do you want to talk about it?"

Buttoning up her coat, Ella smiled at him. "No, Rob. Just knowing that someone else is having . . . is seeing . . ." Her voice trailed off as she struggled and failed to find words to describe the terror with which Karen Trevor filled her. "My psychologist says I'm using Karen as an excuse not to confront the real problems in my life."

Rob laughed. "Snap! I seemingly have guilt issues I'm not dealing with."

They were both smiling, an exclusive little club of Karen Trevor victims, as they walked into the hall. Ella's eyes were drawn yet again to the space at the bottom of the stairs where Lady Harriet's portrait used to be. Rob followed her gaze.

"Karen has a distant cousin who lives in London. Clarissa. By and large, the Wellsley clan has died out. I brought the Lady Harriet portrait over to Clarissa. I suppose I was hoping to get some information from her about Lady Harriet. A vain hope. Clarissa was as ignorant of the history as I am. The funny thing was, she refused to take the portrait, even though I told her it was valuable."

"Did she say why?"

"For a reason I would never have given any credence to before."

Ella watched as Rob seemed to battle with his thoughts. She gauged from his rapid blinking and facial tics that his mind was in turmoil. Yet he remained silent, standing in the very spot where his wife had spent so many hours staring at the Lady Harriet portrait.

"The reason, Trevor? What was it?"

His eyes came to focus on Ella. She looked deep into

them and saw shadows of the confusion and utter terror she herself had endured for the past year.

"She said the portrait was cursed. That it would bring bad luck to her. In fact, it terrified her."

He was staring hard at Ella now, gauging her reaction, waiting for her to scoff, to laugh at this outrageous superstition, to tell him he was insane. But Ella was looking steadily back at him, remembering that she had seen the portrait shimmer and waver before her eyes. She nodded to Rob to continue.

"Harriet's father was an authoritarian man, given to violent tantrums. He was enraged when his daughter ran away with the stable lad. Here in this hall, standing in front of the then newly painted portrait, he cursed his daughter. He said she was dead to the Wellsley family but that she would never know the peace of eternal rest. He then took her pet dog, a Cavalier King Charles Spaniel out to the courtyard and shot it through the heart. Lady Harriet was never mentioned again after that day."

Ella shivered and for a moment superstition was more compelling than logic. No wonder the portrait exuded such sadness and terror. Hatred that intense had power and energy to transcend time. She took a deep breath then. Not my time, she thought. I'm not a Wellsley.

"Is Clarissa Karen's only surviving relative?" she asked.

"There's another distant Wellsley relation somewhere in South Africa, I believe. No one else. Karen was an only child. I had intended doing some research on Harriet. Archive material, certificates, that kind of thing. I've changed my mind now. I need to say goodbye to Lady

Harriet and her secrets."

Ella looked at the portrait of the man in pantaloons and laughed. "They weren't all as beautiful as Lady Harriet, were they?"

"No, but I believe one of the bidders is. Both my housekeeper and Jason Laide remarked on Maxine Doran's resemblance to Lady Harriet."

Ella's mouth pursed. Maxine Doran. Bitch! She turned to face him. "Rob, you now have two people interested in buying Manor House. Do you have a personal preference or do you just want the property to go to the highest bidder?"

Rob shifted from one foot to the other, staring down as if fascinated by the movement of his feet. When he looked up, the haunted look was still in his eyes.

"I think Jason Laide could cope with it. His hide is too thick to feel any of the disturbance, the unhappiness of this house. I want to move out as quickly as possible."

Ella knew exactly what he meant. She had wanted to ask him about Karen. What her interests were, her favourite foods, her hopes, her ambitions. She had wanted to know the details of the woman who had turned her life upside down but the cold blast of air which suddenly filled the hall made her need to escape more urgent than her need to know. She pulled her coat closely about her. Goosebumps appeared on Rob's skin. For one moment Ella thought they would both freeze to death in the vastness of the towering hall.

"Jason Laide is very anxious to close," she said.

The sound of her voice echoed around, bouncing off

the vaulted ceilings and breaking whatever icy spell had gripped them.

"Jason Laide it is then," Rob said as he moved to open the door for her.

He stood in the doorway until Ella started her car. She waved to him as she began to slowly turn the car towards the driveway. He was just a dark shadow in the huge doorway, backlit by the glow from the spectacular crystal chandelier. Ella blinked as beside him she saw the outline of Karen Trevor, hands extended in her pleading gesture. She swerved and mounted the lawn. The car tilted. Frantically Ella spun the steering wheel. In an instant she was back on the driveway. She did not look back again. Leaving Rob to his ghosts, she headed towards Cuanowen and peace.

Chapter 18

The bells of Salzburg's magnificent baroque Cathedral rang out, the peals soft and gentle as if even they were muffled in the snow which blanketed the old fortress town. Jason lay on his back, eyes closed, savouring the morning and the warm sensations wafting from his toes to the top of his head. His body was so relaxed that it felt weightless, part of the fabric of the big comfortable bed on which he lay. Not wanting to break the spell by moving he just opened his eyes and turned them towards the woman lying beside him. She was facing him, knees drawn up, arms folded across her chest. Asleep. Her dark hair tumbled around her beautiful face. He examined her features minutely, from the black semicircles of her curling lashes to the soft curve of her mouth. She seemed vulnerable. Soft and warm and very innocent. He reached out his hand and touched a strand of hair. It slid between his fingers, silky and smooth. Just like Sharon herself. So silky, so smooth, yet always slipping away from his grasp.

He withdrew his hand and the movement woke her. Her eyelids flickered and opened to reveal violet-blue eyes. Jason felt his breath catch in his throat. No matter what happened between himself and Sharon, no matter what their future held, he would always believe that she was the most beautiful woman he had ever met. Also the most infuriating.

"Good morning," she muttered. "Did you sleep well?"

Jason turned impatiently onto his side to face her. This was so typically Sharon. They had fucked each other's brains out last night and now she was speaking to him as if he was a stranger. A guest. Which in a way he was. This elegant house on Junkergassse belonged to her. He just paid for the upkeep. Feathered her little Austrian nest.

"I did. And you?"

"You wore me out," she laughed and the smoky voice stirred Jason to the depths of the soul he rarely acknowledged.

"I suppose you have plans for today. You always have."

Sharon sat up and stretched her arms up over her head. Jason watched in fascination as her breasts rose too, becoming even more pert.

"The choice is yours," she said. "Shopping, skiing, walking. Maybe sightseeing."

"I'm not going on that fucking *Sound Of Music* trip again. Don't even think of it."

"Nor would I," she agreed as she slipped out of bed and put on a silk robe.

The big bed suddenly seemed less comfortable to Jason. He sat up and, punching the pillows into shape, propped them behind his back.

"We must talk, Sharon."

"Sure. What about?"

Even though her voice still held her whispery, caressing quality, the words had a sharp sting. It was as if she believed that they had nothing to talk about, that if she allowed him have a shag every so often he would continue to unthinkingly support her life of luxury.

"Manor House. This house. Our life style. Our future."

"Okay," she said disinterestedly as she tied the belt on her silk robe and pushed her feet into high-heeled mules.

"I want to start a family," Jason announced and then sat back against his pillows, furious with himself for his lack of finesse. He should not have blurted it out, issued it as a challenge.

And judging by Sharon's reaction, that is exactly how she saw it too. She had stood stock still where she was, just staring at him. A clock chimed in the silence. It must be that awful-looking thing on the mantelpiece in the lounge. The one that Sharon said was a valuable antique. A Napoleon clock that had cost a ransom to buy. She said it was a good investment. He had to take her word for that. Just as with so many other things in their lives. He had to believe her when she said her boyfriends were only for amusement, when she said she would eventually settle down, when she said she would one day be a proper wife to him. Eventually was now. No more fucking around. No more using Jason Laide as an ATM machine.

"You're pushing on, Shar. I want a son before it's too late for both of us."

Maybe it was the way the early morning sun filtered through the curtains, or maybe it was imagination but Jason thought Sharon paled. She walked slowly over to the bed and sat on the edge of it, keeping a safe distance away from her husband.

"You're not ready to settle down, Jason. To be a father."

"Jesus! You're the one that needs to settle. You're the one who spends her time globetrotting. And now that we're on the topic, I'm not happy either for you to continue on the way you are. With your boyfriends."

"We agreed. No questions, no jealousy. You have your little dalliances too, Jason. I don't question you."

"That's different. I'm entitled."

"Is that so?"

The way she looked down along the length of her perfect nose at him angered Jason. Throwing back the duvet, he swung his legs onto the floor. His back was to her now but he still felt the coldness of her disdain. He had not meant to drag the topic up like this but, now that he had, he realised there was no other way. The Jason Laide way was best. He turned his head to look at Sharon and he saw as well as felt her disapproval. There was a touch of fear too in her raised shoulders and the defensive folding of her arms across her chest. Enough!

"I'm not asking you to do something unreasonable, Shar. I'm investing a lot of money in Manor House. I want it to be our home. I want my children to grow up there. I want to know I am their father – so no more fucking around. Understood?"

She laughed. The throaty sound stung Jason like a

sharp slap. Bitch!

"And you will give up your girlfriends?" she asked. "Those little trollops you pick up and occasionally beat up?"

"I never beat anyone up. Not really. Just make them behave themselves. Besides, you're not going to tell me what to do. I'll live my life whatever way I want and what I want now is for my wife to stop behaving like a whore."

"What about Maxine Doran? Do you still visit her regularly? "

"That's a business arrangement."

"Really? I didn't know that fashion was one of your many enterprises."

"Maxine's useful. Which reminds me, you must open the vault for me. I need to check on some of the material there."

Sharon stood and began to smooth down her robe. Jason narrowed his eyes in suspicion. She seemed a bit edgy, a tad guilty.

"Actually, I've moved the things I think you're looking for," she said and there was a definite tremor in her voice.

In an instant Jason was standing in front of her, catching her by the arms, shaking her.

"The envelopes! You've moved them? Where to? Why?"

"I-I won't answer un-unless you take your hands off m-me," Sharon said, her voice rattling in time to the violent shaking her husband was giving her.

Jason dropped his hands. He had Maxine Doran and others for that type of treatment. Not his wife. Not usually. But his papers! His videos! They were his life-blood. Sharon had flopped onto the edge of the bed again now and was rubbing her arms and grimacing in pain. Tears filled her beautiful violet eyes.

"I told you about the work needed on the cellar, didn't I? It's starting next week. I had to clear everything out."

"Why clear out the safe? Surely to Christ they're not dry-lining that too?"

"Jason, that cellar is going to be full of strangers next week. Did you really want me to leave my jewellery and your business papers there where somebody determined enough could access them?"

"Jesus! Who are you getting to fix the bloody basement? A gang of safe-breakers?"

"Use your head. Anyone seeing that big safe would know it must be worth breaking into. I've taken my jewellery out and your papers too until the work on the basement is finished. You should be grateful to me. I was only looking out for your interests."

"So where did you put them?"

"In a secure place."

Jason grabbed her again and this time he felt no compunction about hurting her. She had committed the unforgivable sin. His thick fingers slid around her slender throat. He felt her pulse flutter under his hands. He squeezed and heard her gasp of fear.

"Tell me, you bitch! Tell me where you put my property!"

"In the bank. Our Swiss bank. Stop! You're ch-choking me! Stop!"

Suddenly they heard a knocking on the bedroom door. Jason's fingers loosened their grasp. Sharon's hands flew to her bruised throat.

The knocking on the door got more insistent.

"Answer it," Jason ordered.

Pulling the collar of her robe up to cover her neck, Sharon stumbled over to the door and opened it.

Frau Henner stood there, solid and solemn. Her eyes went to Sharon's hands which clutched the lapels of her silk robe tightly around her throat. She raised one dark eyebrow.

"Yes, Frau Henner?" Sharon asked.

"Will you want breakfast in bed or will I serve it downstairs?"

"Downstairs, please. We'll be there in ten minutes."

Frau Henner nodded and turned away but not before she had caught the look of gratitude in Sharon's eyes. There was no need for gratitude. Frau Henner would have gone to the ends of the earth to protect Sharon against her gross husband.

Sharon closed the door and faced Jason. "You heard that. Breakfast in ten minutes."

Sharon made the bathroom before Jason could speak to her or touch her again. She dashed inside, locked the door and stood with her back to it while he pounded on the solid timber. He must have hurt his fist, or thought of another plan or just got fed up with thumping a closed door. For whatever reason the banging stopped but Sharon knew she was living on borrowed time. She, too, must think of another plan. Urgently.

★ ★ ★

Confusion was the first feeling to greet Ella when she woke. The room was strange. An unfamiliar dressing table stood opposite the foot of the bed and oak-veneered built-in wardrobes lined the wall to her right. Even the light was different. Whiter, more piercing than what she was used to. As she lay there, suspended between a state of sleep and wakefulness her attention was caught by a low growling rhythmic sound. It rolled towards her and then whispered away. Her mind engaged. The sea! Cuanowen!

Jumping up, she threw back the covers and ran over to the window. When the curtains were pulled back she was faced with the sight of the Atlantic swelling and receding just one hundred yards from where she stood. The water was grey and windblown. She opened the window and took in a deep breath of the sea-air. It swirled into her lungs, her blood stream, her very soul. Throwing back her head she allowed the damp, salty wind to toss her hair and caress her face.

Feeling clean and refreshed, she closed the window again and looked around the room. It was small. Clean. Adequate. A perfect little bolthole for a woman spending a weekend alone. A woman whose husband was most likely waking up at this very minute and turning towards his mistress to kiss her good morning.

Ella glanced out the window again and watched as white-capped waves rushed powerfully towards the shore only to peter out in creamy puddles on the beach, energy spent, majesty diminished. Her eyes were drawn towards the horizon where big swells of water were beginning to curl and shape themselves into onrushing waves. The ceaseless dance of ebb and flow hypnotised her. Some perceived wisp of wisdom filtered through the salty spray. She couldn't quite grasp it, couldn't fit the ethereal idea into a straitjacket of words. It was something about permanence, about perpetuity, about rushing towards goals only to start all over again, leaving a little of yourself behind each time.

Ella turned her back to the window and began to get ready for the day ahead. Breakfast in Seaview Hotel was served between eight thirty and ten. It was already nine o'clock and her appointment to view the bungalow was for ten. A quick shower later, she followed the smell of rashers and sausages. There were only four other people seated in the dining room on this low-season morning – a middle-aged couple and two men sitting at separate tables. They all muttered good morning and then got back to the serious business of eating a full Irish breakfast. Ella ate quickly and then went back to her room to collect her jacket.

The estate agent's office was in the village of Cuanowen, five kilometres away. As she drove the coast road, Ella remembered all the times she had walked along here. Her steps had been shorter then. And lighter. The protected only child of Helen and Jim Deasy had nothing to fear from life, nothing to weigh her down. The road dipped towards the village and as Ella began the descent she held her breath. At the foot of this hill, just at the entrance to the village, stood her parents' house. What used to be her parents' house. Her home. There had been so many alterations made that Ella recognised her childhood home now only by its location. It had been extended, re-roofed, dormer windows and a conservatory added. She slowed down when passing and peered into the house, admiring the way the present owners had blended the old with the new. There would be a view of the sea from the dormer windows. For an instant she regretted selling but it had been the right thing to do at the time. The money had been a significant factor in getting Ford Auctioneers off the ground. Her parents would have liked that.

The village looked neat and tidy. A contender for Tidy Towns. Flowerbeds, shrubs and litterbins had been placed along the length of the main and only street, the shops looked freshly painted. A picture postcard village. Glancing around for a parking space, Ella was glad to see that at least one thing had not changed. Everybody still parked their cars on double yellow lines. She followed suit and found a space just outside the estate agent's office. Stopping to look at the window display on the way in, she was surprised at the range of properties on the books from farms to holiday homes. And at the prices. Cuanowen had become an exclusive area to live.

The estate agent was waiting inside to greet her, all efficiency and politeness. Ella smiled to herself as he reeled off all the usual patter she knew so well. He was following guidelines. Be informative but not pushy, friendly but not familiar. The system worked well until he recognised Ella.

"You're Jim Deasy's daughter," he said in a tone which was far more colloquial than the one he had been using. It was almost an accusation.

"That's right," Ella admitted, looking closely at him, trying to peel back the years from his face. He was fair-haired, stocky, beginning to bald. "Pebbles Shorten! It is, isn't it?"

A slight blush spread up from underneath his collar. "Well, sort of," he said uncomfortably. "Nobody calls me that any more."

"Of course not. Sorry," Ella muttered, desperately trying to remember his Christian name. How could she have forgotten? Maybe she never knew it. She must have seen it recently on his web page or over the door. He had always been known as Pebbles because of his penchant for collecting piles of little stones. He used to spend hours combing the beach for specimens he thought special. His pockets used to rattle when he walked. Pebbles Shorten had been the first boy ever to kiss her. It had been a fumbling, awkward clash of noses, ending in the barest touching of lips.

"My name is Gavin," he announced.

Ella nodded, remembering now, embarrassed that she had not been able to recall it. It was just that the innocence and freedom of her childhood and teenage years seemed to belong to another era. There were no parallels in the pressurised life she lived today, no space for remembering exploratory kisses on the beach.

"I believe you're in this business yourself, Ella. In a big way."

"We've been lucky. The city is booming."

Gavin, who used to be known as Pebbles, shuffled from one foot to the other, suddenly looking anxious. "Actually, I'm thinking of making the move myself," he said. "I've a good little business here but it's hardly cutting edge."

"It's cutthroat in the city. I'd think carefully about it if I were you, Gavin."

He gave her a look which said that he didn't trust her. He thought she was trying to stave off opposition. The city would swallow him up and spit him out. The pace was so different. The environment so competitive. She had warned him. Let him think whatever he liked.

"Can we see the bungalow now, Gavin?"

He locked up his office and then they both got into his car to drive the two miles to the property. They left the village behind and began the climb up the hills on the south side of Cuanowen. The gradient was steep and the road narrowed as they rose. When they had almost reached the summit, Gavin turned left and manoeuvred the car up a neat laneway bordered by stone walls. Brambles, bare and leafless now, poked up from the other side of the ditches. Ella imagined the summer, lush berries on the brambles, honeysuckle, wild roses. This laneway would be an oasis of colour and scent in the warm season.

The laneway came to an abrupt end and without warning widened into a tarmac driveway. The landscaped gardens on either side were wet and windblown but still attractive. Ella's eyes skimmed over the shrubs and miniature trees, the water feature. Her attention was drawn inexorably to the house itself. It sat at the end of the driveway, solid yet somehow ethereal, the solar panels and glass frontage giving it a light and very modern appearance. She jumped out of the car almost before it stopped. Turning her back to the house, Ella looked downwards over the fields, right down to the cliffs and beyond to the sea. Every direction she turned she was met by views of the restless ocean, rolling, heaving, finding an answering rhythm somewhere deep within her. She felt at one with the motion, humbled by the power, warmed by the sense of belonging. Ella knew then that no matter what Andrew said, she wanted to buy a house in Cuanowen. Probably not this bungalow. Definitely not. It was more clever architecture than a home. But she would have, she must have, a safe haven by the sea.

Chapter 19

Jason had always felt uncomfortable in Salzburg but now the fact that his wife and her housekeeper were conversing in German, or whichever guttural language they were babbling, made him even more edgy. He pushed his breakfast away from him. Sharon was really playing him for a fool. Nobody did that to Jason Laide.

"What the fuck are ye gassing on about?" he shouted.

His coarse voice echoed around the elegant dining room of the Junkergasse house. Both women stopped talking and stared at him. There was disdain in Sharon's violet gaze and an intense flash of hatred in Frau Henner's beady little eyes.

"Frau Henner was just reminding me that I had arranged to go hill-walking with some friends today. They'll be here shortly. Would you like to join us?"

"'*Would you like to join us?*'" Jason mimicked in a cruel impression of Sharon's husky voice. His temper was reaching meltdown. "Get her out of here," he ordered, nodding in the direction of the housekeeper.

Sharon turned and said something to Frau Henner in the language that Jason did not understand.

"Talk English," he snapped.

Frau Henner just nodded to Sharon, turned her back on Jason and walked out the door. He spluttered, specks of saliva spraying over his lips and onto the remains of his breakfast on the table.

"I pay that bitch's wages. Yours too. How dare you treat me like that! What in the fuck are you up to?"

"What do you mean?" Sharon asked, trying to infuse her quavering voice with an innocence which did not deceive Jason for a second.

Getting up he walked around the huge oval oak table to sit beside his wife. He knew his physical proximity was a threat to her. Her delicate frame seemed to shrink more as he pushed his bulk even closer to her. He could smell her perfume, feel the touch of her breath on his face, see the minute beads of moisture that clung to her hairline. He could almost reach out and touch her fear. One part of him, the part which wanted to protect this woman, shrank back from the confrontation. But that was the lesser part of Jason Laide. She was playing some game. He could not allow that. He grabbed her wrist and squeezed his fingers around the narrow span.

"I want my private papers. They're what set up my business and keep it going. They're the reason you live in fucking luxury. You'll go back to that poncy Swiss bank on Monday and get my property. Then you'll personally deliver it to me in Ireland. Or else . . ."

Jason's grip on her wrist loosened and let go. She rubbed her skin and watched as he bowed his head and closed his eyes. She noticed that his hair was thinning. The colour was fading. It was not as flame red as it used to be. His face and body were more bloated. And yet this violent man could be gentle too, loving, generous. He had an animal attraction that she had never experienced with any other man. Not that there had been any other men. Maybe she should tell him the truth. Her hand went to her throat which still burned with the imprint of his fingers. He would kill her. She had left it too long. And he had changed too little.

The front doorbell rang. In the silence they heard the soft patter of Frau Henner's feet as she went to answer the door.

They heard her greet people and laughter filled the hall as they all shared some joke. Sharon tried to play for time.

"Here are my friends now. Why don't you come on the hill walk with us?"

Jason narrowed his ice-blue eyes and stared at her. Then just when she thought her gamble had not paid off, he smiled at her.

"You're nothing without me, Sharon. Just another high-class whore and the world is full of them. I'll meet your friends. Go walking on the fucking hills, yodelling and wearing leather breeches if that's what you want. But don't think for a minute you can fool me. I'll have my papers back and then I'll decide what to do about you."

Sharon nodded slowly. She had always known this day

would come but she had thought it would be at a time of her choosing. She was not really ready now. And she still had not decided how much she would tell him. Then she remembered the reason why she had kept secrets. A smile lifted the corners of her mouth and touched her eyes. She reached her hand out to her husband.

"Deal," she said.

He took her hand and for a moment they smiled at each other. Then fear shadowed her eyes and suspicion his.

Jason went to the bedroom before they left for their walk. His call to Gussie just took a few minutes. By the time Jason was struggling up the snowy hills, Gus had already booked O'Shaughnessy on the early Monday morning flight to Salzburg. He would, of course, have his camera with him.

* * *

Maxine was surrounded by stacks of clothes and make-up. They were piled all over her dressing-table and bed. Daywear, casual, formal, eveningwear, matching shoes, toners, blushers, mascaras. The tools of her trade. But the therapy wasn't working. Usually a spring clean of her apartment filled her with renewed energy. Decluttering her living space also freed up calm space in her mind. Or it used to. No matter how much she sorted and discarded now, her thoughts returned again and again to Manor House, Jason Laide and Andrew Ford. At least Andrew seemed to have got the message. He had not tried to contact her at all today.

She looked at her silent phone and wished it to ring. Maybe she should talk to Andrew. Explain that their relationship had no future. After all, he was married and Maxine herself was . . . she was Marie Murphy, tramp and slut, and had earned every other derogatory term that could be thrown at her. She had sold her right to a decent relationship the first time she had performed for Jason Laide.

Images flashed across her mind. Maxine threw herself onto her bed, not caring that she was squashing and creasing garments which were worth more per item than a month's pay for the average worker. What did the hand-painted silks and woven linens matter when the body they were designed to clothe was used and cheap? She squeezed her eyes shut but like a newsreel the images flickered past. Marie Murphy, fifteen years old, tall, pretty, eaten up by the ambition to escape from her family, from Mountain View Terrace. Jason Laide, with his flame-red hair, stocky and strong, already a powerful presence in the area. Jason with his haulage business, his sharp suits and his coterie of respectful followers in tow. How could she have been so naïve? She had been an intelligent child, always near the top of her class in school. How could she have believed Jason when he said he had contacts in the film world? What had she been thinking when she allowed him to film her? Escape? Fame? Money? And he had reeled her in so cleverly. Just some innocent pictures at first, taken with his home-movie camera in the front room of his house. The three-bedroomed semi-detached that Maxine – Marie – had thought at the time to be the height of elegance and sophistication. When he said the film director needed some shots of her in her underwear to help him make a decision, she had peeled off her clothes. It was just like wearing a bikini and she might be cast in a movie where there were beach shots.

Tears slid out from under Maxine's closed eyelids now as the scenes she tried so desperately to obliterate rolled inexorably on. She had willingly accepted Jason's stories, willingly gone to his house, evening after evening, until finally, on that night, that despicable, horrific night, he had introduced her to alcohol and another girl. A young girl like herself, hungry for money just like her. They had done unspeakable things to each other, naked and sweaty, while Jason had filmed their shame. He had then handed them each twenty pounds. Their thirty pieces of silver. The other girl, who called herself Gail, had gone out and bought some drugs with her money. She was dead now. Overdosed on heroin and found in a squat, a whole two weeks after she had died, decayed and worm-eaten. Lucky bitch. Maxine had got the worst of the deal. She had to live with what they had done in Jason Laide's bed in front of his camera.

Angrily now, full of self-hatred, she sat up and began to throw her beautiful clothes off the bed. She didn't know why, just that it made her feel more in control to treat the symbols of her success with disdain. If only she had waited. If only she had kept her knickers on for just another two weeks.

Fourteen days after Maxine had given Jason Laide control over the rest of her life she reached sixteen years of age. That was the day a representative of the leading model agency in town came to her school to give a talk on modelling as a career. The woman had looked down into the sea of upturned faces in the assembly hall and immediately her eyes had settled on Marie Murphy sitting in the back row, taller, thinner and somehow seeming older than the other pupils. She had offered Marie a place on a modelling course. Free of charge. That was when Marie Murphy had left Mountain View Terrace behind and became Maxine Doran. A glittering career. International fame. Money. Prestige. Despair.

Getting up and walking over to her dressing table, Maxine swept it clean of its overpriced heap of make-up containers. They rolled and slithered, falling softly onto the thick carpet. A cap came loose on a tube of foundation. It seeped onto the carpet, a sun-kissed worm in the cream wool. Just like Jason Laide. A worm. Always crawling through her life, always holding the threat of the video over her head, always sure that she had to do his bidding. Exactly as she had done since first she realised that there had been no film director, no prospect of a screening in Hollywood. No possibility that she would ever again have any self-esteem. She had sold herself, body and soul just for Jason Laide's pleasure. For his convenience. Stupid, stupid child.

Looking around at the mess she had created in her bedroom she felt an even deeper degree of self-loathing. No wonder Jason had found it so easy to manipulate her. No wonder he held onto that video and used it to get her to do his bidding. She had no self-control, no moral fibre.

Why did she never have Jason charged with making child pornography? Silly thought. She would have to admit she was star of the video. All her years of carefully hiding her background and paying her family to stay quiet would come to light. The agency would never have taken her on had they known. They thought her address was the only thing she had to be ashamed of. She had been doing Jason's bidding, accepting it as an inevitable aspect of her life, entertaining those he wanted to impress, sleeping with thugs he wanted to sweeten, introducing him to the high and mighty she had got to know in the course of her work. It had been bearable until she had met Andrew Ford.

The thought of Andrew brought tears to her eyes again. It would have been so much easier if she had never met him, if he had never made her laugh, made her feel loved, made her want to love him back. Jesus! Love! How could she talk about love? Where could she find space in the blackness of her heart for an emotion as unselfish as love? But she had. After all, falling in love with the wrong man was in her genetic make-up.

Leaving the chaotic bedroom behind, Maxine went into the living area and unlocked her desk. Taking out the old red photo album she walked over to the couch and made herself comfortable. As usual the book fell open at the page which held her great-grandmother's photograph. Maxine stared into the lustrous eyes, traced the lines of the beautiful face, steeped herself in the dignity and poise of her great-gran. Harriet also had fallen in love with the wrong man, hadn't she? All those years ago, this magnificent woman had given herself to a Murphy from Mountain View Terrace. Why? Surely she had belonged to a different class. How had she ended up in that poky little terraced house when every bone in her body conveyed refinement? The antithesis of life in the Murphy household. But Harriet had abandoned the mean streets, hadn't she? Just left. Disappeared. Never to be heard of again. Or so Maxine's father said. Where had Harriet gone? Had she been murdered by one of the hot-tempered Murphys? Perhaps her husband. Or had she made a better life for herself, gone back to her own family, found her proper place in society?

Maxine sighed. She had been asking these questions of her beautiful great-grandmother as long as she could remember. Harriet always gazed back at her from the sepia picture, silent, keeping her secrets. But now there was the added mystery of the portrait of Lady Harriet Wellsley in Manor House. The one Rob Trevor had removed. Had Lady Harriet Wellsley become Mrs Harriet Murphy of Mountain View Terrace, wife of Thomas Murphy, the man who had handled horses so well and women so badly?

Maxine smiled at her great-grandmother's photo. "Right, great-gran," she said aloud, "no more messing around. I'm going to track you down. And I'm going to buy Manor House."

The words echoed around the empty apartment and returned to Maxine. Her resolve strengthened. Getting paper and pen, she began to trace back from her father, making out approximate dates. The next time she went to the Registrar's Office she would be prepared. Harriet's secrets would no longer be safe.

Satisfied with her work, Maxine folded the piece of paper and put it into her purse. She felt more energised now, more in control. As she began to tidy up her bedroom and sort her packing for Amsterdam on Monday she brought her clearer thinking to bear on the other problems in her life. Her accountant Charles Rea presented himself as a solution to one of her difficulties. She would ring him on Monday and ask him to represent her interests in the purchase of Manor House. Jason was bound to outbid her. Charles could stall the sale. He was good at bumbling. And this would also mean that she herself did not need to have further contact with Andrew Ford. No. That was wrong. She needed to, yes. How she needed to hear his voice, to touch him, to feel his arms around her! But she could not, would not allow herself to be hurt any more. Nor did she want to hurt Andrew.

Then there was Jason Laide. Everything depended on this trip to Amsterdam and on her hunch being right. It was an outside chance. Jason was so conniving, so violent, that he totally controlled his own environment and the people in it. He had worked hard at covering his tracks which led from the mire to the dizzy heights of legitimate business success. It was Maxine's aim to find his weak spot. To expose him. To destroy him.

Driven by anger, she was working faster now, folding, hanging up, discarding or putting in the laundry. The room was almost tidied when her phone rang. She stood still and listened to the repetitive peal. Walking slowly over to the phone, she wished with all her heart that it was

Andrew calling. Not that she would speak to him. She just wanted to know that he needed to contact her. She glanced at the caller ID and felt equal measures of relief and disappointment. It was Natalie. Bubbly, fun-loving Natalie, her only friend on the modelling circuit. She picked up and listened as Natalie babbled on.

"Maxine Doran, are you still misty-eyed over your mystery man or are you back to normal yet? I feel like a night on the town. How about it? A few drinks in The Mills and then we'll hit the clubs? How does that sound?"

"Great. Pick you up at nine. Okay?"

Natalie was silent for a moment, surprised at how easy it had been to persuade Maxine and understanding that the man who had been making Maxine all dreamy and moody lately was no longer on the scene.

"All the war paint on! We're going to have a serious night, Max. See you at nine."

Maxine was smiling as she put down the phone. Just what she needed. A night of serious fun. Maybe she could absorb some of Natalie's energy and love of life. Maybe she could forget Jason Laide, great-gran Harriet and Manor House for a few hours. She would never forget Andrew Ford though. Not even for a few minutes.

* * *

The only thing more ridiculous than mowing the lawn at this time of year was sitting inside worrying. Sweat dripped off Andrew's forehead as he pushed the lawnmower through the damp grass. There were bare patches where sods had been gouged out of the soft earth but Andrew ignored them. He needed to keep going. He needed the release of all his pent-up feelings.

Maxine was first and foremost in his thoughts. He tried to forget her as he ploughed ahead, mangling bundles of defenceless grass. He had not heard from her since he had let her know Jason Laide was the other bidder on Manor House. It was as if that had been all she had wanted from him. A name on a piece of paper. Once she had it she just disappeared, not answering her phone, not ringing. He must let her know he had put in her bid for Manor House, even though Rob Trevor had been noncommittal. As Maxine's estate agent, Andrew had a legitimate excuse to contact her. He had toyed with the idea of going around to her apartment but had dismissed the thought. Suppose she was there with another man? Of course there would be another man. A woman could not be as beautiful as Maxine Doran and not have men in her life. As the image of Maxine in someone else's arms flashed before him, Andrew gave the lawnmower an extra vicious push. It dug deep into the wet soil, blades screeching as they skimmed a buried stone. Cursing, he switched off the motor and began to dig out the front of the mower. One of the blades was bent and shiny where it had scraped against the stone. Shit! He stood and looked over the lawn. One half was still lush and beautifully carpeted in grass. The other half, the one he had attacked, was as pockmarked as a rugby pitch after a tough match. Ella would be very angry when she saw it. If she noticed. Maybe she would arrive back from Cuanowen in one of her spaced-out moods. The mood where she seemed to float about in isolation, not seeing, not hearing.

Going to the garden shed, Andrew got a shovel. At least he could cover up some of the bare patches. Put some sods over the soil. He was almost finished his camouflage job when he heard the phone ring in the house. Dropping his shovel he ran. It might be Maxine.

"Andrew. You sound out of breath. Have you been out running?"

Andrew took a deep breath and wiped the sweat off his forehead with his sleeve before answering his wife. "I've just been doing some gardening. How are you?"

"Gardening? This time of year? Are you sure you're okay?"

"I'm fine. Have you seen the bungalow yet?"

As she began to tell him about the property, Ella's tone changed from the usual monotone Andrew had become so familiar with over the past year. The more she spoke about it, the more enthusiastic she got. "You should see the views, Andrew! From all sides! It's like being on an island. Just sea, glorious sea all around!"

"You haven't gone ahead with a deal, have you? You promised no commitments until we both decided."

"No. I've made no definite bid on this bungalow. But I have expressed interest in buying here. Actually I know the estate agent. Maybe he could get us a good deal. I might drive along the coastline now and see if there are any bargain properties we could renovate and resell."

Andrew gripped the phone tightly. Some half-remembered details of bi-polar disorder came uncomfortably to the forefront of his mind. One day all black depression, the next on top of the world, making irrational decisions like going on a property-buying spree. Immediately he relaxed his grip on the phone and smiled. What a ridiculous thought! Ella was suffering from Post Traumatic Stress Disorder. It had been diagnosed and confirmed. She would work her way through it. Maybe that was what she was doing now. She certainly sounded brighter.

"No harm in looking, Ella. But remember, no deals without my agreement. What's the interior of the bungalow like?"

"As you would expect. Spacious, light-filled rooms, top-class fixtures and fittings. Maybe you should come to see it for yourself."

Ella held her breath. Would Andrew suggest coming up here tomorrow? His business meeting was tonight. Cuanowen was only about two hours' drive from the city. He could so easily be here in the morning, look over the property and give it his approval. She was sure he would love it. He must.

"I have to go now, Ella. I must get ready for my meeting. Hopefully Pascal McEvoy will be able to shed some light on all the interest in Ballyhaven. Then at least we can make an informed decision about it. Take care. See you tomorrow evening."

Ella switched off her phone. She felt that she too could now make an informed decision about her future.

Chapter 20

The roads were in better repair, the houses more numerous, the traffic more dense but yet Cuanowen had managed to retain the sleepiness of a seaside village clinging onto the edge of the coast. Leaving her car parked outside Gavin Shorten's office, Ella strolled past the main street and down towards the beach. She felt as if she was back in her childhood again. The village had never been a comfortable place for her, its smallness always seeming to close in about her. Maybe it was the twitching curtains. Maybe it was just that she had been a restless child, looking outwards from Cuanowen towards the city life for which she had yearned.

Boarding school had been her first escape. That was where she had learned her lessons in survival of the fittest. She had gone to the closest second-level college at the time. Thirty miles and a whole world away from her seaside home. Just twelve years old, lonely, missing her mother and father, she had been bullied and taunted by older girls and by some of the nuns who ran the school. It had taken all of her first year there for her to find her strength of character, to access the authority and dignity she had inherited from her parents. Jim and Helen Deasy, both teachers in the small Cuanowen Primary School, were the essence of authority. Helen, whose dark hair and hazel eyes she had inherited, was the more assertive of the two, her majestic bearing demanding respect. Her father had been gentler, softer but nonetheless dignified. They had held a respected position in the local hierarchy of Cuanowen and by osmosis their daughter Ella, their only child, had enjoyed that same respect.

The shock of being thrown into the rarefied atmosphere of an all-girl boarding school had destroyed her for a while. She had longed for the protectiveness of her parents and the sea breeze of home. How many nights had she spent crying into her pillow until she discovered that the only way to survive was to be better, quicker, tougher? And she had found that strength. She had shone, academically and athletically, in her five years there, gaining a scholarship to university in her final year. That strength, that sense of purpose had driven her onto a first-class-honours commerce degree, onto setting her sights on Andrew Ford and marrying him, onto founding Ford Auctioneers and making a huge success of it. Her character had stood her in good stead and stayed with her until Karen Trevor had taken it away on that stormy, cursed, death-filled evening.

Ella stood still now on the path that led to the beach, her feet glued to the sandy surface. How had she allowed this to happen? How had she allowed Karen Trevor to infiltrate her mind, to dominate her thinking, to ruin her life? The accident had been a horrible tragedy. It was a cruel and savage act of violence with terrible consequences. But one of the consequences should not have been Ella's strength, her self-belief, her very sanity. It had been an accident. Not her fault. So why was she torturing herself by paying this price, by throwing away the life she had worked so hard to create for herself? Ella's feet began to move. She did not consciously direct them but yet she knew where they would lead her. Off to the left, up the narrow road, under the arch of yew trees and into the graveyard.

The marble headstone seemed shiny and new, surrounded as it was by ancient lichen-covered stones. Her mother and father had been buried in the old part of the cemetery where members of the Deasy family had been interred for generations. Ella knelt down on the kerbing and read their names. *James Deasy and his wife Helen*. Mam and Dad.

Her eyes filled with tears as she read the date of their death. *19th November.* All the memories of that day came flooding back. First phoning them to say goodbye before they left for Rome. They had been excited and happy. Even her mother had been uncharacteristically chirpy. They had been planning this trip for months. They would start their grand tour in Rome, St Peter's and the Trevi fountain, then on to Venice, Pisa with its leaning tower, the beautiful shores of Lake Garda. Helen had their itinerary drawn up and planned to the last detail. They had even gone to classes to learn Italian. Sounding like two teenagers, they prattled on to Ella about their tour, throwing in Italian phrases, taking the phone from each other, both telling her to take care, that they would ring her regularly from Italy and that they would see her soon. That they loved her.

Ella had been busy that morning. Closing a sale. She had thought of going back to Cuanowen to take them to the airport but Ford Auctioneers had been little more than a struggling idea at the time. Every sale counted. So she had settled for a phone call to her parents. She and Andrew had been celebrating a successful sale when Ella heard the first news reports. An Irish plane bound for Rome had crashed over the Apennines. The sickening feeling that it could be her parents' flight, the frantic phone calls, the shock when she discovered that they were indeed listed as passengers, the despair when she was told there were no survivors of the crash. She had taken consolation then from the fact that Helen and Jim had died together while on their way to the country they had always wanted to visit. Probably holding hands, being dignified, thinking of their daughter. Ella had borne their loss with dignity too, her tribute to the fine people they had been. She had looked at their lives together, at how united they had been, at how they would have wanted to die at the same time. Examining every aspect of the disaster she had found all the positives in the situation. Just as her parents would have expected her to do. She had never once, not even in her darkest mourning, allowed herself to dwell on the fact that she had been too busy to go to see them before they left. Before they died.

Tears dribbled unchecked down her face now. Her lips began to move and she heard herself mutter repeated apologies to her parents. To their headstone. "I'm sorry. I should have come to see you." The words spilled out over and over, uncoiling from the depths where they had hidden ever since the plane had slammed into the mountainside. The space inside where her guilt had lived for so long began to feel empty. The void was instantly replaced by a fierce longing to see Helen and Jim once more. To snuggle into the warmth of their embrace. To be safe. To be loved and protected. To bask in their unconditional love.

Hot tears cooled on her cheeks. Sobs became convulsive little breaths. Scattered thoughts became rational analysis. She had blamed herself and buried her shame deeply so that she would not have to feel it. She had wanted to be successful. Yes, of course. She was driven, ambitious. But she had never wanted to become the person who would choose completion of a deal over a last goodbye. She knew her parents would never have blamed her. They would have accepted and forgiven. Ella stood now and leaned towards the headstone. She laid her forehead on the cool marble. At long last she forgave herself.

Walking back under the arch of yew trees, Ella dried her eyes and blew her nose. She rejoined the path leading to the beach and soon the tarmac gave way to soft sand underneath her feet. The tide was on the turn. Far out over the wet sands she could see the sea begin to push inexorably towards full tide, each wave depositing a frill of foam progressively closer to the shore. It took her only a second to decide which direction to go. Turning to her left she headed for the distant rocky promontory known locally because of its shape as the Dog Rock. A favourite haunt of shore anglers when mackerel was in season. She had been forbidden to go there as a child. At full tide only the very tip of the Dog remained above water. A strong current swirled around the base of the rock and there had been several drownings from Dog Rock over the years.

As Ella reached the rock and settled herself comfortably into the curved space which formed the Dog neck, she remembered that this was where Pebbles Shorten had head-butted her all those years ago in his awkward attempt to kiss her. She had been so full of confidence and hope then. What had happened to her? How had she become this shadow of herself? Where had the laughter, the loving, the fun gone? Where was the substance of the person who was Ella?

She looked out towards the horizon. The sun was beginning to dip low. Soon the western sky would be orange-tinged. Another day over, another cycle complete. Just like Mam and Dad had completed their allotted timespan. A shuddering sigh escaped her and floated onto the breeze. Her parents would not recognise the woman she had become. The shell of the person she used to be. The questions still buzzed around in her head. She knew now the answers were in there too. She did not need Peter Sheehan or any other doctor to diagnose her illness or to dignify her condition by giving it a title. Post Traumatic

Stress Disorder. But that's not what Peter Sheehan really thought, was it? He knew. She had seen it on his handsome face, read it in his clear, green eyes. He was trying to push her towards the answers he had guessed at. The answers she had hidden from herself.

Leaning back against the Dog neck for support, Ella closed her eyes and raised her face to the breeze. The ebb and flow of the ocean sounded louder now that she could not see it. The hissing murmur was accompanied by the clamour of questions demanding answers. First, Karen Trevor. The eternally suffering, never-dying Karen with her terrified eyes and her mouth so wide open in a scream. What did she represent? Why did Ella's mind constantly conjure up this image, why did she allow Karen to invade her life, her home, her very existence? "You're a victim of your unwillingness to face your problem," Peter Sheehan had said. Well, Peter smart-ass Sheehan, Ella thought I am facing my problem now. My problems. Here on the Dog Rock. Formulating the thought gave her strength. She knew, had known all along what Peter meant. She was using Karen, using the accident, to stop time in its track. A ploy not to move on. Not to move away from her marriage. Her failed marriage.

A wail, sharp and full of pain, rang out over the rocks, the seaweed, the shoreline. It was whipped away by the wind and headed out to sea. Ella was not sure the awful sound had come from her until she felt tears on her face and saliva drool from her mouth. The sound rang out again, this time deeper and full of fear. It was the death knell of a marriage, the end of a failed relationship. It was the destruction of her life plan. It was fear of the future. A future that could be alone and lonely.

Screwing her eyelids tightly shut Ella watched images of Andrew pass before her, memories of special moments they had shared. She remembered the first time she had seen him. It had been in a lecture theatre in college. Both freshmen, both ambitious, both clever, they had gravitated towards each other. What neither had admitted was that their union was a logical decision more than an emotional one. Yes, each found the other physically attractive but they were essentially an alliance of ambition. The marriage of the most likely to succeed. And succeed they had. In the field of commerce.

Memories, sharp and painful, slithered out of their hiding place, each one adding to her determination to unearth the next. All the firsts were there. First kiss, first time they slept together, first flat they shared, first office, first sale, first big contract with the Cox brothers. First time she realised that she and Andrew had a very successful business partnership but a cold and shallow emotional life. It had been at one of the interminable parties they always attended. One of the places to see and be seen. Andrew had casually introduced her to a potential client as his business partner. Not as his wife. Not as the woman who shared his home. What shocked Ella most at the time was that Andrew had not even realised he was hurting her. This was how he saw her, how he viewed their relationship.

That slip of the tongue had forced her to examine her own feelings. The examination had been almost complete, her decision almost made when the accident had happened. When Karen Trevor began to haunt her. When she allowed the mirage of a dead woman to block the thoughts she did not want to face. She remembered now that Peter Sheehan had led her to realise just what her problem was. The reason why she needed Karen Trevor as a focus in her life. There would be no more hiding behind a dead woman. And no more ignoring the fact that Andrew was having an affair. Maxine Doran. Supermodel and look-a-like of Lady Harriet Wellsley. The final nail in the coffin . . .

It was the sound of water lapping against Dog Rock that woke Ella. Realisation dawned very quickly. She was marooned. The tide had come in and cut off her access to the shore. When she tried to move she discovered she was numb and stiff. Dragging herself up, she stood and looked around her. The sun had almost disappeared beneath the horizon and the tide was three-quarters up the rock. Underneath the notorious currents of Dog Rock swirled and eddied. She must have slept for well over an hour. Maybe more.

She was a strong swimmer but from here the shore seemed a lifetime away. Besides she was stiff and cold. Her legs began to tingle as circulation returned. Ella flailed her arms, beating them against her body to instil some heat. She hopped on her tingling feet, trying to dance the pins and needles away. All the time the tide was rising, the dusk falling, her fear growing. Would she have the strength to fight that current? Peering into the depths of the water lapping against the rock she knew the undertow would drag her down. The cold would take her breath away. She would die quickly. Ella Ford did not want to die.

Heat surged through her body, her lungs drew in a huge breath of air. She had not survived a road crash and coma just to drown in Cuanowen. She could cling onto the very tip of the rock. Try to keep herself warm until the tide went out again. She scanned the body of water between her and the horizon. It was relatively calm but the swells were big. She had lost touch with the natural rhythms of nature but it seemed to her this might be a spring tide. When she looked skyward her fears were confirmed. The silver crescent of a new moon glimmered palely. She remembered this meant that the earth, the sun and moon would be in line, the gravitational pull of the sun and moon combining to contribute to high tides. It would drag an increased volume of water towards the shore. Dog Rock would probably be covered. Her stark choice brought panic. Dive in now and drown. Stay here and be washed off. Why, oh, why hadn't she brought her phone? It was in her car outside Shorten Auctioneers. Locked in. Useless.

Turning, she looked back towards the shore. Only a hundred yards of freezing, heaving water away. One hundred impossible yards. The strand was shrouded in dusk, overshadowed by the dark walls of the cliffs. She shouted for help but her voice came back to her, sounding weak and hysterical. Besides, the village was a kilometre from the beach. Who would hear her? Unless someone had decided to walk their dog along the strand. Or maybe a young couple, seeking the privacy of the sheltered sand dunes. She shouted again, louder, more desperate this time. The wind was getting stronger and blowing seaward. It carried her voice towards the horizon where only a sliver of yellow light was now visible. If only she had her phone. Or even a torch. Something to attract attention. An icy wave lapped over her feet. She pulled herself higher up the rock, huddling close to the Dog-ears now. The pain in her feet was intense as wind and water combined to freeze them.

Ella suddenly realised that even if there was somebody on the beach they would not be able to see her clinging to Dog Rock. The light was too dim and her clothes too dark. Her jacket was navy, her jeans and sweater dark blue. She would fade unseen into the falling darkness. Unless . . . Frantic now, Ella struggled with almost numb fingers to unhook her bra. It was white. The straps tangled in her sleeves, the water lapped at her shins, her fingers were stiff but panic drove her on. When her bra was finally off she began to wave it over her head and shout for help.

She shouted until she was hoarse and then she just continued to wave her bra. At one stage she laughed and knew there was hysteria in the sound. Ella Ford. Sensible, sophisticated, ambitious Ella Ford, sitting on a rock in the middle of an ocean waving her underwear over her head! Her knees were under water now. There was nowhere else to go. Darkness had almost engulfed Cuanowen. It was time to make a decision. Dive in or float away. A quick controlled ending or a desperate clinging on until the last minute. Ella realised then how very much she wanted to live. How much more she needed to do, how she wanted to change her life. She began to pray. A meaningless babble of words and pledges and promises. She bargained with whatever deity would listen, all the time waving her bra about. She would be kind and forgiving, she would donate her profits to charity, she would help old ladies cross the road and even forgive Andrew his affair. If only she survived.

The water was at her waist level when, in the distance, she saw the lights of a car approach along the strand road. It came to a stop in the tiny car park to the left of the strand. She began an even more frantic waving of her bra. The lights of the car were switched off. God, Ella prayed, please don't let it be a couple who can see nothing but each other! A small circular beam shone through the darkness. The driver had got out of the car and had a torch. The light wavered as the holder of the torch walked towards the strand. Ella screamed. Fear forced a sound from her hoarse throat. The beam of light moved around, searching. It moved to the left of her, to the right. She shouted again, knowing that she was fighting for her life. The beam came back towards her and focused on her waving white bra. She spun the garment so frantically that she almost toppled into the black depths.

A voice carried on the wind. She could not hear the words but she recognised the deep tone. It was Pebbles Shorten. She tried to shout back to him but her vocal chords refused to work anymore. As the water inched up her ribcage she was struck by the thought that her rescue could be too late. By the time Pebbles had gone for help she would be gone under.

A numbing weariness gripped her and she had to struggle against the need to close her eyes. The next minutes were spent fighting the weight of exhaustion, fighting the little voice in her head which said that she could let go now. Just as her eyelids began to droop she heard a new sound. A rhythmic splash. It got nearer to her. It was then she remembered Shorten's rowing boat. They always kept it moored at the little cement strip the locals grandly called the jetty. She could hear the paddles splash, hear the scrape of timber on rock as the current tossed the little boat, hear Pebbles shout to her to hang on, to hold her hand out to him. When she tried to move she found her legs had gone numb. With a combined effort of push and pull, somehow she and Pebbles managed to land her safely in the rowing boat. The last thing Ella remembered was a man's coat being wrapped around her. She closed her eyes then and allowed herself the sleep her body craved.

Chapter 21

Andrew was the first of the group to arrive in the pub. Saturday night revellers already packed The Mills. The air was thick with the smell of alcohol, perfume and aftershave. As usual the young and beautiful were here in force, showing off their designer labels and toned bodies. A DJ in a far corner was talking over the music he was playing, speaking some type of American-English. The whole place seemed to be throbbing to the rhythmic beat. Andrew walked quickly through the crowds and made his way to the first floor.

The upstairs lounge bar was quiet. Just a few couples here and there, lolling on the overstuffed chairs, conversing in low tones. Mozart played softly in the background. Andrew ordered his drink and found a table for three in a far-off nook. The others would find him here when they arrived.

Glancing at his watch, he realised he was early. And nervous. Of course he knew both men well. They had been in college together. They were friends. Of sorts. Tonight he must make that friendship work for him. Without being too obvious. But how in the hell was he going to broach the subject? "Tell me about the Gambling Bill, Pascal. Oliver, have you been lying to me about planning in Ballyhaven?" Words, which had always been Andrew's forte, spilled aimlessly around in his head now.

The first part of the evening would be fine. It would be the usual enquiries after family, discussions of mutual friends, tales of their time together in college. But the conversation must be steered around to Ballyhaven. Should he mention the fact that two of the bigger players in the city had recently put in bids on the fifty-acre site? He knew what they would say. 'Take the highest bid, Fordie.' End of conversation. But that would not answer any of the questions. It would not tell him why both the Coxes and Jason Laide were offering way over the odds for a site with no planning permission. Unless they knew something Andrew did not. Something Pascal MacEvoy and Oliver Griffin most probably did. He patted his pocket to make sure the piece of paper he needed was in there.

Andrew finished his drink and ordered another. He was trying not to think about Ella. Trying not to worry that she was committing them to another purchase in Cuanowen. He should not have allowed her to go there alone. Despite his efforts, a frown creased his forehead and his lips pursed as thoughts of Ella and her mental state would not go away. She was a loose cannon. Off the rails. Befriending Jason Laide! Jesus! Everyone, including pre-accident Ella, knew that Laide was someone you respected for his power but never befriended. The man had no friends. Just major and minor enemies. It was difficult to get a straight answer from Ella these days but it would definitely seem that she had made some promises to Jason Laide regarding the Ballyhaven site. As far as Andrew could gauge, she had committed nothing to writing but for Jason Laide that would be a mere detail. If she had promised him the site in Ballyhaven then Andrew was going to have one hell of a struggle to secure it for the Coxes. But if Gary and Noel wanted it, they must have it. No matter what.

"That face would turn milk sour, Fordie!"

Andrew started in fright.

Oliver Griffin was standing over him, a big grin on his face.

"Any sign of McEvoy yet?" Oliver asked.

Andrew shook his head. "No. He was never on time for anything, was he? I'll get the drinks in. The usual?"

Andrew walked to the bar and took advantage of the few minutes alone to get his thoughts together. He decided his best bet was to wait and see how things developed. He was just bringing the drinks back to the table when Pascal McEvoy arrived.

"Sorry I'm a bit late, lads. Had to drop my son off in town."

"He must be at that awful teenage stage by now, is he?" Oliver asked.

"Hugh's thirteen and is convinced the world revolves around him and his social life. Having a Big Mac in town with his friends is the height of his ambition now. Being a parent is more about chauffeuring them around these days than anything else."

"You can say that again," Oliver agreed. "That and supplying pocket money."

They passed over the topic of children quickly, all aware that Andrew could play no part in that particular conversation. Not that it worried him. Or Ella. Probably. They had never really discussed the issue.

"How is Ella these days?" Pascal asked. "I hear she's working as hard as ever. She had a great escape, didn't she?"

Andrew just smiled in answer. What could he say? Yes, Ella escaped the accident with her life intact but with her mind in pieces!

Oliver Griffin held his glass up in salute. "To great escapes!" he said.

Andrew noticed that the hand holding the glass had a slight tremor. He examined Oliver more closely. His face was lined and he suddenly realised that Griffin had lost a lot of weight.

"Gym or road-running, Oliver? You seem to be very trim."

"Just working hard. The best diet ever."

"Talking of work, I wanted to ask you about Ballyhaven," Andrew blurted.

As soon as the words were out of his mouth he regretted them. Both other men were looking at him in annoyance as if he had committed some horrible social gaffe. He had. It would have been more acceptable to spit in his drink rather than to so obviously look for inside information like this. He had meant to be much more circumspect. But it was out now and what surprised him most was that Pascal McEvoy's reaction seemed to be as intense as Oliver's.

"What's your interest in Ballyhaven?" Pascal asked sharply.

"Fordie owns a fifty-acre site there, right in the centre of –" Oliver stopped mid-sentence and exchanged glances with Pascal.

That surreptitious little exchange was enough to convince Andrew that his suspicions had been right. There was something going on in Ballyhaven. Both these men knew about it. So did the Coxes and Jason Laide. So why the secrecy? Why had Oliver lied? No longer worried about their opinions, Andrew decided to lay his cards on the table. He cleared his throat.

"Right. I think it's time I knew what's going on. In recent weeks I've had two exceptionally good offers on my Ballyhaven site. I haven't put it on the market. They approached me. It's just fifty acres of poor agricultural land. No residential permission. No planning that I know of, yet two very astute business people have offered me big money for my site. What do you say now, Oliver? Are you still insisting that there are no plans for the area?"

Oliver drained his glass. "Another drink?" he asked.

Both Pascal and Andrew shook their heads. Oliver went to the bar to buy his own drink.

Andrew turned to Pascal. "Does this have anything to do with the new legislation on gambling?"

Before Pascal had time to reply, Andrew reached into his inside pocket and pulled out the newspaper article he had clipped from the business section of yesterday's paper. He unfolded it and placed it on the table between them.

"This report claims that the new Gambling Bill will allow gaming machines in pubs and more importantly that it will open the way for a super casino or casinos to operate here. I respect this journalist. Finnegan is never sensationalist and never wrong. He asks why all the cloak and dagger and I'm asking you the same, Pascal."

Pascal leaned back in his chair and, hands in trouser pockets, stared up at the ceiling. Andrew wanted to hurry him up, to demand an answer but knew his best tactic was to sit and wait. Eventually Pascal lowered his gaze and looked directly at Andrew.

"There's no cloak and dagger. How could there be? You know the way our legislative system works. A Bill has to go through five stages in the Dáil. As well as that it has to be examined in the Senate too. There are so many committees and sub-committees that nothing is secret. Nor should it be. But there is an urgency."

"What do you mean?"

"All I'll say is that there is a need to regulate gambling here. You know how the loopholes in the present laws are being used. Private clubs are effectively operating as casinos. That must stop. We must have more transparency. Another factor is that since 9/11 our tourism has taken a big downturn. A super casino would attract a lot of visitors."

Andrew took his paper clipping and carefully folded it.

Pascal had not really answered his question. He was prevaricating, skirting around the real issues of revenue and control. He was talking political-speak. These were reasons for changing the laws, for bringing them up to date, but they were not urgent.

"And why so quickly? Why now?" he asked.

Pascal laughed. "Always the sharp one, Fordie, weren't you? I won't go into detail but I'll just say we are taking this opportunity to pass our own legislation before it's imposed on us. This way we can have more control over the whole process."

Andrew nodded, assuming Pascal was talking about EU influence. As he was meant to assume. He did not care what the reason was. His real concern was the connection with Ballyhaven.

Oliver arrived back, splashing his drink over as he parked it on the table.

"Just in time," Andrew said. "Now tell me what Ballyhaven has to do with the new gambling legislation."

Oliver looked in Pascal's direction and raised his eyebrows. The politician nodded.

"Well, after a lot of debate it was decided to grant a licence for just one super casino," said Oliver. "The real McCoy. A custom-built gambling resort."

"In Ballyhaven?"

Oliver nodded, not seeming even slightly ashamed that he had lied so much before now.

"And my fifty acres is bang in the middle of the development area. Am I right? As soon as permission is granted for the casino my fifty acres become a prime site."

"The whole area will be designated as a custom-built gambling resort," Pascal said. "Under licence, granted with very strict criteria. It will be, in effect, a little Vegas. We have a raft of legislation to enact first, including some amendments to taxation, finance and planning law but we are confident that tourists will flock there. More tourists, more revenue, more employment. Everyone's a winner."

Andrew pushed his beer mat around in circles, occupying his fingers while his mind worked overtime to assimilate the new information. The super casino promised to be one of the biggest projects ever undertaken here. And it seemed like his fifty acres was crucial to its development.

"Why Ballyhaven?"

Oliver shrugged. "Proximity to the city, yet far enough away. Airport nearby and motorway. No major developments there so minimal disturbance to existing facilities."

"And cheap land for whoever is quick enough to snap it up before development. It seems like I'm sitting on a goldmine."

"Maybe. Maybe not," Oliver said. "Yours is just one site in the area. There are others that could just as easily be developed. I'd take the best offer now if I were you."

Pascal checked his watch and stood up. "I'd better go and collect Hugh. I don't want him hanging around the city centre. Sorry to cut it short, lads. We must arrange another night out. A proper one."

They shook hands and promised to meet again soon. Andrew and Oliver were silent as they watched Pascal walk away. Tall, straight, debonair, Pascal was wearing his age well. Andrew knew he himself was too. Oliver was the one who looked a bit worn, a bit battered and bruised by the passing years. The shaking hand was noticeable again as Oliver raised his glass to his lips. He looked like a man with a lot of worries on his mind. Putting the glass down with a thud, he leaned towards Andrew.

"This development is going to be huge, Fordie. One of the biggest undertakings ever in Ireland. As well as the casino itself, there will be hotel accommodation, amusement park, health spa, retail park. You name it, the Casino Village will have it. It will take someone with huge resources to handle it."

"Or a syndicate."

"Maybe. But someone like, say, Jason Laide, just for instance, would be the right person. He could finance the whole thing."

"He's in haulage for Christ's sake! Surely the most suitable person for this project would have to be an experienced developer. Anyway, why are you canvassing for Jason Laide? What makes you think he might be interested in the Ballyhaven site? Do you know him?"

Oliver just sat and stared, his mouth pursed in a tight line as if trying to hold in any more indiscreet words. He looked shifty and uncomfortable. Even a little desperate.

"Are you involved with Jason Laide, Oliver? Are you telling me I should sell to him?"

In reply Oliver gave a little snort. "You know damn well I'm in the Planning Office. I work for the Government. Nobody else. I'm just saying you should take the best offer going now. If you wait you might not do so well under a compulsory purchase scheme."

Compulsory purchase? No way! The Government might be backing this scheme but they could not be seen to be the prime movers behind a casino. Unless they wanted to turn the whole island into a gambling state.

Andrew looked at the man he had trusted as a friend and for the first time ever that trust was wavering. Griffin was lying about the compulsory purchase. He must be. And no matter how he denied it, Oliver seemed to know that Jason Laide was interested in Ford's fifty acres. The Coxes obviously knew the Ballyhaven plans too and probably a whole raft of insiders had been informed at this stage. A wink and a nod. Some of them, any one of them, would be more suitable than Jason Laide. Andrew stood.

"I must be off, Oliver. I have a lot of paperwork to catch up on. Maybe draft an ad for my site in Ballyhaven. Put it on the open market and see who comes out of the woodwork."

"I wouldn't if I were you," Oliver said quickly.

Andrew heard an unspoken warning in the words.

The two men looked at each other but neither offered a hand to shake. A line was drawn in the sand. Their friendship stood coldly on either side of that line. Both knew that Jason Laide was firmly parked in the middle.

* * *

Anger quickened Andrew's step. He hurried down the stairs and sliced his way through the noise and packed bodies of the ground-floor bar. Out on the street, he took a minute to breathe in some of the cool air. Where to now? A taxi home to his empty house? He shivered. He could not face it. Not just yet. A quiet pub somewhere seemed like a good idea. A few drinks to help him relax. The streets were busy. Taxis flashed past, all full. He began to walk. Behind him he heard someone laugh. Not just someone. He would know that voice anywhere. He whirled around towards the direction of the voice. Maxine stood on the pavement, just a foot away from him, shimmering, beautiful, another very attractive girl by her side. She smiled but he saw a momentary shock in her eyes. As if he had been the last person she'd wanted to bump into.

"You look like a man in a hurry, Andrew," she said. "Too busy to join us for a drink?"

He felt his anger from the meeting dissipate as he looked at her. She was wearing a full-length knit coat unbuttoned to show underneath a very short skirt and an even shorter top. His eyes were drawn to the toned and tanned area of her bare midriff. Her skin gleamed in the streetlights. He knew what it felt like to touch and he had to stop himself from reaching out now and running his hands over her glorious body. Her blonde hair was loose and being gently tossed by the breeze. A waft of her perfume blew towards him and robbed him of his last vestige of control. He struggled to find some smart, sophisticated words, a casual remark but the sight of Maxine looking more beautiful than he had ever seen her robbed him of speech.

"My friend and colleague, Natalie," Maxine said, turning to the girl by her side. "Nat, meet Andrew Ford. He's an estate agent."

Andrew offered his hand to Natalie but all the time his attention was on Maxine. He could not, would not let her slip away again. "Yes. I'd love to join you for a drink," he said.

He caught Natalie's fleeting frown of annoyance and guessed that he had ruined a girls' night out. Tough! Back inside The Mills, they found standing space at the back of the ground-floor bar. Andrew battled his way to the bar and bought drinks. When he arrived back at last, Natalie had gone.

"She met some friends. They're off clubbing," Maxine explained. "Do you mind?"

Andrew looked into her deep blue eyes and smiled. Her reciprocal smile gave him the answer he wanted.

"Will we go some place quieter?" she asked.

"Ella is away. How about going back to my house?"

Maxine hesitated for just a moment before abandoning her drink and leading the way through the crowds towards the door.

The first taxi they flagged stopped for them, the traffic lights were green all the way, the journey to the outskirts of town was speedy. They held hands in the back of the car and did not speak. Nor did they speak when Andrew opened the front door of his home and led Maxine into the house he shared with Ella. Closing the door, he took her in his arms and they kissed with a passion that did not need words. They both knew they would not go to the master bedroom. That would be cruel, crass. They kissed and caressed on each step of the stairs, littering the steps with items of discarded clothing. When they reached the guest bedroom, they were no longer making choices, no longer in control. Their need for each other had taken over. Andrew took Maxine with all the passion of a man in love and Maxine responded in kind. Their union transcended the physical. It was a meeting of spirits. It was fate.

They lay quietly in each other's arms for a while, revelling in the closeness. Their heartbeats slowed and their feelings gave way to thoughts.

"I vowed never to see you again," Maxine whispered.

Andrew held her more tightly. Sadness and guilt tinged the perfection of the moment. He had never wanted to cheat on Ella. She did not deserve that. Nor did he want to offer Maxine the sleaziness of an affair.

"I vowed never to let you go," he whispered back into the silkiness of her mane of blonde hair.

Maxine pulled herself up and, leaning on her elbow, looked down into his face.

"Andrew, there are things about me you don't know."

"I don't need to know anything except that I love you."

"No. Bad things. Really bad. I'm not who you think I am."

"You're the most beautiful woman I've ever met. You're intelligent, funny, astute. Do you need me to go on? I love you. If you have secrets, Max, I don't care. If sharing makes you feel better, go ahead, but there's nothing you can say that would make me change my mind."

"Do you really mean that, Andrew?"

He moved to kiss her, to hold her in his arms and reassure her but she sat up and swung her legs out over the side of the bed. Her back to him, she hung her head, allowing her hair to form a veil about her face. Her shoulders were raised and her hands were gripping the edge of the mattress tightly. Some instinct told Andrew to lie still and wait. This was Maxine's struggle. Her choice. When she turned towards him, there were tears in her eyes.

"My name is Marie Murphy," she said softly "I come from Mountain View Terrace."

She spoke for twenty minutes, stopping only to blow her nose or brush away the tears that tracked down her face and dribbled over her chin. She gave him the facts. No explanations or apologies. Just the bare unvarnished truth of a deprived, unhappy, ambitious child manipulated into making a pornography video. Of a successful young woman haunted by her past. Of a ruthless man who was blackmailing her with the depraved video. Threatening to publish if she did not do his bidding.

"Now you know, Andrew. I'm not the type of woman you would want to have in your life."

Andrew cradled her in his arms and gently stroked her back. Her sobs eased until they became no more than soft sniffles. He kissed the tears away from her face.

"Do you want to tell me who that blackmailing bastard is?" he asked.

Maxine stiffened. "No. Don't ask, Andrew. It's better you don't know. I have a plan. I think I can deal with him. But I don't want you involved. "

"I'll help you, Max. You don't have to fight him alone. I'll always be there for you."

She smiled wanly at him. "I don't feel alone any more. But this is a situation I must sort myself. And if I can't, at least you won't be hurt by it."

"But he's blackmailing you! I can –"

Maxine raised her hand and placed her fingers gently over his lips. She did not want to discuss it any more. They lay together then, both exhausted by the emotion of Maxine's confession. They slept, arms entwined, bodies close together as if they were afraid to let each other go, even in sleep.

They slept so soundly that they did not hear the front door opening, or the tread on the stairs, or see the flash of the camera as O'Shaughnessy photographed them. He crept quietly away, making sure to close the door gently behind him. A satisfied grin flashed across his face as he sat back into his car. A great night's work. What a stroke of luck! He had just been returning from taking shots of the politician's little brat buying some merchandise when he happened past The Mills and saw Maxine Doran getting into a cab with Andrew Ford. The Boss was always interested in whatever the supermodel was up to. He couldn't believe his luck when the pair went into the house, forgetting to lock the door after them. Yes. Jason Laide would pay him well for this night's work.

Life was rosy for O'Shaughnessy. He had his trip to

Salzburg to look forward to now. Gussie had rung only an hour ago to say everything was arranged from flights to accommodation. All O'Shaughnessy had to do was get his ass over there on Monday morning, trail Sharon Laide and take a few shots of whatever she was up to. Obviously Jason's old lady had angered her old man. Foolish woman. Jason was a good boss but a very dangerous enemy.

Chapter 22

There was no waking-up process for Ella. One moment she was in a deep exhausted sleep, the next she was awake, fully aware that she was in Seaview Hotel outside Cuanowen and that she had almost drowned last evening. The room was exactly as it had been yesterday morning. The same white light, the same dressing table and wardrobe, the same rumble of tide in the background. Yet Ella perceived it differently. She saw dust motes swirl in the light, felt the texture of the pillow underneath her head, heard the hissing curl of the waves in the tidal din. It was as if her senses too had woken from a long sleep. So long. Over a year.

Someone tapped on her door. Ella pulled the duvet up around her chin and called "Come in!".

Mrs Langford, proprietor of Seaview Hotel popped her silver-haired head around the door.

"Just checking that you are alright, dear. You gave us all rather a fright last night."

"I'm fine, thank you." Ella smiled. "I'm so grateful to you for all your help, Mrs Langford."

The older woman's rings glinted in the light as she waved her hand dismissively. "Not at all, dear. I just called a doctor for you. Gavin Shorten was the hero of the hour."

Ella nodded. How would she ever be able to thank Pebbles? If he had not noticed that her car was parked a long time outside his office, if he had not guessed she had gone to the strand, if he did not have access to a boat … She shivered.

"Yes, indeed. I was very lucky and Gavin was very brave."

"Actually, he's in reception at the moment, Mrs Ford. I just popped in to let you know and to ask if you would like breakfast in your room."

Ella threw back the duvet and jumped out of bed. Her toes curled as they savoured the softness of carpet under her bare feet. She was awake and gloriously aware. She was alive! She smiled at Mrs Langford, seeing beyond the make-up too heavily applied and the staggering amount of jewellery. It was the kind eyes and the prim little mouth that could never utter a harsh word on which Ella focused.

"Thank you so much, Mrs Langford, but I'll take breakfast in the dining room. Perhaps you would ask Pebbles, sorry, Gavin, to join me, please?"

The old lady nodded in approval. Beryl Langford respected the spirit of get-up-and-go. It had been her yardstick in life. It was what gave her the strength to run her little seaside hotel alone now that her husband Archie had passed on. She gently closed the door of Ella's room and went to reception to talk to Gavin.

When Ella entered the dining room, Gavin was already seated at a little round table which fitted snugly into the bay window. His back to the door, he was looking out over the sea. Ella walked up behind him and put her hand on his shoulder.

"Gavin, how can I thank you enough? You saved my life."

He blushed, mumbling something in an embarrassed undertone which Ella did not catch. She stooped to kiss him on the cheek at the very moment he raised his head to look at her. Their noses clashed and they both laughed.

"We never did get that right, did we?" Gavin said.

Ella smiled her agreement as she took a chair opposite him.

"How are you feeling this morning, Ella? Any after-effects?"

She leaned towards him and her eyes were intense, sparkling. "I feel great. Better than I have for a long time." She hesitated a moment before adding, "I haven't been well for a while. I had an accident, a car crash, over a year ago. It has been a difficult time."

"What in the hell were you doing out on the Dog Rock? Didn't you know the tide was coming in?"

Before she could answer, a waitress arrived in with heaps of toast and a pot of tea and coffee. She fussed around, offering cereals and fruit juice and taking orders for the ubiquitous full Irish breakfast.

"Well?" Gavin prompted when the girl had hurried off towards the kitchen.

Ella thought back over yesterday evening and remembered her sadness and guilt after her visit to her parents' grave.

"I had a lot to think about. Dog Rock seemed like a good place to do my thinking. The tide was well out. Then I fell asleep."

"Jesus! Sitting on a rock, the tide coming in around you and you fell asleep! The city must have affected your brain, Ella."

Ella frowned. Wise words indeed. The city had affected her brain, her heart, her very soul. She had found there the identity she had craved. Ella Ford was a successful businesswoman, married to a handsome man, living in a fine house in a good area. She had achieved everything she had gone there to find. Money, respect, security. So why did she feel so empty? Why had she used the excuse of her accident to withdraw from the things she had convinced herself she held so dear? Peering over her shoulder, she looked out to sea. It was sparkling in the morning sun. Smooth, beautiful, inviting, its icy death-inducing coldness now hidden.

"I'm sorry," Gavin muttered. "That was a bit churlish of me."

He was blushing again. Ella reached across for his hand and squeezed it. "You're right, Gavin. The city has changed me and I don't really like the person I've become. I've a lot more thinking to do."

"Not on Dog Rock, I hope!"

Ella laughed with Gavin but inside she was not laughing. She was making a solemn vow to herself. Whatever happened in the future, whichever painful decisions she had to reach, she would never ever allow herself to reach the depths of despair and self-pity that had led her to almost lose her life on Dog Rock.

* * *

Maxine's hair was fanned out over the pillow and her face was even more beautiful in sleep. She looked younger. Vulnerable. Andrew stayed perfectly still, just watching as she slept, noticing how her dark eyelashes curled, how her breasts rose and fell with her soft breathing.

He tried to imagine what she had looked like as a fifteen-year-old. Probably as beautiful as she was now but less sophisticated. He felt his face flush with anger as he thought of what she had told him. What kind of low-down criminal could have used her like that? The bastard should be locked up. Worse. He should be tortured, his nails dragged off with a pliers. One by one. He should suffer the agonies of the damned. Andrew realised his fingers had clenched into fists. He loosened them out. Rage was not going to help Maxine. She was determined not to tell him that man's name, that animal's name, but he would find out. Sometime. Somehow.

Maxine stirred. Her eyelids fluttered open and Andrew was struck yet again by the blueness of her eyes. They were cornflowers and deep lakes, Mediterranean skies and violets. She smiled at him and he kissed her softly on her lips. Her hands slipped around his neck and pulled him close to her.

"Do you hate me now?" she whispered into his neck.

"I hate *him*," Andrew replied with vengeance. "I wish you'd tell me who he was and I'd soon have him under lock and key."

Maxine pulled abruptly away from him and sat up, panic in her staring eyes. "You must promise me that you'll stay out of this. He's a dangerous man and a powerful one too. He could hurt you, Andrew. Physically and in your business. Please promise me."

"But what he did, what he's doing is illegal! He shouldn't get away with it."

"Don't you think I know that? But what I did was disgusting. He didn't force me. I wasn't beaten or kidnapped. I did it to try and escape my family and Mountain View Terrace. And I have continued to do what he has asked of me. Because I wanted to protect my career. I must take responsibility too."

"You were only fifteen then. And now you're being blackmailed."

Maxine flopped back against her pillow. Her smile tinged with bitterness. "I'm no longer making excuses for myself and I don't want you to either. I must solve this alone. Try to earn back my self-respect. Get revenge. And I think I know how to do it."

Andrew looked at the stubborn set of her mouth and knew any further discussion of this topic would be pointless.

"Are you still interested in buying Manor House?" he asked. When she nodded he told her he had passed on her offer to Rob Trevor. "He didn't seem too enthusiastic. Of course he has the other offer in already. From Jason Laide. You know that."

"We'll talk about it again when I come back from Amsterdam," Maxine said and it seemed that another subject was closed.

Looking at his watch Andrew was surprised to see that the morning was already half over. They had slept late.

"What time is Ella due back?" Maxine asked.

A cold shiver rippled down Andrew's spine. Ella. His wife. Mrs Ford. The depressed and traumatised Ella. How was he going to tell her he no longer loved her? That maybe he never had. What was going to happen about the business, the house, the investments they shared? A cordial agreement or years of wrangling in family courts? Whatever happened he was sure of one thing. He loved Maxine Doran, also known as Marie Murphy, with a passion so deep that it would not be denied. He did not care what had happened in her past, how many men, or even women, she had slept with. He would be fair to Ella, give her the share of the wealth she had helped create but his future, all the rest of his life belonged to the beautiful woman who now lay beside him.

"Don't ever leave me, Max," he whispered.

In reply Maxine covered his lips with hers. It was lunchtime before they came downstairs.

* * *

Even though the Junkergasse house was centrally heated Sharon could always sense a slight drop in temperature when it was snowing outside. More than that, she had developed an ear for listening to the quietness of snow. It was a stillness more than an absence of sound. Without looking out the window now she knew the city of Salzburg would be deeply carpeted in a thick snowfall. Too early yet on this Sunday morning to have tyre tracks or footprints ruin the pristine whiteness.

Sharon slipped quietly from the bed even though Jason would not have noticed if she had put on hobnailed boots and trampled all over the bedroom. She leaned over him, worried now that maybe she had given him too much sedative last night. He was pale but then Jason always had that pasty white complexion which evoked days and nights spent in smoke-filled rooms. Misspent days and nights. His breathing was quiet and even.

Wrapping her warm robe tightly about her, Sharon left her husband to his drug-induced sleep and padded down to the kitchen. Frau Henner was standing by the sink, her back to the door. Her shoulders were tense, raised closer to her neat grey hair than usual. Sharon sighed. Now she was going to have to deal with Frieda's disapproval as well as everything else.

"Morning, Frieda," she said as she went to the percolator and poured herself a mug of coffee. Frau Henner was the only person Sharon knew whose moods were reflected in her back. The face would be impassive. Non-judgemental. The back was furious.

"*Guten Morgen*," she muttered as she continued

vigorously scrubbing the pot she had in the sink. At the rate she was wielding the pot scrub she would shortly rub a hole in the saucepan.

Sharon sat at the table with her coffee and waited for the storm to break. It was a short wait. Saucepan in hand, Frieda swung around to face her employer.

"I do not approve of drugging people," she said in the precise English she always used when she was angry. "And I do not like being drawn into your deceptions. You are just building up a house of lies. It's all going to tumble down and you are going to get crushed underneath. And not just you –"

"I know, Frieda, I know," Sharon interrupted. "But it's almost at an end. If everything works according to plan, we'll soon be free of Jason Laide. I'm very sorry to involve you in all this. Your family too."

The saucepan landed on the draining board with a bang. Frau Henner dried her hands and walked over to the table. Sitting opposite Sharon she fixed her with a sympathetic gaze.

"I know why you are doing this, Sharon. I don't mind pretending to be nothing more than a housekeeper but . . ."

Sharon's hand shot out and she grabbed the older woman's damp fingers. "You're so much more, Frieda. I couldn't manage without you."

"I know that. Your husband doesn't. He has no idea of my role here and for the first time, Sharon, I'm starting to believe that he should."

"No, no and no! I can't tell him. You know how

dangerous he can be!"

"Then why are you are still married to him? I could accept it at first but since I've got to know him – well, I don't understand any more why you are still his wife."

Sharon bowed her head. Frieda was right of course. Especially now, since she finally knew what Jason had in those envelopes she had so obligingly stored for him. The filth and cruelty. The downright evil.

"It's not entirely your decision, is it?" Frieda asked. "Other people have rights. Your husband for one. And don't look at me like that! Of course he should be told. What if he finds out? I'm amazed you have got away with it for so long."

Sharon raised her head now and looked at Frieda. "I suppose I hoped for a long time that things might change. Then I could have shared everything with him."

Frieda snorted. "What is it they say about a leopard changing its spots? You're an intelligent woman. How could you ever have believed that your husband would change? You fooled yourself. "

Sharon stood and walked to the door. With her head to one side she listened carefully for any sounds from upstairs. There were none. She closed the door and went back to her place at the table.

Leaning towards Frieda, she whispered. "I'll tell him as soon as the house deal on Manor is through."

"And why do you have to wait for yet another house?"

Sharon was asking herself the same question. Why should she wait for Manor House to be signed, sealed and delivered? Because, of course, half the property would be hers. Security. The payoff for the years she had stayed married to Jason, all the time building up the property portfolio. And what did that make her? There was a name for women like her, wasn't there? Tears sprang into her eyes as she looked across at Frieda Henner. The only person in the world she really trusted.

"We'll need all the money we can get to protect ourselves, Frieda. Our safety will come at a high price."

The kitchen door burst open and Jason appeared in the doorway, barefoot and still groggy-looking.

"What in the fuck did you give me to drink last night, Sharon? I have a shit of a hangover!"

"*Sturm*," Sharon replied without blinking an eye. "It's new wine, semi-fermented. An Austrian speciality. It has some kick, hasn't it?"

Sharon was proud of her lie until she saw the look of disgust on Frau Henner's face. She looked away from Frieda and then poured coffee for Jason. While he was drinking it she went and got him some paracetamol. Then she massaged his shoulders. She would have done anything at that moment to make him feel well enough to catch his flight back to Ireland.

"How am I going to fly with my head throbbing like this?" he asked.

Sharon redoubled her efforts on the shoulder massage.

He glared at Frau Henner and nodded towards the door. When she had left the kitchen, he turned to his wife.

"Now, Sharon. No more fucking around. When are you coming home? And by home I mean back to Ireland."

"I'll be back some time next week. I have a few things

to organise here first," Sharon said and gave his shoulders one last pat.

His hand clamped onto hers like a vice. He dragged her around to face him, his eyes blazing in his pale face. His hand slipped up along her arm and came to rest at her throat, exactly over the bruises he had left there yesterday.

"You'd better have my business papers with you. The ones you stole from me. Do you hear me?"

"Y-yes. I-I'll have to go to Switzerland and collect them before I come home."

"You wouldn't try to trick me, Shar, would you?"

She shook her head, unable to squeeze any word past her constricted gullet.

"'Cause if you did, I'd kill you. You know that, don't you?"

She nodded more vigorously this time.

"So get back my fucking property! Don't give me any more bullshit about keeping it safe for me. Understand?"

He let her go then and laughed into her face. She knew she was paler than him now. Rubbing her throat she staggered back from his reach and then reeled up the stairs. Frau Henner met her on the landing and gave a quick, consoling hug.

In less than two hours Sharon had brought Jason to Salzburg Airport and stood watching as he went through into the boarding area. She waited until there was no more sign of him in the queue, then exhaled a shuddering breath. But it was not a sigh of relief or triumph. Not yet. She had a lot to organise before she could catch a plane for Ireland. Before she could set herself free.

Chapter 23

Maxine's flight to Amsterdam was at six o'clock on Monday morning. Andrew insisted on driving her to the airport. It was still dark when he went to her apartment block to collect her. There was an awkwardness between them.

"Did Ella get home all right last night?" Maxine asked when what she really wanted to know was if there had been a reconciliation between husband and wife.

"Yes. It was very late though. She left it until the last minute to drive back from Cuanowen," Andrew replied when what he really wanted to say was that he had not yet told Ella he was going to leave her.

The unasked questions hung in the air. They were silent as they left the city behind and headed towards the airport. Then suddenly, as if both were responding to the same signal they spoke together.

"Are you looking forward to –?"

"Will you be –?"

They laughed and the weight of silent guilt and treachery disappeared. They chatted easily about Maxine's assignment and she told some amusing stories about the more famous excesses of DiAngeli.

"How can he be so off-the-wall yet so successful?" Andrew asked. "Everyone who is anyone wears his designs, don't they?"

"It's his eccentricity that gives his designs their flair. Besides, most of his odd behaviour is for the media. He's really a very shrewd man. His designs, especially his bags, are a good investment too. They'll increase in value a lot because he produces very few of any particular line. He signs some of his work randomly. It's just a matter of looking out for a signed piece and waiting for DiAngeli to die."

Andrew was impressed yet again by Maxine. When it came to shrewdness she seemed to be a match for DiAngeli or anybody else. Maybe he should have more faith in her plans for Manor House.

"Do you want me to up your offer on Manor House? Are you willing to go head to head with Jason Laide?"

Maxine turned towards him and Andrew took his eyes off the road for long enough to see anger flash in her eyes. "Yes. I want Manor House and I intend to have it. But wait until I come back to make any increased offer. I've instructed my accountant to act on my behalf if necessary but I'd prefer to handle it myself. I have other things on my mind now. Just leave it for a while, okay?"

Andrew wondered if she understood how close Jason Laide was to closing the deal. Laide too intended to be the owner of Manor House. Ella seemed to be representing Laide's interests pretty well. He would just have to stall things until Maxine was ready. Besides, Laide must be spreading himself thin between Manor House, the new pub, his interest in Ballyhaven and the proposed casino. Unless he had limitless resources.

The control towers appeared on the horizon. Soon it would be time to say goodbye to Maxine. That, as far as Andrew was concerned, was the most important item on the agenda now.

"You'll ring me?" he asked.

"Every day."

"You'll take care?"

Maxine laughed. "How can you ask me that after all I've told you? I'm from the toughest part of the tough side of the city. I've been making my way in the world since I was fifteen. I can take care of myself."

"You don't have to any more. I'm here to look out for you."

Maxine reached her hand across and laid it on Andrew's. The contact brought warmth and security. She smiled at him and sighed with relief and contentment. She felt young again. Strong. Not yet proud but she would be. She had someone who believed in her, someone who knew her most humiliating secrets but still loved her.

"You'll talk to Ella?" she asked as the car came to a halt in the short-stay car park of the airport.

Andrew nodded his head. Yes. He must talk to Ella. He should have last night but she had been very tired after the drive back from Cuanowen. An excuse. He could have told her while they were making supper, or when they were going through their routine of locking up the house, or even as they had lain side by side on their bed, not touching but each very aware of the other. He had not had the courage. He looked at Maxine now and found all the courage he would need.

"Yes. I'll tell her."

Maxine leaned across and kissed him, not caring now who saw. Everyone would know very soon that Maxine Doran, supermodel, and Andrew Ford, estate agent, were an item. A commitment. A real relationship. A partnership for life.

* * *

When Ella woke, she heard the sound of the tide echoing in her head. She sat up and smiled. She must have been dreaming about Cuanowen. She shook her head to clear it. The sleepy coastal village of Cuanowen had no place in her head this Monday morning. It would have to wait in line with all the 'to be decided' issues.

Beside her the bed was empty. Andrew had told her last night that he had an early start this morning. Important negotiations to prepare for. He had looked shifty, uneasy, as if he was lying. She had lied too when she told him that she'd had an uneventful weekend in Cuanowen. Near drownings, heroic rescues and new perspectives on life were not mentioned.

Ella threw back the duvet and padded into the shower. When she was dressed she would think about her marriage. Must think about it.

Showered, she put on her dressing-gown and went back into the bedroom. Standing in front of the full-length mirror, she stared at her reflection. A dark-haired woman stared back at her, wet hair curly, a scar visible on her forehead, hazel eyes bright and observant, lips full and softly pink without lipstick. There was a vulnerability about the reflected image. Maybe it was the way the big white towelling robe dwarfed her or maybe it was just the fact that she looked younger, more innocent, without make-up. Ella took a step towards the mirror, so close that her breath formed little patches of condensation on the shiny surface. She peered over the shoulders of the image. Above, beneath, left and right. The two-dimensional image was alone in the mirror. No spectre looming. No wide-eyed terror or mouth open in silent screams. No Karen Trevor.

Ella winked at her reflection and laughed out loud as she saw a flash of the Ella that used to be. She dressed carefully, choosing a white lacy cami-top, pink, cropped jacket, jeans and very high heels. Twirling around, she admired her choice. She looked vibrant, sexy, her hair now sleek after straightening, the scar hidden by her fringe. The antithesis of the solemn businesswoman image she usually portrayed. Going to her jewellery box she searched through the discreet pieces until she found the earrings she was looking for. She had bought them in Greece on one of the rare holidays she and Andrew had taken. They were bigger and brighter than she normally wore but had seemed right for the sunshine and blue skies of Athens.

They seemed right now too. She popped them on and shook her head. The gold hoops jangled. The happy sound, redolent of sunshine and lazy days on the beach filled Ella with energy and the return of the confidence she had not known she had lost. Her step was light as she went downstairs to grab breakfast before going into work.

★ ★ ★

For the first time ever Jason Laide felt that he was not fully in control of his life. His waking-up thoughts were ones of anger. Sharon! Bitch! He felt, somewhere deep inside, that Sharon had somehow outmanoeuvred him. He leaped out of bed but the thoughts of betrayal stayed with him. Why in the fuck had she removed the tapes and papers from the Junkergasse vault? He didn't believe her cock-and-bull story about the cellar, even though he had seen for himself that it was being cleared out. He didn't like the close relationship between Sharon and that grey-haired battle-axe called Frau Henner either. They were on first-name terms. Sharon and Frieda when they thought he wasn't listening.

Stepping into the shower, he turned it on full. He did his best thinking with gallons of hot water cascading over him. He had been careless. Too trusting. Thinking back over his weekend in Salzburg now, he realised that Sharon had shagged him to exhaustion, nearly killed him climbing bloody hills with those poncy friends of hers and then managed to get him blind drunk on that stuff she called *Sturm*. She had done everything to avoid a face-to-face confrontation and to muddle his thinking processes. And she had succeeded. He should never have left without his tapes and papers safely back in his hands. He had behaved the same way he had always done – he had trusted in the fact she wouldn't dare step out of line. Now he wasn't sure. Why had she done it? What in the fuck was she up to? The thought that Sharon might want to leave him crept into his mind again. Again he blanked the thought. Not acceptable. Not allowed.

Squeezing some shampoo onto his hand, Jason carefully rubbed it into his hair and gently lathered it. On top of everything else he was going bloody bald. Maybe he should consider hair implants? Annoyed with the pettiness of this thought in the face of real problems, he stuck his head underneath the shower and rinsed. A fistful of faded red hair swirled down the plughole. Fuck! Even more insecure now, he got out and dried himself off.

When he was dressed he sat at the kitchen table with a cup of tea and ran through the inventory of the Junkergasse vault in his mind. There were videos. The first one he had made of Maxine Doran and that junkie girl. The one who had OD'd. And plenty of the high and mighty with their trousers down around their ankles. Those tapes were worth their weight in gold. They had ensured licences, contracts, attention when it was needed and a blind eye when that had been called for. The documents were priceless too. Amongst them Oliver Griffin's IOUs and details of his offshore accounts. His stash was irreplaceable so why had he been so stupid as to allow anybody else, even his wife, especially his wife, to have control over them? Trusting was for fools.

Sharon said she had put them in a safety box in their Swiss bank. Jason stirred his tea as he thought about this. He could check. He could contact the bank. He dismissed this idea. They would not deal with his query on the phone. He would have to go there himself.

Well, at least O'Shaughnessy would be watching her movements. Nobody could hide from that man or his telescopic lens. If Sharon had any secrets, they would soon be uncovered. Jason's mouth tightened. Sharon should never have put him in this position. It wasn't easy knowing that O'Shaughnessy would probably see Mrs Jason Laide with one of her young studs. But O'Shaughnessy knew it was more than his life was worth to ever repeat what he saw. Jason glanced at his watch. O'Shaughnessy should be landing in Salzburg just about now. Finding his way to Junkergasse, watching the comings and goings of Sharon and her po-faced housekeeper, focusing his lens, reporting back.

Jason stopped stirring the tea which was by now lukewarm. Standing up he went over to the sink and emptied the cup. He had no appetite for breakfast. He must go to the warehouse depot and talk to Gussie. He began to feel a little better as he thought of Gussie. Now there was a man he could trust. With him since the early days, Gussie had served his interests well, never asking questions, never doubting. He needed to go to the depot anyway to check that the latest delivery of merchandise from Dirk Van Aken had gone smoothly. Jason looked over his shoulder as he thought about the packets which had been hidden in the gaming machines. Then he smiled at his own paranoia. Did he really believe there could be someone in his kitchen reading his mind? That operation – the Holland-Ireland shuttle as he liked to think of it – was foolproof. This was only the third run but already he regretted not setting it up years ago. It was the backbone of his organisation, the goose which laid so many golden eggs for him. And would continue to do so.

The swagger was back in Jason's step as he locked the house and went out to his car. He would talk to Gussie. And then he would call to see that crazy estate agent, Ella Ford. Mad as a hatter that woman was. Always falling over and having accidents. Back in control again, Jason revved up the car and sped towards town.

* * *

The sight of his depot completely restored Jason's battered self-confidence. It was operating smoothly, lorries coming and going, loading, unloading. The public face of Laide Transport. Respectable, hardworking and very profitable.

Having made his customary visit to the front office pricks in suits, Jason crossed the yard to warehouse six. As he approached he straightened his shoulders, knowing that Gussie would be sitting on his high stool, watching his boss through those hooded eyes. He went into the little office and closed the door behind him.

"Morning, Gus. Everything okay?"

Gus just nodded his head and waited for Jason's next

question. This was one of the qualities Jason liked most about his old friend. He knew his place.

"The gaming machines. Were they delivered?"

Another passive nod. Jason glanced around before going on. He peeped through the glass panels on the office door into the warehouse beyond. It was empty of people and not even Jason suspected the boxes and crates of listening in on his conversation. It was safe to talk. He turned back to Gussie.

"The merchandise. Safely distributed?"

Gussie got up off his stool and walked over to the grey steel locker where he kept his coat, lunch box and flask. With one powerful heave he pulled it forward and disappeared behind it. Jason listened to the soft clicks as Gus entered the code that would open the wall safe hidden behind the locker. Turning his back on the office, Jason kept watch out into the warehouse until he heard the scrape of the locker being pushed back into place.

"All there minus the lads' payouts," Gus said handing Jason a bulky envelope full of money. "And this too," he added, pushing a camera into Jason's hand.

Switching on the camera, Jason scanned the digital images. He smiled. O'Shaughnessy had done well. The images told the story of that politician prick, McEvoy, dropping his son off in town and then the same boy with his friends, handing over money to a dealer in exchange for a tiny plastic bag of white powder, then the TD picking his son up again. Properly edited, this series of pictures could show that Pascal McEvoy had deliberately set up his thirteen-year-old son to buy a few hits for him.

Dynamite! Pascal McEvoy was in Jason Laide's hands now.

And to add to the triumph, O'Shaughnessy had also captured some great pics of Maxine Doran and that snotty bastard Andrew Ford. Jason laughed out loud as he examined the images of Maxine asleep, one hand thrown back up on the pillow, the other around Andrew Ford's neck, cradling his head on her bare breasts. Fuck!

This was better than sex. In his hand Jason held the key to getting the licence for the super casino. He had them all over a barrel. Oliver Griffin could not help himself. He would never be in a position to pay Jason back what he owed him now and yet he kept on gambling, kept putting his faith in one huge win to get him out of trouble. Idiot! That was planning sorted. Almost. It would be as soon as he got Griffin's IOUs back from Sharon. Bitch!

Pascal McEvoy would have to protect his son and his reputation. He would do anything to keep these pictures away from the media. He would willingly ensure that licensing conditions contained nothing which could prevent Jason Laide's name being considered. The only one to be considered.

And Andrew Ford, that snobby prick with the mad wife, he would be more than happy to sell his Ballyhaven site to Jason as long as these pictures of him with his bit-on-the-side stayed out of public view. And out of his wife's view too.

A hot flush of excitement had spread over Jason's pale face. Reaching into the envelope, he took out a bundle of notes and handed them to Gussie.

"Good work, Gus. Here's a bonus for a job well done.

And put that camera back in the safe."

As Gussie was stowing the camera away Jason's expression changed. He looked from the camera to Gussie.

"What in the fuck is this doing here? Why isn't it in Salzburg with O'Shaughnessy? I want pictures. Proof! And I want all my wife's movements logged. I hope he knows I'm not sending him on a bloody holiday!"

"He took his other camera with him. Said it was better. I warned him like you told me to. And he'll ring in with reports."

"Good man, Gus. Get those pictures you have of the politician and the estate agent printed out for me now."

Jason relaxed again. Back in control. He was grinning as he left the warehouse and crossed the yard. He was still smiling as he left the depot to make his way to Ford Auctioneers.

* * *

Ella parked and then through force of habit stood still at the front door of Ford Auctioneers. On the third step. In the very spot where she had spent an entire year sloughing off the mantle of Karen Trevor before facing work. Before facing reality.

She held her breath and listened to the sounds. Traffic noise, snatches of conversation, a siren wailing in the distance, busy footsteps. A breeze swirled around her, tossing her hair and jangling her earrings. She let her breath out in a long sigh. It was an exhalation of relief. No black cloud chilled her skin or froze her mind. The fog had lifted and in the clearness she could see the wasteland of the past year. A whole year of her life spent hiding behind the spectre of a dead woman.

Sure now that she had returned from her self-imposed exile into terror, Ella closed her eyes and dared Karen Trevor to appear, dared her to scream and bleed and plead and refuse to die. Squeezing her eyelids tightly shut she looked into the darkness and saw nothing but vaguely swirling patterns of blacks and greys. No open mouth, no terrified eyes. No Karen Trevor. Karen was dead. Long live Ella.

A hand crashed onto her shoulder.

Ella's eyes flew open and she jumped with fright.

"What in the hell are you up to now? Is it this Chinese exercise thing or what?"

Beside her Jason Laide's face was distorted in a grin that was both cruel and mocking. Ella blushed and failed to find an answer to his question. What could she say? I was just trying to see if Karen Trevor had really gone back to her grave?

"I must say you're looking well," he remarked, flicking his pale blue eyes from the top of her head to the pointed toes of her high-heeled shoes. His gaze came to rest on her breasts.

Ella self-consciously pulled the edges of her jacket together and raised her chin defiantly.

"Good morning, Jason. How was your trip to Salzburg?"

The grin faded as his lips tightened into a straight line.

"Fine," he said abruptly, then turned to climb the steps ahead of her and hold the front door open.

Head held high, she preceded him into her office.

When Andrew looked up from the papers he was examining, his expression was cross and tufts of his hair stood up ominously. Harbingers of a bad mood.

"So you decided to come into work at last," he greeted her before he noticed Jason Laide trailing in her wake. Andrew's expression changed to one of guarded welcome and his hand went instinctively to his hair to tidy it. Ella waved Jason to a seat in front of her desk while she settled herself into her chair. Then, feeling more in charge now that Jason was in her domain, she smiled at him.

"What can I do for you, Jason?"

"Close the deal on Manor House. We're messing around with it for too long now. I want it over and done with."

Ella opened her mouth to reply but she was not quick enough. Andrew beat her to it. Leaving his own area of the office he came and sat on the corner of Ella's desk, his long legs stretched in front of him.

"Not so quick, pal," he said and even to Ella's ears he sounded patronising. She winced, knowing how angry her husband's tone would make Jason. Knowing how awesome that anger could be.

Jason's voice was quiet when he spoke but that very quietness seemed to emphasise his anger, as if it was coming from a great depth. "Listen, *pal*, I was talking to your wife, in case you didn't notice. She's dealing with the Manor House purchase for me. But since you're so anxious to stick your oar in, what about your site in Ballyhaven? Ella has agreed to sell it to me."

"Hang on a second, Jason," Ella spluttered. "I told you that site is in joint ownership. I wouldn't, I couldn't agree to sell without Andrew's say-so."

"Really? You should have thought of that before you shook hands on the deal. In front of witnesses."

"Enough!" Andrew said, standing up and towering over Jason. "Don't try to be divisive. It won't work. You know damn well that agreement isn't binding. Don't try to bully your way into getting what you want."

Jason laughed, sat himself back in his chair and stared fearlessly up at Andrew. Hands in his trouser pockets he began to jingle change, the sound sharp and annoying in the tenseness of the office.

"True," he said at last. "No need at all for bullying. I'll get what I want anyway. I always do."

Andrew chose to read that as an apology. Or at least as much of an apology as he was ever going to get from this thug. He sat again on the corner of Ella's desk. And tried to smile at Jason. The man was, after all, a client.

"Why are you interested in the Ballyhaven site? I didn't think fifty acres of agricultural land in the county would hold any interest for you."

"How in the fuck could you know what interests me?" Jason snapped. "I, on the other hand, have an in-depth knowledge of your interests."

Ella felt her muscles tense as if preparing for a blow. She was. She had heard the threat in Jason's voice even if Andrew had not.

"What are you talking about now, Jason? I'm just trying to establish why you would want fifty acres in Ballyhaven."

"None of your goddamn business. All you need to know is how much I'm willing to pay. And what a bad enemy I could make if I'm pushed too far. "

Andrew stood up again but this time he walked across to his own desk and picked up the papers he had been working on. If he did not have something to occupy his hands there was a strong possibility that he would lash out at the smug face of Jason Laide.

"As far as Manor House is concerned," Andrew said as calmly as possible, "I'm afraid your engineer's report is still being examined. Also you should be aware that there's another offer in on the property. That bid is higher than yours."

Jason, small in stature, though very muscular, seemed to swell in his chair. His eyes changed from pale blue to a clear icy hue. Ignoring Andrew, he turned his stare on Ella.

"Why in the hell didn't you tell me I'd been outbid? Who's bidding against Jason Laide? Forget that engineer's report. I'll take the bloody place as is. And I'll top the other offer."

Ella felt rather than saw Andrew's warning gaze. It was telling her not to make any agreement. To stall Jason Laide. He was, of course, protecting Maxine Doran's interests. Protecting Maxine Doran. Pig!

"Certainly, Jason. As you wish. But I'll have to get back to Rob Trevor."

"And our other bidder," Andrew added.

Jason stood and pushed his chair back under the desk. He turned to face Andrew.

"I hope you enjoyed your weekend, Andrew. You certainly looked as if you were having a good time."

Then he turned and walked out of the office, leaving both Fords staring after him.

"What in the hell was all that about?" Ella asked.

Andrew didn't answer. He didn't have to. They both knew that they had been threatened by Jason Laide.

"Well?" she prompted. "The weekend. What was he talking about? What did you get up to?"

"We must talk, Ella. We have things to sort out."

So! Now she knew. Andrew had spent the weekend with Maxine Doran. Jason Laide knew too. There were certainly things to sort out. Like separations and divorces, ending marriages, saying goodbye . . . Ella's phone rang and she grabbed it as if it was a lifeline.

"This is Dr Sheehan's secretary, Mrs Ford. We have a cancellation this morning and I was wondering if it would suit you to come in earlier than you had planned."

Ella frowned. She had completely forgotten her follow-up appointment with Peter Sheehan after her most recent visit to the hospital. She looked up at Andrew and saw the concern and sadness in his eyes. The pity. She wanted none of it. She spoke into the phone.

"Yes. That's fine. When will I come in?"

"Now, if it suits you."

"See you in ten minutes then."

Ella put the phone down, grabbed her bag and walked

out of the office she shared with her husband. Outside, the breeze tossed her hair again and jangled her earrings. She tried to recapture the buoyant mood of earlier but a huge lump of overwhelming sadness lodged in her throat. She swallowed hard and hurried off to keep her appointment with Dr Peter Sheehan.

Chapter 24

Jason broke every rule of safe driving as he crossed the city from Ford Auctioneers to the complex which housed the Planning Office. It was time to get tough with those snotty Fords and he knew just how to do it. She would be easy. She was almost over the edge anyway. He was a different story. Jason sensed a core of steel underneath the polite veneer of Andrew Ford. The prick needed a good kick in the arse to wake him up to reality. Breaking yet another rule of the road, Jason tapped in Gussie's mobile number and spoke to him as he drove along. Satisfied that he had a nice surprise organised for Andrew Ford, he turned his attention to Oliver Griffin.

"I'm sorry, Mr Griffin is at a meeting," the receptionist told him when he arrived at the Planning Office.

"Give me a piece of paper," Jason demanded. Tongue between his teeth he carefully penned a note. "Get that to him. It's urgent."

The girl hesitated at first but then she read the anger

in the pale blue eyes. "I'll see what I can do."

Jason sat into one of the plush chairs, knowing that he would not have long to wait. The look on Oliver Griffin's face as he followed the girl into the reception area was gratifying. It was a mixture of outrage and blind panic.

"Mr Laide," he said, barely concealing the quiver of fear in his voice, "would you like to come into my office?"

Jason stood and followed Oliver along endless acres of green-carpeted corridor lined by identical doors leading off left and right with regular monotony. They came to a door with a plaque marked *'Head of Planning'*. Oliver ushered Jason in and then firmly shut the door before letting all his indignation and utter horror pour out.

"What in the hell are you doing here, Jason? We have an agreement. Our business is private. You're not supposed to bother me at work."

Jason watched as Oliver Griffin unravelled in front of him. Even his suit seemed to bag and wrinkle as the man shrank into a defensive ball, face pale, fists bunched.

"Bothering you, am I?" Jason asked with a smile.

Oliver plopped onto his chair behind the desk. It was more a falling down than a sitting. He clasped his hands together and put them up on the desk but still they shook.

"I know I'm a bit late with payments but my youngest has First Holy Communion soon."

"Aah! Nice white frock, clothes for the family and meal out. Sacraments are expensive these days, aren't they?"

Not knowing how to answer, Oliver bowed his head. He could try begging. It had worked before. He should be humble, show gratitude but he had not yet lost enough self-respect to do that. But time was running out. Laide had upped the ante by coming here. He could never deny now that he knew the creep.

"You know what I want, Chief Planner," Jason said sarcastically. "And it's not your piddling little repayment, even though I'll have that too."

The shaking travelled from Oliver's hands right through his body. He put his feet up on the footrest under his desk, afraid that his shoes would tap out the rhythm of his shivering on the floor. He now owed Jason Laide almost half a million. Half the value of his home. All built up over the years by a grand here and a grand there. How could he have been so stupid? So sick. So gullible. He thought of his daughter, with her blonde curls and baby soft skin, eyes shining with the excitement of her First Holy Communion. He thought of his wife, making a production out of the day. Only the best would do, which in her view was the most expensive. Tricia bought price-tags, satisfied that whatever was attached to the highest tag was the best. He could sell the house. Clear his mortgage and his debt to Jason Laide in one sweep. Owe nothing. Own nothing. Have nothing. And then what? He cleared his throat to shift the choking fear.

"I've given you what you asked for, Jason. I let you know which area was being targeted for the casino. I can't do any more."

"Don't fuck around with me, Griffin. You can tell your politician buddy McEvoy that my name is on that licence. Nobody else is to get a look in."

"How do you think that could be done? Stipulate that only jumped-up criminals may apply for the casino licence?"'

Both men sat in shocked silence, Oliver shocked that he had had the stupidity and lack of wit to speak the truth and Jason that his once pliable lackey was fighting back. Sweat broke out on both of them. With Oliver it prickled his back and armpits. On Jason it formed tiny beads around his receding hairline. Outside the office phones rang, doors banged, people laughed and had indecipherable conversations. Inside, all was silent. A standoff. Oliver's last vestige of self-respect kept him from apologising. Jason's self-image would never allow him to accept an apology. Griffin had marked his card.

"You've fucked up good now," Jason said at last. "I could call in your markers. I could and I will destroy you. What's your wife going to say? Your shitty work colleagues? Your snobby friends? The high and mighty Oliver Griffin, Chief Planning Officer. A gambler. A debtor. A cheat and liar. And you've the gall to talk down to me! You'll end up a hobo. Living in a cardboard box."

Oliver bowed his head. He could not bear to let Jason see the tears in his eyes. He blinked. The hot, salty liquid trickled out of the corners of his eyes. Raising his hand, he brushed the tears away as quickly as possible but not, he knew, before the thug watching him had witnessed yet another sign of his weakness.

"Not much point in blubbering now," Jason sneered. "You're in too deep. You should have thought of this when you placed your first bet. What was it? When did you start? The poker school in college, was it? Or maybe you were still in short pants when you started."

Oliver's mouth gathered into a tight, bitter line. He had not started gambling until he had met Tricia. Until she had taken to spending what they had not got. It had begun as a desperate attempt to increase his income, a blind faith in luck. Horses, dogs, cards. It had ended up in desperation. If only he had cut his losses early on. Got help, counselling, before the adrenalin rush of the chance to win had became the only hope in his life. He was gone past blaming Tricia now. She too was a victim of this mania. This sickness. Except that she didn't know it. Yet.

Oliver lifted his head. He shivered again as he was speared by the full gaze of Jason's cruel eyes. There was no mercy in this man. No honour.

"I think it's time to tell the truth, Jason," Oliver said, hating the whine in his own voice. "The help I can give you is limited. I've told you where the casino is going to be built. That gives you a head-start. I can't do any more. Andrew Ford's site is crucial to the whole development. It's in the centre of the area being earmarked for the casino. If you already own that when the project is put up for tender, then you would have a big advantage. But I can't guarantee that you will get the casino licence. Maybe they will opt to grant the development to one person and the licence to run the casino to someone else. I don't know and I can't do anything about it. Neither can Pascal McEvoy."

"You fucking liar! You've led me up the garden path!" Jason thumped the desk. Pens rattled in the holder and papers shook in the trays. Beads of sweat glistening, veins standing out on his forehead, eyes bulging, Jason Laide was awesome. "I want it all! I want the site, I want to develop it according to my own plans and I want the licence to run the casino. Do you understand? I want it all! And half a million in IOU's says you'll bloody well get it for me."

Oliver sat back in his chair, subconsciously trying to put distance between himself and the violent man sitting across from him. For the first time he actually looked into Jason Laide's eyes and saw shrewdness, cruelty, but no intelligence. The man was a moron. He did not have any grasp of the intricacies of the legislation, the licensing system and the planning involved in the super casino project. Oliver had assumed a man as successful in business as Laide appeared to be would have researched the procedures. Or at least have somebody do it for him. He must have legal advisors and accountants in his employ. The respectable face of Laide Transport. Oliver had always believed that Jason was in charge. That he knew the overall picture and had contacts in all the other departments where decisions were being made. His childish, desk-thumping outburst had shown a different side to Jason. A very ignorant and stupid side. Not the behaviour of a man in control. Nor of a successful entrepreneur.

Oliver felt a little confidence, a little hope return. Jason Laide was still a backstreet boy. A petty criminal trying to punch above his weight. His transport business was a huge success, yes. There were rumours of art collections and property portfolios. But he was basically a very stupid, if lucky, bully. How in the hell did he think he was going to get this project when he had no history in property development or gaming? It was then that Oliver remembered the Dutchman. Van Aken. Dirk Van Aken. A continental version of Jason Laide. They had met in the little rabbit warren of a house where Jason liked to conduct meetings. What had they said that day? Wasn't it that Van Aken had a business supplying gaming machines? Yes. Oliver remembered now. The proud, almost childish boast of Jason as he announced that Dirk owned the biggest gaming machine company in Europe. And that he would be supplying equipment for the casino which both thugs were certain they would be running in Ballyhaven. They were in it together, Laide and Van Aken. A partnership of silk suits, gold chains and shady histories.

"Are you going to apply for this licence in your own name or are you forming a partnership with Van Aken?"

"None of your fucking business!" Jason shot back.

And Oliver knew then that Jason did not really know what to do. He knew just one way. Bullying, blackmail, cheating. Nothing mattered as long as he got what he wanted.

"You do realise that all the information will be in the public arena very soon. There will be a lot of interest in that licence. Many people will apply and each will be scrutinised for income tax compliance and source of funding."

Jason threw back his head and laughed. "You! Advising me on money matters! That's rich! I have people I pay huge retainers to sort those things for me. I have no worries there. The money problems are yours."

Oliver stood. They would be wondering at the meeting where he had got to. He leaned his hands on the desk for support and tried to look as if he was in command of the situation.

"Go and talk to your expensive advisors, Jason. They'll confirm what I've told you. What you should have known. You can bid for the licence but nobody, and I mean nobody, can guarantee it for you. You can bully me all you like but it won't get the licence for you. Remember too that other bidders will be trying to use whatever influence they have. I'm sorry but I must go now."

"You ponce! You'll make sure I get that licence. You and that political friend of yours. Tell McEvoy that I was asking for him. And his son. Terrible what kids get up to these days. And your payment better be passed on to me before the weekend. Or else . . ."

Oliver managed to hold himself together while he ushered Jason out of his office and back to reception. As he watched Jason strut toward the lift to the ground floor, Oliver's knees began to feel weak. When the doors of the lift closed, bile rose in his throat. Jesus! Pascal's child! Laide had something on Pascal's child! And he was evil enough to use it. Pascal should be warned. Oliver barely made it to the bathroom before the vomit spewed out of his mouth.

* * *

There was no waiting in reception today. No flicking through magazines. Ella was ushered straight through to

Peter Sheehan's office. He came out from behind his desk, hand proffered in greeting. He was wearing jeans and a moss green sweater which enhanced the green of his eyes and his well-defined muscles. Ella blushed when she realised that she was staring at him. But then he was looking closely at her too.

"You look very well, Ella," he said. "Sit down and tell me how you feel."

Ella sat and glanced around the room, trying to find something on which to focus. Maybe the big window with the view of rooftops and scudding clouds through the slats of the cream Venetian blind. Maybe not. The abstract paintings, all rusts and greens with daubs of yellow. No. Her eyes were drawn back again to Peter Sheehan. The clearness of his green gaze reminded her of spring. The translucence of a leaf with the sun shining through its newly unfurled greenness. A lime-tree leaf perhaps. Tall and straight. Yes. Peter Sheehan was a lime tree. And he wanted to know how she felt.

"I nearly died."

"Yes," Peter agreed. "You were lucky to survive the accident."

"No. Not that. I nearly died this weekend. I almost drowned. The water was rising and rising and I was stranded on a rock."

He said nothing. Just sat there waiting for her to go on. Waiting for her to speak her most intimate thoughts. To explain herself. To put sounds to her innermost feelings. To pour out her fears and hopes wrapped up in vowels and consonants. The sounds of suffering. All the pain of the past year, the blackness, the coldness, the terror, the haunting, welled up in her throat. It was a hard, hot lump and it was choking her. She opened her mouth to gulp for air and words came tumbling out.

"I've been unhappy for a long time. I thought I wanted this life. The business, the status, the money. It was what I had worked so hard to get. I couldn't let myself admit that my life was empty. Pointless. No warmth. No friendships. Just business contacts. No love. Only a business partnership. I worked harder, made more money, became more successful. And pretended more."

The lump in Ella's throat began to hurt. Tears filled her eyes and then spilled over. Peter Sheehan reached into his desk, took out a box of tissues and wordlessly pushed them towards her. She loosened a wad of tissue and dabbed at her eyes but the tears continued to flow and the words to tumble.

"You were right when you said the answer to my problems lay in what I wasn't facing. I believed Karen Trevor was haunting me, taking over my life. But it was the opposite way around. I was taking over her death. Using the accident as an excuse not to take responsibility for my future. My only way forward is to admit that I have taken the wrong path. And not just in career choice. Andrew and I have a close bond. We care for each other. But it's not love. It was a union of ambitions. Not his fault. Not mine. Just a mistake."

Sobs wracked Ella's body now as the lump in her throat dissolved in a flood of scalding tears. Unstoppable, unrelenting, the torrent flowed, carrying with it the flotsam and jetsam of disappointment, fear and failure.

"I let my parents down. I wasn't there for them when I should have been. I let Andrew down. I'm not the wife he expected me to be. I let myself down. I've been weak and self-indulgent . . ."

Peter's hand shot up, palm towards her. "Whoa there! Not so fast, Ella. You seem to have a lot of guilt issues. Let's break them down. Take them one at a time. Your parents, how did you let them down?"

Ella grabbed another bunch of tissues and tried to dry her face. The tissue turned into a sodden mass instantly. She mopped again with a fresh bunch. Where were all the tears coming from? From their hiding place, of course. When had she last cried? Really cried with the abandon and relief of a child. It must have been during her first term in boarding school. Before she had become strong and ambitious. Before college, the city, Andrew, her parents' accident. Peter Sheehan sat still, watching, waiting for her answer. Her words were hiccoughed out, mixed with sobs and gasps for breath.

"Once I left for college, I rarely went back to Cuanowen to see my parents. I was an only child. They idolised me, yet I didn't make the time to see them. They died in a plane crash. Together. My last farewell to them was a phone call. I never thanked them. Never really told them how much I loved them."

"Did they come to see you much?"

"No. They did come to visit of course. Every Christmas time. Maybe a summer visit too. But no. They didn't like the city."

"Did they ever tell you that you should visit them more? Were they unhappy not to see you often?"

Ella stopped twisting the bundle of soggy tissues in her hand. She stared at Peter Sheehan but she was not really seeing him. She was too busy looking back. Remembering little snatches of conversation, cameos of time she had spent with her parents. Gradually a picture emerged of a couple who were very contented to be together and extremely proud of their daughter. She could not recall one, not even one occasion when they had said they were unhappy with Ella or that she should visit them more often. They had never wished her anything but happiness. So why had she tortured herself with guilt? If they had not felt neglected by her, why had she looked back and regretted not visiting them more? It was, of course, because she had needed them more than they needed her. And she had been afraid to admit that need. Until now.

"To answer your question, Peter, no. They never said I was a bad daughter. Never made any demands on my time. They gave me what they believed would arm me for life. Education and independence. And then they got on with their own lives and allowed me to do the same."

"So why are you guilty?"

Ella smiled, conscious of how gross a mess she looked at this stage. Even her waterproof mascara must be running in muddy streaks down her face.

"I'm not. I'm regretful. I know I should have gone to see them more often. They would have liked that. It would have made me a stronger person too. I probably didn't want to compare my relationship to theirs."

"Aah! Your marriage."

The lump in her throat began to grow again. Hotter, harder this time. Ella fought the urge to swallow it, to allow it back into its hiding place. To wallow in darkness behind the spectre of Karen Trevor. She opened her mouth to speak but no sound emerged. It took huge effort, both physical and mental to push the first word out.

"Affair."

Peter Sheehan did not react. He sat, watching cat-like with those green eyes. Sleek and powerful like a tiger. Or a cheetah. Prepared to pounce but willing to wait.

"Andrew is having an affair," Ella said more strongly this time. "And the saddest part is that I've told myself I'm jealous. But I'm not. I'm disappointed. Furious that he's lying to me. But not jealous. What does that mean?"

"What do you think?"

Annoyed, Ella sat up straighter and leaned towards Peter Sheehan. "I see. The psychiatrist game now, is it?"

"Psychologist."

"Whatever! I'm not a procedure. A theory. I need your input, not a series of questions throwing my problems back on me. I've carried them alone for too long. Do you realise that a worry is heavy, that sadness has weight? I can't do this on my own."

Ella heard the anger in her own voice and realised she was transferring blame unfairly onto Peter Sheehan. Another cop-out.

"I'm sorry. That wasn't fair. The truth is Andrew and I have been together since we were freshmen in college. We have become a habit. Our business, Ford Auctioneers, is our child. We created it, nurtured it and have watched it grow. But that's not enough any more. For either of us."

"Have you spoken to Andrew?"

Ella shook her head. "Not yet. But I will."

"What about the marriage counselling I spoke about? Would you like me to give you some contact numbers?"

Ella stood and tried to gather any bit of pride she had left together.

"I've gone through hell to get to this stage of honesty, Peter. I don't need anybody else to tell me about my marriage. It's easy. Andrew and I don't love each other. Not in the way my parents did. Not in the 'til death us do part way. That's what I have to face. Alone. I won't be hiding behind Karen Trevor any more."

Peter nodded and a slow smile spread across his face. His eyes crinkled at the corners and years seemed to fall away as his white teeth flashed. He looked very young.

"I'm waiting for you to fire me again, Ella."

She responded to the twinkle in his eye and laughed too. The sound startled her at first. It was a genuine chuckle, full of warmth and enjoyment. Another visitor from her past.

"You're fired! Your job is done. The rest I must handle myself. But thank you."

"You don't have to be alone. I'm always here for you, in my professional capacity or . . ."

Or what? He was still sitting in his cat-like pose, ready to react. It would be nice to feel there was someone to talk to. Somebody on her side. Even if it was only her psychologist.

"May I ring you?" he asked.

"Yes. Please do," Ella answered before picking up her bag and making straight for the bathroom.

When she looked in the mirror she was horrified. Her mascara had indeed run and her eyes, nose and cheeks were red and puffy. It took her fifteen minutes to repair the damage to her make-up. Then she picked up her bag and, chin up, went to try to repair the damage to her life. And this time, she was not going to hide behind any spectres, real or imagined.

Chapter 25

Frau Henner's home was as solid and practical as the woman herself. There were no unnecessary frills and flounces. Set on the rocky slopes of the Mönchsberg Mountain, it overlooked the roofs and spires of the old town of Salzburg. The house was warm, clean and functional. Sharon loved being here. She liked the safe feeling of the heavy Germanic furniture which somehow seemed to fit perfectly into the compact rooms. It was now, as it had been since she had met Frieda, her refuge.

Sharon finished the hot chocolate Frieda had made for her and laid her head back against the headrest of the big leather chair. She would love to close her eyes and sleep. For just ten minutes. A little oblivion. A Jason-free, decision-free oasis.

"Well," Frieda said, "what are you going to do? You know you can't go on like this any more. It's not right. Not fair on –"

"I know! I know!" Sharon cut in impatiently and

immediately regretted her brusqueness. She smiled an apology at Frieda. They understood each other well enough to preclude the need for words. Sharon's hand went automatically now to her throat and lay protectively over the area Jason had bruised. Frieda saw the movement and immediately tried to push her advantage home.

"You see! He nearly killed you. Are you going to wait for him to find out? What do you think he'll do then? Pat you on the head?"

"Yes, I do believe he would. With a hammer."

"So! Are you just going to wait for that to happen?"

"Of course not. But it's not as simple as I thought it would be."

"Divorce him. How complicated is that?"

Sharon did close her eyes now but it was not to grab some badly needed rest. It was to review her situation, yet again. Everything swam around in her head making her feel dizzy and nauseous. She opened her eyes to find herself under the stern gaze of the woman who had become the only constant support in a life that was crumbling apart.

"You haven't told me everything, have you?" Frieda asked.

Sharon bowed her head. She was ashamed to meet the questioning grey eyes. Ashamed to admit that she had been so misguided, so stupid as to marry a man like Jason Laide. Ashamed of the secret she had kept for the past few days. Ashamed to share what she had found in the safe in Junkergasse. Frieda leaned down towards her now and laid her strong hand on her shoulder.

"It's the envelopes, isn't it, Sharon? The ones you asked me to keep here."

Sharon nodded. "Papers, photos, videos. Filth, blackmail, dirt!" Relieved now to get at least one of her guilty secrets off her mind Sharon continued more vehemently. "He's evil, Frieda. I knew when I married him that he was a rough diamond. There was a time when I thought that quality attractive. But I never knew he was so unspeakably bad. Never knew what he was storing in the safe in Junkergasse. What you now have hidden in your attic. No wonder he was angry with me. That little stash must be worth a fortune to him."

"He's blackmailing people?"

"Yes. He seems to have something on almost everyone. Affairs, visits to brothels, evidence of bribe taking, stacks of IOUs. He has people from every walk of life under his control. Even a pornographic video of a leading supermodel when she was little more than a child. He's vile! I can't believe I helped him. How could I have been so naïve? I couldn't have been, could I? I must have known these things he was asking me to stash for him were at the very least illegal."

"You had other things on your mind," Frieda said calmly. "Besides, it could be to your advantage now. This stack of blackmail material will give you a lever. Something to fight him with."

"No. I can't do that!" Sharon said quickly. "That would make me as twisted as him. I'm going to give these things back to the people he is torturing. I must break the stranglehold he has over their lives. Try to make amends for my part in it."

Frieda walked across the room and slowly eased herself into an armchair opposite Sharon. She folded her hands together on her lap. Chair and woman blended to become a unit. Restful. Strong. Sharon smiled at her.

"You're going to lecture me now, aren't you?"

"I'm going to try to advise you," Frieda replied quietly. "Of course you must free those people your husband has treated so badly but you must protect yourself first. Have you decided to stay here when you have divorced him?"

"I can't, can I?"

"He'll track you down wherever you go, especially when he knows everything."

"No! Never! He can't know. He must never know."

Levering herself up from the depths of her comfortable chair, Frieda came and stooped down in front of Sharon.

"He has a right to know, Sharon. Besides, if you tell him yourself, he loses some of his power. You can't spend your life running away."

"But he won't give me a divorce if he knows. He'll take control. Exert his evil influence . . ."

Frieda stood up abruptly. "Get your coat. We're going to the hospital. You need treatment for that bruise on your throat. You need evidence. I'm your witness to domestic violence. And the collection of blackmail material in my attic is your insurance. Now get yourself ready and come on."

Sharon put her hand on Frieda's strong arm. "I'll go to the hospital with you. But I must, must, free those people

Jason has been blackmailing. I had a part to play in that too. I'll never rest until I've tried to right that wrong. Will you help me?"

Frieda smiled and hauled Sharon out of the chair. "You're a very stubborn woman. You should be worrying about yourself now, not other people. But of course I'll help you any way I can. Now come on to the hospital. No more delaying."

Obediently, Sharon put on her coat, picked up her bag and allowed Frau Henner to lead her north to the Landeskrankenhaus Hospital.

They did not notice O'Shaughnessy as he tailed them, discreetly taking photos.

* * *

Andrew swept a stack of paperwork aside and propped his elbows on his desk. He could not concentrate. The threat of Jason Laide's words this morning had been quickly followed by a phone call from Gary Cox. A strident Gary Cox whom Andrew had never encountered before. The implication was that the Cox brothers' continued association with Ford Auctioneers depended on their getting the Ballyhaven site. Hobson's choice.

Cox's threat was clear. A huge drop in turnover for Andrew and Ella. Jason Laide's threat was murkier and more terrifying. What in the hell was he hinting at? He knew about Maxine obviously, but how did he intend using the information? By telling Ella?

Andrew dropped his head onto his hands as he

thought of his wife. He must talk to her this evening, but which Ella would she be by then? The one who was in a perpetual fog, eyes glazed, withdrawn, out of touch with reality or the person who went scurrying around the place, making questionable deals and having accidents? Or maybe the different Ella he had seen briefly this morning, bright-eyed and smiling. Until Jason Laide had made his veiled threats. Then she had been the fleeing Ella, running away from reality, from life.

A knock on the office door startled him. He straightened up and ran his hands through his hair just as one of the girls from the front office came in. She was carrying a large white envelope.

"A courier dropped this in for you, Andrew. It's marked for your attention so I don't know what it's about."

The girl placed the envelope on Andrew's desk and stood there. Some instinct told Andrew that he needed privacy before opening the delivery.

"That's fine, thank you," he said to the girl, giving the impression it was something he had been expecting to be delivered.

It was. His hands shook as he tore open the flap. The shaking spread to his body as he drew out the photograph. It was in colour and very clear even though it had been taken at night, as he and Maxine had slept in the guest room of his home, naked, entwined, sated. He picked up the envelope and shook it, then ripped it flat open just to be sure. There was no note. He grabbed the internal phone and buzzed the front desk.

"Who delivered that envelope?"

"A courier. He wore a helmet and leathers so he was obviously a bike courier. He didn't have a delivery docket though. Is there a problem, Andrew?"

"No, none at all," Andrew lied and then put down the phone.

Fuck! Laide was really prepared to play hardball. And it wasn't just Andrew's reputation at risk. Maxine's career could suffer too. And what would this do to Ella? Damn Jason Laide!

The door opened again. Andrew grabbed the photo and quickly flipped it upside down. Ella stood in the open doorway, her eyes puffy, her nose slightly red but her shoulders thrown back and her chin held high.

"More secrets, Andrew?"

"Just sorting through some stuff here," he answered as casually as possible. "Time for a spring clean, I think."

Picking up the photo, picture side turned into his body, he walked over to the shredder and watched until the last millimetre had been drawn into the churning blades. When he looked up, Ella was still standing at the door, her gaze steady.

"I agree, Andrew. It's time for a spring clean. Why don't we go some place we can talk? We can't keep putting it off for ever."

Andrew looked at the woman who had shared his bed, his business, his life for so long. For the first time he felt not just regret but a deep sadness at the thought of a future without her by his side. He nodded his head slowly.

"You're right, Ella. We must talk. Where?"

"How about the Ballyhaven site? It's quiet and private there. And we still own it."

Andrew smiled at the irony of the location she had chosen. He shut down his computer. He would not be doing any further work today. By tacit agreement, they each took their own cars. There was after all, a strong possibility that they would be going in different directions by the time they had finished the spring clean of their lives.

* * *

Ella was first to arrive at the broken-down gate which was the most convenient entrance to the Ballyhaven site. She opened the boot of her car and hesitated for a moment before taking out a box and opening it up. Then she kicked off her high heels and put on the expensive red leather shoes Jason Laide had given her in the hospital, glad now that she had felt uncomfortable enough about the gift to hide it in her car. Not a good match for her pink jacket but then colour co-ordination was the least of her problems at the moment. She watched as Andrew approached, his face solemn. He was driving slowly. Not something that came naturally to him. Nothing about this situation was natural.

He got out of his car and stood in front of her.

"Will we walk?" he asked.

Silently Ella headed for the gate and scaled it with ease. She was getting good at this. Andrew followed and they set off. They did not have to discuss the direction. Both knew they were headed for the glade. The place which had once been special to them.

Ella glanced around her as she trudged along. It seemed to her that nature was setting a very apt backdrop to the death of her marriage. Underfoot, the ground was sodden, needing to be ploughed through rather than walked on. The red leather shoes were by now frilled by layers of squelchy mud. The sky was grey, low, promising rain and darkness. Ahead the trees of the little glade they used to call their forest stood stark against the skyline. Today they seemed cold and unwelcoming, their very stillness a judgment.

Ella led the way to the big oak and, mindless of the damp ground underneath her, sat with her back against the gnarled trunk. Andrew sat down beside her. A crow squawked, nearby the brook gurgled, a twig snapped, a pigeon filled the air with its plaintive coo – but Ella and Andrew were silent. Prepared speeches were forgotten as they sat side by side and each absorbed pain from the other. Andrew reached for Ella's hand and held it tightly. She returned the pressure of his fingers.

"I'm so sorry, El," he whispered.

"Do you love Maxine Doran?"

His lips moved but no sound came out. Ella squeezed his hand.

"Yes. I do," he whispered. "How long have you known?"

Ella withdrew her hand and turned to face her husband. There were tears in his eyes. His beautiful dark-blue eyes with the curling lashes. She lifted her hand and touched his cheek.

"A while. But I didn't allow myself to admit it until recently. I'm glad it's out in the open now. I want you to be happy, Andy. You've been good to me. But we're not right for each other. We're a business, not a relationship. We both deserve better."

Ella watched as disbelief and relief chased across his face. Her words seemed to lift a weight from him. He raised an eyebrow.

"You've met someone too?"

"In a way, I have." Ella smiled at his puzzled frown. "Not a man. I've rediscovered Ella Deasy and I want to get to know her better. If that sounds like weird psychobabble, it probably is. It's very difficult to put logical words to the illogicality of my life for the past year."

"It's bound to have been confusing. You had a very serious accident. I didn't always have the patience I should have had with your slow recovery."

"Aah! The accident. My excuse. My shelter."

"What do you mean?"

Ella picked up a curled leaf from the ground and began to smooth it out. It crumbled in her hand. Rubbing her palms together to free them from the debris of the decayed leaf, she took a deep breath.

"Andy, can we be really honest with each other at this stage? It might be more painful now but it would mean we could both go forward with a clean slate."

He nodded his agreement and then Ella tried to explain to him – and to herself – why she had married him in the first place, how she had come to realise that she did not really love him as a wife should a husband, how she now knew that their relationship must end.

"Peter Sheehan somehow unlocked the paralysis in my mind. I think he did it by very skilfully and calmly encouraging me to find the answers myself. "

"Yes. Post Traumatic Stress Disorder is his field."

"But that wasn't the problem. Not really. Yes, I was getting flashbacks to the accident but not of the crash itself. What haunted me and took over my life was the ghost of Karen Trevor."

"Ghost!"

Ella laughed as she saw the expression on Andrew's face. He was clearly thinking that she was still crazy.

"Of course not," she said quickly. "There are no ghosts. I allowed my imagination run riot. I obsessed about Karen Trevor, saw her everywhere. And she was always in the throes of dying. Screaming. She took over my life."

"So all the times you were pale and shaking and terrified, you were seeing Karen Trevor? Or thought you were."

"True. I could hardly tell you that, could I? Even on my worst days, when Karen shadowed me from dawn to dusk, when I could feel her coldness on my skin, when I believed she would suck the life from me, I still knew that she was a secret I should not share. So I stayed silent instead. Eventually I admitted to myself that I was using these illusions as an excuse. I didn't have to move on from the time of the accident as long as the haunting was happening. I was hiding behind Karen Trevor and what I was hiding from was my life in general and my marriage in particular."

"It wasn't that bad!" Andrew protested.

Ella smiled at him. "No. We were very happy while we were building up the business. Remember? We were happy when we bought this site. Another acquisition for the Fords. But why do you think we never seriously planned a family? Wasn't that always a vague plan off in the distant future? Why were our conversations always about work and never about us? We agreed to be honest today, didn't we?"

Andrew lowered his head and stared at the ground for what seemed like a long time. When he looked up he seemed older.

"Honesty it is then. You're right. We worked so hard to compensate for the lack of passion between us. We're a good team. In business."

"Exactly. But a balance sheet is cold comfort. You've obviously found what I couldn't give you."

"About Max. I didn't deliberately . . . I never went out to . . ."

It was dusk now, that time of evening when the last rays of light pierced encroaching darkness with a red intensity. A beam pierced through the treetops and lit the area where they were sitting. Ella stared at her husband and knew that she had caused some of the white hairs and fine lines on his forehead. The last time she had really looked at him, a long time ago now, he had been raven-haired and smooth-skinned. They had scarred each other in a silent, cold way.

"You lied to me, Andrew. I'm disappointed about that. But I'm not jealous or resentful. Does Maxine love you?"

"I think so." Andrew hesitated before adding, "She's had a lot of trouble in her life. She has her secrets too."

"Talking of secrets, what were you trying to hide from me in the office this afternoon?"

Andrew shifted his position and suddenly seemed very intent on staring at the sunset. "A photograph," he mumbled.

"Of you and Maxine?"

He didn't answer.

"Andrew, remember we're being honest here . . ."

"It was taken while we were sleeping. Someone must have followed us and broken in."

"Of course the paparazzi would be interested in whatever Maxine was up to. She usually manages to avoid them pretty well. How come they found her this time?"

"I don't think it was the papers. Why would they send it anonymously to me?"

He did not have to mention Jason Laide. Ella remembered Jason's cryptic remarks this morning. Hints about Andrew's weekend. Jason was obviously prepared to stoop even lower than she had thought to get whatever he wanted. She looked down at her muddy red leather shoes and realised that her dealings with that thug had made the situation dangerously complicated.

"Why does Jason Laide so desperately want this site? He has already bought the pub in Ballyhaven village. What's going on here? Did you find out anything new from Oliver Griffin and Pascal McEvoy?"

By the time Andrew had finished explaining the new Gambling Bill and the plans for designating Ballyhaven as a custom-built gambling resort, the last rays of sun had disappeared. Ella at last understood why Jason had targeted their fifty-acre site. And why the Coxes wanted it too. And there would be many other bidders once the proposed bill was in the public domain. Laide and Cox just wanted to beat the rush. But Laide would make sure that he was the one who came out on top.

"Does Jason know that Maxine is the other bidder for Manor House?"

Andrew shook his head. "I don't think so. Unless you told him?"

Ella's angry look was answer enough. It was getting very cold now. Pulling her jacket close about her, she moved a little nearer to Andrew and peered up into his face.

"Here we go again, Andy, talking about business when we should be discussing us. What are we going to do about our marriage, our future?"

"What do you want to do?"

"I want a divorce."

Her words, loud and clear, seemed to echo around the glade. They were both shocked by the baldness of her statement. Andrew stood and held his hand out to her. She felt stiff, cold and damp when she got up. Standing close together, they shared the sadness, the sense of failure.

"If you're sure," Andrew said, implying that there was another way when they both knew there was not. Sorting out the details would take time. Division of assets and finances. But there was no division of opinion. They both knew their future would not be spent together.

Ella shivered. The glade was no longer a place of shelter and beauty. It was dark and threatening, each tiny sound magnified in the stillness.

"We should go home now, Andrew. Have a shower and something warm to eat before we get pneumonia."

Andrew took her hand and together they picked their way through the rough terrain of their fifty-acre site. Each step they took brought them further away from a marriage which had not worked. By the time they reached the gate they were each engrossed in thoughts of their own separate futures.

Chapter 26

Maxine stood on the balcony of the Royal Theatre Carré and looked out over the river Amstel from which Amsterdam had derived its name. It was already dark though it was only seven o'clock in the evening. She looked towards the lights of Magere Brug, the Skinny Bridge, and wished that Andrew was here with her to share this moment. She would love to tell him the myth of the Magere sisters who supposedly lived on opposite sides of the river and had this bridge built so that they could more easily visit each other. Even more she would like to tell him how much she missed him and wanted to be with him. Sighing she turned her back on the beauty of the darkly flowing river and prepared herself to return to the war zone the theatre had become since DiAngeli had arrived.

Chaos reigned inside the Carré. DiAngeli was prancing about, wringing his hands, shouting, tying his hair into a ponytail and then immediately ripping off the band and shaking the long white mane loose. He was as manic as Maxine had ever seen him. She sat quietly on her own in one of the plush red theatre chairs and watched as egos clashed. From her vantage point it was hard to decide if the eccentric designer or his highly paid supermodels were winning the battle of wits.

"This theatre was designed for circus acts," he whined, tears in his voice. "Why can't you see that? Since 1894 they have circus acts here and you tell me you won't co-operate. I have paid a ransom to rent Carré and now you all make trouble."

"I'm a model," Céline, the cream of French models, hissed. "I refuse to go on a trapeze."

A chorus of models, their agents, make-up artists, photographers, hairdressers, stylists, set designers, carpenters, electricians and everybody else concerned with the show joined in the argument. Maxine smiled to herself. Experience told her how this argument would end. What she did not know was how long it would take to settle. Time was moving on. The show was scheduled for tomorrow at three and they had not even had a rehearsal yet. Besides, she was meeting Dirk Van Aken at nine o'clock.

Leaving the relative peace of the body of the theatre she walked towards the stage where everyone was shouting and nobody listening. DiAngeli, stopping for a moment to twist the band around his ponytail, saw her coming.

"Maxine. You have worked for me many times. Tell them! Tell them they must show my designs the way I want. Only DiAngeli knows how DiAngeli designs should be shown!"

Maxine walked over to the little man with the big ego. Stooping she kissed him on the cheek. The group fell silent, each trying to second-guess DiAngeli's reaction.

"I know this collection has been inspired by a circus theme," Maxine said. "I've seen the ruffled collars, baggy pants, sequined body stockings. I also know you don't really expect the most successful and expensive models in the world to do trapeze acts, ride elephants, tame lions or whatever else it is you are asking. Am I right, Mr DiAngeli?"

His anger seemed to leave him in a rush of breath. He grinned and Maxine could see humour and shrewdness in equal measure reflected in his eyes.

"You know me too well. Don't blame me for trying though. It would have been spectacular."

Maxine smiled back at him, knowing that he was ready to behave sensibly now.

"So since you want a circus theme and you knew you would never convince your models to risk life and limb, you have hired a circus act? Professionals?"

"The works. Acrobats, clowns, trapeze artists. All tumbling and spinning around the theatre while you beauties glide along the catwalk. *Magnifico*?"

The protests began again but this time they were not as heated. DiAngeli produced the circus act he had had in waiting and rehearsals began in earnest. Maxine thought it safe then to ring Taxicentrale and order a car for later. DiAngeli was right about one thing. The collection and the show promised to be '*magnifico*'.

Tempers had cooled by the time rehearsals were over. While everyone else was regaining their equilibrium Maxine was growing more nervous by the minute. Her hands shook as she refreshed her make-up and brushed her hair. Her taxi was waiting when she arrived at the front entrance of the theatre. She hesitated for a moment, not sure she was up to meeting Dirk Van Aken again. Then she threw back her shoulders and took graceful strides towards the car. She must. Van Aken was her last, her only chance.

⋆ ⋆ ⋆

The journey was too short. Even before she had finished her pep talk to herself, Maxine's taxi pulled up outside the Moko bar. She felt her knees shake as she walked in. It was busy, with many customers occupying the range of designer chairs for which Moko was noted. In the far off right-hand corner, sitting on a chair which looked too delicate to support his weight, sat Dirk Van Aken. Maxine felt his piercing gaze from across the room. Forcing herself to smile, she headed in his direction. When she stood before him, hand held out in greeting, he stared at her from head to toe. Especially toe. God, no! A foot fetishist! He looked up from her gold strappy sandals with the three-inch heels and smiled.

"Very good, Maxine. I see you don't intend going out walking tonight."

He reached out for her hand then and shook it.

Maxine tried to return his handshake but her fingers refused to co-operate. Dirk was grinning at her, enjoying her discomfort.

"Have you eaten?" he asked.

"I have, thank you, but you order dinner if you want."

"No. I've already eaten. Follow me. There's someone I would like you to meet."

Maxine's instinct was to run for the exit, to race back to the safety of her hotel. Not an option, she told herself, and followed Dirk across the bar and out onto the terrace. It was quiet there with only a few people braving the chilly night to sit by the canal. Tables lit by lanterns were scattered about and Dirk headed for a table right by the edge of the terrace where a woman sat alone. She was dark-haired, well-built, with broad cheekbones. Maxine stood still beside the table. No way! Absolutely no way was she going to get involved in a trio!

"My wife Greta," Dirk said, laying his hand on the woman's solid shoulder. "Greta, this is Maxine, the model who blistered my feet by walking me from one end of her city to the other."

The woman laughed and held out her hand to Maxine.

"At last I meet the only person who has made my husband take exercise. Do sit down, Maxine. I would love to hear about the exciting world of modelling. I believe you are here for the DiAngeli show?"

The woman's voice was warm, her smile welcoming, her English only slightly accented. Confused, Maxine sat while Dirk ordered fruit-flavoured vodkas for them. There was something very unsettling about this scenario. Maybe it was just that it was so unexpected. She had anticipated sleaze. Van Aken looked no different. He still wore his silk suit and an array of gold jewellery. But yet Maxine sensed his respect for his wife, a wholesome connection between himself and the woman with the Slavic cheekbones which was so far removed from the foot fetishes and group sex she had feared that she blushed. She had never thought of Van Aken as a faithful husband. Thinking back to his trip to Ireland now she realised she had not been as clever then as she imagined. She had believed that her extensive walking tour had tired him out. That physical exhaustion had prevented him from pawing her. From running his slimy hands over her body. From humiliating her as Jason Laide did. It seemed now she may have been wrong. Maybe. And she had also assumed that if he had a wife she would be a stereotypical gangster's moll. This woman was . . . Maxine struggled to classify Greta as she examined the open, honest face and the full figure dressed in well-cut but unremarkable clothes.

"Is DiAngeli really as eccentric as he likes people to believe?" Mrs Van Aken asked.

Maxine smiled, remembering the chaos of tonight's rehearsal. "I think he likes to cultivate the mad genius image but behind it all he is a very astute businessman. He's difficult to work for but it's worth it just to wear his beautiful clothes."

"And the money," Dirk said. "His models are the highest paid, aren't they?"

"Believe me, we earn every cent of it!" Maxine laughed.

"Dirk brings everything back to money," Greta said but her tone was indulgent rather than critical.

Maxine seized the moment, not giving herself time to think. "Talking of money, that's why I wanted to see you, Dirk. I need some advice."

Leaning back in his chair Dirk laughed so loudly that heads turned in their direction. "I'm disappointed, Maxine. I knew you wanted something from me but never guessed it was just advice."

Greta turned her dark eyes on her husband and immediately he stopped laughing.

"I'm sorry," he said. "Go ahead. Ask."

Now that she had the opportunity Maxine was afraid to speak. Even though Dirk had this lovely warm woman by his side and even though he was probably not the lecher she had assumed him to be, he was still a friend and business associate of Jason Laide. That made him a dangerous man. If she said a wrong word, gave him the wrong impression, she could be in serious trouble. Even worse than she was in already. She cleared her throat.

"As you know, modelling is not a lifetime career. I'm looking to the future and I intend investing some of the money I've made. I'm going into the hotel business but it's a huge outlay. I have to take a business partner. I know Jason Laide is an associate of yours. Would you advise me to go into partnership with him?"

Dirk put his elbows on the table and moved closer to Maxine. His eyes and his jewellery glittered in the lantern light. Greta sat calmly beside him, sipping her vodka. As the Dutchman stared, Maxine became aware of the low buzz of conversation of the other patrons, the lap of the canal water, the rapid beating of her own heart.

"Why are you afraid of him?" he asked.

"I don't know what you mean."

"Don't lie to me. I saw the way you cringe in his company. I knew that you were afraid of me too but had to do what Jason told you. And we both know what he meant when he asked you to entertain me. You're a successful woman. You don't need him in your life. Has he got some hold over you?"

"No. He has not," Maxine said quickly. "I just know him for a long time."

"Then you should know not to go into business with him."

"*You* did."

Dirk picked up his glass, swallowed his drink in one gulp and put the glass back on the table with a sharp rap. Maxine was furious with herself. She had made him angry now. She looked towards Greta, silently pleading with her to calm her man.

"Another drink?" Dirk asked and before they could reply he had gone to the bar. Greta was staring across the table but Maxine could not read the expression in her eyes.

"What did you hope to gain from tonight, Maxine? Did you think you could get some information about Jason Laide by sleeping with my husband?"

Maxine felt the familiar heat of tears well up. Why was she sitting here, being quizzed by a gangster's wife, humiliating herself? Closing her eyes for one second she visualised Andrew. So handsome, so kind. So very good. Her eyelids flickered open and she felt stronger.

"What exactly is your husband's business link with Jason Laide?"

"Dirk supplies a wide range of commodities and Jason transports them to the Irish market."

"You're going to tell me gaming machines and other innocent things. Just like Jason has a haulage business. But Jason owns property all over the world, he has art collections and a seemingly endless supply of cash. I think his transport company is just a front."

"And you believe my company is just a front too," Dirk said from directly behind Maxine.

She jumped with fright. He must not have gone to the bar at all, instead staying in the shadows behind her to listen. Deciding that denying what she had said was pointless, she nodded her head in agreement. Dirk laughed and sat down again, wriggling into the chair to make himself comfortable.

"I think you should stop bullshitting, Miss Doran," he said in a voice that was quiet but menacing. "You've obviously come here to get some dirt on Jason Laide. Nothing at all to do with setting up in the hotel business. I don't blame you for that but if you think you are going to involve me or my company, you're making a big mistake. You're out of your depth, you silly woman. You know I could pick up the phone now and call Jason. How would you like that?"

Maxine's shiver of fear was answer enough.

Satisfied that he had her full attention, Dirk continued.

"I'm glad I went to Ireland to find out how Jason operates there. I saw for myself how reckless and stupid he is. In fact, I'm severing all links to him as soon as our current agreement is through. He's heading straight for disaster. I'm not going to get involved in his new project. Neither will he, unless he can run it from behind bars."

"Dirk has made some enquiries," Greta explained quietly. "That's why he went to Ireland. Your government, specifically your Criminal Assets Bureau, are beginning to show an interest in Jason Laide's affairs. His days are numbered. He's not going to bring us down with him."

Maxine could not help the smile of satisfaction which slipped across her face. For the first time ever she thought of Jason in gaol. She had often wished him dead but spending endless days and nights in prison was a far better punishment. She imagined his pasty face up against the bars, his icy-blue eyes pleading for freedom. But that might take a long time. Years of investigation, following paper trails, fighting in the courts.

Her smile faded. She had come here hoping, praying, Dirk Van Aken would confirm her suspicion that Jason Laide was involved in drug distribution. That he would give her evidence which she could throw in Jason's face, swop for the vile video of young Marie Murphy. Dirk was right. She was a silly woman. Had she really believed that Van Aken was going to admit he was the supplier? Which of course he probably was. But he and his wife were a very clever team. They would not have left any traces of their involvement. Nor would they ever give her anything to hold over Jason's head. Honour amongst thieves. She picked up her bag and stood.

"I'd better get back to my hotel. I've an early start in the morning. It was nice meeting you, Greta. Thanks for your time, Dirk."

Greta smiled at her and reached out to shake her hand. "Take care, Maxine. Don't go having any silly accidents."

Maxine looked into the woman's dark eyes and saw an impassiveness there. A detachment she had not guessed at. A fitting mate for Dirk Van Aken.

"We'll be following your career with interest," Dirk added.

The comment was full of threat. Maxine was tempted to assure them that she would never repeat any of their conversation or admit that this meeting had taken place. Instead she turned and walked away, knowing that any pleading would put her in an even weaker position. She was almost to the exit when she remembered something. A niggling question that needed an answer.

She went back to the table where the Van Akens were sitting, both now staring at her with the same impassive gaze. A match made in hell. Quelling her fear she asked her question.

"What's the new project? What's Jason getting involved in now?"

"Read your newspapers," Dirk said. "You'd better go now. Your car is waiting to take you to the Amstel Intercontinental."

"But I didn't order . . . How did you know where I was staying?"

"I have many friends both here and in Ireland. Take

care, Maxine. Goodbye."

When Maxine got outside the same taxi driver who had collected her from Carré was waiting to bring her to her hotel. Only when she was sitting in the car did she realise how very foolish her meeting tonight had been. The taxi was confirmation that Van Aken and his deceptively matronly wife were every bit as frightening as Jason Laide. She looked anxiously out her window, trying to remember landmarks, wondering if she was being driven to the Intercontinental at all. She even considered jumping out of the moving car. When at last the taxi pulled up in front of the hotel, she jumped out so quickly that she almost fell.

The first thing she did when she got to her room was to have a stiff drink. Then she rang Andrew. She needed to hear his voice. When she discovered that Andrew's phone was switched off she cried. It was a long, lonely time before Maxine finally slept.

* * *

Sharon Laide knelt on her case to close it. It was bulging. She hoped to spend only a few days in Ireland but had to allow for the fact that it could be weeks. Depending on how quickly she would be able to organise things. Depending on how Jason reacted.

Hauling the case off her bed she threw herself down and closed her eyes. The familiar smells and sounds of her Junkergasse home assailed her senses. She would miss this place so much. She hated leaving, even for a short time.

There was a calm atmosphere, a safe feeling about the old house which made her feel that here in Salzburg she had at last found her place. And it was more than just the three-storey nineteenth century building with the magnificently ornate fascia in which she lived, beautiful as that was. It was the hills and rivers, the winter snow and summer flowers, the clean air, the music, the history, the timelessness of Salzburg. And of course, above all, it was the presence, the precious existence, of the person she loved above all others. Maybe the only person she had ever really loved in her whole life. Her body shuddered as tears began to flow. How was she going to bear the separation?

A hand gently touched her hair. Sharon opened her eyes and smiled through her tears at Frau Henner. Frieda. Her rock.

"I see you're packed. What about these?"

Sharon looked at the bundle of files and padded envelopes Frieda held towards her. Jason's sorry pile of filthy blackmail.

"I'm taking them as hand luggage," Sharon said, sitting up and swinging her legs onto the floor. She took some tissues from the box on her bedside table and dried her eyes.

Frieda was looking suspiciously at the canvas holdall sitting on the bed beside Sharon's case. It was stuffed with tissue paper. "And what about this? What are you up to now?"

"I'm going to lose that," Sharon explained and then laughed at the expression on the other woman's face.

"Jason's expecting his 'business papers' as he calls them. I can't give them to him because I'll be handing them back to the people he tormented. And the rest, the accounts of his illegal financial dealings, they're in the bank vault in Geneva where I put them yesterday, so he can't have those either. Although he won't care much about that. He pays accountants and lawyers to square his books."

Frieda put her hands on her hips and stared at Sharon. "That still doesn't explain why you need to lose a bag stuffed with tissue paper."

"I have to make Jason believe that I've made every effort to bring his papers to him. I'll check this bag in for the flight and then dump it somewhere in the airport in Ireland. Then I'll report it missing."

"He will go mad if he thinks you lost his property."

"He'll blame the airline. Bullying them will keep him occupied while I'm contacting the people I need to. And since you told him yesterday when he rang that I had gone to Geneva, he won't suspect me. He'll be convinced I went there to take his documents out, not put them in. The terrified little wife, doing as she's told."

Frieda's frown of puzzlement changed to one of concern. "Why don't you think about your own safety and go straight to the police before it's too late?"

"I know him, Frieda. He's not a murderer. A thug, yes. But he'd never kill me. That's ridiculous."

"He tried to strangle you! Even now, you're not admitting the truth about the man you married!"

Sharon nodded slowly. Frieda was right. How could she admit the truth? The consequences of accepting that

Jason was a criminal and a potential murderer were unthinkable. She had laughed with him, talked with him, made love with him . . .

"You remember what they said to you in the hospital?" Frieda asked.

Sharon remembered too well. They had been so kind but very adamant in their warnings. With his penchant for putting his hands around her neck, Jason could so easily kill her, whether he meant to or not. "It was clever of you to insist on me going to the hospital," she said. "Is there anything you don't know about? I'm glad you were so familiar with the Austrian laws for medics, the ones you call Ärztegestetz. Especially the bit that makes it mandatory for the doctor to report an actionable assault to the police. I would never have gone to the hospital myself. "

"At least it's some threat against him. He'll be arrested and charged if he tries to come back to Austria. It would have been wrong not to go. You let him get away with it for too long."

Getting up, Sharon walked over to the window and looked out beyond the little courtyard onto the street below. The frosted cobbles were glistening in the streetlights. A young couple were walking along, arm in arm, heads close together. Just as she and Jason had once done. She turned her back on them, walked over to Frieda and hugged her. She felt safe in the warm embrace.

"I'll look after everything while you're gone," Frieda said. "All you have to do is rid yourself of Jason Laide and come back safely to us."

Sharon tried to smile but the fear gripping her whole body was affecting her facial muscles. Pokerfaced, she picked up the phone and rang Jason to inform him she would be on the early flight in the morning.

He was excited, a touch of the old Jason.

"And what about my business files?" he asked. "Did you get them? When I rang yesterday that old bag of a housekeeper said you were in Switzerland."

"Yes, Jason. I have your material."

"That's my girl. Wait until you see Manor House. Fit for a princess. As a matter of fact, I'm going to get on to the owner this minute. Fuck the estate agents. Those Fords are useless. I'll finalise the deal myself. You'll be coming home to a mansion. Nothing too good for Jason Laide's wife! Isn't that right?"

"That's right, Jason," Sharon agreed. "See you soon." She put down the phone.

"Are you going to tell him everything?" Frieda asked.

Sharon put her head on Frau Henner's shoulder and cried until there were no more tears left.

Chapter 27

On first waking Ella felt dizzy. As she looked around her bedroom and noticed the shafts of morning light, heard the trilling of a thrush from the garden, noted the empty space in the bed beside her, she realised her light-headedness was caused by relief. She had done it! She had clawed her way out of the long dark tunnel where she and Karen Trevor had spent the past year.

Jumping out of bed she ran to the long mirrored panels of the wardrobe doors and examined her reflection. The woman she was looking at was brighter, more animated than she had been for a long, long, time. She tried a smile. The reflection beamed back at her. Ella twirled, feeling so light that she almost believed she could fly. She could do anything now. Achieve anything. Be anybody she chose to be. She stopped mid-pirouette. The arms which had been raised in a graceful arch fell to her sides. She looked again at her empty bed and the enormity of her decision to end her marriage struck a lonely, fearful chord.

Walking slowly, she went to the window and drew back the curtains. It was raining. Just a shower now but darker clouds were massing on the western horizon. The lone thrush perched on a top branch of the bare cherry tree sang bravely on, bill raised to the heavens. Ella knew then that she would miss this garden and the house which had become little more than a bed and breakfast. She would miss Andrew. Mourn the death of their hopes and ambitions, their dream of a perfect life in the perfect little world they had created for themselves. All that perfection had not been enough. For either of them.

Going back to the mirror she examined her reflection again and this time she saw the dark shadow of pain in her eyes. Maybe Peter Sheehan was right. Perhaps she should go for marriage counselling. Or more appropriately, divorce counselling. Divorce was, after all, one of the most traumatic life events. Andrew would have his supermodel to help him through. If he needed help. Probably not. He was the one who had somebody to turn to, someone with whom to share. Fuck him! Her reflection was angry now. Ugly. This was not the image she wanted to see. Not the Ella she wanted to live with for the rest of her life. She forced herself to smile again. Better now.

This smiling woman, dark-haired, attractive even without her make-up, was someone who could cope with divorce, selling her home, buying a new one, leaving the business she had helped build up from scratch, starting a new career, putting a major accident and a year of deep depression behind her.

Ella took a deep shuddering breath. She could do it. She must. But first she must deal with Jason Laide and Manor House and the mess the much-sought-after Ballyhaven site had become. She winked at her reflection. The woman in the mirror smiled back and Ella knew that she would somehow, somewhere, find the strength to carry on.

* * *

Andrew had come into the office early to get a head-start on work. Or so he had told himself. He had spent the past hour just sitting at his desk thinking about the conversation he and Ella had had last night. Discussing their future. Dismantling their marriage. Ever since he had met Maxine he had wanted his marriage to end. He should be happy. And he was. Except for the deep feelings of regret which would not go away and the memories of the young Andrew and Ella, so full of hope and confidence in their future together.

The office was quiet. Staff would not be here for another half an hour. Annoyed by his confused thoughts, Andrew stood and began to pace. Ella had been the soul of reason and understanding last night. She did not want a huge settlement, instead suggesting that she put her share of the business up for sale, sell their home and the Ballyhaven site, then split whatever was left after the mortgage was paid. When she had outlined her plan for moving back to Cuanowen, Andrew felt she had been thinking of this for a long time. Maybe that, rather than the accident, had been the reason for her mental condition during the past year. This thought was the most upsetting. Had he been that unapproachable? Had he been so self-obsessed that he had not seen why Ella was suffering? The answer obviously was yes. He had gone willingly along with the idea that all her problems had been caused by the accident. Even now, it was difficult to admit that he could have been . . .

The ring of his phone was very loud in the silent office. He reached to pick it up quickly in order to still the jarring sound.

"Is that you, Ford?"

"It is," Andrew answered coldly, resenting the way Jason Laide addressed him and hating the lout's guts for sending that photo of Maxine and himself. Even though he had not had much time to think about it since, he knew it was Laide who had done that. Who else would be low enough?

"What do you want? Your photo back maybe?"

"Ah! Come on now, Andrew. You must admit it was a nice shot. You should be proud to share it. With Mrs Ford. And why stop there? "

"I could have you prosecuted, you prick."

"For what? You hardly think I took the photo. I just passed it on. Thought you should know it's out there. It could be used by someone with less scruples than I have. Maybe some low life would send it to the papers."

Jason was enjoying himself. The sound of his mocking laugh echoed down the phone. Andrew could imagine his pale face split by a big toothy grin. The man was ugly inside and out. It was difficult to know whether he would carry through on his threats or not. He seemed more the type of bully who enjoyed threatening rather than carrying out. But yet . . .

"What exactly do you want, Laide?"

"Now, now, I don't like your tone. I'm a client. Have some respect. And talking of respect, that's why I'm ringing you now. Out of respect. I want to let you know that I got fed up waiting for you and your accident-prone wife to close the deal on Manor House. I've just been with Rob Trevor. The deal is done. Manor House is mine as soon as the paperwork is through. My solicitor is working on it as we speak."

If Jason Laide had been expecting a shocked reaction he was not disappointed. Andrew spluttered and stammered before finally getting his words together. "You can't do that! You can't just go off and make a deal behind our backs."

"I can and I did. Ask Rob Trevor. Just to show there are no hard feelings I'm going to pay you a bonus, but there's a condition attached. Want to know what it is?"

"Laide, you can shove your bonus. You're not getting Manor House. Another client has outbid you. Rob Trevor knows that too."

"But he doesn't want to sell to Maxine Doran. He couldn't bear the thought of a trollop like her in his house. She would probably put a red light over the lovely double doors and open up for business."

For the second time in as many minutes Jason had stunned Andrew. So! Rob Trevor had obviously told him about Maxine's offer on Manor House. Andrew had to bite hard on his lip so as not to shout at Laide. Outraged by the slurs cast on Maxine, he had never felt so incensed. Some instinct told him that being ignored would offend Jason Laide more than rising to the putrid bait he was dangling. The thought of offending Laide helped Andrew silence his need to defend Maxine.

"I take it you agree with Rob Trevor's opinion then?" Jason said when he realised Andrew was not going to answer him.

"What do you want, Laide? What is it you're after?"

"Ballyhaven of course. I want those fifty acres. If you just wise up and sell them to me, then you could be saving yourself and other people a lot of trouble."

"What in the hell are you on about now?"

"Well, we all have secrets, don't we? Even people like your buddies Pascal McEvoy and Oliver Griffin. They might thank you for keeping me happy. Not to mention the woman who calls herself Maxine Doran."

"You bastard! You're trying to blackmail me. How dare you drag my friends into it! And Maxine. You piece of scum!"

Andrew heard Jason's sharp intake of breath on the other end of the line. He was no longer amused.

"I'm on my way to the airport to collect my wife. I'll call into your office later. We'll talk then."

Jason clicked off the phone, leaving Andrew standing with the receiver in his hand.

He was still standing there five minutes later, staring at the phone. All the pieces began to fit together as he recalled the conversation word for word: "the woman who calls herself Maxine Doran." His knees buckled. He sat and ran his hands through his hair. Fuck! Why hadn't she told him? Why hadn't Maxine told him that Jason Laide was the piece of filth who was blackmailing her? The pig who had filmed her when she was little more than a child. She knew Jason had put in a bid for Manor House. Andrew himself had told her that. Was this why she wanted the big old house so badly? To spite her tormentor? Or maybe she was working with him. Maybe she had told the photographer where to find them?

Andrew dropped his head into his hands. Even more than Jason Laide's threats, the thought he could not handle was that Maxine had used him. He could not, would not, believe that. What they had shared had been real. But how real was Maxine Doran? The girl who used to be Marie Murphy.

He glanced at his watch. It was almost nine o'clock. Any minute now the staff would be here, chattering and ready to start the day's work. For once Andrew was happy to leave it to them. He would ring Rob Trevor first to confirm Laide's claim and try to reverse Rob's decision if he could. He should contact Oliver and Pascal to warn them about Laide but that would have to wait. He had more important things to do. He was going to the Registrar's Office to find out just who Maxine Doran was and where she had come from. Only then would he be able to decide where he and this girl who was once called Marie Murphy were going.

* * *

Sharon waited for a feeling of belonging to swamp her. She was home. Standing on Irish soil. But all she felt was terror. Wishing she was back in Salzburg. The baggage conveyer belt was empty by now. Passengers from the Salzburg flight had collected their luggage and drifted one by one out through the Arrivals exit.

She wheeled her case towards the ladies' cloakroom, the canvas holdall balanced on top, her hand luggage gripped tightly in her free hand. Going in, she turned her back on the mirrors and leaned against the vanity unit. Her phone was still switched off. Jason would be trying to contact her. She could picture him, scanning faces, anxiously watching new arrivals, beginning to panic as he checked and rechecked the monitor. He would probably make enquiries to be told that yes indeed, the flight from Salzburg had landed thirty minutes ago and all passengers were now disembarked. Sharon closed her eyes and took some deep breaths.

"Are you feeling all right?"

Embarrassed, Sharon opened her eyes and smiled at the elderly woman standing in front of her. She seemed like a kindly person and Sharon had to quell the temptation to spill out her troubles to this stranger. The gentle little lady with the white hair who was still standing waiting for an answer!

"I'm fine. Thank you for your concern. Just tired from the early flight."

"Are you sure?" the woman asked anxiously. "Maybe

you should go and have a nice cup of tea. You'll feel better then."

"Yes, you're right," Sharon agreed, straightening herself up and pretending to check her hair and make-up in the mirror until the old woman finally toddled off, leaving Sharon alone in the cloakroom.

Quickly, before someone else came in, she secured her precious hand luggage onto the handle of her suitcase, opened the canvas holdall and scooped out the bundles of tissue paper. Balling them up as tightly as possible, she threw them into the disposal bin for paper towels.

Then working with shaking fingers, she ripped off the airline tag, tore it into tiny pieces and shoved the sticky little ball into her handbag. Glad now that she had had the foresight to remove the stiff base from the holdall before packing it, she found that she was left with an easily foldable piece of canvas.

A toilet flushed. Sharon started. She had not realised there was someone else here. She dashed into a vacant cubicle, shoving her wheeled luggage ahead of her, and continued her folding of the canvas holdall. When it was scrunched as small as she could make it, she lifted the lid on the sanitary bin and breathed a sigh of relief when the holdall slipped in easily. It was gone. Lost. All she had to do now was make the loss official.

The bureaucracy of the Lost And Found department took another twenty minutes but Sharon didn't mind. At the end of that time she had a piece of paper in her hand to say her canvas holdall had been booked onto the flight in Salzburg and appeared not to have arrived in Ireland.

As she walked through the Arrivals exit her legs shook. She and Jason saw each other immediately. His normally pale face was flushed red. He raced towards her, coming inside the barrier.

"Where in the fuck have you been?" he greeted her. "Everyone else from your flight is gone ages ago."

"They've lost one of my cases," Sharon said, and she did not have to act the anxiety in her face and voice. "I had to go to lost luggage and fill out endless forms."

"Stupid bastards," Jason muttered. "No hassle. You can buy whatever you need until your case turns up. Anyway you must have plenty to keep you going with what's in there." He glanced at the overstuffed case she was pushing.

He grabbed the case from her and began to push it towards the exit. Sharon followed on, clutching her hand luggage tightly, willing him to ask the question so that she could get it over with. He continued on ahead of her complaining about the weight of her luggage, wondering if she had brought "some of her bloody statues" as he called the sculptures she had so carefully collected for the Junkergasse house. His car was, as usual, illegally parked close to the exit so they did not have far to walk. Opening the boot, he heaved the case in and slammed the lid shut. He just abandoned the trolley then and jumped into the car. Sharon barely had time to tie her seat belt before he took off, driving too fast through the airport, driving manically when they reached the motorway.

"I have a big surprise for you, Mrs Laide. You're going to love this. I closed the deal on Manor House this morning. It's ours, bar the legalities. Would you like to see it now?"

"I'm tired, Jason. Do you mind if we just go to our old house first so that I can have a rest. It is still ours, isn't it?"

"Well, the buyers haven't moved in yet if that's what you mean," he answered sulkily. Sharon knew she had ruined his surprise and that his mood would be bad now. It would get worse. And since he had not asked the appropriate question she would have to volunteer the information.

"Jason. The case that's gone missing . . ."

"What about it? Your make-up or something? Do you want to go shopping?"

"Your papers were in that case."

Rubber screeched as Jason jammed on the brakes. The driver behind them pressed on his car horn and kept it depressed. Sharon closed her eyes, aware just of blaring horns and squealing rubber and waited for the inevitable crash.

"You mean you've lost my property? My livelihood? My insurance? You stupid bitch!"

Sharon opened her eyes and looked across at the man she had once thought so exciting. She shuddered. He had somehow avoided a crash and was driving on but he was seething with anger, eyes flashing, beads of sweat on his forehead.

"Surely you must have made copies of these things if they are that important to you?"

"Of course not, you moron! That was the point. Only I had them. That's what made them so valuable. Have you any idea what you've done?"

The temptation to answer that question was so strong

that Sharon had to press her lips firmly together. Holding it all inside, the disgust, the fear, the need for vengeance, she cleared her throat before she spoke, her voice soothing and steady by sheer force of will.

"They promised me they'd have my case back soon. Probably by tomorrow."

"Soon! Probably! For fuck's sake! What were you thinking of? Why did you let those sensitive papers out of your sight? Why didn't you keep them in your hand luggage? What have you in there? Your fucking perfumes and make-up?"

Sharon clasped her holdall close to her. Her hands were shaking. "Yes. I'm sorry, Jason. But it struck me that some of that material – the tapes – might have caused some problems coming through customs."

He scowled but she saw she had scored a point.

"And I did tell you that your things were safe in the bank vault," she went on. "You should have left them there. Why do you need them now?"

"None of your business. My property and nothing to do with you. I should never have let you anywhere near it. I'll get onto that fucking airline as soon as we're back at the house. I'll sort them!"

"I don't think that would be such a good idea, Jason. I've already dealt with it by reporting the loss and filling in all the necessary forms. If you make a huge fuss it might arouse suspicion about the contents. You wouldn't want people opening the case and rifling through your things, would you? But suit yourself. I'll give you the reference number if you want it."

"Fuck!"

Sharon glanced at her husband again. He was pale now, more than pale. Ghastly. They drove the rest of the way in silence.

Pleading tiredness, Sharon went straight to the master bedroom when they got to the house. She locked the door behind her. The room was tasteful, sparklingly clean and soulless. She threw her holdall onto the four-poster bed and opened it up. Carefully she loosened Jason's files and videos from the underwear in which it was wrapped. His blackmail stash. His video of Maxine Doran.

Picking up the haul, she walked into the adjoining dressing room. This was hers. Jason never came in here. Not as far as she knew. She dragged out a stool and standing on it put the papers and videos up in the highest press. That was as safe as she could make them for the time being.

A thump on the bedroom door made her jump so that she nearly fell off the stool. She pushed the stool back in its usual place and rushed to open the door to Jason. She must, must, keep him as calm as possible until she was ready. Until her work was done.

* * *

Never one to behave as expected, DiAngeli was all calmness and maturity this morning. Rehearsals in the Royal Theatre Carré were rolling ahead with military precision. A big surprise to those who had not worked with him before. The show was coming together very well. By three o'clock this afternoon it would be the slickest, most inspired fashion show of the season.

The manic little designer always pulled it off, Maxine thought, as she stood quietly in the wings, waiting for her cue to make a trial run on the catwalk. She felt uncomfortable, glancing about her continuously, wondering which of the cameramen, stagehands, theatre cleaners were in Van Aken's employ, very aware that she had now put herself in danger by bringing herself to Van Aken's attention.

"Maxine! You're on! C'mon, c'mon! What's wrong with you this morning?" shouted DiAngeli's second in command who had by now assumed the role of hysterical artist so that his boss could don a mantle of calm.

Maxine sighed and strode towards the stage and improvised catwalk. Her stride had an edge of anger. She was disgusted by the naiveté she had displayed last night and worried by the fact that this morning Andrew's phone was still switched off. She had thought of ringing his office. But what if he had deliberately switched off his phone to avoid talking to her? Maybe he had got back with Ella. Maybe they were together in bed this moment, having a glorious reconciliation.

"Maxine! Oh, my God! What are you doing? Turn! Sashay! Hips, girl! Hips!"

Maxine brought her attention back to her work. A flicker of light up in the gods told her she was being watched. Perhaps Andrew Ford had abandoned her but she believed that Dirk Van Aken had not.

Chapter 28

Ella glared at Andrew's mobile phone. It was sitting on his desk, switched off, as it had been for the past four hours. Wherever her husband had gone he certainly did not want to be contacted. Ella would have believed he was with his girlfriend had he not told her last night that Maxine Doran was working in Amsterdam. She buzzed the front desk.

"You're sure Andrew didn't say where he was going? Or that he didn't leave any message for me?"

"Absolutely sure," the girl answered with barely concealed impatience. "He left shortly after I arrived. Just told me to keep an eye on things until you got here."

Ella put down the phone, embarrassed that she had interrogated the girl yet again. She desperately needed to discuss Manor House with Andrew. He had left her with no option now but to wait until he came back from wherever he was.

Ella had been angry with Rob Trevor when he rang

earlier. Neither he nor Jason should have gone behind her back and closed the deal on Manor House without her. Rob could have told Jason Laide to work through the proper channels. She shrugged then. What the hell! Jason got his mansion, Rob got his money, the Fords' commission was still on the table and Maxine would be the only loser. And maybe Andrew too. He had seemed very anxious to secure Manor House for the supermodel.

Ella drummed the desk impatiently with her fingers. Where in the hell was Andrew? If only he hadn't forgotten his phone. He might be with the Coxes or some other client. So why hadn't he left a message for Ella as to his whereabouts? As he always did. She could ring around. Her hand reached towards the receiver and then dropped again as Andrew stormed through the door.

"Well, good afternoon," she said, watching as he took some sheets of paper out of his inside pocket and threw them on his desk. Trouble, Ella thought as she noted his dark eyebrows drawn together, the tight line of his mouth and his hair standing in peaks.

"What's wrong?" she asked.

"Jason fucking Laide!"

Ella was stunned by the vehemence of the answer. Then she remembered the photo Andrew had tried to hide from her. They had suspected Jason of being behind that.

"The photo of you and Maxine?"

"No. Well, not just that. He's bought Manor House. He went to Rob Trevor at the crack of dawn this morning and signed some sort of agreement."

"I know. Rob rang. I don't think there's much we can do about it. Jason paid a hefty deposit too. In cash. I realise Maxine wanted to –"

"She has a right!" Andrew shouted, beginning to pace now, distractedly running his fingers through his hair. "She's a Wellsley. She should have, she must have that house."

"What are you talking about, Andrew? Would you calm down?"

He sat at his desk and dropped his head onto his hands. His stillness was even more intense than his frantic pacing. Ella stood and walked over to his desk. Laying her hand on his shoulder, she felt the knotted muscles and tremors of anxiety.

"I can't explain it all, Ella, but I've been to the Registrar's Office and done some research. It turns out that Maxine's great-grandmother was Harriet Wellsley."

"The woman in the portrait in Manor House?"

"Yes."

Ella's hand slipped off Andrew's shoulder and fell to her side as she thought about Harriet Wellsley. The beautiful woman in the portrait. The black sheep of the Wellsley clan. The woman who resembled Maxine so much. The woman who had obsessed Karen Trevor. She remembered Rob's description of Karen standing in front of Harriet's portrait for hours on end. Just staring. It seemed as if the lady Harriet was reaching out to fascinate them all again. She shivered.

"I don't understand," she said. "Why did you have to do research? Did Maxine not tell you?"

"I don't think she knows."

Ella sat. She needed time to think. If Maxine Doran was Harriet Wellsley's great-granddaughter, then she had been related to Karen Trevor. And if that were true . . .

"Does Maxine have inheritance rights? Is Manor House hers by right?"

"I don't think so. Of course a solicitor would have to verify but as far as I know Harriet was disinherited quite legally by her family. Disowned. But now you can understand why Maxine must have Manor House, can't you?"

Ella nodded agreement just to pacify Andrew but she still did not understand.

"Does Rob know that Maxine is a Wellsley?" she asked.

Andrew stood up and grabbed her hand. "Let's find out. Maybe he does and that's why he sold so quickly to Jason Laide. We're going to see him this minute."

"Wait! Slow down, Andrew. Better ring first to see if he's available."

"No! Come on. We're not going to give him a chance to avoid us."

He caught Ella by the elbow and steered her out the door. She allowed herself to be led along. Her husband, soon to be her ex-husband, was in no condition to be left alone.

* * *

Oliver Griffin sat at his desk with the office door locked and his phone off the hook. Words had always come easily to him. Until now. He stared from the photograph of his wife and children to the blank sheet of paper in front of him. The hand holding the pen shook. Ever a man for protocol he was anxious to follow correct procedures. That was the trouble. Other than the instinctive knowledge that you penned rather than typed a suicide note, he was unsure of how to proceed.

Lowering the pen onto the paper he wrote the date. Then *Dearest Tricia*. He smiled at the irony of the juxtaposition of the word 'dearest' with his wife's name. What an unfortunate combination Tricia's expensive shopping habit had made with his gambling addiction. Hating himself for being unfair, yet again, wanting to at least face the truth now, he bent over the page and gripped the pen more tightly.

'I'm sorry to tell you I have run up debts of half a million euro. I gambled too much and lost too often. The money is owed to a very ruthless man. Sorry. Take care of the children. And yourself. Love, Oliver.'

He stared at the spidery writing. At the self-pitying note. I owe. I go. Take care. You clear up the mess because I can't. Tears welled in his eyes and spilled over. A large drop plopped onto the page and landed over his name. He watched hypnotised as the word Oliver became all blurry and edged in wavering blue. Tie-dyed. Duck-egg blue streaked with violet. Just like his young daughter's eyes. Her clear, innocent eyes, gleaming now with anticipation of her First Holy Communion Day.

A loud sob escaped from deep within the place where Oliver Griffin hid all his fears. Shoulders shaking, he put his head in his hands and cried as he had never cried before. He wept for his wife, his children, for opportunities lost and for shame. Why oh why had he not stopped in time? Why had he not asked for help, told the truth? The answers rang in his head, loud and clear. Because he was weak, vain, selfish. Stupid! Driven only by his need to experience that thrill, the incomparable feeling of putting everything on the line, of confronting fate, of believing in his own ability to outwit chance.

Even now, as he sat here drenching his suicide note in tears, his heart beat fast with recollections of his triumphs. He'd had many wins. Poker games, horses, dogs, blackjack, roulette. There had been some glorious winning nights in the Eureka Club. In the place where he had first met Jason Laide. Nights when even the croupier had applauded Oliver's good luck. But smiles and cheers had disappeared with the winning streak. There were polite conversations at first, the management pointing out that Mr Griffin had run up considerable debts. Then there were gentle reminders. Finally threats and demands. Pay up or be disgraced. That was when Jason had come to his rescue. That was when Oliver Griffin, Chief Planner, had sold his soul.

And now, at last, Oliver fully understood that his gambling was a fire which needed perpetual stoking, his life a disposable commodity for Jason Laide to use or abuse at will, his only escape the one he was planning to take tonight. A leap from the bridge into the freezing, polluted waters of the river would douse the fire. Feet tied together and weighted. A quick plunge to the muddy bottom. A mucky end to a murky life.

Oliver took a deep breath and sat up straight. Only a few hours left before he could safely make his way to the bridge and prepare for the biggest step of his life. He already felt a sense of relief. An unburdening of responsibilities he could no longer shoulder. The page on the desk was crumpled and soggy. Full of self-loathing he snatched it up and tore it to pieces. Oliver Griffin had made a mess of his life but he was determined to orchestrate his passing with all the control he had lacked in his living.

Taking out a clean sheet of paper, he began again. He had the date written when there was a knock on his door. He sat very still, barely breathing. Whoever it was knocked again. He began to get angry now. He had warned his secretary that he was not to be disturbed. What in the hell was she doing at his office door when he had told her stay away? There was another knock, louder, more urgent this time.

"Oliver! Let me in. I must see you."

It was Pascal McEvoy. The panic and desperation in Pascal's voice were audible through the thickness of the door. Oliver knew then that Jason Laide had carried out his threat to involve Pascal's son in some type of sleazy blackmail scheme. Jason Laide! He should be the one with his feet tied together falling headfirst into the freezing water. Scum!

"Open up, Oliver! It's urgent!"

Pascal was not going to go away. Oliver wiped his eyes and patted his hair. He put the dated page into the pending tray. He would get back to it. As he rose he felt old and weary. When he opened the door, he was shocked to see that Pascal looked older, wearier.

"I've been trying to contact you for hours. What in the fuck are you doing locked in here?"

"A lot of paperwork to get through. I needed peace and quiet," Oliver answered and felt like crying again so strong was his need for the very peace and quiet about which he had just lied.

"Look at this," Pascal said, passing a large envelope to Oliver. They both sat down and Pascal watched as his friend fumbled with the envelope before finally drawing out an eight by ten photograph. Oliver examined the picture closely. It had been taken in the city centre. At night. At the side entrance of a fast-food outlet. A narrow street running off one of the main thoroughfares. A group of teenagers stood laughing and chatting on the left-hand side of the shot. In the centre of the picture, a few yards away from the group was a man wearing a woolly ski hat, his back to the camera. Facing the lens, features clearly shown, was a fair-haired boy, young teens. His hand stretched out towards the older man, open and ready to receive the small packet of white powder the man was passing to him.

"Jesus! Your son? Hugh?"

"That's my boy all right," Pascal said. "The stupid little bollocks."

"Christ! He's only a child. How long has he been on drugs?"

"He's not. He was just bribed into acting as go-between."

"Really? Are you sure?"

"Yes. It's taken me all last night and most of today to get the truth out of him but I know he's being honest now. He's too terrified to be otherwise. This picture was dropped off at my home late last evening. Motorbike courier. Real gangland stuff. That's Hugh in the picture all right. He's not denying it. But he was buying for the older boys. Just acting as a stooge, the little idiot. He was promised a place on the rugby team. That's how fucking cheap my son sold his life away."

Oliver glanced at the pending tray with the yet to be completed suicide note. Christ! How well he knew about selling life away! How cheap was it in the end? An IOU, a place on a rugby team? Jason Laide, the vile criminal he was, had set himself up as the arbiter of life and death. Oliver had chosen his path, had lied and cheated, had allowed himself be drawn into Laide's clutches. But a thirteen-year-old child!

Pascal was staring, his eyes narrowed in his pale face. "I want an explanation, Oliver," he said reaching inside his pocket, pulling out a piece of paper and passing it across the desk.

Oliver scanned the terse, typed message: *'If you want to keep this out of the media contact your friend in the Planning Office.'*

The paper fell from Oliver's hand. It was as if he had already taken the leap from the bridge and was falling through the dark void towards an unknown endpoint.

"Jason Laide's behind this," he mumbled.

As soon as the words left his mouth he knew the

sentence was incomplete. Jason Laide had organised the picture-taking, the delivery, the destruction of a child's life but none of it would have happened if Oliver Griffin hadn't involved this piece of filth in all their lives in the first place, if he hadn't met him in the Eureka Club, if he hadn't taken the first loan, if he hadn't placed the first bet . . .

"Do you mean Laide, the transport guy?"

Oliver nodded silently. Words were stuck in his throat. Words of apology, of explanation, of excuse. They were choking him. He coughed, cleared his throat yet still the words pressed on his windpipe. Sweat broke out on his forehead.

"You'd better talk, Oliver. And quickly. I'm on my way to the police with this. It's only out of respect for the friendship I believed we had that I came to you first. What is all this about and why has my son been dragged into it? And what in the fuck have you got to do with covert surveillance and blackmail?"

Oliver was incoherent at first. Half-formed words, half-finished sentences. His mouth was dry, his heart thumping but gradually, admission by admission, the lump in his throat eased and the words began to flow more easily. Confessions of gambling debts, deceit and utter stupidity tumbled out. Pascal never took his eyes off Oliver's face as his onetime friend told his story of addiction.

"So you're a gambler, Griffin. What has that got to do with my son?"

Oliver glanced at the pending tray again. He would

not have to write his final note now. Pascal could tell his story for him. Every grotty detail from his indebtedness to Jason Laide to his foolish promise that he would deliver the casino licence for him.

"The casino licence . . ."

"You told him I would guarantee his name on the casino licence?" Pascal asked incredulously.

Oliver nodded, suddenly too tired for any more words. His body ached as if he were bruised and battered all over. He could not look at Pascal, could not meet the disdain in his eyes.

"Why in the fuck did you promise something you knew you could not deliver? I wouldn't be swayed anyway but you know the system. What you were promising was impossible. We're not a banana republic. Even if I'd wanted to, I couldn't have done that. What did you think I'd do? Buy off the whole government? Surely Laide understood that too. He must be an intelligent man. He couldn't have got as far up the ladder as he has if he was that inane."

Oliver looked up and cringed in the face of Pascal's glare. He must find the strength to make one last effort to be understood. To be pitied.

"The only thing Laide understands is cruelty. He bullied his way to the top. He finds weaknesses and exploits them. I presented mine to him. He thought your son was your vulnerable point. He's trying to get to Andrew Ford as well. He wants Ford's Ballyhaven site. And yes, before you ask, I told Laide about that too."

Oliver focused on the picture of his wife and family on his desk. Then he reluctantly looked at Pascal McEvoy. At his old friend. He saw all the disgust and contempt he had expected in Pascal's eyes. But nothing like the disgust and contempt he felt for himself.

Oliver closed his eyes and longed for the feel of the bridge parapet underneath his feet, for the rush of wind as his body sliced through the air, for the impact of his contact with the water, for the coolness of the depths, the darkness, the oblivion. He stored the image, the feelings, then opened his eyes. Pascal was still glaring at him. Oliver's jump into the void was taking far longer and the chasm was deeper than ever he had imagined.

* * *

Sharon woke with a start, not sure where she was. The yards of frothy voile draped on the posts over her bed soon told her that she had been sleeping in the *Ideal Homes* parody her Irish house had become. She jumped out of bed. It was late afternoon. How could she be wasting time sleeping when there was so much to do? The answer of course was that her exhausted body could not have taken a minute more of restless wakefulness.

Going into the bathroom she laid her make-up out on the vanity unit. Bottles and jars lined up, some with the lids off. She quickly tied her hair up in a bun and put on a towelling robe. A glance in the mirror satisfied her that she appeared to be a woman about to spend hours applying make-up. Or so Jason would think should he come into the bedroom. Probably not likely. Jason had got what he wanted from her earlier. Roughly and cruelly. A punishment for not having his files.

Sharon locked the bedroom door before taking down Jason's treasure trove of videos and files from the top press. She smiled as she saw how conveniently, and stupidly, Jason had left contact numbers for all his victims. A blush crept up her neck and face now at the thought that she had at one time admired Jason for his intelligence. What did that say about her own IQ?

Shrugging off her discomfort, she began to tap in numbers, confirming the appointments she had already made, leaving voicemail when there was no reply. If everything went according to plan she should have this raft of cruel blackmail back to its rightful owners today. Then she would be ready to tell, not ask, Jason Laide that she wanted a divorce.

Having not yet got a reply from Maxine Doran's number, she tried again when she was through with her other calls. As she sat listening to the ring tones she imagined that Maxine must be at some glamorous location, probably on a beach, Caribbean maybe. Blue skies, warm, gently lapping sea . . .

"Hello. Maxine Doran speaking."

Sharon dragged herself back from her daydream. "Hi, Maxine. Sharon Laide here. How are you?"

"Actually I'm busy, Sharon. Just waiting to go on stage for a final bow at a show. Is there something I can do for you?"

Sharon noted and understood the coldness which had crept into Maxine's voice. She had always put Maxine's aloofness down to conceit. Just another misjudged assumption. The girl must hate her, believing that she was Jason's partner in crime.

"I'd like to meet up with you, Maxine. I'm back in Ireland for a little while. I know we don't really know each other. We've just met socially. But there's something I'd like to discuss with you."

"I'm in Amsterdam. Sorry."

Sharon frowned. She began to have doubts about her plan. How much was she going to have to reveal in order to persuade Maxine to meet her? How much should she reveal? Perhaps Maxine was happy with the status quo. Maybe she had a fixation on Jason. A Svengali-type relationship. It was not unknown. A sick bond between victim and perpetrator. But the girl was at least entitled to make a choice.

"I'm going to have to trust you here, Maxine. You mustn't tell anybody about this call. I've recently come across a piece of property which belongs to you. It's quite old. Maybe eight or nine years. Very explicit. Do you know what I mean?" There was silence on the other end of the line. "Maxine?"

"Yes. I'm here. What do you want, Sharon? Are you doing Jason's dirty work for him now?"

"No! I want to give you back your property. You see why I have to trust you not to say anything? You know my husband, maybe even better than I do. He can't be told about this. Please meet me."

Sharon heard somebody call Maxine's name.

"I've got to go," Maxine said quickly. "I'll be back in Ireland tomorrow morning. I'll contact you."

The phone went dead just as Sharon heard the front door open and then bang loudly. Jason's tread across the hall was heavy. She just had time to put the files back and unlock the bedroom door before Jason hurtled into the room.

"Christ! Are you still dolling yourself up? C'mon! I'm spending a fucking fortune on a bloody palace for you and you can't even be bothered to come to see it."

"Just five minutes and I'll be with you," Sharon said as calmly as possible. Her hands shook as she quickly applied make-up and put on her clothes.

Jason stared as she slipped into her navy Dolce & Cabaña suit and added Swarowski earrings and a scarf to hide the bruising on her neck which was by now bluish yellow. She had not mentioned that she had been at the hospital in Salzburg and Jason couldn't ask her about it. How could he explain O'Shaughnessy to her? Or maybe he should. Let her know that he would always be watching in future as he should have been in the past. Not that O'Shaughnessy had reported much to Gussie other than the visit to the hospital and the trip to Geneva to get the papers and tapes she had now so stupidly lost. No visitors to Junkerstrasse except Frau Henner's family. That bitch was living well off Jason. Taking over. Moving her bloody family in. Sharon and that lump of a woman were too close. That would have to change too.

"Are you sure you're feeling all right?" he asked.

Sharon glanced at him as if he had no right to ask that question. "I'm very well, thank you. Do I look unwell?"

"You look the part," he announced. "Lady of the

manor. Lady of Manor House."

She stood and examined him from the top of his thinning hair to his beige-leather cowboy boots. She smiled at him. "You look the part too."

Considering himself complimented, Jason allowed the frown on his forehead to relax a little. It must have been the old bag of a housekeeper who had needed the hospital visit. Sharon just accompanied her. That must have been it. Pity they hadn't kept the old bag there.

He took Sharon's arm and led her out to the car, the pressure of his fingers biting into the soft flesh on the top of her arm. He meant business.

And so do I, thought Sharon as she and Jason headed in the direction of Manor House.

Chapter 29

It seemed to Ella that Manor House was in a different time zone to the world outside. Glancing through the narrow window of the study where she, Andrew and Rob were sitting, she could still see traces of daylight in the sky. It was not yet night out there. But in here, behind the three-foot-thick walls it was already dark. The desk lamp which Rob had switched on bathed the three of them in an eerie greenish glow. The corners of the room were solidly black, hiding bookshelves and secrets. Harbouring the undead. Ella shivered.

"Are you cold, Ella? I'll turn up the heating," Rob, ever the gentleman, said.

Ella shook her head and smiled at him, noticing his gauntness. Rob was becoming a pale unkempt shadow of the man he had been a year ago.

She glanced at Andrew. Her husband had the stubborn set to his chin she recognised all too well.

"Okay," said Andrew. "Let me get this clear with you,

Rob. You signed some piece of paper this morning agreeing to sell Manor House to Jason Laide. And you won't reconsider, even though I'm sure my client would top the offer. Is that about right?"

"Yes. That's it. Done and dusted. Even if I wanted to consider Maxine Doran's offer, I couldn't now. But I don't want to anyway. The sooner I leave this place, the better."

"If the offer was from someone other than Maxine would you be thinking differently? Are you afraid of any rights she might have?"

"What are you talking about?" Rob asked, apparently bewildered. "Rights to what?"

Andrew studied Rob Trevor's face, the paleness of his skin and the haunted darkness of his eyes. He looked sick. Troubled. But not shifty. This was not the demeanour of somebody trying to deceive. Could it be possible that Rob, like Maxine herself, had not known of the bloodline which stretched from Lady Harriet Wellsley all the way down to Marie Murphy? That's what Ella believed. Besides, Andrew could not really talk about it without Maxine's permission. Why did she have to be in Amsterdam now of all times? And why hadn't he thought to contact her before coming here? Andrew felt his pocket for his phone and realised he had left it in his office. He must somehow stall this sale without telling Rob what he knew. He smiled at the gaunt man sitting in front of him.

"I mean, maybe the fact that Maxine so resembles the portrait of Lady Harriet is an omen. Don't you care about what happens to Manor House after you have left? How do you think Jason Laide will fit the role of Lord of the manor?"

"I really don't care what happens to this mausoleum after I escape. Ask your wife about it. Ask her about the hold this place exerts over fragile minds. She'll tell you. I can't take any more of it and I'm sure Jason Laide is a match for the powers that be in Manor House. It should be a good battle."

Ella sat back and observed Rob, from the nerve which ticked underneath his eye to the bony shoulder-blades visible through the thin fabric of his fine cashmere sweater. She had to draw on all her newfound mental resources not to be dragged into the maelstrom of fear, anger and depression which surrounded him. She could so easily fall back into the clutches of her nightmare year. Wallow in the powerlessness of it all. And how much worse must it be for Karen Trevor's husband? He had lost both wife and child. He had lost his future. She leaned towards him.

"I understand what you're talking about," she said softly. "But you can't get through this by just selling off Manor House and you can't do it alone. I was helped by a doctor. I don't see Karen any more, Rob. I'm free. Why don't you talk to him? Dr Peter Sheehan. I can give you his number."

"No! No, thank you. I'm sure your doctor is very proficient at what he does but I don't need him or any doctor. I just need to get out of here. Out of this house, this country. That's all I need."

"You can't run away from what's inside your head, Rob. Think about what I said."

Ella understood exactly where Rob Trevor's mind was at the moment. It was in the dead and dying world of Karen Trevor. In the place where Ella had found herself trapped for over a year. Until Peter Sheehen had helped her free herself. Handsome, green-eyed Peter Sheehan. Broad-shouldered, tanned, well-muscled, Peter Sheehan . . . Ella blushed guiltily as if the two men in the room could read her thoughts. She picked up her bag and stood. Andrew stood too but he was not yet ready to give up on convincing Rob to change his mind.

"Maxine Doran is out of the country at the moment but she will be back tomorrow. Would you at least wait until I've spoken to her?"

Rob was very still as he appeared to consider Andrew's request. The sound of a car engine disturbed the quietness. Headlights pierced the darkness of the garden. Gravel crunched and brakes squealed as a car was driven at speed towards the house and then parked opposite the front door.

Going over to the window Rob peered out into the darkness.

"Jason Laide," he said. "His wife is with him. I'd better let them in."

"Have you met Sharon Laide?" Ella asked.

Rob shook his head.

"You'll like her. She's a very nice lady."

Andrew raised an eyebrow and smirked. Ella frowned at him as Rob excused himself to go open the front door.

"I know what you're thinking but you're wrong," Ella whispered.

"How could you describe Sharon Laide as a lady? In the first place she's married to Jason which says a lot and secondly what about all the boyfriends she's supposed to have abroad? Toy boys by all accounts."

"You should be the last one to believe rumours," she said sharply and regretted the words as soon as they were said. If there had been rumours, which there must certainly have been, about her husband and a certain supermodel, they had been true, hadn't they? Closing her eyes for an instant, she struggled to recover the state of understanding and forgiveness she and Andrew had reached yesterday.

"I'm sorry Ella. Really sorry."

When she opened her eyes again she smiled at him. "Let's not fall out over Sharon Laide. Anyway, maybe you're right."

Voices echoed in the hall outside, Jason's being the loudest and roughest. Ella glanced around at the ageless study. A place of mahogany bookcases, solid oak bureaus and quiet culture. Jason's crudeness was a travesty. She caught Andrew's arm.

"Let's go," she whispered. "I don't really want to be here with the Laides."

She was too late. Jason came barrelling into the room, pushing ahead of his wife and Rob.

"Ah, the Fords!" he said and managed to make his words sound as insulting as if he had cursed them. "What are ye doing here? This is my property now and I don't remember inviting either of you. Unless of course my lady-wife did? Well, Shar, are you issuing party invitations already?"

Sharon walked forward and held her hand out to Ella. "Nice to meet you again, Ella. Thank you for selling our other property so quickly."

Ella glanced from the beautifully tailored navy suit to the pink blush of embarrassment on Sharon's cheeks and knew her assessment had been right. Sharon Laide was a lady. What in the hell was she doing married to this corrupt thug?

"You're welcome, Sharon. How did your ski trip go?"

"Keep the chit-chat for the party," Jason interrupted. "I want to know about Ballyhaven. When are ye going to sign it over to me?"

"We're not," Andrew said firmly and even Jason heard the note of anger in his voice.

Jason walked across the study to stand in front of Andrew, having to bend his head back to look up at the taller man.

"What in the fuck do you mean? Your dozy wife agreed to sell it to me. It's mine every bit as much as this house and the pub."

"What pub? You never mentioned buying a pub," Sharon said.

Jason rounded on her. "Since when do we tell each other everything? I don't ask you about all the arty-farty things you spend my money on, do I? Mind your own business."

"Excuse me but –" Rob said feebly.

"Shut up, you, too!" Jason shouted. "I'm talking to Ford. Well? The Ballyhaven site? Is it mine? I've played fair up till now with you and your cronies but I could get dirty, you know."

"You mean you could have photos of my husband and his girlfriend delivered to our office, is that it, Jason?"

Jason turned to stare at Ella. The room was quiet except for the creaks and groans and whispers of the old building. He seemed confused, not quite sure how to respond.

"You know about Maxine Doran then?"

"Maxine Doran?" Rob and Sharon chorused together.

"I do," Ella replied. "So what were you saying about playing dirty? You'll have to do better than that."

"And I fucking can! I could send the photo to the papers. How would you like that? And what about your poncy friends, Ford? The politician and the planner. I could destroy them. And I will unless they do what I want."

"You mean unless you get the casino licence?"

"So you know about that too. A cosy little old boys' club. Keeping it for one of your own, are you? We'll see about that!"

Sharon went to Jason's side and caught him by the arm. "Why don't you show me around the grounds of our new home, Jason? And while we're walking you can tell me about pubs and casinos and whatever it is about Ballyhaven that's upsetting you so much."

There was a tension-filled moment as Jason seemed to waver between blowing up or collapsing. Sharon smiled at him. He went for the quiet option and allowed himself to be led out into the hall. Sharon threw an apologetic look in Andrew and Ella's direction and signalled to Rob to follow them.

"I'll just show Mr and Mrs Laide out first," Rob said to Ella and Andrew. "Then I'll join you."

"Well, do you still think you made the right decision?" Andrew asked Rob when he came back to the study.

"Perfect." Rob smiled. "You can tell Maxine Doran sorry but Manor House is sold."

Ella smiled too. She understood Rob's reasoning. Only someone of Jason's insensitivity could live in this house of ghosts. But Sharon was different. Though if her past history was anything to go by, she would just be a visitor here.

Rob escorted them to the front door.

Before getting into the car, Ella looked back at Manor House. It was towering over them in the darkness, watching them. She stared at the front door where Rob stood framed in the light spilling out from the hallway. Squinting her eyes, she dared Karen to appear. Just as she had before. Rob remained the only one standing forlornly in the huge doorway.

"C'mon," Andrew said impatiently. "I must contact Pascal McEvoy and Oliver Griffin. They need to be warned about Jason Laide."

Ella gave a last glance at Manor House. All she saw was an imposing old house and a very lonely man. Peter Sheehan had done his job well.

* * *

Oliver was on autopilot. Being led along. Just sitting

quietly in the passenger seat of Pascal McEvoy's car. Not putting up any protest. Weak and snivelling, welcoming the numbness which was beginning to invade his overwhelming self-loathing.

"Where in the fuck is Ford?" Pascal fumed, throwing down his phone as he failed to contact Andrew yet again.

They were parked in front of the darkened offices of Ford Auctioneers and Estate agents. Looking at the man sitting beside him, Pascal knew he would have to make a decision soon. Oliver had the appearance of someone about to go into a catatonic state. An easy escape from responsibility. Tricia Griffin would have to be told what was going on. What had gone on without her knowledge. The police should be informed. Jason Laide should be hung drawn and quartered. A public hanging. A washing of all their dirty linen in public . . .

Pascal put the key in the ignition of the car and quickly did a U-turn.

"We're going to Fordie's house. He must be there even though he's not answering his phone," he told the semi-comatose figure slouched in the seat beside him.

There was no response from Oliver, no reaction as they approached the tree-lined road where Andrew and Ella lived, no objection until Pascal parked the car in Ford's driveway.

"I'm not going in," Oliver said, glancing at the lights in the front windows. "I need to go. There's something I must do."

Pascal opened the door on the passenger side and caught Oliver by the arm. "Get out," he said. "We'd all like to run away from this but we can't."

There was no fighting the anger in Pascal's voice. Oliver reluctantly got out and allowed himself to be led towards the Ford's front door. For more humiliation, more recriminations. The call of the river was loud in his ears. The pull of the coldness and nothingness unbearable. He would have run if he had the strength. His leg muscles twitched but his feet remained planted as he watched Pascal ring the bell. The door was opened by a very agitated-looking Andrew Ford. So much upset, so many people, scared, angry, desperate. And all because Oliver had allowed Jason Laide to pay his gambling debts. All because of Jason Laide. All because of Oliver Griffin.

Andrew ushered them into the kitchen where Ella was making coffee.

"Tea? Coffee?" she inquired and the normality of her question seemed incongruous in the suddenly tension-filled room. She looked from one to the other of the men. The three friends. The students who had gone their separate ways but had never cut the bonds of their college friendship.

"I was just about to ring you both," Andrew said. "You should be warned. Jason Laide has tried to blackmail me. He has a photograph of me in a – in a pretty compromising position. I think he may try to get at both of you as well."

"Tea for me, please," Pascal said. "And coffee, strong and black, for Oliver."

Andrew stared, taken aback by Pascal's calm. "You knew?"

"Yes."

Ella busied herself making tea and coffee and putting a precooked pizza on to heat. She listened as Pascal and Andrew spoke, noticing that Oliver was staying very silent. By the time she had placed drinks and slices of pizza in front of each of them she had heard the whole sorry saga of Oliver's gambling addiction, his indebtedness to Jason Laide, his rash promise to ensure the proposed casino licence for Laide. Jason Laide seemed driven by his need to be the sole owner of the casino. At any cost. He was determined to buy the Ballyhaven site. As he had bought the pub there. But Manor House didn't fit into that picture at all.

"Where's he getting all the money?" she asked, doing a quick mental calculation on just how much Jason was spending now and how much he had pledged to spend in the future on the development of the casino project. "I know he has a very successful haulage business but he seems to be able to lay his hands on huge amounts of money without any problems. Who's backing him? He couldn't be in this alone, could he?"

"Some pretty unsavoury people, I'd say," Pascal answered. "You just have to look at his modus operandi – blackmail, bullying – to know that. I made a few discreet enquiries today from Revenue. It seems our pal Jason has his fingers in a lot of pies. For one thing, he's a majority shareholder in the Eureka Club. So, you see Oliver, he lent you money to pay back a debt you owed to him anyway. And probably claimed tax relief on it. He had all this planned well in advance."

"How could he have known about the Casino Village?" Ella asked. "Isn't that legislation very recent?"

"He didn't," Pascal answered. "He just knew that having an executive of the Planning Board in his pocket was bound to come in handy at some stage. And he was right, wasn't he?"

A sound came out of Oliver's mouth. It was halfway between a sob and a laugh. Then he sealed his lips again and looked down at the pizza he had not touched.

"So these are our options as I see them," Pascal continued on, ignoring Oliver's little outburst. "We can go to the police with the photographs both you and I were sent, Andy. The one of my son and the one you got of . . ."

Ella smiled first at Andrew and then at Pascal. "It's okay. You can say it. Andrew's mistress, girlfriend or whatever he wants to call her. Maxine. Maxine Doran. I know about them. And I wish them luck. You may as well know now too that Andrew and I have agreed to divorce. But Maxine is only one of the reasons. Breaking up our marriage is not one of Jason Laide's triumphs."

They were all silent, nobody else as comfortable with Ella's announcement as she herself was. Oliver muttered an "Excuse me" and asked for directions to the bathroom. When he had left the kitchen Andrew immediately leaned towards Pascal.

"What in the fuck was Griffin thinking about? It's his fault we're all in this mess."

"Not so quick with the condemnation, Andy. Laide would have come after us anyway to try to get this casino licence. You have the land he wants, he thinks I have the political clout he needs. And of course Oliver's addiction made him vulnerable."

"It's made us all vulnerable, hasn't it?"

"Enough of the blaming. We'll have to decide where we go from here. How are we going to handle this?"

Bravo! thought Ella as she listened to Pascal, disappointed that it was not her husband showing some sympathy for the addiction which obviously had totally ruined Oliver Griffin. She cleared off the table and put fresh coffee on to percolate as Andrew and Pascal debated their options. To go to the police or not. To go public or not. To take the excruciating embarrassment of having Andrew's affair, Pascal's son's dabble with drug-dealing and Oliver's gambling become public knowledge.

"That's what Laide is depending on," Ella pointed out. "He believes you will all put your public image ahead of principle."

"Even if we did feel like that, and I must admit my instinct is to protect my son, I still can't and won't get that licence for him. Oliver should never have pretended that I could. If only . . ." Pascal stopped speaking. "Where is he? Where's Oliver?"

"He went to the bathroom," said Ella.

"He should be back by now."

Ella went to check. A blast of cold air hit her when she went into the hall. The front door was open.

"He's gone!" she called back over her shoulder.

Hurrying to the door she checked the front garden, then went to the gate and looked up and down the street.

It was deserted. No Oliver.

When she came back into the kitchen Pascal was already on his feet, putting on the jacket he had draped on the back of his chair.

Oliver's phone was sitting on the table.

"His phone's here. He can't have gone far," she said. "Maybe he just wanted a breath of fresh air."

"So he snuck off without saying anything? I don't think so," said Pascal. "He's not thinking logically at the moment. In fact, he's in a bad way. We'd better split up and search for him. He needs help."

Ella and Andrew grabbed their car keys. A quick consultation decided which direction each should take. The three cars drove out onto the road. Pascal would go west in the direction of Oliver's home. Andrew was to head north towards the Planning Office in case Oliver had decided to go there. Ella could head south or east. South towards the airport or east into the city. She hesitated, trying to put herself in Oliver's mindset. The road to the airport wound through some nice landscaped areas before joining up with the motorway. Some quiet, secluded areas. Probably what Oliver would be looking for now. The city centre would offer no peace or calm, even at this hour of night. Decision made, Ella drove away in the direction of the airport while Oliver strode with determination eastwards towards the city centre. Towards closure.

* * *

The three-way phone communication between Ella,

Andrew and Pascal became increasingly more agitated. There was no trace of Oliver Griffin. He was not on his way to his office or on the road to his home. Ella was not as sure about the airport road. She was driving slowly, peering into the darkness on either side of the road. There were many little areas where someone could easily hide from passers-by if they wanted to. But yet how far could Oliver have got on foot? Ella had come out onto the motorway leading to the airport by the time Andrew contacted her again. He had rung Tricia on some pretext. Oliver was not at home. Tricia said he was at a business dinner.

"Shit!" Ella said. "He must be gone in the only direction we haven't searched. He could have walked almost as far as the city by now. It's only three kilometres. He could have flagged down a taxi or got a bus. I think we should all head towards the city centre. Will you let Pascal know? We'll meet up by the train station. Okay?"

Andrew grunted a reply as Ella turned off at the next intersection and headed back towards the city centre. The further she drove the more convinced she became that Oliver had got some form of transport into town. How in the name of God were they going to track him down? She was remembering snatches of the scene in the kitchen tonight. How had she not noticed Oliver's down mood, his silence, his detachment at the time? Too occupied with the unfolding story of his gambling addiction, she had missed the signs. How humiliated and guilty he must feel at this minute. How desperate.

Town was quiet, even for a week night. Ella kept her

eyes peeled on the footpaths as she headed towards the railway station. She saw couples, groups of teenagers, some people sleeping in doorways, two gardaí on the beat but no sign of Oliver. Turning right to drive along the quayside, she glanced at the bridge spanning the river. She jammed on her brakes and pulled in to the side. A dark figure was hunched over the bridge, elbows on the parapet. He appeared to be staring into the murky depths of the river. Ella knew. She was too far away to see his face, his hair, his tormented expression but Ella knew she had found Oliver.

She quickly let Andrew know, then locked the car and began to approach the hunched figure. Instinct told her that she would have to move cautiously. Her legs shook as she crossed the wide bridge, terrified that Oliver would decide to act before she could reach him. She got within three yards of him. He was still. Just staring. Not even noticing her approach. Should she wait until Andrew and Pascal got here? Just keep watch. He knew them better than he did her. A young couple began to cross the bridge. They were engrossed in each other and did not seem to notice the man leaning over the parapet and the woman who was intensely watching him. They passed by. Where in the hell were Andrew and Pascal? Oliver moved. Just a repositioning of his feet but it was enough to make Ella act. She crossed the few yards between them and stood beside him.

"Are you all right, Oliver?" she asked gently.

He turned to face her and she was shocked by the devastation on his face. It seemed that he had aged ten years since he had left the kitchen in Ford's house. In the yellow glow of the neon street lighting he looked like a man in the end stages of a terminal illness. Ella reached out and laid her hand over his on the stone parapet. His skin was icy cold.

"I need help," he muttered.

"And I know just the person to give you the help you need," Ella replied.

Tucking her hand into his arm she gently tugged him away from the parapet. He offered no resistance. They had begun their slow walk back to her car by the time Andrew and Pascal arrived.

"Back to our place," she said and warned them both with a look not to say anything.

Oliver seemed to be very detached by now. He got into Ella's car, allowed his seat belt to be tied and allowed himself to be driven to her house without saying a word. Back in the kitchen Ella sat him down and placed a cup of hot, sweet tea in front of him. He smiled at her. It was a wan smile but it was the first sign Ella had seen that Oliver still had some hope.

"I was thinking about jumping," he said.

Ella sat opposite him and caught his hand. "You know, Oliver, that I've been through a pretty tough time lately. The accident and other things. There were times in the past year when I felt like giving up but I found someone to help me. His name is Peter Sheehan. Would you like me to ring him for you now?"

Oliver's eyes filled with tears. "What have I done, Ella? I've ruined my marriage, my children's lives, my friends.

How could any doctor help? I've destroyed so many lives."

"Your addiction to gambling has done the damage. Why don't you talk to him about it? He won't judge you, just as he didn't judge me."

Oliver nodded. A barely perceptible dip of his head. Ella seized the moment and dialled Peter Sheehan's number. His hello sounded sleepy. For an instant Ella imagined him in bed, his torso bare, his hair tousled. She rushed on, ashamed of her thoughts in the circumstances.

"Sorry for ringing at this hour, Peter, but a friend of mine is in trouble. He needs help. Your help. Can I bring him to see you?"

Ella heard some rustling and she knew Peter was throwing back the duvet, swinging his legs onto the floor. His thighs would be tanned, muscles well defined.

"Where is he?"

"Here in my home."

"Okay. I have your address. What are we talking about here? Emergency situation?"

"Exactly."

"I'll be with you in ten, fifteen minutes."

Ella put down the phone and turned her attention back to Oliver.

Andrew and Pascal, both looking pale, walked into the kitchen. She told them about Peter Sheehan. Not everything. Not about her fantasies. Her imaginings. And in the middle of a crisis! That was something she would have to think about later.

* * *

It was a very long night. Peter admitted Oliver to hospital for observation. Ella went to the hospital with them while Andrew and Pascal went to see Tricia. Having tried to explain Oliver's situation to his wife as gently as possible, they then brought her to visit her husband. He was sedated. Enjoying an artificial calm while all around him was chaos, guilt and regret.

Feeling that Oliver's room was crowded since Tricia, Andrew and Pascal had arrived, Ella tiptoed outside and sat in the corridor. Her eyelids drooped. She jumped when Peter Sheehan sat beside her on the upholstered seat.

"Is he going to be all right?" she asked.

"He has a long road ahead but yes, with support he should be fine. What about you? How are you feeling?"

Ella looked into his clear green eyes with the dark lashes. She could not find words for how she was feeling. Tired, sad, emotionally drained. Yes. But also warm and comfortable in his green gaze. She felt safe sitting beside Peter Sheehan. She smiled at him.

"I'm fine, Peter. Thank you for helping Oliver."

"No problem. You look tired. You should go home."

Ella agreed. Going back into Oliver's room she saw that Andrew was comforting Tricia. It wouldn't be right to drag him away.

"I'll drive you home," Peter offered. "Your house is on my way."

Ella said her goodbyes quickly. She was anxious now to get out of the hospital, away from the suffering which was evident in the lines and furrows on Oliver's sleeping face and in the heartwrenching sobs of his wife.

In Peter's car she lay her head back against the headrest and closed her eyes. She was lulled on the journey by the smooth hum of the engine and the clean smell of Peter's aftershave. Maybe it was deodorant. Anyway it was nice. Like a summer meadow. Full of sunshine and the promise of harvest.

Ella woke with a start. Peter was gently shaking her arm. They were outside her front door.

"Andrew and I are going to get divorced," she said and then cringed with embarrassment. What had possessed her to come out with that announcement? Spitting it out as if it was something of which to be proud. As if it mattered to Peter Sheehan. Lowering her head to hide her shame, she grabbed her bag off the floor with one hand and opened the car door with the other.

Peter's hold on her arm tightened. "How do you feel about that?" he asked.

Ella pulled her arm away and put one foot on the ground outside. "I'm not your patient any more."

"Just what I wanted to hear you say, Ella. I wouldn't dream of being unprofessional."

The meadowsweet smell engulfed her as Peter leaned close. She felt his breath on her face, the warmth of his skin as his fingers brushed her cheek. She closed her eyes and savoured the sensations. His lips touched hers. A butterfly caress. A thunderclap. A bolt of lightning. Opening her eyes she looked into the clear green of his. She saw compassion and understanding there. She thought she saw passion too but her judgement was being impaired by her racing heart.

"May I call you sometime soon?" he asked.

"Please do," she answered and then she levered herself out of the seat and closed the car door in case she kissed him again. And again. She watched as he turned the car in the driveway and then drove away. She did not hear Andrew come home. She was sleeping too soundly and dreaming too sweetly.

Chapter 30

It was still dark when Jason woke. Looking at his watch he saw it was six o'clock. He hated dark winter mornings. Maybe when everything was fixed up he would take a sun holiday. In a lively Mediterranean resort full of sangria and young girls wanting to have a good time. He'd show it to them!

He glanced at the sleeping woman on the other side of the bed. His wife. Wriggling closer to her he leaned on his elbow and examined her beautiful face. Her dark hair was spread out on the pillow, her lashes black and curling. She had the delicate bone structure of generations of good breeding. Except, Jason thought angrily, this classy mare doesn't breed. Until now. She was on her last chance. No more fucking around the world for her. That was all right when he had been so smitten he'd tolerate any behaviour from her. And while he'd had other interests to pursue himself. Not any more. He'd bought a fucking palace for her. He was going to own Ireland's first and only super casino and he must have children to pass it all onto. If she couldn't, or wouldn't produce, he'd get rid of her. Replace her. Destroy her. Bitch! He was tempted to wake her now and let her know who was boss in this marriage. But he had too much else to do. Not least to track down his missing papers. He glared at his sleeping wife again. Stupid bitch! She should never have left those things out of her hand. Only she would consider her make-up more important than anything else. Though he had to admit she had a point about the danger of taking them through customs. Far more risky in bulk than when she was carrying them to Salzburg one by one.

Jason rolled out of bed and threw on some clothes. It was going to be a bad day. He knew it. His anger was boiling up and the sun had not yet risen. Going down to the kitchen he put on the kettle and made himself a cup of tea. He always felt better with a mug of sweet tea in his hand. Just like his mother. Nelly. That scrap of a woman who had borne eight children and lost four of them to sickness when they had been only babies. Lost them to poverty. To deprivation. To dampness and dirt and hunger. To injustice. To a class system which had allowed inner-city babies die and upper-class kids be coddled and protected. His father, big and rough and red-haired, had sneaked off to England and left his wife to her mourning and to deal with her surviving children as best she could. Nelly Laide had had no pleasure, no happiness in her life. Except a cup of sweet tea.

Outside the kitchen window, Jason noticed the sun struggling to surface through a sea of dark cloud. He drained his tea, got his jacket and checked his inside pocket. Assured that his precious notebook was snug inside, he smiled to himself. It wasn't that he feared Sharon would read it if she found it. He knew how to deal with her anyway. It was just that the less anybody knew about his deal with Van Aken the better.

He got his car keys and then hesitated after he had put the key in the ignition. Where should he start? The airport? He had got the details from Sharon last night and the all-important reference for her piece of missing luggage. But maybe she was right when she said that creating a fuss would arouse their suspicion. They were all hyper about security now. Suppose they started asking too many questions, maybe searching the bag when it finally turned up. A fine film of sweat broke out on Jason's forehead at the thought. He'd wait another day. Give Sharon a chance to work her charm on them. Anyway he had other things to do. He must set up another deal with Van Aken. Expenditure was heavy now with one thing and another. Gussie at the transport depot should be his first stop. All the money should be in by now from Dirk's last shipment. He'd have to collect that and bring it to the accountant's plush office so that the cleaning-up process could begin. The laundering. Some would appear to have been won in the Eureka Club or earned against ghost transport contracts for Jason's legitimate business interests. Some would be spirited into foreign accounts, the rest to shell companies. The process of legitimising the money so that Jason could access it and spend it as he wished and not have to look over his shoulder. His anger smouldered again now. He knew all those pricks in suits, including his accountant, were ripping him off. Someday he'd prove it and then they would pay the price. Someday when he had everything he wanted. When his children were grown. Posh, well-educated children who had never known a day's hunger in their lives.

Angrily he revved the engine and shot down the driveway. He didn't like remembering where he had come from. It made him feel inadequate. A bit like Sharon made him feel.

He tried to concentrate on the day ahead as he sped along the road. There was the business of the casino. That snotty Andrew Ford and his peculiar wife. The muscles on Jason's jaw twitched as he thought of that clique. The Fords, Oliver Griffin, Pascal McEvoy. Shits, the lot of them. Looking down on him. Thinking they were better than him but all they were was more educated. When he had the Ballyhaven site and the casino licence secured he'd destroy the lot of them. Just for the pleasure of it. Maxine Doran too. The whore who thought she was a cut above.

By the time Jason arrived at the transport depot he was in better humour. The anticipation of vengeance delivered had lightened his mood. He passed the offices. They were still in darkness. He headed towards warehouse number six at the rear of the lot. Gussie, he knew, would be in his little office at the back, already sitting on his high stool, watching everything through his half-closed eyes. A genuine smile lit Jason's face. Gussie was a real friend, maybe the only one he had. He had stayed faithful since the early days, never demanding, always happy to take what he was given, always ready to obey orders without question.

The smile faded as Jason walked past the stacked crates and boxes in number six warehouse. Gussie's office was in darkness. He looked at his watch and checked the time. Ten past seven. It was unheard of for Gussie to be late. Jason tried the door. It was open. He went in and flicked on the lights. His mind registered the fact that there was something wrong but it was some seconds before he realised that the office had been cleared out. The vacant stool was there, like a throne without a regent, but everything else was gone. No posters, the girlie ones Gussie liked, on the walls, no overalls hanging up, no ledgers. Not even a pen.

Dashing across the little office Jason caught the grey steel locker and heaved it out from the wall. The door of the safe hidden behind it swung open. Jason shoved first his hand and then his head into the safe. It too was empty. Except for a large envelope. Shaking now with an anger deeper than he had ever before experienced, Jason tore the envelope open and pulled out a bunch of photographs together with a single sheet of A4 paper. The top photo showed Sharon and Frau Henner – O'Shaughnessy's work in Salzburg.

He had to read the letter in Gussie's distinctive handwriting twice before he could begin to make sense of the contents. Even when he understood the words he could not comprehend their horrendous treachery. He put the letter on the stool where he could read it without having it shake in his hand. He went through it for a third time.

Dear Jason,

I'm sorry to have to do this to you but for my own safety I have no alternative. As you know by now I have left. I've gone abroad and there is no point in trying to find me.

Because we are such old friends I am going to warn you even though I've been told by some powerful people to keep my mouth shut. The authorities are onto you. Revenue and police are watching your operations. You've been splashing too much money around. If only you had kept a low profile you could have had it all.

As you never paid me enough for the risks I was taking on your behalf I've taken the money from the safe. A nice little nest egg. Thank you.

One last word of warning. Dirk Van Aken knows too. He's breaking all links with you. Stay away from him or he'll fix it so that you can't implicate him in your mess.

Goodbye

Gussie

PS O'Shaughnessy arrived back last night and handed in these photos – enjoy!

Shag the photos! They weren't important now. Gussie's treason overshadowed everything else. Jason tore the letter into shreds and then kicked the stool. He slammed the door of the safe and thumped the steel locker. His hand hurt and tears of rage prickled behind his eyelids. Closing his eyes he pictured Gussie's face. Long and woebegone with drooping eyes and mouth. He imagined kicking that face in, running a knife across the scrawny neck, watching blood spurt from the wound, seeing the life drain out of the man who had once been his friend. His only friend.

And what the fuck was that about the authorities and Dirk Van Aken? Who was watching? Was he being followed, listened in on, his privacy invaded? No way! Bullshit!

Jason picked up the phone. The only way to find out about Van Aken was to ring him. Even as he dialled, Jason was certain that he would prove Gussie to be a liar. An opportunist. Just trying to put him off the trail. He must have been planning this rip-off for years. How much had he salted away since they had started working together, Jason the young entrepreneur and Gussie his stooge?

Thoughts of Gussie were pushed aside as Jason listened to a dispassionate voice on the phone droning on in a foreign language. He tried again with the same result. This time Jason understood. Dirk Van Aken's number was no longer in service. Logic kicked in then. So Dirk had changed his phone and forgot to let Jason know. He could ring the business number. He did. With as little success. There was no getting beyond the switchboard. After his third attempt, the receptionist explained in reasonably clear English that she was under instruction not to put Jason Laide from Ireland through to the great man himself. Fuck him!

Jason shoved O'Shaughnessy's photos into their envelope, thrust it in his pocket and ran through the warehouse, knocking a pallet of boxes as he caught them with his elbow. The forklift driver had to swerve to avoid ploughing through his boss. Jason drove across town and arrived on the doorstep of his accountant at the same time as the man himself.

"Have they been on to you? Have they asked to see my books?"

"Who? What are you talking about? Jason? You'd better calm down and come in."

"The fucking law. The Revenue. They're after me. Don't tell me be calm! Have you got my ass covered or not?"

Embarrassed, the man glanced around him to make sure nobody had overheard the rantings of the most lucrative but most despicable client he had. Opening the door he ushered Jason inside as quickly as possible. The full story of Gussie's treachery and the letter he had written tumbled out as Jason strode over and back across the office. The accountant sat back in his chair, watching as the man who prided himself on being a bully dissolved into a quivering mess.

"Well, that's it," Jason said. "Am I covered? I've paid you enough to regularise my accounts. Have you done your job? Would my accounts stand up to scrutiny?"

"Certainly," the man answered. "As long as you were telling me the truth. I took everything you told me in good faith. If you gave me an invoice for over a hundred grand on a delivery of nappies, I believed you. Why shouldn't I? Hopefully the tax inspector will too."

Jason sat and bowed his head. At that moment he knew his accountant was not going to protect him in any way. If any irregularities in contracts or overseas accounts were uncovered, the man would deny all knowledge. And he would have the paperwork to back up his claims. Jason was on his own. Just as he had started out. The runt of the litter. A small man with big ideas. He could argue with the prick sitting smugly in front of him now. Point out that he had advised on shell companies and overseas accounts, that he knew, and had always known that Jason had unearned income. That he had gladly taken under-the-counter cash bonuses to keep his mouth shut. The biggest mistake Jason had made was in trusting. He had trusted Gussie and he had trusted this stuffed shirt. He had trusted Sharon. He stood up slowly now, fear making his legs feel heavy.

"You'd better pray that they find nothing to investigate. I'll drag you down with me."

The man laughed into Jason's face.

Jason turned his back on him and walked out to his car. He was trying to keep his temper at bay. Be calm. Conserve energy. He had a big battle ahead and he must, he had to, emerge the winner. He headed for the airport. Discretion be damned. He'd get his papers back from those pricks. He'd get everything he needed and more. And then he'd get his revenge.

* * *

When Sharon woke she lay very still, listening for the snores, the snorts and snuffles that would tell her Jason was lying on the other side of their giant bed. The room was quiet. Jason-free. A good start to the day. Throwing back the duvet she got out of bed, took her phone out of her bedside locker and dialled Salzburg. She smiled when she heard Frieda's rich, calm voice.

"*Guten Morgen*, Frieda. How are you? How is everyone?"

Nodding as Frieda spoke, Sharon listened, agreeing to take care and ring again as soon as possible.

When Sharon had dressed she went to the top press in the dressing room and took down the bundle of files. Today she would be giving them back to their rightful owners. Freeing them from Jason. As soon as she had made contact with the final two, the model and the planning officer, then she herself could also be free of the monster.

Sharon's hands began to shake. She would never be free of the lout if she did as Frieda said she must. If she told the truth. He didn't deserve honesty. Deceit was his way of life. Sharon's head dropped. She could not meet her own eyes in the mirror, knowing that she had perpetrated the biggest lie of all. An unforgivable deceit. Frieda was wrong though. Jason must never know the truth. The consequences would be too horrific. Not for herself but for the person she loved with all her heart and the part of her soul which had not been contaminated by her stint as Mrs Jason Laide.

After ringing for a cab, Sharon got her coat and ran downstairs. She tapped her foot impatiently as she waited in the hall for her car. There were so many wrongs to be righted and so little time. Lucky that Jason was preoccupied buying up half the city. How foolish and vulgar was his display of wealth! Did he really think he was going to get away with it? And what were his advisors, those professionals he paid to protect his image, thinking of? His accountants and lawyers. How could they allow him to buy a mansion, a pub and bid for a fifty-acre site all within a few weeks of each other? The answer to that of course would be that Jason paid them to advise him and then went his own way anyhow. If anyone knew how pigheaded he could be, it was his wife. The woman who had gone to sleep with an exciting man and woken up with a monster. A long sleep. But she was awake now.

The cab beeped outside. Sharon shook her head to clear it of her dark thoughts and then walked quickly outside to the car. She had no time to waste.

⋆ ⋆ ⋆

Ella was up and had breakfast made long before she heard Andrew stirring. He was pale and shaken when he came into the kitchen. She handed him a mug of coffee as he smiled wanly at his soon-to-be-ex-wife.

"Some night last night! How are you feeling this morning?" he said.

Knowing it would be insensitive to tell him how invigorated and hopeful she felt, Ella evaded answering his question, instead asking one of her own. "How was Oliver when you were leaving?"

"Still sleeping. The longer he sleeps the better. He'll have to face the music when he wakes."

"Did you and Pascal decide what to do? Are you going to the police?"

Andrew ran his fingers through his hair and swallowed a long draught of his coffee.

"What do you think?" he asked.

"I think Jason Laide is a criminal. He must be stopped," Ella answered without having to consider her reply. She knew immediately by Andrew's expression that he did not agree. "Surely you don't want him to get away with blackmail and bribery and God alone knows what else, do you Andrew? It's not as if we can do business with him now after all this –"

"Of course we can't do business with him! And I think the bollocks should have the book thrown at him. But what about Oliver and his family? And Pascal's son? And of course myself. And Maxine . . . well, more Maxine than anyone else."

"Why Maxine?" Ella asked in surprise. "Does he have something especially damning on her. Something more than her affair with you?"

Andrew looked away, avoiding her eyes. She knew then that it was really Maxine Doran whom her husband wanted to protect. Jason Laide must have been blackmailing her too. For an instant Ella felt sad. Andrew must love his supermodel very much to compromise his principles like this. More than he had ever loved his wife. Andrew stood up and put his mug into the dishwasher.

"I'm going to the airport to meet Maxine now. The early flight from Amsterdam is due to land shortly. Can I tell her Manor House is hers if she wants it? Do you agree?"

"I do, but what about Rob Trevor? He's already made a deal with Jason, hasn't he?"

"He'd change his mind if he knew about Laide. If we explained that Jason had blackmailed and bribed his way to prosperity."

"I think you're wrong, Andrew. Rob would be

convinced then that Jason and Manor House belonged together."

"That's such a crazy notion!"

"Not so crazy. It has its own logic. Rob is not very well at the moment. He's grieving and guilty and he's looking for someone or something to blame. He believes Manor House in general and Lady Harriet Wellsley in particular are to blame for the death of his wife and child. He thinks Jason Laide is insensitive enough to handle the unseen influences of the house. "

"He's lost the plot!" Then he noticed her expression. "You don't believe him, do you Ella?"

Ella looked out the window at the rain-filled clouds. They hung low and black, threatening a downpour as severe as the day she had had her accident. That life-altering, life-ending crash. Turning back to face her husband she struggled for words to describe her feelings.

"I really don't know what to believe about Manor House, Andrew. There are so many coincidences, all drawing us towards that house. First my accident and Karen Trevor's death. Her son's too. Then your relationship with Maxine who you say is really Harriet Wellsley's great-granddaughter. Did you know that Karen had developed some sort of obsession with Harriet's portrait before she died? Rob said she used to spend hours just staring at it."

"Really? Is that why Rob got rid of it, I wonder?"

"Probably. Then there's the Jason Laide connection. You have implied that he has some hold over Maxine. And, it appears he's the new owner of Manor House. It just seems like we're all going around in a big circle and Manor House is at the centre."

In two long strides Andrew was standing in front of Ella, holding her arms and peering into her face. "Are you feeling all right, Ella?"

"Don't patronise me!" Ella said, angrily pulling away from him. "Just because I suffered from depression doesn't mean everything I say is off the wall."

"You know that's not what I meant. But listen to yourself. Manor House is controlling our lives. Really!"

Put like that, Ella had to agree she did sound a bit off. But Andrew didn't have all the facts, did he?

"I told you about Karen Trevor. About how she haunted me, waking and sleeping for a year after the accident."

"Of course she did. It was a horrible experience for you. It's just that I thought you were over it."

"I am," Ella said firmly. "You can go off and live happily ever after with your girlfriend with a clear conscience."

"So now we're getting to the truth at last! You don't love me any more. You've even said you never did but you don't want me to be happy with anyone else. That's it, isn't it?"

"Oh, for God's sake, Andrew! I thought we had reached an agreement. Yes, I'm hurt. I'm sad and I'm sure I'll be very lonely for a while. But jealous or resentful? No. I should be. If our marriage had meant anything, I would be tearing Maxine's hair out by now."

"So, it meant nothing to you. Is that what you're saying?"

Ella shook her head. That's not what she had meant to say at all. "It's just that it didn't mean enough. For either of us."

Clouds closed in and the first spatter of rain hit off the windows as Ella and Andrew stood in the kitchen of the home they had shared together. They stared at each other. Ella knew she had hurt Andrew with her last remark and he understood how hurt she was by his betrayal. There had been too much hurt. Too much pain. Any words they would say now would be too bitter and too late.

He put his arms around her and held her close. Eyes closed, she leaned her head on his shoulder. She felt his heart beat and his chest rise and fall with each breath he took. She felt his regret and his guilt, his wish that things could have been different. They both knew they had reached the boundary now. They were about to cross a line which would see their paths divide. Andrew's lips touched hers. A parting kiss with none of the elemental force of Peter Sheehan's caress. Ella stood back and smiled at Andrew.

"You'd better go. You don't want to miss Maxine at the airport. I'll call to the office first and then go to the hospital to see Oliver."

"Would you talk to Rob Trevor? See if you can persuade him?"

Ella hesitated. She didn't want to try to dissuade Rob. He was doing what he believed to be right for his peace of mind. Maybe she would just talk to him, see how he was.

"Okay. I'll go to see Rob. But I won't bully him. You

can scoff all you like but there's something very odd going on with Manor House and I don't blame him for wanting to escape."

"Coincidence. One coincidence after another," Andrew muttered as he gathered his jacket and car keys.

Ella went to the front door with him to wave him off. The cold wind whipped around her. She shivered and pulled her dressing-gown close, raising her hand as he drove off. He didn't see her. He was already leaving his wife behind and focusing on his future. On Maxine.

Chapter 31

As Ella waited at the interminably red traffic lights her eyes were drawn to a puddle in the street. A little dint in the tarmac immediately to her right had filled up with rain. The water looked black but something about the way the needles of cold rain broke the scummy surface reminded her of Cuanowen. The ocean would be wild this morning, buffeted by the gales now sweeping the whole country. Dog Rock would be submerged. Pebbles Shorten would be sitting at his desk in his estate agency wishing he was in the city. In Seaview Hotel Beryl Langford would be supervising the cooking of full Irish breakfasts, and all over the little village, from Main Street to the surrounding hills, eyes would be drawn towards the sea, the majesty and power …

A driver hooted impatiently behind her. The lights had turned green and Ella's daydream of Cuanowen was holding up the flow of traffic. Waving an apology, she headed off in the direction of the office. When she got out of her car, she made a dash for the door, glancing at the name over it: *Ford Auctioneers and Estate Agents*. How proud she had been of that sign! She still was but it no longer represented who she was. It was just a signpost to the wrong path on which she had allowed ambition lead her.

Inside business was running smoothly. The staff were responding well to the challenge of being given more responsibility. Sly little glances and conversations aborted as soon as she appeared. Ella knew that they were all speculating about the unusual comings and goings of their bosses. She smiled to herself as she realised they probably thought she was having yet another mental breakdown. How surprised they would be if she told them the breakdown was of her marriage and that the Fords were embroiled in suicide attempts, blackmail and corruption.

Phone messages were piled up on both desks. Mostly from the Cox brothers. She had expected something from Jason Laide. Loud, bullying demands that the deal for the Ballyhaven site be closed immediately. There was nothing from him. Maybe the combined charms of his wife and Manor House were civilising him.

Ella felt the start of a tension headache. She sat at her desk and massaged her forehead, thinking that Andrew should be here instead of dashing off to the airport. Her fingers stopped moving as she analysed her feelings of resentment towards Maxine. Was she jealous? Surely not. Wasn't she leaving Andrew because she didn't love him any more? So why the anger? Her frowns eased when she found her answer. She was frustrated, anxious to begin her new life, eager to tie up all the loose ends here and be on her way. All these delays were keeping her from moving forward, sucking her into the mire of deceit and greed from which she so desperately needed to escape.

Ella sat up straight, pulled her chair forward and picked up her phone. It was time she began to actively put the plans for her future into motion. As she tapped in the Cuanowen number she said a quick prayer to her mother and father. A positive response to this call was vital. Even a maybe or a promise to think about the proposition would do for now.

By the time Ella put the phone down again she knew her prayers had been answered. Not completely. There would be negotiations, bargains to be struck, conditions to be agreed. But the principle had been accepted. The path to her new life had been forged and this time she knew, in her heart and soul, that her feet would not falter.

It took longer to placate Gary Cox. He eventually agreed to a meeting in two days' time on condition that he had a final, and preferably affirmative, answer by then on the Ballyhaven site. Ella agreed wholeheartedly. Everyone concerned needed closure and the sooner the better.

Secret looks were exchanged between the staff as Ella left the office again.

"Will Mr Ford be in today?"

Ella hesitated for a moment before answering. Then she decided.

"Actually he's collecting his girlfriend from the airport. He'll be in later."

She turned her back on the shocked faces and, head

held high, walked out into the rain and wind. She was smiling.

* * *

All eyes were on Maxine as she emerged through the Arrivals exit. Women looked in envy and men in awe. She had eyes only for Andrew Ford. He hovered anxiously by the exit, grabbing her luggage, leaning forward to kiss her on the cheek as soon as she reached the barrier. He seemed tense, his hair ruffled, his face pale.

"Why did you not answer my calls?" Maxine asked as they walked towards the car park.

Andrew stood, his hands on the luggage trolley. He stared at Maxine as if he couldn't think of a convincing answer to her question. She began to walk away. He chased after her, standing in front of her, deliberately blocking her view so that she could not see Jason Laide as he rushed towards the airport doors, pushing people aside as he stormed along. Andrew wondered if the bastard had been going to meet Maxine, to torture her again. Jason disappeared into the airport building, leaving a trail of disgruntled people in his wake. Maxine began to walk ahead again.

"Wait!" Andrew said. "You've no idea what's been going on. It's been chaos here. And I've found out something you need to know."

"Likewise," Maxine answered. "Let's go to my apartment and exchange the need-to-knows."

They were silent as they loaded the luggage into

Andrew's car, as they drove along the motorway, as they pulled up outside Maxine's apartment and unlocked her front door. Inside, there was an awkwardness between them, a lack of trust they had not experienced before. They sat in the lounge, one on the couch, the other in an armchair and regarded each other cautiously.

"You first," said Maxine.

"I've been to the Registrar's Office. I traced your family tree. The Murphy line."

He thought Maxine flinched. That her mouth twitched, her eyelids blinked. He must have been mistaken. Her voice was very cool.

"And?"

"And Harriet Wellsley is your great-grandmother. There's no doubt. Her marriage certificate shows that in 1901 Harriet Wellsley of Manor House married a stable lad named Thomas Murphy with an address at 6 Mountain View Terrace. Your great-grandfather Thomas. She was sixteen at the time. They had a son John who married Eileen Shaw. Your grandparents. John and Eileen had a son Paddy. Your father. Am I right so far?"

There was no mistaking her reaction now. Maxine was white-faced and looked close to tears. Andrew went to sit beside her on the couch. He held her close and felt her body shake.

"I knew it," she muttered over and over. "I always knew it." Suddenly, she pulled away from him. "When did she die? Where?"

"That's the peculiar thing. I searched and searched but there's no record of her death. Harriet Murphy is registered as the mother of John born in 1902. Nothing after that. No more children. No death certificate. No paper trail at all. She just disappeared. From official records anyway."

"According to my father she upped sticks and left one day. Why would she do that? Especially since she had a son. John. My grandfather."

"You've spoken to your father about this? Did they search for her or report her missing?"

"I think they were just glad she was gone. That's the impression my father gives anyway. My father was born in 1935 and he never met Harriet. Not that he can remember anyway. His memory is a bit impaired. To be honest it's pickled in alcohol so I can't rely on what he says."

"Did he know she was Harriet Wellsley?"

"I don't believe so. Though he seemed to recognise her in the photograph of the Manor House portrait. The one you gave me."

Andrew put his hands on Maxine's face and gently turned her so that they were looking directly at each other. "Manor House, Max. I have two things to tell you about it and I don't think you'll like either. Firstly, Harriet's father died shortly after she left Manor House. I looked up his will. Luckily there was a copy in the National Archives. She's not mentioned in it at all. He had obviously disinherited her. I'm sorry, but you have no rightful claim on the property."

"But I –" Maxine began before Andrew interrupted her.

"The second thing is that Jason Laide has made an agreement with Rob Trevor. They went behind my back. It seems Mr Laide is set to be the new owner of Manor House."

"He most certainly is not!" Maxine said and this time Andrew could not stop her talking until she had told him all about her meeting Dirk Van Aken.

"How could you put yourself at risk like that, Max? He could have killed you."

"I had to. I must stop Jason. I wanted to find something to threaten him with. He can't keep ruining my life like this."

She stopped then, her eyes huge in her pale face. She was perfectly still, waiting for Andrew's reaction.

"I know he's the one. I figured it out," he said quietly. "The blackmailer. The one with the video of you."

Maxine nodded. "Yes. He's held that cursed video over my head since I was fifteen years old. People look at me and think I'm a success. Now you can see, Andrew, what I really am. Just a tramp who made good. Jason Laide's tart."

Andrew moved to draw her close to him. The intercom buzzed. He looked at Maxine, eyebrow raised.

"Are you expecting someone?"

She shook her head. In fact her whole body shook. What if it was Jason? No. It couldn't be. He'd just barge up. Her relief was short-lived. When she picked up the intercom she heard Sharon Laide's husky, cultured voice asking to be allowed up.

Maxine heard herself agreeing, found herself buzzing

Sharon up, opening the door for her, offering her a seat.

Assured, beautiful, so well dressed and elegant, Sharon sat into an armchair and coolly regarded Andrew and Maxine.

"It's nice to meet you again so soon, Andrew," she said, "but would you mind excusing us for a moment. I have something private to discuss with Maxine."

"I have no secrets from Andrew. He's staying."

Sharon looked from one to the other of them and then smiled. "That's good, Maxine. There have been too many secrets. That's why I'm here. I can't explain it all to you but I've recently discovered that my husband has some property which rightly belongs to you. I've come to return it."

Sharon reached into her bag, took out a padded envelope and offered it to Maxine. She sat there, hand outstretched while Maxine just stared, afraid to take the packet, terrified to open it, to find out if it really contained the video. *The* video.

"Take it. It's yours."

Maxine stood and walked slowly towards Sharon. Taking the padded envelope she squeezed it gently all over, feeling the hard outline of a rectangular box inside. A video? Fingers shaking, she ripped the paper and dropped it on the floor. In her hand she held a video labelled in Jason's childish handwriting: *Marie Murphy aka Maxine Doran*.

"Have you seen it, Sharon? Do you know what's on it?"

Sharon lowered her head. She seemed ashamed to

meet Maxine's eyes. "I'm sorry," she said softly. "I did see it. Not all of it. Just enough to know you were very young and very drugged when it was made."

"Drugged?"

"Yes. Didn't you know? It's obvious. Isn't that usually how these despicable things are done?"

"You should know that. You're his wife."

"Did he make copies?" Andrew asked.

"No. My husband likes to control everything himself."

Sharon stood. She seemed less tall, less assured than when she had come in. She picked up her bag.

"I understand how you must feel, Maxine, but please believe me, I knew nothing about this. As soon as I found out I arranged to return it to you. And you can be assured this is the only copy. Destroy it. Keep it. Give it to the police. It's up to you now."

"Wait!" Maxine said as she walked over to the television set and switching it on, slotted in the video.

All three pairs of eyes were riveted to the screen as the tape rewound and then flickered into life. The camera panned around a small untidy bedroom before focusing on a double bed which seemed too big for the space available. Two young girls, dressed only in underwear, lay on the bed, one dark-haired and painfully thin, the other with blonde, cropped hair and a stunningly beautiful face. The young Maxine. Already the figure of a full-grown woman but the vulnerability of a child in her smile. The girls were giggling, drunk, or maybe, as Sharon had suggested, drugged. A male voice, unmistakably Jason's, muttered something. The dark-haired girl reached her hand towards Maxine.

The screen went blank. Maxine had switched it off. She looked at Andrew, searching his face for signs of rejection and disgust. All she saw was anger glittering in his eyes.

"You're sure this is the only copy?" she asked Sharon.

"Certain. He wouldn't trust anyone but me with his 'insurance policies' as he called them. This is why I had to ask you not to say anything. When Jason finds out about this and the others too . . . Well, I think you know how he'll react."

"Why in the hell did you marry him?" Andrew asked.

Sharon looked solemnly at him, speaking slowly as if she was just finding the answer to the question herself. "I married him because he was the most exciting man I had ever met. He was different, stronger, more vital, than anyone else I had known. Marrying him wasn't the problem. The mistake was staying married to him. But I had my reasons."

"Money," Andrew spat. "Properties and holidays. A jet-set lifestyle. And now Manor House. But he's not getting that. I won't allow it."

Maxine laid her hand on Andrew's arm to calm him.

Sharon was standing by the door now, tears visible in her eyes.

"What are you going to do, Sharon?" asked Maxine. "You know he's dangerous."

A brave smile flitted across Sharon's face. "I'll be all right. I have just one more person to see and then I can settle affairs with my husband."

Maxine crossed over the room and stood in front of Sharon. "You do know you're not alone, don't you? Other people want to see your husband get his just desserts too. I've been given to understand the Revenue Commissioners and the Criminal Assets Bureau are interested in exactly how Jason is making his money. Jason's partner in crime, maybe you know him, a Dutchman named Van Aken, has abandoned him. Van Aken masquerades as a gaming-machine supplier but, like Jason, his real source of income is drug-dealing."

"Drug-dealing!" Sharon's face was drawn with shock.

Maxine leaned towards the elegant woman and hugged her warmly. "I'm sorry," she said, "but it's true. And I'm very grateful to you for giving me back the video. For giving me back my life. Thank you, Sharon."

Sharon just stared at Maxine, her eyes still glazed with shock. Everything was beginning to make a cruel type of sense to her now. Jason's recent uncontrolled spending, his vulgar display of wealth. Her own utter stupidity. How had she not known that Jason would inevitably get involved in pedalling drugs?

In one fluid movement Sharon had opened the door and closed it gently behind her. Maxine turned to Andrew. "I'm going into the bedroom," she said. "Watch that video and then tell me if we have a future together."

"Stay just where you are," he said.

Maxine stood and watched as Andrew walked into the kitchen. She didn't know why he had gone there or why he had told her to stay. She just knew that the future course of her life was about to be decided. She moved to the kitchen door.

Andrew glanced at her standing in the doorway, watching him. She looked young and very vulnerable. Just like the little girl in the video. Her eyes were gazing steadily at him. Questioning. Going to the knife block, Andrew picked out a sharp carver and brought it into the living-room. He picked up Jason Laide's video and began to prise open the casing.

"What are you doing?"

Andrew looked up at Maxine. There were tears in his eyes. "I love you, Maxine Doran. I don't care what's in this video. It would make no difference to how I feel."

"No, Andrew! I need you to watch it! Y-you don't realise –"

"It doesn't matter. Nothing matters except the fact that you're the woman I've waited all my life to meet. I love you whether you're Marie Murphy or Maxine Doran. I always will."

"B-but if we're to be together I need you to know everything about me!"

"I know everything. Everything that matters."

The cover loosened now, he began to unwind the tape from the spools. It slithered snake-like over the tiled floor. He went to the kitchen again and poked around until he found a scissors. Then he came back and carefully began to chop the tape into tiny sections.

"Do you want to help?" he asked Maxine.

She walked slowly towards him. He held the scissors out to her. Her hands shook as she snipped and cut. After five minutes the floor was littered with tiny fragments of tape. Fragments of Maxine's nightmare. She sank to her knees and cried like the baby she had been when Jason Laide destroyed her life. Andrew stooped down beside her and put his arms around her. He stroked her hair and kissed her wet face. They cried together for the hurt Maxine had suffered, for Andrew's pain of knowing and for the joy of having found strength and forgiveness in each other.

★ ★ ★

Ella scanned the hospital car park anxiously. She suddenly laughed at herself. Not only was she looking for Peter Sheehan's car in the public parking area when he would obviously have a reserved space in front of the hospital but she was silly enough to be looking out for him in the first place. He probably kissed women all the time, held them in his strong arms, drowned them in his clear green gaze. He most likely had forgotten their kiss last night. Hopefully he had forgotten that Ella Ford had trembled in his arms, that her heart had beaten wildly against his chest. "Silly cow!" Ella muttered to herself as she found a space and parked her car.

The main entrance to the hospital was five minutes' walk from the car park, so Ella was composed by the time she reached the building. She caught a lift to the third floor. Oliver's room was right at the end of a long corridor. As she approached it, the door opened and Sharon Laide came out. Head down, she walked past Ella, apparently without even seeing her. Feeling slightly taken aback, Ella continued down the corridor and entered the room. Naturally, Oliver and Sharon had met socially but Ella had not realised they were on hospital visiting terms.

Oliver was asleep. He still had a greenish pallor but some of the frowns on his face had softened. They did not seem as deep as they had last night. Ella had to fight the temptation to lie down on the bed beside him. She was suddenly exhausted, all the drama of last night beginning to catch up with her. Andrew must be worn out by now.

Easing the newspaper and book she had brought for Oliver out of her bag she tiptoed across and put them on his locker. She took one last look at him and crept out of the room.

Knowing that a duty roster would be on display in the lobby, she deliberately went out a side door. She would not lower herself to reading the roster, spying on Peter Sheehan, trying to find out if he was in the building. Anyway, he was most likely in his private clinic, making pots of money and charming his female patients out of their neuroses. This growing obsession with him must stop. She was nothing but an ex-patient to him. Angrily, Ella kicked a stone ahead of her. How could Peter Sheehan ever take her seriously? He had seen her at her most vulnerable. At the time when Karen Trevor had been her constant companion. Besides he hadn't cured her. Not really. She had done that herself. On her own. Just like she was going to organise the rest of her life. No more depending on anyone else, no more trusting and being vulnerable. Catching up with the stone, she gave it another kick.

"Therapy?"

Ella jumped when she heard the voice coming from behind her. She did not have to turn around to know that Peter Sheehan's green eyes were regarding her with professional interest, wondering about her stress levels. She twirled around to face him.

"Yes! I'm angry, Peter. I'm tired and hurt and fed up of being around here. I want to go. To get out."

"And why don't you?"

"I have things to do first. People to see. Arrangements to make. Then I'm going home. To my real home. Cuanowen. I should never have left there."

"Are you running away?"

Ella opened her mouth to answer. To shout at Peter Sheehan. To tell him how she resented his remark. How wrong he was. The energy suddenly drained out of her as she realised she was angry at herself and not at him. Angry because she had wasted a whole year of her life in a self-induced cocoon of depression. She smiled at him.

"No. I'm running towards, not away. How is Oliver doing?"

"I'm just going on duty now. I'll let you know as soon as I see him. I was going to ring you anyway. Would you like to come to dinner some evening? "

Ella looked down at her shoes and saw a scuffmark where she had kicked the stone. She wanted to see Peter again. Just once before she went away. No harm in that. Except of course that it would be pointless and she didn't need any more complications in her already convoluted life.

"Sure. I'll ring you sometime, Peter."

"The brush-off? Well, if you change your mind, you have my number."

They turned and walked in different directions. Away from each other.

Ella was pleased with herself, knowing she had made the right decision. Peter Sheehan was a very attractive man and she had no business around attractive men until her life was back on track. Which reminded her of Andrew. She rang him and reported on her visit to the sleeping Oliver and the arrangement she had made with Gary Cox.

"I'm meeting Pascal shortly. We'll be going to visit Oliver then. Trying to sort out the mess." He sounded tired. Down.

"Are you all right, Andrew?"

"I'm fine. At least I will be when Jason Laide is behind bars. I've found out that he's involved in drugs, Ella. He's reportedly under investigation. We can't afford to deal with him. You must warn Rob Trevor too. When are you going to Manor House?"

Ella glanced at her watch. It was lunchtime and she was hungry. "I'm just going to get something to eat, then I'll head out to see Rob. Are you sure about Jason? They're pretty heavy accusations."

"I'm sure. Look, I'll give Rob a quick call. Just to warn him. Then you can fully explain the Jason situation to him when you get there."

"Sharon Laide has been to visit Oliver too. I was surprised. She left his room just as I came in but she didn't seem to see me." There was silence on the other end of the line. "Are you still there, Andrew?"

"Was Sharon talking to Oliver?"

The question sounded urgent.

"I don't know. He was sleeping when I went in. But perhaps he fell asleep while she was there."

Ella heard Andrew give a long sigh. She couldn't decide whether it was a sigh of upset or relief. Maxine was probably with him. Let her decide.

"Keep in contact," she said. "I'll ring you as soon as I've spoken to Rob."

As Ella switched off her phone she realised she might not love Andrew Ford enough to stay married to him but adjusting to life without him was going to be very difficult.

Chapter 32

Sharon tried Jason's phone for the third time even though she knew by now that he had switched it off. She was beginning to panic. The last thing she needed was for Jason to disappear before she had sorted things with him. Maybe he had found out that the authorities were watching him. Running away wasn't in his nature but self-preservation was. Shit!

Everything had been going so smoothly. Ahead of schedule. Oliver Griffin had been the last person she had needed to contact. He had been difficult to track down. She eventually had to ring his wife only to find that Oliver had been hospitalised after an accident. A few tactful questions later she had known where to find Oliver. She had gone to the hospital, given him his IOU's and sat with him for a while – it was the least she could do. It would all be wasted effort now if she could not find Jason and talk to him face to face. Closure was what she needed and must have.

She drove back to the depot and asked again if he had called. She got the same answer as she had previously. "He was here early this morning, ma'am. We haven't seen him since."

Sharon sat back into her car and tried to think where he could have gone. He had so many businesses. So many boltholes. If he felt threatened he would hide. No. He wouldn't. He would fight! Fight for what he thought was his by right and at that minute Sharon knew what he would fight hardest for. Manor House. She turned the car and headed back through the city, out into the suburbs and beyond.

When she got as far as the narrow road bordered by stone walls, she slowed down. The road was dangerous, windswept and flanked by quickly filling channels in the heavy rain. But more importantly, she was almost there now and certain that she would find Jason. She must decide. Frieda's words echoed in her head: "He has a right to know." Sharon thought about Salzburg and about her life there. How precious it was. How she must protect it. Frieda said she must tell the truth. But the knowledge now that he might be a drug-dealer made everything more dangerous. As she turned onto the long avenue leading to Manor House the battle was still raging in her head. It was only when she saw Jason's car parked on the sweep of driveway which fronted the house that she finally made up her mind.

As Sharon stood on the steps at the magnificent double doors waiting for an answer to her ring she thought with sadness of Karen Wellsley. They had grown up together, gone to the same school, the same ballet classes and music lessons. That's where the similarities had ended. Karen had been the quiet one, always on the outside of their group, the girl who rarely smiled and never laughed. The girl who had grown up to become Karen Trevor. The woman who had died so tragically at such an early age.

Sharon heard footsteps approaching the door from inside and then some fumbling as the big latch was unhooked. The door was opened by a grey-haired, middle-aged woman wearing a navy pleated skirt.

"Good afternoon. My name is Sharon Laide. I'm here to see my husband if I may."

The disparaging glance the woman gave as she held the door open said everything about her opinion of the Laides. She waved the visitor into the hall and then, hands folded neatly in front of her, went to get Jason.

As Sharon waited in the huge hall she looked around and upwards, admiring the flooring, the staircase, the magnificent vaulted ceiling. She was reminded of the time she had been at Karen Wellsley's birthday party here. A party everyone had seemed to enjoy except the birthday girl and the grumpy housekeeper. Sharon smiled and nodded her head. Of course! The housekeeper. The same woman who had reluctantly opened the door to her today. Just grumpier and greyer now. No wonder she resented the Laides. This woman had given a lifetime of service to the Wellsleys. A strong gust of wind swirled around the house and whistled as it rushed down some of the many chimneys here. Sharon shivered at the eerie sound. This was why Karen Wellsley had always seemed so solemn and sad. She had been shaped by this house. This mausoleum.

Sharon was just about to examine the portraits hanging along the stairway when the sound of raised voices drifted over the whistle of the wind and out into the hall. Jason's voice was loudest and most angry. She walked in the direction the housekeeper had taken and followed the sound until she came to an open door. The grey-haired woman was standing in the doorway, her hands still neatly folded, while inside the room, which was a study, Jason was hovering over Rob Trevor, spitting fury at him.

"It's mine, you fucker! I want it now! "

"Will you please refrain from using that language in my house? Remember there are ladies present."

Jason turned around and glared at the women standing side by side in the doorway. His face, flushed and bloated with temper, twisted into an ugly sneer as he looked them up and down.

"I don't know about your housekeeper," he said "but my wife's no lady. She's anyone's as long as they can afford her."

"Mr Laide! Control yourself or leave immediately, please!"

Rob was standing now, taller than Jason but immeasurably weaker both physically and mentally.

Jason laughed into his face. "Who's going to make me? You? Or your stone-faced housekeeper?"

"Me," Sharon announced, stepping forward and catching Jason by the arm. The feel of his tensed muscles underneath her fingers frightened her. She must get this maniac out of here before he caused real harm. Leaning close to him she whispered into his ear. "I have something important to tell you, Jason. We need to talk privately."

"Let go my arm," he said roughly, pulling away from her.

Sharon grabbed him again and this time her hold was firmer. Her temper was beginning to match his in intensity but it was colder. More steely.

Rob sank back onto his chair, looking pale and very upset. She leaned towards him.

"I'm terribly sorry, Rob. Would you excuse my husband and me for a moment? We need to talk."

Rob seemed relieved that they were going, even for a short time. "Feel free to use the drawing room. Betty will show you the way."

Sharon tugged at Jason's arm and was surprised that this time he offered no resistance. Betty, as the housekeeper was obviously named, straight-backed and still with her hands folded, led them along the corridor towards the hall. Stopping outside a magnificently carved ornate door she opened it and stood aside for the Laides to enter the room. Her disapproval was apparent even in the soft click of the door closing behind them.

The drawing room was vast and would have been bright if it were not for the thick velour drapes and the greyness of the day outside. The air had the musty tang of a room seldom used. Sharon glanced around and pursed her lips in a silent whistle as she made a rough estimate of the value of the faded décor. The fireplace was marble, the furniture rosewood, the tapestries Persian, the embossed wallpaper hand-painted silk. Grand relics of a gentler age.

"Jesus! This is like a museum," Jason said, hunching up his shoulders and pulling his jacket more tightly around him.

Sharon did the same. The room was freezing. And eerie. She jumped when the wind blasted down the chimney, bringing with it more cold air and the smell of soot. Walking over to a chaise longue with faded lemon silk upholstery, she sat and indicated to Jason to sit beside her. He remained standing.

"What in the fuck do you want to talk about? You never did have much time for conversation with me, did you? Why now?"

Just the opening she needed. Sharon took a deep breath and then jumped at the chance.

"Very true, Jason. We really have nothing much in common. That's why I think we should end our marriage. I want a divorce."

She had to clasp her bag tightly in her hands to keep them from shaking. Jason seemed to stop breathing. His face went from red to purple as he stood stock still, staring at her with the icy-blue eyes she had once believed so intelligent. Sharon thought he might get a heart attack, a stroke, a brain haemorrhage but she could not move to help him. Eventually Jason took in a huge gulp of air and strode across to stand in front of her. She was eye level with his chest which was heaving now, drawing in oxygen at double rate to compensate for his moment of paralysis.

"Bitch!" he shouted and his voice echoed around the

huge room, joining with another blast of wind which had screeched its way down the chimney. "Bitch! Bitch! Bitch! You go when I decide. You don't tell me what to do. Nobody tells Jason Laide how he should live his life. Not you, not fucking Van Aken or that ponce Rob Trevor, or Andrew Ford and his snotty friends! Not even Gussie. Twisted bastard. Judas!"

"You seem to have made a lot of enemies, Jason."

His hand shot out and made sharp contact with her face. Her cheek stung. Tears welled in her eyes but she held them back. There would be time for crying later. Later, when she was in Salzburg, in her home, with the people who loved her and whom she loved deeply in return. Loved enough to down-face this animal now. Raising her hand she soothed the cheek which was already red and swollen with the mark of her husband's hand.

"I think you had better sit down, Jason, and listen to me. We can settle this here and now or we can go through the courts. How do you feel about the law poking about in your affairs? Maybe even your Dutch connection. The choice is yours."

Jason sat, choosing a seat opposite her. It was a huge green leather armchair stuffed with horsehair. His legs barely touched the floor because the chair was so big and his legs short.

Footsteps sounded in the corridor outside. A gale swept in around their feet as the front door was opened and then quickly closed again. Voices filled the hall – the housekeeper's low tones and the lighter tones of a younger woman, sounding, Sharon thought, exactly like Ella Ford. They passed by the drawing room door and then their voices faded as they walked along the corridor to where Rob Trevor had his study.

The room was quiet again except for the sound of the wind and Jason's laboured breathing. Not the peaceful quiet of Junkergasse. Sharon closed her eyes for a second, drawing on her inner strength. When she opened them again she felt strong enough to face Jason.

"I knew straight away, even during our honeymoon that I should never have married you."

"Then why in the fuck didn't you leave?"

"Because I was afraid of what you would do. Just listen, Jason. It's not easy and I'm not very proud of my part in it so just let me speak while I have the courage. When we came back from honeymoon I planned to leave you. But then things changed."

"They certainly fucking did. You went whoring all over the world. At my expense. I was a fool to fall for your talk of open marriage and all that crap."

"Yes, you were," Sharon agreed. "Because none of it was true. I never went on safari or to South America, to San Tropez, or to any of those places where I told you I was partying and having grotty little affairs. All the time I was making a home in Salzburg."

Salzburg! Salzburg! A shiver ran down Jason's spine as he thought of the big, dreary house and the steely gaze of Frau Henner. Sour old bag. He remembered O'Shaughnessy's photos. He had shoved the envelope into his pocket in Gussie's office without looking at them.

Time to take them out now and see exactly what Sharon was up to in the place she called home. He flicked through them, his face getting redder with each shot he examined.

"I knew it!" he shouted, jumping out of the big chair and almost toppling as his feet made contact with the floor. "I just knew there was something going on between you and that butch-looking housekeeper in Junkergasse! That Frieda person. You're a dyke! Christ! My wife is a lesbian! And I have proof! Look! O'Shaughnessy caught the two of ye at it!" He thrust a stubby finger at the top photograph.

She glanced at it. It was a close-up of Frieda and her. Frieda was hugging her, consoling her after the ordeal she had been through in the hospital. How much worse the ordeal would have seemed had she known one of Jason's goons was spying on them.

"You sent someone to spy on me!"

"Yes, he even followed you to Geneva when you went there to get my papers out."

Sharon laughed and the light heady feeling of laughing into Jason's face gave her more strength. "I went to Geneva to put your papers in, you idiot! They're in a vault there and, if anything happens to me, my solicitor is under instruction to give them to the police."

"That's what you fucking think! I'll be over to Salzburg in the morning. I'll sort that!"

"Try if you want to but you'll be arrested the minute you land. There's a warrant for your arrest in Salzburg. Frieda and I went to the hospital after your last visit to

Junkergasse. The staff were horrified by the marks of your fingers around my neck. The doctor was obliged to report it to the police under the Ärztegesetz law relating to domestic violence. I was happy to follow up with my official complaint. You nearly choked me, you animal!"

In a movement that was surprisingly quick and fluid Jason launched himself at Sharon, dropping O'Shaughnessy's photographs onto the floor. She jumped to her feet just as he leapt on the chaise, red-faced and panting. She had felt his hands around her throat before and it was never going to happen again.

"Your bullying tactics won't help you now," she said as she faced him. "Your papers and videos weren't lost in transit. I've returned them all to their owners. You can't torture those people any more."

She braced herself for Jason's reaction. A scream, a roar, maybe a kick. He was silent, staring at the floor. She followed his gaze and her eyes came to rest on O'Shaughnessy's scattered photos. Her heart almost stopped. One picture, the one mesmerising Jason, lay face up. It had been taken at the airport as she had said goodbye to Frieda and to the most precious person in her life. She was holding him close to her, not wanting to let him go. A fierce protective instinct galvanised her into action now. She swooped down to grab the photo.

Jason's foot stamped onto her fingers. She cried out with pain and fear. He lunged down beside her and prised the photograph from under her hand.

Wind whistled, timbers creaked, time moved on but neither Sharon nor Jason noticed. He stared at the photograph and she stared at him. Gathering up the other photographs, he scrutinised them. He looked up at Sharon and down at the photos again.

"You whoring bitch!" he breathed. "This is your son!"

Sharon nodded her head. Just the slightest little dip to acknowledge the little boy who was the centre of her life.

"Jesus! You lying bitch! You can't have a son. When were you pregnant? Where did you have the baby?"

"In Salzburg. I was seldom anywhere else."

"Who's the father? Tell me or I'll kill you now!"

This was it. The secret Sharon had tried so hard to keep had to be revealed. She could attempt to lie but now that Jason knew of the existence of the child the risk was greater. And yet she couldn't say the words. Not all of them. Not the full truth.

"He's my son and mine alone. Nothing at all to do with you. I don't want you near him. Don't ever try to see him or I'll make sure you end your days in jail."

"He's wearing a hat in all the photos. What colour is his hair?"

Sharon and the man she had once loved gazed at each other in silence. She shook so much that her teeth chattered but no word passed her lips. Jason seemed to deflate as the meaning of her silence sank in. His purple flush of rage was replaced by a ghastly white pallor. He flopped onto the chaise and leaning forward hung his head. He knew. He did not need to be told that the little boy in the picture had a shock of red hair. Just like his father.

When he looked up there were tears in his eyes.

"How old is he?"

"Almost four," Sharon said. "He's a beautiful boy. Very clever. He's fluent in both German and English.

"Who's looking after him now?"

"Frieda. She has always taken care of him when I'm not there. She's my son's nanny not my lover."

He dropped his head again. Sharon felt a pang of guilt. She had been very devious. She had plotted and planned for so long. She should have told Jason in the beginning and faced the consequences. Yet she had wanted the best for her child. That's why she had spent so many years converting Jason's assets into legitimate investments. Tolerating his brutality in exchange for security for her son. Fifty percent of all Jason owned when she divorced him. That had been before she knew of his involvement in drug-dealing and blackmail. But now she felt guilty by association. Dirty.

Jason looked up at her again, his eyes still watery.

"Where do you hide him when I go to Salzburg?"

"Frieda's daughter and son-in-law keep him in their home. You met them, remember? They brought you hill-walking. It was never a problem. You rarely visited and seldom stayed long."

"What have you told him about his father?"

"That he's very busy travelling around the world making money. I'll be honest with Harry when he's old enough to understand."

"Harry? Harry."

Jason's shoulders began to shake. Sharon watched as the bully, the blackmailer, the drug pusher cried. She walked across and sat beside him. Tentatively she put her hand on his shaking shoulders. He leaned against her and she felt his hot tears on her neck.

"You were so wrong, Shar. I would have been a good father to him. I would have given him everything I didn't have when I was a child."

Tears welled in Sharon's eyes now too. What had she done? What in the name of God had she done?

"When would you have told me if I hadn't seen this photo?"

"Not until he was a lot older. Until he could decide for himself whether he wanted to see you or not."

"If you had been a better wife and I had my son here I would have made different decisions. None of us would be in this mess now."

Sharon pulled away from him. He was doing it again. Confusing her. Fooling her. Nobody had made him into a blackmailer and drug dealer. That had been his choice and he would probably have made the same choices even if he had known about Harry from the beginning. She opened her bag and took out a photograph of Harry, smiling, his red hair gleaming.

"Here take this. It's better than any your spy has taken. You can keep this photograph, Jason. But don't ever come near us."

Jason stared at the picture of his son. A mirror image of himself at the same age stared back. But Harry was stronger, better nourished.

"What are you going to do?" Sharon asked. "For Harry's sake I'm not going to turn you in to the police but other people may. For instance Maxine Doran or Oliver Griffin."

Jason looked up at her and smiled. "I think I'll go on safari."

Then he wiped his eyes on his sleeve, hauled himself up off the chaise longue with the lemon upholstery, kissed her on the cheek and walked out of the room holding the picture of his son in his hand.

Sharon sank back onto the seat he had just vacated and cried for Harry. What cruel mistakes both his parents had made.

* * *

Even in the dim light of his study, Ella noticed the hollows underneath Rob Trevor's cheekbones. The man seemed to be rapidly caving in. Ella sat, not even sure if Rob was aware of her presence.

"Quite a storm brewing up outside," she said but, getting no response, she tried again.

"Is that Jason Laide's car I saw parked at the front of the house?"

Rob looked up and his eyes glittered with an anger Ella had not guessed he could possess.

"Yes. The thug is here. Could you believe he threatened me with violence? I don't know what would have happened if his wife had not calmed him down."

"Sharon is here too?"

"They're in the drawing room. I should have thrown them out. I don't want that man anywhere near me."

"Did Andrew ring you this morning?"

"He did. He told me there may be an investigation into Laide's business affairs. That I would be well advised not to deal with him. I withdrew my agreement to sell to him. That's why he went berserk."

Pity tugged at Ella's heart. In Rob's obvious distressed state it must seem to him that he could not get rid of Manor House. That it was holding on to him, sucking him into its dark corners and creaky attics. She reached across and gently stroked his cold hand.

"Maxine Doran really wants this house. She'll buy it from you and then you can get on with the rest of your life."

"She died nearly twenty-five years ago."

"Rob, what's the matter with you? She's not even twenty-five yet. Maxine is alive and well. And with my husband."

"No. No. I mean Lady Harriet Wellsley. I changed my mind about investigating Lady Harriet. I hired a private detective. I had to. I wanted to understand before I left here why Karen had been so obsessed by her. All those hours spent staring at Lady Harriet's portrait when she should have been talking to her child. And to me."

Rob's gaze went off into the distance again. He really appeared to be at the limits of his stress tolerance. Ella squeezed his hand to remind him she was there.

"And? What did this detective find out?"

"He emailed this morning. In the early nineteen hundreds Lady Harriet married a stable hand named Murphy. She stayed with him for twenty years in some little hovel in the inner city. The Wellsley clan, of course, disowned her. It seems she had been saving pennies here and there for the twenty years. When she had enough together she bought her passage to South Africa and . . ."

Rob paused again. This time Ella left him to whatever thoughts he had until he was ready to continue.

"The Wellsleys have distant cousins in South Africa. They own a big plantation. Harriet lived out the rest of her days with them. She never spoke about Ireland. They didn't even know she had a son. She was ninety-nine years old when she died."

Ella thought of the beautiful young girl in the portrait, full of youth and beauty. What a sad and lonely outcome all that promise had.

"Where's the portrait now?" she asked.

"I burnt it."

Ella stared at him. My God! What was that painting worth?

"I took it out of the frame this morning, brought it to the courtyard, poured petrol on it and watched as it crackled and curled. And I'll tell you, Ella, I felt such relief when there was nothing left of it but a handful of ashes. I must be insane. Of course I am. Mad with guilt and grief. But I believe Lady Harriet Wellsley was trapped by her father's curse. She was undead. Now, she is gone. I think I heard her . . ."

Rob stopped talking. Whatever he had thought he heard, he decided not to pass on. Ella reached for his cold hand and held it in hers. She too felt relief that the beautiful portrait with the very ugly history was no more.

But Rob was still haunted by ghosts. She saw them in his eyes. The ghosts of his wife and child. He seemed very much alone with his torturous memories.

"So what now, Rob? Are you satisfied that Karen's problems had nothing to do with the unfortunate Lady Harriet? Will you be able to put all this behind you?"

"Of course not. I lost my wife and child. I'll always believe though this goddamn house had something to do with the way Karen was. The way she died. I can't wait to get out of it. In fact I won't wait any more. I'm going to London to live. Leaving in the morning. You and your husband can sell the house for me. Betty will look after it until the new owners arrive."

Ella jumped at the sound of a loud crash. "Damn!" Rob muttered. "Bad storm. Another slate gone."

Ella shivered. She stood, anxious now to leave here and get home before the storm got too bad. She extended her hand to Rob. "Good luck in London, Rob. I hope you'll be happy there."

Rob stood up and walked around the desk. He stooped and kissed her on the cheek. "Thank you, Ella. You've been very kind to me. I hope you'll be happy too."

Thoughts of Cuanowen and her new life plan ran through Ella's mind. Yes. She would be happy. After the sadness of her failed marriage had eased, after the accident and Karen Trevor had become a distant memory. After she had settled into her new job.

Rob walked with her to the door. As they passed the drawing room Sharon Laide emerged, red-eyed and very pale except for one livid patch on her left cheek.

"Are you all right, Sharon?"

She nodded her head in reply to Ella's question. "I'll be fine. I just need to get back to Salzburg."

Rob cleared his throat. "Mrs Laide, there's the matter of your husband's deposit on this house. I'd like to return it. Will I give it to you now? It's cash."

"I'll bet it is. Give it to Jason, please. I don't get involved in his financial affairs. Goodnight."

Rob shrugged and raised an eyebrow as Sharon turned and walked out through the hall. She struggled with the latch on the big door. Rob opened it for her and both she and Ella went out together into the storm. It was already dark, the thick wads of black cloud smothering what light there might have been. The strong winds were swirling sheets of rain in all directions. They ran for their cars, holding their coats over their heads.

Ella jumped into her car and wiped the rain from her face with a tissue. She looked out at the windswept old house and sighed with satisfaction. This would definitely be the last time she would lay eyes on it. She felt strong enough now to stare into its granite face and not be touched by its coldness.

Just as she turned the key in the ignition Sharon pulled up beside her and hooted. She indicated for Ella to lead the way. Ella waved back and put her car in gear. They drove in convoy down the avenue and out onto the narrow road with the stone ditches and overflowing channels. They drove slowly and carefully until they came to the hairpin bend. The bend that Ella knew so well. Every stone and bramble. The bend where over a year ago she had been critically injured and Karen and Ian Trevor had lost their lives.

The bend where Jason Laide's car now lay embedded in the stone wall, lashed by wind and rain. The bend where Jason lay crushed and broken in his car. His head a bloody mess. A picture of a little boy clutched in his hand.

The bend where Jason Laide lay dead.

Chapter 33

Sharon rode in the ambulance taking her husband to the city hospital. As Ella watched it disappear off into the distance, blue light now switched off, she realised for the first time that she was drenched to the skin, freezing and beginning to feel the onset of shock. When a paramedic bundled her into the emergency car to drive her to hospital she did not object.

"Is there anyone you would like us to contact for you?" the paramedic asked.

Ella shook her head. She would ring Andrew herself as soon as her fingers thawed out. For now she just wanted to be alone with her thoughts. Her increasingly nightmarish thoughts. Images of Jason Laide's smashed head floated before her eyes, interspersed with the too familiar images of Karen Trevor bleeding and dying.

She looked out the passenger window at the accident scene. In the lashing rain police were measuring and writing reports, the flashing blue lights of their patrol cars bouncing off the twisted metal of Jason's car.

"That's the second fatal crash at that corner in just a year," the paramedic said as he steered his car carefully past the police cordon.

Ella didn't answer him. She was desperately trying to hold onto the strength she had lost for so long and had just recently rediscovered. She squeezed her eyes shut and forced herself to imagine Cuanowen. The beach, the sea, the rocks, the deep pools teeming with marine life. The future.

The rest of the journey passed with Ella counting the beats of the windscreen wipers, noting the buildings they were passing, listening to the crackling reports on the car radio and every so often taking her mental journey to Cuanowen. Everything and anything to stop her thinking of what had happened on that cursed stretch of road.

In the hospital Ella was quickly and efficiently checked over, dried off and heated up. When she rang Andrew to tell him what had happened some instinct told her he was with Maxine. She assured him that she was all right and there was no need for him to come to the hospital.

"My car is still at the accident scene. Would you collect it?" she asked.

"Of course. Then I'll collect you from the hospital on the way home."

Home. Where was that? Not the house she had shared with Andrew. Not the house in Cuanowen she had shared with her parents. She didn't have a home to go to, did she?

"No, thanks, Andrew. I must go to Sharon. See if there's anything I can do to help."

"Of course. I can't say I feel sorry about Jason. But I do pity Sharon. Just as well she was here and not away on one of her trips. Are you sure you're okay, El? It must have been awful for you. Like history repeating itself."

"Yes, yes, I'm fine," she answered more impatiently than she had intended. It was just that she still wasn't sure of the answer herself.

A care assistant provided dry clothes for her from the stock of donated items the hospital kept for such emergencies. Ella shrugged off the hospital gown she had been given and dressed herself in a brown skirt with box pleats and a polka-dot blouse. "You'd better keep yourself warm," the care assistant said, handing her an oversized Aran sweater. They both laughed at the finished effect. Before she left the Accident and Emergency, Ella had to listen to the advice the nurse was giving. Yes, she'd watch out for any vomiting, headache or signs of delayed shock, she promised, before making her way to the morgue.

She found Sharon, still wet and ghostly white sitting in the corridor outside the mortuary door. A nurse was seated beside her but Sharon looked very much alone. In her hand she was holding a photograph. It was bloodstained. The same photo that Jason had been clutching in his dead hand. Ella nodded at the nurse and then sat on the other side of Sharon, slipping her arm around the shaking shoulders.

"I did love him once," Sharon whispered. "He wasn't all bad. He didn't deserve this."

Ella squeezed Sharon's shoulder. It was shaking more now. She exchanged glances with the nurse.

"I think you should see the doctor soon, Mrs Laide," the nurse suggested.

Sharon continued on talking as if she had not heard her. "It's my fault, you know. I never told him about Harry. Not until this evening in Manor House. He was looking at the photo. That's why he crashed. I know it." She held the blood-soaked picture out to Ella.

The child in the photo could not be anyone else but Jason Laide's son. He had red hair, pale skin, light blue eyes. A mirror image of his father. Ella stared. She had never known Sharon and Jason had a child. If what Sharon was saying was true, neither had Jason. No wonder he crashed the car, no wonder he took his eyes off the road. He had died because he and Sharon could not be honest with each other, not because, because . . .

Ella suddenly took her arm from around Sharon and stood up.

"Sharon, go get checked out. See the doctor. Change your clothes. Then we'll meet and I'll help you make arrangements."

Responding to the new authority in Ella's voice, Sharon nodded agreement and stood up. Just as the nurse put her arm around her to lead her away, a paramedic came towards them, a little leather notebook in his hand. Ella recognised him as being the person who had attended to Jason at the accident scene tonight.

"Excuse me, Mrs Laide," he said. "This fell out of your husband's pocket while we were putting him into the ambulance. I thought you might like to have it."

Sharon reached out and took the bloodstained

notebook. Hands shaking she flicked it open. The first words she saw were Dirk Van Aken, written in Jason's distinctive, semiliterate scrawl. A glance told her there were times and dates and amounts recorded. She handed the notebook back to the paramedic.

"Thank you but I don't want it. The police may though. Would you see that they get it, please?"

Then she turned her back on all the surprised faces and walked with dignity down the corridor towards the treatment centre.

* * *

Sharon's house was like a command centre. She rang Salzburg as soon as she arrived back from the hospital. Frieda immediately agreed when Sharon asked her to bring Harry to Ireland for his father's funeral. Andrew and Pascal called to the house, leaving Ella's car outside for her and then going to the funeral home to make burial arrangements on Sharon's behalf. Worried about how pale and weak Sharon looked, Ella tried to convince her to go to bed but Sharon was immediately on the phone again, asking her solicitor to call and see her. He must have lived nearby because ten minutes later Ella opened the door to him.

He listened carefully as Sharon told him what she knew of Jason's affairs.

"Just as well you bought your Salzburg home with your own money," he said. "I have a good idea that Jason's assets may be frozen while investigations are ongoing. And afterwards some or all of them may be disposed of."

"I had no idea he was involved in drug dealing. I thought he was just an astute, if dodgy, businessman. Am I in trouble? I'm all that my son's got. What will happen to him if I go to jail?"

The solicitor had tried to reassure Sharon. The more he spoke about the laws Jason might have broken and the possible repercussions of his crimes the more fearful Sharon became. He rambled on and on, quoting the Criminal Justice Act 1994, the Proceeds of Crime Act 1996, the Prevention of Corruption (Amendment) Act 2001 until eventually confusion replaced fear in Sharon's mind.

Then, after all the waffle, he just patted her on the hand and said, "You'll be fine. Nothing to worry about. You haven't committed any crime. You may have unwittingly benefited from the proceeds of crime though and that could cost you. We'll meet tomorrow and prepare your statement for the police."

"I'm not going to mention anything about the blackmail."

The solicitor opened his mouth to object but Sharon gave him one of her most withering looks.

"I'll be asking you to defend me against any charges of fraud or benefiting from proceeds of crime, or whatever it is you were talking about. I did live well on Jason's earnings and I never asked where they came from. That's fair and I'll take that on the chin. But if you as much as mention blackmail, I'll deny it. There's no evidence now anyway. It's all been returned to the rightful owners. Over.

Caput. Understood?"

Ella watched in admiration as Sharon, so distraught by the events of tonight and the possible years of legal wrangles ahead, fought tooth and nail to protect the people Jason had hurt most. And she won her battle. This one at least.

By the time the solicitor left the house Sharon was near collapse from shock and exhaustion.

"Bed!" Ella said and this time she was not going to take no for an answer. Ella tucked Sharon into the four-poster bed she had shared with Jason.

"A lot of people will be glad my husband is gone," Sharon said. "He has caused so much unhappiness. I'm very grateful now for my home in Salzburg and for my son. I'll never come back here again."

Ella opened her mouth to contradict her but, when she thought about what Sharon had said, it was probably true. Instead of answering she stroked Sharon's hair until she saw her eyelids droop. Then she tiptoed out of the room.

In the kitchen she had just made a cup of coffee for herself when the front doorbell rang. She rushed out not wanting the noise to waken Sharon. She stood still inside the door. Suppose it was one of Jason's friends. He must have some pretty unsavoury connections. It couldn't be Andrew. He had said he would not call until the morning. The bell rang again. Shit! She quickly opened the door and scowled at the caller. Her expression changed when she saw who it was.

"Peter Sheehan! What are you doing here?"

He stepped into the hall and caught her by the arms, peering into her face. "Are you all right? Why didn't you call me? "

"I didn't want to bother you. We weren't brought to your hospital. St John's was nearer. How did you know I was here?"

"I rang your house. Andrew told me. I couldn't believe this accident happened at the same spot as yours. I thought you might need me."

Ella looked up into his clear green eyes and knew that his supposition had been right. She did need Peter Sheehan. She needed to talk to him, to know he was listening but not judging, to see him smile, to watch the crinkles at the corners of his eyes. She suddenly became aware of how she must look in her second-hand clothes. Embarrassed she turned and led him into the kitchen.

"Coffee?"

"Yes, please."

They were silent as she prepared the drink for him. She blushed, conscious of her box pleats, polka dots and knobbly Aran sweater.

"Why did you ring my house anyway?" she asked, handing him his coffee.

"Because I'm still waiting for an answer to my dinner invitation."

Ella smiled. How petty a dinner date seemed now! She sat at the table opposite him.

"I've been busy, Peter. Maybe we'll have dinner before I leave."

"Leave? What do you mean? Where are you going?"

"Home. To Cuanowen. I thought I told you."

"You did and I asked if you were running away. Are you?"

"You mean you thought I was just reacting to my situation. Everything. The accident. Karen Trevor. Maxine Doran. Divorce. And now Jason Laide." Ella leaned her elbows on the table and looked at Peter steadily. "You're wrong, Peter. I'm taking control. Acting, not reacting. I have plans."

"I'm glad to hear that, Ella. How about you tell me your plans?"

She did. She told him about her phone call to Mrs Beryl Langford, the owner of Seaview Hotel near Cuanowen. How she had offered to buy fifty percent ownership in the little hotel and run it in partnership with Beryl. And more importantly that Beryl had accepted her offer.

"She's a lovely lady, Peter. A widow. I know we'll get on together. But she's too frail now to continue on alone. The hotel has huge potential she's not able to develop. This arrangement suits us both so well. I'll learn the hotel business from someone who is vastly experienced and Beryl will hopefully benefit from my business know-how. The hotel will be our home too."

"No more auctioneering so?"

Ella shook her head emphatically. "No more anything to do with the life I have been living. It almost destroyed me, as you know. This is a clean slate. Beryl and I, running our Cuanowen hotel, working together, living together. Expanding the business. Walking on the beach. Perfect."

"There's no perfect lifestyle. Are you sure you're not just trying to have the relationship with Beryl you never had with your mother?"

"Oh, for Christ's sake, Peter! Stop analysing me! It's taken me long enough to get to this stage. Don't start putting doubts in my head now."

Peter reached his hand across the table and caught hers. Quite subconsciously their fingers intertwined and locked together. Ella felt a shiver run through her. A shiver of excitement.

"I'm not trying to put a damper on your plans, Ella. I just needed to know that you're sure. I want you to be happy."

His thumb was distracting her. It was gently rubbing her palm and sending signals all over her body. She withdrew her hand. This handsome man must be well versed in the techniques of seduction and at this moment Ella felt very vulnerable to his charms. Peter Sheehan, with his green eyes and long black lashes, was a complication she did not need in her life. It was just Ella and Beryl until she felt confident enough to trust her instincts again. If ever. They had let her down when she believed Andrew Ford was her partner for life. She stood up.

"More coffee?"

Peter stood too. They stared at each other across the table. Her resolve weakened. When he moved towards her and put his arms around her, she laid her face on his broad shoulder, breathing in his meadowsweet scent. He slipped his hands underneath her knobbly Aran sweater and gently massaged her back. She felt the heat of his hands through the fabric of her polka-dot blouse. Her tensed muscles relaxed as she leaned against him, secure in his arms. Protected. Safe from harm. From accidents. From illusions and fantasies of dead people who were not dead at all.

She was safe from everything except the response of her own body as Peter brought his lips to meet hers. Her eyelids closed as she savoured the warm sensation of his kiss. It was not until she felt his tongue slip into her mouth that she broke the contact and quickly pulled away from him.

"I'm not ready for anything like this, Peter. You know I'm not. Andrew and I have to say goodbye, to finalise our divorce, sell our home, decide what to do about our business. And Ballyhaven. We've been together since we were students. I'll need time."

Peter raised his hand and gently pushed a stray strand of her dark hair off her face. He smiled at her and his eyes crinkled at the corners in the way she was beginning to like so much. Putting his hand on her shoulder Peter gently pushed her back down on her chair.

"Sit down. I'll make coffee. And of course you're right. You need time and space, Ella. But will you promise me you'll keep in contact with me? Maybe I can go to see you sometimes. Cuanowen isn't the end of the earth. In fact I'm quite interested in a consultant's post in the Western Regional Hospital. That's only twenty miles from Cuanowen."

"We'll see," Ella said and watched as Peter filled the

kettle and got out clean mugs and a jar of instant coffee. A man who knew his way around the kitchen. Had he always looked after himself? Surely someone as attractive and kind as Peter Sheehan had a history. Someone special, or maybe a string of special somebodys in his past. How could she respond so strongly to a man about whom she knew nothing? He was leaning against the granite counter top now, waiting for the kettle to boil.

"Do you think it was all coincidence?" she asked. "Manor House and Karen Trevor and the influence they seem to have had on my life?"

"Maybe."

"That's not an answer."

"There isn't a right answer. Who knows? You can take every event that led us here and put it in a logical sequence. Manor House is just an old building which happened to be the home of Karen Trevor, who happened to be involved in a car accident with you."

"And I happened to be married to a man who is having an affair with Maxine, who turns out to be a relation of Karen's. Coincidence? Then Jason Laide, the man who was killed tonight in the very same spot as Karen Trevor, was trying to buy Manor House. Coincidence?"

The kettle boiled. Peter made the coffees and brought them over to the table. He spooned sugar into his mug and stirred thoughtfully.

"Yes. I'd have to agree. A lot of coincidence. But there are probably a lot of logical explanations too."

"I must work out the answer for myself, Peter. And it

wasn't just me. The unhappiness of the past year seems to have spread out and affected a lot of people. Like Oliver Griffin. You saw him. The man was desperate."

"He has a gambling addiction. Nothing at all to do with Karen Trevor or Manor House. He has agreed to start counselling by the way. And why are we talking about other people when all I really want to talk about is us?"

"Us? Is there an us?"

"I want there to be but it's up to you, Ella."

Needing to look away from the distraction of Peter's eyes, Ella bowed her head and looked down at the table, examining the whorls and knots in the timber. She could not possibly get involved with anybody now. Her newfound confidence was too fragile and the hurt of Andrew's unfaithfulness too raw. Nor could she bear the thought of never getting to know Peter Sheehan, his likes and dislikes, his hopes, his dreams. She looked up and smiled at him.

"I'd be more like your patient now. I need time to settle into my new life. "

Peter caught her hand and their fingers entwined again. "You know where I am if you need me," he said.

He stood then, stooped to kiss her on the cheek and let himself out of the house that used to be Jason Laide's home.

Tiptoeing into the master bedroom, Ella checked on Sharon before going to the guest bedroom herself. Jason's widow was sleeping peacefully. All the unrest, the cruelty, the viciousness that Jason had brought into their lives seemed already to be losing the power to hurt and disturb.

Ella removed her hospital clothing and snuggled down underneath the fluffy duvet. She felt exhausted. Totally drained by the events of the past days, the past year. She slept. She dreamt. In her dream she was running, alone, wild and free along the strand in Cuanowen, cool wind in her hair and warm sand beneath her feet.

Ella woke with a smile on her face and hope in her heart.

Epilogue

Two years later

The narrow pathway leading onto the beach was stony and bumpy. Ella kept running, her trainers absorbing the shock as her feet pounded the hard surface. She slowed as she hit sand, starting her warm-down. When she was cool enough, she sat on a rock and sighed with satisfaction. The route she had chosen to run this morning had been punishing but she felt great now that she had finished it.

Taking off her baseball cap and loosening her hair, she turned her face up to the sun. She closed her eyes and absorbed the warmth while listening to the gentle rhythm of the sea. A gull screeched. She opened her eyes immediately. She loved to watch the graceful swoop and dive of the gulls. She was just in time to see the bird break the surface of the water, dip its beak and soar again.

Unknotting the laces on her trainers, she kicked them off and walked barefoot towards the water. The tide was almost full in. She dipped a toe into the sea and quickly drew back. It was freezing! Ella stepped a little from the water's edge and began to jog along the sand. Just a gentle canter. The sun shone on her face and the wind blew her hair back from her face. She felt free and wild, at one with the sea and sand. At peace with herself.

A quick glance at her wristwatch shattered her dreamy peace. Jesus! It was already after ten o'clock. The run had taken longer than she had realised. Beryl would be fussing. And how! She would be driving the staff to distraction. Ella put her shoes and cap on again and headed back towards Seaview Hotel by the coast road, trying to run faster than her legs wanted to carry her. Hearing a car approach her from behind on the narrow road, she hugged the ditch. The car drew up beside her and slowed down to match her speed.

"I thought you'd be too busy for running today," Pebbles Shorten said. "What time is this big do on?"

A stitch in her side took Ella's breath away. She bent over, trying to ease the sharp pain.

"Jump in," he said. "I'll drop you back to the hotel. You're hardly going to greet the Minister for Tourism in a tracksuit and baseball hat, are you?"

Ella sat in gratefully. "You're a darling, Pebbles! I've stayed out too long and there's so much to do before all the guests arrive. You and Norma will be coming, won't you?"

"You bet!" he laughed. "Nobody in Cuanowen is going to miss the official opening of the revamped Seaview Hotel. Anyway, since Norma and I will be the first to hold our wedding reception in the new function room, I don't think wild horses would keep the future

Mrs Shorten away."

They rounded a sharp bend now and the land began to slope gently downwards. Beneath them, about mile away on their right-hand side, the newly painted Seaview Hotel glowed in the morning sun. Ella felt her heart beat faster as she looked down at the end result of all the planning and hard work she and Beryl had done over the past two years. Seaview was sleek and modern now but yet they had managed to retain the old-world warmth and charm which had first attracted Ella. A harmonious blend of old and new. Just like herself and Beryl. Most of the time.

"I suppose the Minister will have a retinue with him." Pebbles said. "And a bloody big car."

"He'll have a police escort maybe but Pascal McEvoy has no interest in pomp and ceremony. He'll probably just stay long enough to cut the ribbon. Unfortunately we're opening up the same day as the super casino in Ballyhaven that all the fuss has been about. Pascal has to officiate at that too. He won't want to miss the photo opportunities there. Do you know it's built on land Andrew and I used to own?"

Pebbles grunted a disinterested reply. Super casinos did not impinge on Cuanowen life. Ella tried at conversation again.

"Andrew and his wife will be here too. You know, my ex-husband? He and Pascal McEvoy went to college together."

Pebbles did not comment on this topic either. But then he always went silent at the mention of Andrew's name. Like Beryl, he believed Andrew had broken Ella's heart by marrying Maxine Doran. Nothing Ella said ever changed their minds. She had learned to ignore their tightlipped disapproval of Andrew. None of the Andrew and Maxine things mattered any more.

As they drove into the grounds of the hotel Ella saw that the length of red ribbon had already been strung across the entrance to the new extension. Typical of Beryl! The ribbon was in place but the hors d'oeuvres had probably not yet been started. Ella gave Pebbles a quick peck on the cheek. Somehow they managed to bash noses. They both laughed.

"We'd better give up on this kissing business, hadn't we?" Pebbles laughed. "I hope you do better with your doctor boyfriend. I certainly do with Norma."

"Much, much better," Ella smiled and then felt herself begin to blush as she recalled just how much better she and Peter Sheehan did with 'the kissing business'.

Pebbles waved as he drove off. Ella stood and watched him go. The man who had been the first to kiss her and the one to save her when she was clinging to Dog Rock by her fingertips. Holding onto life by a thread. She shivered. Today was not for looking back. Today was for welcoming the future. She was already mentally ticking off to do's as she climbed the steps to the entrance of Seaview Hotel.

* * *

Beryl was in a right dither. Her hair wasn't right and

she couldn't find the pearl and ruby brooch her husband had given her as a present for the last birthday they had shared together. Ella sat her down and brushed the silver silky hair, then handed her the ivory and ebony box where the old lady kept her jewellery.

Beryl smiled up at her. "Thank you, dear. I'm getting to be rather a nuisance, aren't I?"

Ella stooped down and hugged the old lady close to her, breathing in her lavender scent. "Never, Beryl. How could you be? You're my rock. And my business partner."

"I don't have anything more to teach you now. You're going to be one of the best hoteliers in Ireland."

"You've taught me so much, Beryl. I'll never be able to thank you enough. You've restored my trust in human nature."

"Really? I didn't do much. You're the one who's put in all the work."

"Remember when I rang you two years ago, confused, just coming out of a depression and a marriage which had never worked? You trusted me then, didn't you? You took my word that I'd pay you for my share of the hotel when I had my financial affairs with Andrew settled up. You gave me a home, Beryl, as well as a career. So don't ever again say you could be a nuisance to me. I won't listen."

Beryl looked in the mirror and patted her hair. She glanced at Ella's reflection and smiled. "Yes, dear. We're a team. And we both look lovely. I really like that suit on you. Cream is perfect with your colouring. Sort of bridal, do you think?"

"Don't start matchmaking again! You only gave up on

matching me off with Pebbles Shorten when he got engaged to Norma. Now you've started on Peter Sheehan since he moved to the Western Regional Hospital. I'll admit Peter and I are good friends. Maybe a bit more . . ."

"Cyril was my best friend and we were married for forty years. Your husband should be your friend. You're making a good start with Dr Peter Sheehan. Is he coming today? I invited him, you know."

Ella laughed in exasperation. She could never stay cross with Beryl for long.

* * *

Adrenalin had kept Ella on a high all day. She had organised catering and entertainment with flawless efficiency, supervised staff, mingled with guests and generally handled the whole ceremony with great aplomb. It had been a success from the ribbon cutting by Minister Pascal McEvoy to the chicken vol-au-vents and the myriad of other things in between. She was proud of what she and Beryl had achieved but she was also suddenly very tired.

Most of the guests had left by now. Stragglers had retired to the bar where a singsong was starting up. Ella went to the door of the bar, looked them over and decided they could be left to their own devices. Anyway Beryl was in there with them sipping her glass of port. They were in good hands. Fresh air was what Ella needed now and a few minutes' peace and quiet.

As soon as she got to the front door she took in a huge

breath of the cool evening air. Crossing the lawn, she walked to the low stone wall which marked the border between Seaview Hotel and the coast road. At the other side of the road was a sheer drop of black cliff face. And beyond the cliffs, the ocean, tinged by the red of sunset, tossed and turned in its ceaseless rhythm of ebb and flow. Ella's eyes travelled over the breadth of the vista and she began to feel its depth. Its timelessness. Its imperviousness to human joy or tragedy. Her parents' deaths had not stopped the tide. Her accident, the nightmare of Karen Trevor's death and the yearlong replay of her dying, the violent end to Jason Laide's violent life, the break-up of her marriage, none of these had altered the course of a single wave. The powerful emotions of grief and fear and black despair she had felt had, after all, been powerless.

"It is beautiful, isn't it? I'm not surprised that you don't miss the city."

Ella jumped with fright.

"Sorry," Andrew said. "I'd forgotten how you drift off into a world of your own."

She turned to him and smiled. "Andrew, thank you for being here today. It meant a lot to me. Especially since I'm sure you'd like to have been at the casino opening. Did the Coxes mind you not being there? "

"The Coxes got what they needed from me. The Ballyhaven site was what they wanted. I'm sure they don't care whether they see me or not."

Ella's ears pricked up. Was that a note of cynicism she heard in Andrew's voice? He had always been a touch conceited, a touch dishonest. But cynical, never. Maybe he was just learning realism and finding it a difficult lesson to absorb. She glanced at him and noticed that the boy was gone. Andrew had a new maturity. The look of a man who had responsibilities and took them seriously.

"A pity Maxine couldn't make it," she said, "but I understand that she needed to be with her father. I'm glad they've found each other again."

Andrew ran his hand through his hair and Ella remembered the danger signal. She braced herself as he spoke.

"Her father is sick. That's true. And she's caring for him."

"But?"

"But the real reason she's not here is because she's not feeling very well herself at the moment. Actually she's pregnant."

Ella looked out to sea again. The tide rolled on, not skipping a beat.

"Congratulations. I'm happy for you both," she said before she had time to analyse her words. She listened to them as they rolled out into the calm evening and she knew they had come from her heart. She was glad for Andrew and Maxine. Glad that they had found each other, glad that they had not bought Manor House which had by now been demolished to make way for a housing estate, glad that Maxine ran a small restaurant in town while Andrew had a new business partner in the estate agency. Glad that they were going to have a baby.

"You'll make a great dad."

"What a thought! Me a daddy! Thank you, Ella. Thank

you for everything."

Ella turned to look at him. At her handsome ex-husband. At the man with whom she had intended to spend the rest of her life. She smiled at him.

"We had some interesting times, didn't we? Not all good but interesting. Which reminds me, how are Oliver and Tricia getting on with their shop?"

Andrew shook his head and grinned. "If anyone had told me Griffin would end up being a convenience-store owner, I'd have said they were crazy. How wrong can you be? The best thing he ever did was to take early retirement from the Planning Office. And getting his gambling under control, of course."

Andrew took a step towards her. He still wore the same aftershave. It came to her on the evening breeze, carrying with it memories she had thought long dead. He raised his hand and gently touched her hair.

"And you, Ella. Are you happy here? Have you found the peace you were looking for?"

"I love the hotel. I like meeting people and I like the challenge of building the business up."

"I was talking about Peter Sheehan. Beryl told me."

Ella laughed. Beryl had probably had her prissy little face on while she told Andrew that Ella had a man in her life. She might even have said "So there!".

"Yes. Peter and I are seeing each other. When we can. He works long hours and so do I. But the time we get to spend together is special. Very special."

Andrew kissed her on the cheek. Just a brief touch of lips, a brush of bristle on smooth skin and he was gone.

She remained standing by the wall and waved to him as he drove across the driveway and out onto the road. Home to his wife and child.

The sun was very low on the horizon now, night beginning to push the light from the sky. Snatches of music drifted out from the bar. Maybe she should join them, sing along but maybe she would take five more minutes to herself. Just five minutes of quiet at the close of a perfect day.

Almost perfect. Peter should have been here. She knew he would have been if he could. There must have been an emergency in the hospital. Or perhaps with one of his private patients. Someone desperate teetering on the edge of disaster, like Oliver Griffin had once been. Like she herself had been. Peter was a rescuer of lost souls. She was worried. What if something had happened to him? What if he never came here again? No more walks along the beach, no more warm hugs and shared jokes. No more thunder and lightning kisses. Ella turned and walked quickly towards the bar. She mustn't let anything, or anyone spoil her day. Not even Peter Sheehan.

She had just reached the entrance to the hotel when Beryl came towards her, walking a little unsteadily.

"Now don't be cross with me, dear," she said "but I have a confession to make."

Ella had to wait then while Beryl hiccoughed. She must have really pushed the boat out and had three glasses of port.

"What have you done, Beryl? Besides getting a little drunk."

"I forgot to tell you that your young doctor rang earlier. You were busy with the Minister at the time."

"And?"

"And he was very sorry but there was an emergency at the hospital. He'll be here as soon as he can. Are you cross with me now, dear?"

Ella laughed as Beryl staggered slightly. She must get the old lady to bed before she had an accident.

"No, Beryl, I'm not cross. How could I be? This was a great day. And you've just made it perfect."

Ella hugged Beryl and then held firmly onto her arm. They stood together in the doorway and turned to face the sea.

The lap of the tide hissed gently against the cliff wall, the sound of singing from the bar rose and fell in a rhythm of its own. The sun finally dipped beneath the horizon and the evening star shone with a cold light. Ella smelt the sweetness of turf-smoke. She heard the distant sound of a car driving along the coast road which lead to Seaview Hotel. It was the high-powered whine of a Ferrari engine. Peter Sheehan's Ferrari. She noted it all. Committed it to memory. Treasures to be recalled for as long as she lived.

The smells, the sounds and the sights of the night Ella Ford finally found peace.

The End

If you enjoyed *Ebb & Flow*

try *As Easy As That* also published by Poolbeg

Here's a sneak preview of Chapter one–

As Easy As That

The contrast had a certain beauty. Warm blood on cool silk. Kate threw the stained scrap of fabric into the laundry basket. She sat on the side of the bath and waited for the tears to come. Her eyes remained dry. She was beyond crying. Getting up she opened the cabinet drawer, took out her pristine pregnancy-testing kit and threw it against the mirror. It bounced off the glass and tumbled into the washbasin, then lay there, taunting her, mocking her failure. Their failure.

The front door opened. She heard Fred drop his briefcase on the hall table with a thump. He called up the stairs.

"Kate! Sorry I'm running so late! Are you nearly ready?"

She stared at the battered pregnancy-testing kit, then picked it up and put it back into the drawer. With eyes closed, she whispered, "Next time. Please let it be all right next time!" When she heard him walk up the stairs, she quickly plastered some cleanser onto her face. She smiled at him as he came to the door.

She was playing the game. His rules, his game, where work was priority and a family happened. Or not.

"Just about to shower now. Your clothes are ready in the bedroom. Busy day?"

"The meeting with Super Store went on and on. Pernickety crowd. But I think we just about clinched the contract. It's small but I can't afford to turn it down."

"Well done, Fred! You'll feel like celebrating tonight then."

He took a step towards her and slipped his hand inside her robe. "Want to know what I feel like doing tonight?"

"Not really," she smiled as she pushed him gently away.

Kate stood under the shower and tried to make her mind as empty as her belly felt, tried to stop the grieving for a baby that had not been conceived, tried to wash away the fears and doubts. It was party time and her party-time husband was waiting.

The Cochranes' house spoke of a need to advertise their new-found wealth. Everything from the electronically controlled gates to the porticos and pillars on the house displayed an abundance of spending power and a terrible lack of taste.

"No doubt about it, there's money in muck," Fred remarked as they parked the car in Cochranes' courtyard.

Kate flipped down the mirror and checked her hair and make-up. She peered at her reflection, trying to find some connection with the sophisticated image. From the carefully made-up brown eyes to the sleek dark hair, she seemed every inch the sophisticate. A look of effortless elegance achieved through heroic efforts with hair-straighteners and an armoury of cosmetics. A mask. Snapping the mirror back into place, she looked at her husband.

"We've got to talk, Fred. We –"

He kissed her on the lips and smothered her words. She gave up. He was probably right. Now was not the time. But there just did not seem to be a right time for Fred to discuss . . . their problem. How could he be so insensitive? So selfish?

She slipped into her role as beautiful wife of the advertising executive and linked his arm as they made their way towards the vast foyer of the Cochrane mansion.

"Fred! Kate! Welcome. You look wonderful, Kate!"

Sheila Cochrane grabbed their hands, kissed their cheeks and dragged them into the lounge all at the same time. It was as if she had read rules one to ten of hostess etiquette and was trying to apply all of them at once.

A quick glance around the huge reception room told Kate all she needed to know. Carefully arranged on and around the state-of-the-art furniture were the same tanned faces and honed bodies that had peopled the last party. And the one before that. And probably the next twenty.

Drawn to potential business like a magnet, Fred zoned in on the retail group. Nigel Greenway, the car-sales supremo, owner of a string of garages, was holding court in front of the bay window. A circle of respectful disciples surrounded him.

Kate watched as Fred slipped into a slot which seemed to have been reserved for him. He shook hands, smiled, struck a pose halfway between subservience and assertiveness and suddenly became the moon orbiting the retailing super-planet. His handsome features were animated, his body tensed, the hunter ready to pounce on any business prey. This was his milieu; this was what Fred was about.

"Kate Lucas! How do you do it?"

Kate turned around and smiled when she saw Patty Molloy. They touched cheeks and stood back to look at each other.

"You're always perfection itself, Kate. Not a hair out of place or a spare ounce of flesh!"

Kate smiled at the petite woman standing in front of her. So tiny and yet she had produced three children in quick succession. Number four was obviously well on the way.

"You look great yourself, Patty. When's the baby due?"

"The next, and last, baby Molloy is due in a month's time. I love them all dearly but enough is enough. I feel like a baby-making machine at the moment. Anyway, I'm boring. Tell me about life in the fast lane. I see a lot of your boss on television these days. Must be exciting in your office."

Exciting? Yes, there had been a lot more work to do lately in Richard Gordon's law office. Research, cross-referencing, press releases. Being personal assistant to the leading trial lawyer in the country was demanding, especially since he was defending in the highest profile case in years. But exciting?

"It's very busy in the office, Patty. A lot of nose to the grindstone and very little else. How are the children?"

"They all take after Brian so they're a handful. And stop changing the subject. Did he do it? Did our sainted minister murder his mistress?"

Trust Patty to put the question everyone else only hinted at. She looked like the others, tanned and toned, but she had a directness unique in their circle.

"I've no idea what the man did or did not do," Kate replied with a smile. "Anyway, I couldn't tell you even if I did know."

Patty shrugged. "Worth a try! I believe he strangled the poor girl and thought he could get away with it. You could tell me the results of the DNA tests. It'll be in the papers soon anyway. Was the baby his?"

A bell rang.

"My God! A dinner-gong!"

They both laughed and then changed their expressions to suitably solemn as they joined the procession into the dining-room and the lavish buffet.

Sheila Cochrane knew how to choose a good caterer. The food was delicious, as was the wine, and conversation flowed.

It would have been a good party except that the host, Gus Cochrane, became coarser and louder with each drink. Sheila was visibly nervous. She knew her husband's veneer of culture was alcohol-soluble. When his voice reached a certain pitch, it signalled the end of the party and people began to gather themselves together to leave.

"I think it's time I went home," Patty said, standing up

from the comfortable couch she and Kate had found for themselves.

Kate stood and kissed Patty on the cheek. "Take care, Patty. And do tell Brian we were asking for him."

Patty replied with a little wave as she waddled off to thank her hosts. Kate glanced around and noticed that Fred was still talking to Nigel Greenway. Or at least he was still listening to the great man. She flopped back onto her seat again. Fred would not thank her for interrupting the sermon. She began to get the uncomfortable feeling that somebody was staring at her. Then she noticed Gus Cochrane weaving towards her, at great speed considering his condition. Immediately she got up from her seat and beckoned to Fred but he was too engrossed in Nigel Greenway to see her. Then she was smothered in a wave of alcohol fumes as Gus Cochrane stood unsteadily in front of her.

"Katie Lucas!" he roared. "When're we going to see little Lucases? Are you afraid to ruin your figure or's Fred shooting blanks?"

The loud comment stopped all conversation. The room fell silent.

Sheila went to her drunken husband and grabbed his arm. "Time to go to bed, Gus. Party's over."

"Let me go, woman!" he snapped. "I just asked a civil question. Maybe they've a problem I could help with!"

Fred crossed the room quickly and took Kate's hand. He squeezed her fingers and she could feel some of his strength transfer to her. Ignoring Gus, they turned to Sheila.

"Thank you very much for the evening," said Fred. "It was very nice."

"The meal was beautiful. Thank you," Kate added.

Little beads of sweat were gathering on Gus's forehead and trickling down the creases of his porky face. Kate and Fred walked away from him.

"Fred! Fred! Listen to me!" the drunk man spluttered.

"Good night, Gus."

"No. Listen! If you can't do the job, I'll do it for you. I'd no trouble getting Sheila pregnant. A favour to a friend so to speak and . . ."

Kate clung onto Fred's hand as they headed for the door, praying that she could control the tears until she got to the car.

Suddenly Fred let go of her hand.

"I won't be a minute. You go on ahead," he said casually.

In panic, Kate watched her husband make a beeline back to Nigel Greenway. Then she ran and did not stop until she reached her car. She leaned against the door, shaking with embarrassment and anger. Gus Cochrane! That big ignorant pig! The foul-mouthed lout! He might have made money from his waste-disposal empire but he was still a piece of filth! And why was Fred taking so long? Why was he making her wait here alone?

Patty came walking towards her.

"Are you okay, Kate? I saw what happened."

"I thought you'd gone."

"I had to go back to use the bathroom. I was passing the reception room when Gus Cochrane started shouting at you. I hope you're not going to let that drunken oaf upset you. God! The man is vile!"

Kate straightened herself up and smiled. "No, of course

not. He's not worth bothering about. Did you see Fred? Is he on his way?"

Patty took Kate's hand and squeezed it. "Why don't you sit into my car for a few minutes? I saw Fred talking to Nigel Greenway. He'll probably be a while."

Without saying a word Kate went with Patty. She did not trust herself to speak. There were no words for the hurt she felt. No decent words. They sat in silence.

"Like some music?" Patty asked, moving her hand towards the stereo.

Kate nodded. The soundtrack of *The Lion King* filled the emptiness.

"The kids love it," Patty explained.

At that, Kate lost her control over the tears which needed so badly to well up and spill over. Would she ever be able to say something like that? *The kids love it*. Would she ever feel the warmth of her baby snuggling into her, guide tiny feet towards their first step, buy school uniforms, help with homework, read bedtime stories? Month after month and still the pregnancy-testing kit remained sealed.

"Fred doesn't care. He's too busy building up his client accounts to worry about having children."

Kate sat bolt upright in shock. How had these words left the safety of her head? 'The Circle of Life' played on. And on. What must Patty think? What would Patty say and to whom would she say it? She saw Fred approach the car, keys in hand.

Patty turned to her. "I hope it works out for you, Kate. Remember Fred is no different from other men. They define themselves by their careers. It doesn't mean he cares less."

"Thanks, Patty."

"And don't worry. I won't say anything to anyone else."

Kate gave her a grateful hug and got out of the car.

Fred talked non-stop all the way home. He had almost secured a big advertising campaign with Nigel Greenway.

"This could be one of our biggest yet. He'll be opening two new garages up-country in the spring and he wants a national campaign for the launch. Multimedia. Television, radio, press, the lot!"

He was still talking about the Greenway contract as they got ready for bed. Kate nodded every so often but he really did not need her input. Gus Cochrane's insult obviously had not hurt him at all. Nor did he seem to realise how much it had pained her. So she just listened to his enthusiastic babble until she could take it no more.

"Night, Fred."

"Night, sweetheart. Aren't you glad now that we went to Cochrane's dinner party?"

She turned her back on him and tried to sleep.

Also published by Poolbeg

Parting Company

Mary O'Sullivan

On the surface Claire Hearn has lived a charmed life with success at work and at home. But now everything she holds dear is starting to fall apart.

Just why is her ambitious husband Brendan flying off to a secret meeting in Bonn? And how come his boss, Claire's father Frank Dawson who is valiantly fighting to keep the family business afloat, has no idea what Brendan is up to?

As her marriage disintegrates before her eyes, Claire channels all her passion into her research which is on the brink of an important breakthrough. But little does she know that powerful people have set their sights on this discovery and want it for themselves.

With tragedy and heartbreak threatening to engulf her world, Claire will need to keep her wits about her as she comes up against the glamorous and dangerous Yvette Previn and the multinational she represents.

But as the web of intrigue starts to unravel Claire must remember to protect the most vulnerable thing of all . . . her heart.

ISBN 978-1-84223-270-5